THE BEST OF FAMILIES

By Ellin Berlin

The Best of Families

ELLIN BERLIN

GARDEN CITY, NEW YORK

DOUBLEDAY & COMPANY, INC.

All of the characters in this book are fictitious, and any resemblance to actual persons, living or dead, is purely coincidental.

THE BEST OF FAMILIES

1

It's a dismal, cloudy November morning and I'm glad my sister Julia is staying with me; I mind morning weather. It can rain all it likes in the afternoon if the day will only begin with sunshine.

As a rule when she is in New York Julia stops at the Plaza but when Bertie is away on one of his shooting weekends she comes to Manhattan House to keep me company. As she drinks her orange juice she doesn't even glance out the window; she has always been more of an indoor person than I am and weather doesn't bother her.

"Thank goodness for orange juice," she says. "Do you remember those awkward, partly peeled oranges impaled on forks at breakfast when we were children? Oh, and that reminds me . . ." She fishes in a pocket of her wrapper and pulls out a letter that looks rather voluminous. "This will take you back; I've been meaning to show it to you all weekend. I better read it to you; Adele had one of those difficult spidery hands. It would take you hours to decipher it—it did me."

"Adele who?"

"I haven't the faintest idea. Some first-name friend of my mother-in-law. I was clearing out some of the drearier Victorians from the upper shelves in the Dower House and I found this. Mrs. Henderson had a trick all her life of using letters as bookmarks and forgetting them. I find one every once in a while and usually they're boring; but this is sort of fun."

Julia puts down the letter and her empty glass. She butters a popover and reaches for the coffeepot.

"What's the letter about?" I ask.

"Us. Us in 1903. Oh, there's some Chicago gossip about people I never heard of which I'll skip. Adele seems to have been a girlhood chum of Mrs. Henderson. Let me finish this popover, though I shouldn't, and I'll give you the Cameron family as observed by a visitor from the West."

Julia wipes the crumbs from her fingers and between sips of her second cup of coffee reads the letter.

"Let me see . . . Chicago . . . Chicago . . . Here's the New York part. 'The senator's cousins, the Somebodies'—I couldn't make out the name, probably those connections of the bishop's Martha Henderson used to stay with—'were more than kind to Paul and me during our New York visit . . . the Diamond Horseshoe lived up to our expectations . . . took Paul to the Union Club while Mrs. Somebody and I did the shops . . . absolutely nothing to compare with dear Marshall Field's . . . a delightful dinner party at Mr. and Mrs. Ogden Mills's . . .' Ah, here we are:

" 'The most characteristic New York affair was an afternoon tea on our last Saturday at Mr. James A. Cameron's. This sort of New York house is harder to get into than Buckingham Palace —much harder, to judge by some of the Americans, even from our fair city, who are received at Court. I really get no satisfaction any more out of having been presented; besides, it doesn't do one any good with the people who count, certainly not with New York's tight little inner circle. A curious thing to me is that the newer people are more snobbish as well as more ostentatious than the ones who have run New York society since the Dutch lost New Amsterdam—I can admit to you that I enjoy a little ostentation if it's well done—I don't see the point of having a lot of money if one never lets it show—and the Fifth Avenue mansions of some of the recent millionaires are breath-taking, the last word inside and out. The members of the old families aren't snobbish, at least not in the usual way. They are merely completely unaware that there are any people to know except themselves and those they choose to accept.

"'I may say I was amazed to learn that Mr. Cameron is someone they chose to accept in his youth. He fits into the old New York pattern as if he'd been born to it. Of course, he did marry a Turner and her mother was a Gore, but he himself comes of very plain stock. He was born on a farm in the Catskill Mountains near a place called Delhi—fortunately for him his forebears were solidly Protestant, Scotch I assume from the name. He was sixteen or seventeen when his parents were killed in an overturned wagon on a mountain road, and he had no brothers or sisters, such a blessing for a man on his way up! Obscure relations can be a real embarrassment. You remember those frightful, common cousins of the . . . of the'—I can't make it out—'and poor Belle and that impossible old Irish grandmother of hers who lived forever. Anyway, Mr. Cameron was left alone in the world and he sold the farm—I don't imagine he got much for it —and came to New York and put himself through Columbia College and law school. He did nicely as a young lawyer, some well-known firm, I forget which, took him on, but he didn't stay with the law. He made his fortune on the stock exchange and it's one of the important New York fortunes, not in the Vanderbilt or Morgan class, but impressive all the same. Mr. Cameron's investment house is a power in Wall Street. According to Paul he is a veritable genius in money matters, has what they call the Midas touch.'"

Julia laughs and says, "Pa would have been amused by those flowery phrases. Remember how he used to say he was born lucky with an inherited bent for hard work and a knack of seeing how things in general are going?"

"He had a taste for understatement."

"The truth is Pa had taste, Nell. And that's a rare commodity in any circle at any time."

"We were the ones, Julia, who were born lucky."

"So we were. Let's get back to Adele and look at ourselves."

"'This all came later after he married Eleanor Turner. She inherited money from her family and that gave him his start in the financial world. Only his start, Paul says, but a start was all James Cameron needed. I've been told, though, that the marriage was a love match, and after meeting him and seeing the Sargent portrait of her I can believe it.' She darn well better believe it."

Julia's eyes look misty. I wonder if she's going to cry. Our generation cries more easily, with less embarrassment than the ones that have succeeded us.

Julia doesn't cry; she pours more coffee into her cup and says, "You can't possibly remember them together, Nell, you weren't three years old when Mother died, but I do. Our house was different from most people's. Father and Mother laughed a lot together and finished each other's sentences and gave each other a secret look in front of us the way children do in front of their elders. In a lot of houses it was only the children who had fun together. Very few were as close as Maud and me, but they were together, and as often as not their parents were separated by more than the length of a dining-room table. Not Father and Mother. And this seemed perfectly natural to me. I just thought other children's families were peculiar. I didn't know then that marrying with love is a rare and fortunate thing. Well, you live and learn."

While Julia hunts for her place in the letter she says, "Pa was pretty wonderful to keep everything the same for us after Mother died, though that seemed natural to me too. I guess every happy family takes itself for granted. We certainly did.

"Here we are: 'The Cameron house is in a part of town that has become very smart, the Sixties—the East Sixties of course. It's a big house with more than twice the average New York twenty-foot frontage, but I was disappointed by the plain façade. These New Yorkers have a passion for drab, brown stone which is beyond my comprehension! However, the interior is spacious and high-ceilinged, with a wide, red carpeted stairway curving up from the entrance hall. The dining room on the ground floor seemed a large, well-appointed room from the glimpse I had of it, but I didn't get a good look. We went directly to the second floor where Mr. Cameron and his daughter were receiving. This floor opens up splendidly for entertaining. The front room, the parlor they call it, is so perfectly proportioned that its size is not oppressive. It's handsomely but comfortably furnished, none of the stiff-backed Victorian heirlooms I had expected, but there's a Steinway grand and some fine pieces that add dignity. My mouth watered over an eighteenth-century secretary that must have cost a mint, unless it was inherited, which it probably was. A few ancestral portraits, needless to say, but fairly good ones. The most interesting was a small head of Lucy Gore in a powdered wig. She's much prettier than in the well-known print. One can easily believe she was the belle of Washington's court. However, the painting that dominates the room is the Sargent. Mrs. Cameron must have been a flawlessly pretty woman, pink and white skin and blond hair but not a china doll by any means. Her lips are soft and full and there's character in her firm little chin. She's slim and light-footed. Clever of the artist to make one see the latter. There's a suggestion of motion in the way she stands as if she might at any second take it into her head to run as lightly and quickly as a girl across the sun-splattered lawn out of one's sight. It's a completely daytime picture, and I had a momentary fancy that I was looking through a window instead of at a framed canvas. But, my dear, Mrs. Cameron is dressed too unsuitably for words! Can you imagine wearing a shirtwaist and skirt to have your portrait done? That's what she has on, a plain white shirtwaist and a yellow and white striped linen skirt and no hat or gloves though it's an outdoor setting. I do think this is carrying simplicity too far even for these New Yorkers who make a cult of it. It certainly would never go down in Chicago. And Mrs. Cameron could be as extravagantly luxurious as anybody when she chose: across the hall from the parlor next to the library there's as elaborate a conservatory as I ever saw in my life, palms and exotic flowering plants and an Italian marble fountain, the base decorated with gilded birds and fruit.

" 'The affair was a large one and I can't match names to faces except in the portraits, but among the guests as well as on the walls there were Gores and Kings, Turners and Jays and Bronsons, the *crème de la crème* as the saying goes, though I think this group would prefer our old French teacher's pet phrase, *les gens bien*. The older people were conservative in dress and manner but friendly enough so that Paul and I didn't feel that we were outsiders at Madame Tussaud's with the waxworks ignoring our presence. There must have been over a hundred guests and at least half of them were young, very attractive, most of them, and smartly turned out. I do think the modern styles are exceptionally becoming to the younger generation. Clothes today have a purity of line—almost a severity wouldn't you say? —that shows off a youthful figure to advantage.

" 'The tea was in honor of the eldest daughter of the house, a last debutante festivity before Lent sets in. I'd been told that Esther Cameron is the beauty of the year but even so I wasn't quite prepared. She is the loveliest creature imaginable, with more fire than the mother, blazing red hair that shines like gold, and enormous, dark-lashed eyes that are almost the color of corn-flowers. Several ladies informed me that her hair and eyes come from the Gore side. Perhaps, but New Yorkers are over fond of giving every face a pedigree and I think this girl has a beauty and look of her own. Odd, isn't it that beauty by itself is never enough? Some other quality is necessary, a glow, a loveliness. I can't put a name to it, but whatever it is Esther Cameron has it.

"'Her father is obviously proud of her, but then this hard-headed businessman is touchingly proud of all his girls.' This is where you and Maud and I enter the scene, just walk on parts, but as Adele describes us I can see us.

"'Julia and Maud who can't be more than ten and eleven respectively put in an appearance in adorable black velvet dresses with pale blue satin sashes. They are well-behaved children but I detected a spark of mischief in Julia. There was an occasional wicked gleam in her blue eyes and a hastily smothered whoop of laughter as she whispered with her sister that led me to suspect that Julia's demure party face is not the one she wears at all times. Even the little one, sweet and rosy in Irish lace with pink bowknots on her shoulders, was brought down from the nursery for a few minutes.

"'The three younger children have the mother's fair complexion and her blond hair, though in varying shades, Maud is almost a towhead. Like both parents they are blue-eyed, not the remarkable color of Esther's eyes but a nice clear blue with no hint of gray. Julia and the baby are pretty children, and I think they'll grow up good-looking, but Maud, I fear is doomed to plainness. It's so unfair that a fractional difference in the size and placement of a woman's features can make the difference between prettiness and plainness. Poor Maud. Listen to me, if you please! I'm the last person who should pity her. I'm the plain one in my family and I wouldn't trade Paul for either of my brothers-in-law. Of course Mother was a great help to me in landing him. It must be hard for a man to bring up a family of girls and it could be terribly hard on them though I don't believe so in this case. What struck me most about all four of these children is that they are happy. A seventeen-year-old is still in many ways a child, though I don't suppose Esther thinks so any more than you and I did when we were that age. Four happy young sisters. It was a nice thing to see.'

"That's all there is about us except a few sentences about the refreshments being delicious and Pa being a perfect host and sending Adele and her husband to their hotel in his motorcar, which she says was quite a novel experience. Pa always was an automobile man. Remember how he never would use one of the carriages except on special occasions like Easter Sunday?"

Julia picks up the letter again. "Let me make sure. Yes, that's all. There's just a play-by-play account of the trip home . . . the train was hours late getting in to Chicago, and she's utterly worn out by the journey on top of the round of entertainments in New York but wants to dash off these hasty pages with her love and is 'ever aff'ly Adele.' "

Julia puts the letter back in her pocket. "That takes us back a lot of years, doesn't it?" She gets briskly to her feet and says, "Let's bring the papers into the living room and return to 1968."

She settles herself on a sofa and is quickly immersed in the Sunday *Times*. I take my *Times* to the other sofa and separate the sections, putting the ones I mean to read beside me and dropping Business and Finance, Classified Advertisements, and Sports on the floor.

I pick up the first part of the news section, but I don't look at it. I think about Adele's letter and all of us when we were young. I don't remember myself in 1903. As Julia would say, I couldn't possibly and yet in a way I can. Even before that I can remember some things. When Adele called the Sargent a completely daytime picture she reminded me of an early puzzlement I thought I had forgotten. I've grown fond of the painting: I like knowing what Mother looked like, and it pleases me to see her when we stay with Julia at Henderson. It's fair that she should be the one to have the portrait now; this is how she remembers Mother. The lady standing on the grass in the sunshine was a stranger to me when I was little. She got in my way when I tried to remember Mother. The recollection I tried to hang on to was of Mother in the night nursery, when because of my early bedtime I had her to myself. I remembered or thought I remembered a sweet scent of sachet and cologne when she came into the darkened room. I tried to remember how she looked when she came through the door, but I never succeeded, she tiptoed too quickly out of the oblong of light to my crib on the other side of the room. Adele was right. She did move as quickly as a girl. I remember her voice, but I don't remember anything she said to me except my name and even that I perhaps imagine. But I do remember—though I am old and she is years away and young I do remember now this minute that she was never in a hurry with me. She stood beside me with her hand against my cheek and I don't remember never did remember being left alone while the door closed behind her. She must have stayed with me until I fell asleep. It's not much but it's nice to have even a small recollection of her that isn't secondhand, wasn't told me by the others.

The event in the early years of which I have a clear recollection is Esther's wedding to Richmond Scott. Julia wouldn't believe me if I said so, and in a sense she'd be right because I don't so much remember that day in May as know it by heart, the way I know nursery rhymes and hymns I can't remember learning.

I know the date: May 4, 1904. Julia would laugh and say of course I do, Aunt Lucy or someone told me later, but on this she'd be wrong, the date was part of the day as I described it to myself and to anyone who would listen.

"The wedding was on the fourth of May, exactly a month after my fifth birthday," I would begin, "and I was the flower girl . . ."

I went over the tale often enough for my seven- or eight-year-old self to keep it intact for me. Even if all I have is the memory of a memory, I haven't forgotten it.

Esther's dress was creamy white to match Mother's lace. Except for her hair blazing through the veil she was all creamy white. Even her bouquet of orange blossoms and rosebuds was softer than dead white.

While the procession was forming at the back of the church, I stayed close to Esther though with her train almost as long as she was tall and the lace folds of her veil making it hard to see her face, she didn't seem like Esther; she was the Bride, the first I had ever seen. I studied her admiringly and I saw that her bouquet was shaking, and that worried me. Perhaps my basket of camellias would be too heavy for me to hold steady all the way up the aisle. I was the only flower girl. The bridesmaids would go up two by two. Esther would have Father, but I would walk alone and must be specially careful to do everything right. Esther saw how anxiously I was looking from her flowers to mine and back again. She was the one of my sisters who quickly noticed when I was worried by things like the array of silver at Sunday luncheon or passing cups and saucers without spilling when Aunt Lucy presided at the tea table. Today Esther was like someone not quite real and I was startled when she murmured something about my not needing to be scared. I'd be all right. I'd be a perfect flower girl. Then she spoke louder and her voice was cheerfully comforting as it always was when I was dismayed by an unfamiliar grown-up situation. "I'll be all right too, Nell. It's just that all brides are nervous."

I was all right. I held my basket carefully and did not swing it. I didn't teeter as we walked in the funny, lagging step we had rehearsed. And when we got to the altar I could see and enjoy everything.

Mr. Scott was a heavy-set, sandy-haired, blue-eyed man, and I thought him handsome and imposing in his wedding clothes. This was a tribute, since he and the best man and the ushers, in their formal attire, were as alike as policemen. Their faces were a blur far above me. I have a more distinct recollection of Mr. Scott because before the ceremony began he bent down and smiled at me in a fatherly way and patted the crown of my leghorn hat. This embarrassed me and I turned away.

During the ceremony I looked mostly at Esther. I'd never seen her so pale. There wasn't even a faint glow of pink in her cheeks. She looks like the Snow Queen, I thought, but I thought this only for a minute, because Esther was nice as well as beautiful, which the Snow Queen certainly was not. And Esther was as brave as a queen. Even though all brides are nervous, when it was her turn to speak her voice didn't waver and when Mr. Scott put the ring on her finger her hand was as steady as his.

The reception at our house was never as clear in my mind as the ceremony at St. Thomas'. There was a confusion of voices and music, and the parlor was a strange place to me. This was the first time I had seen it transformed into a ballroom with the comfortable everyday furniture and the oriental rug banished to the cellar.

The light from the twin chandeliers was reflected in the parquet floor and in the silver gilt bowls that were filled with American Beauty roses. For a gala occasion those bowls were placed on carved pedestals between the windows. This was my first sight of them and they delighted me.

I remember the tiered wedding cake. I couldn't forget it; it was taller than I was. The red-coated musicians also made a deep impression on me. They played very fast, and the guests twirled to waltztime like figures on a music box.

I think I remember that when Father drew back the curtains to let some air in, daylight came in too and dimmed the chandeliers, but maybe I add that from a later recollection. Pa was always a great one for fresh air.

I was allowed to stay until after Esther and Mr. Scott were driven away in a shower of rose petals and a hail of rice, and when the last guests had gone I was not taken up to bed but allowed to go by myself to the nursery where Mademoiselle was waiting and this was a fine, proud end to a fine, proud day.

It wasn't quite the end. When I paused on the third floor to catch my breath I heard someone crying in the sitting room. I ran in, too startled to be scared until I discovered the person crying was Aunt Lucy. For Aunt Lucy to cry was a frightening thing, she was the one who comforted us when we cried. She was our mother's sister and our rock of strength and second in our hearts only to Father.

Before I could back out of the door Father came through it with a glass of champagne in his hand. He gave the glass and his handkerchief to Aunt Lucy and sat down in an armchair and took me on his knee, and asked me why I was crying. I wasn't old enough, he said, to cry at weddings.

I told him I was scared at Aunt Lucy's crying.

"Aunt Lucy never cries, Pa."

"Nothing to be scared about, Nell, all women cry at weddings."

All women cry at weddings. All brides are nervous.

I had acquired two mysterious grown-up facts, but there was

no time to ponder them. The day and my recollection of it were over. Father carried me up to—

"For the love of Mike, Nell, who do you think is dead at long last?"

I jump at the sound of Julia's voice.

"Augie Wenger, that's who," she says.

I look for the obituary in my paper while Julia goes on talking. "A cerebral hemorrhage, according to the *Times*. Wouldn't you know he'd get off lightly even in his dying? I don't believe he had a sick or sad day in his life. It's a respectful obituary, complete with photograph. The Wenger Corporation, the first August von L., and pioneer days in California, Augie's clubs, the usual thing. Nothing about his marriages except that he's survived by his widow, two daughters by a previous marriage, five grandchildren and one great-grandchild. Let's see what's in the paid notice: 'Wenger, August von L. suddenly at his residence, November 22, 1968 . . .' and listen to this 'mourned by his devoted wife.' As the young would say, how corny can you get?"

"Perhaps she was devoted to him, who knows?"

"Who knows and who cares?" Julia lets the paper slide to the floor as she stands up. "How you can be so calm about him even now, Nell! And about her."

"Because it is now. Then was a long time ago. We were a long time ago, Julia."

"I'll concentrate on now thank you very much and leave then on the floor with Augie. I don't want to be reminded of the trouble he brought on our family. Well, I better hurry and get my bath or I'll be late for church. I'm meeting Dotty Guarrigue at St. Thomas' and we're lunching at the Colony Club. See you later."

Julia disappears down the hall into the guest room and I find Augie's obituary and the photograph. I can scarcely recognize him in the white-haired, aging man, but the very changes in him remind me sharply and unexpectedly of Augie as he was when I first saw him. I guess a sudden, unlooked-for death can take you back through the years like a time machine.

Adele's letter was agreeably nostalgic. It recalled the hazy, early days of which I have only scattered and incomplete recollections, but Augie's obituary brings me back with a jolt to the years that are in focus, that are as unblurred as the ones I am living now.

2

Maud once told me rather dogmatically that seven is the age of reason. It may be so, though I think children much younger than that reason according to the data available to them. Still, there is a turning point when the fog over the grown-up landscape lifts. It may quite possibly be at the age of seven. By the time I was that age our family was no longer a maze in which I uncertainly felt my way. I knew my way. And, as I look back, my recollections present themselves in an unbroken sequence of time and place. I can see, plainly and without interruption, my sisters and me in the long young years. It's hard to believe that those years weren't in reality very many but only seemed so as they went slowly by. They still seem long when I think about them and they are agreeable—better than agreeable, they are lovely to remember.

In addition to our family world I had a splendid contemporary world of my own.

In recent years there has been an awareness and a fear of gangs of boys and of girls too, a rapidly increasing fear of their murderous violence. I think young gangs have not always been evil. Harmless and even good things can go bad. Among our elders' quotations a favorite was "lilies that fester smell far worse than weeds." They had many such cryptic tags with which they stopped a conversation that was in danger of becoming unfit for the ears of children or servants.

I had a gang in New York and in Southampton. A group of friends, exactly like oneself, of one's own sex and age, is a bulwark to a child. Women usually outgrow the need for it. Men never do, or they wouldn't seek the refuge of their clubs or be Masons or go off on outlandish excursions to the ends of the earth.

I had two gangs, though they overlapped. I had my friends in my class at Spence and of my age in Southampton. With them, I moved as freely and unself-consciously as one goldfish in a bowlful.

In the summer and in the winter our days were bounded by a timetable. We always knew where everyone was.

In Southampton our first stop in the morning was at the Meadow Club where some took tennis lessons and the verandah was an agreeable meeting place for all. When the weather was fine we moved on to the beach. We quickly outgrew the afternoon sessions at the beach and left the ocean to the little ones and their nurses. In the afternoon we played at someone's house —blind man's bluff or living statues or whatever was the currently popular game. Sometimes we went to Peconic to enjoy the warm and unintimidating bathing. We were accompanied practically everywhere by Mademoiselles and Fräuleins and an occasional English Miss Somebody. However, they kept to themselves and so did we and the summer days were pleasant for all.

In New York there was school in the morning and the Mall in Central Park in the afternoon except on dancing class days. Spence girls had the freedom of the esplanade and we could roller-skate up and down its entire length or we could play hopscotch or prisoner's base in any unoccupied space. The Brearley and Chapin girls kept to the opposite ends of the Mall, and woe betided any member of the rival school who trespassed.

The war between the two schools started, as wars often do

start, because they were neighbors. Spence was at some distance from them on West Fifty-fifth Street. It's a pity that when Chapin and Brearley moved uptown they should have chosen sites within two blocks of each other. Spence is again outside the battle area beside the old Carnegie house on Ninety-first Street. In the summer vacations there was a truce—still is, I suppose. In Southampton there were girls from both schools as well as from Spence and from smaller establishments. Spence's neutrality was strengthened by our having boarders which set us apart and also meant that a large section of our school went home, mostly westward, for vacations and was never known or judged or quarreled with in the summer.

Not being by nature a fighter, I was glad I went to Spence. I liked the week days at school and in the Park. I liked the Saturday luncheon parties. At every place there was a favor, a bunch of violets with a red rose in the center, a box of Huyler's chocolates or a small china ornament. Afterward we went to a matinee, to the Hippodrome or the play or occasionally to the opera if a mother or grandmother had a box and the opera was a suitable one.

In those years Maud and Julia entered their teens and Esther was a married lady with a baby, but she still was one of us. She came often to stay in New York or in Southampton when Mr. Scott was in Chicago or San Francisco for the bank or in Canada or Scotland for salmon or grouse.

Esther's baby was a delight to me. In the first place I helped to name him. His official name was Richmond Scott, Junior, and Esther sometimes called him Richy or Ricky.

"Rikki," I said. "That's it! Rikki Tikki Tavi can be his whole nickname."

"So it can," Esther said. "Rikki Tikki Tavi is a fine name, he'll like it."

Mr. Scott did not consider it a fine name. "The boy will feel a fool later with a nickname like that," he said. "Furthermore he'll get called Mongoose or more probably Goosey at the Browning School and at Groton."

"It's only for now, Richmond," Esther said. "Isn't Rikki all right for now?"

Mr. Scott said there was no harm in Ricky (I was sure that was how he spelled it in his head) or Rick. Rick wasn't a bad name for a small boy but Esther was to forget this Rikki Tikki Tavi nonsense. Young Richmond was not to be saddled with anything so absurd.

It was only in the nursery at our house or Mr. Scott's that Esther and I called Rikki *Rikki Tikki Tavi,* and it was a fine name. We were right about that—it had a rhythm to it. Rikki liked to hear it and say it. Esther gave him a drum on his second birthday and I can hear him beating it in time with the syllables: *Rik* ki *Tik* ki *Ta* vi.

I thought it clever of Rikki to know this was his nursery name and not to expect it to be used in more formal rooms, and I praised him to Esther.

She laughed and said, "He's clever but not that clever. Rikki Tikki Tavi isn't yet a name to him as much as it's a nursery game, a nursery rhyme without meaning but with a swing to it, like 'A diller a dollar a ten o'clock scholar.'"

I must have looked disappointed, because Esther told me not to be. "Cheer up, Nell, Rikki will understand your fine idea one day. When he's old enough we'll read the story to him. Richmond's right about school, you know, but I think Rikki will be privately amused and pleased to have been called after Mr. Kipling's brave little animal."

I loved Rikki from the time he was a fat, pink baby with his hair brushed in a long thick gold crest on the top of his head.

Even before he could talk I enjoyed playing with him. His blue eyes would look from me to the toy I held out to him and back to me again, and he would utter a stream of loud, cheerful gibberish. I always answered him, since probably he thought he was talking and I enjoyed our one-sided conversations, though naturally it was more interesting for both of us when he began to talk intelligibly. However I was interested in Rikki at every stage and fond of him. I suppose what I loved best about him was his age. At last someone in the family was younger than I was.

By the time I was nine years old Maud and Julia treated me, not with more affection—they were usually kind and friendly unless they were provoked—they treated me with greater confidence, as if I too were to some degree a person. They hardly ever stopped talking when I appeared. They discussed their clothes and their parties and their friends in front of me. They shared small family jokes with me. They shared their youthful world with me. It is the Cameron world I remember best, the world in which we were young and gay and at peace.

It suddenly occurs to me that probably every happy family grows up in a serene world like ours, but I always think of us as being like the families in our books. Families in books are the only ones we know intimately besides our own and remembering is like reading a child's book. Children reread more than we do. Remembering is like reading a book in which we know everything that will happen and can change nothing. No one sensible would want to change anything. *If only* is an illusion and a folly. Who knows that another pattern of events would have been better or even as good? At any rate, this is the pattern that is and in remembering it, as in reading a familiar story, we can go as slowly as we please and put off the end of a chapter as long as we wish. That is exactly what I'm doing. A chapter was about to end for us, though we didn't learn for some time that that particular Easter Sunday had begun or ended anything.

It occasionally rained on Easter Sunday, but, looking back, the day seems almost always to have burst on us in a blaze of sunshine.

Lent was over at last. People kept Lent then, kept it in visible ways, I mean. There were sewing circles for the ladies and children "gave up" something more or less faithfully. There was little or no lavish entertaining during that season. Certainly there was none among what Pa affectionately called the Old Guard. New spring clothes were not worn until Easter morning. The outward aspects of winter remained until that day.

The light colors that bloomed on Fifth Avenue were as much a sign of spring as the first forsythia in the park. The ladies' costumes were mostly gray or fawn or navy blue, but their hats were trimmed with crisp ribbon and tulle and ornamented with feathers or multicolored flowers. The ladies wore real flowers too, violets or orchids or gardenias pinned at the waist. Their kid gloves were white and their gold mesh bags glittered. The gentlemen formed a becomingly dark background, but their sober morning dress was brightened by a carnation or gardenia in the buttonhole of their lapels, and their silk hats, as they were raised and lowered in greeting, flashed in the sunlight.

The Easter parade was like a processional dance, a ballet of spring come to city pavements. People went to church more in those days, at least they went more formally and regularly. Sunday best was a reality and on Easter in every neighborhood a lady's Sunday best was as new as she could afford, even if it was only the hat that was new or retrimmed.

I remember Fifth Avenue because that was where we walked. We were driven to church, but we walked home. We admired ourselves and our friends and acquaintances, but the day still kept a not entirely secular meaning. Lent was over, winter was over. Easter and spring were here in their glory. My daughter Roberta insists that it must always have been a rather absurd outdoor fashion show, but it was better than that. "Happy Easter" was more than an ordinary polite greeting. Later, Roberta's description was correct. After the First World War, the Easter Parade was a fashion show that slowly became absurd. Finally it ended in travesty.

In 1908 the Easter skies were not bright. The April morning was cold and rainy. The rain had stopped when we came out of church, but the clouds were still heavy and Julia suggested that we drive home, but Pa said a little walk in the fresh air would do us good. The carriage could follow in case of a shower.

In spite of the threat of rain the Avenue was crowded and we progressed slowly, not at the brisk pace that Pa preferred. We had gone only a few blocks when he was stopped by an acquaintance who introduced a young companion and we had our first sight of Augie Wenger.

I don't remember who introduced Augie to Father. Father introduced him to us and invited him to join us for luncheon at the house.

Augie had recently arrived in New York from San Francisco where he had been born and brought up. The Wenger fortune had started with gold and then had been solidly built on California shipping and real estate but Augie had business and family ties with New York. His mother had been one of the New York Jameses and he had letters of introduction to Father which he had intended to present after Easter.

At luncheon Augie told us that Mrs. Wenger and their little daughters were in Burlingame. They would come East in the autumn and in the meanwhile Augie would see what houses were available here or in Boston. Probably, he said, they would rent something in Boston to begin with, as that was Mrs. Wenger's native city. Eventually he hoped they would make their home in New York. New York was the only other American city for a San Franciscan.

I was not paying much attention to the conversation. My mind was on the food. Our Easter menu always included ham, a meat never served at nursery meals, and Saint Honoré, a rare and favorite dessert.

It was my first sight of Augie on Fifth Avenue that stayed with me. He bowed over Esther's hand and when he straightened up they stood quite still, facing each other.

Augie's slightly foreign ways, which were never exaggerated, were not considered affected, because his grandfather Wenger had been born in Vienna. Augie's manners were correct, but they had more warmth than anyone else's. A conventional phrase on his lips sounded as if he meant it. He seemed really to want to know how you did. If he helped even a child on or off with her coat, she felt that his whole attention was on her. It was said of him that when he lifted his hat to a lady on the street he made her feel that he had walked along that street at that hour solely in the hope of catching a glimpse of her.

Augie's social gestures were never careless or routine. When he sent flowers they were not the usual ones: the corsage of orchids or the two dozen long-stemmed American Beauties. He sent spring flowers to a dowager and scarlet camellias rather than lilies of the valley to a debutante. He would even send flowers to a child, a colonial bouquet or a basket of small roses to a little girl whose father had proposed him for a club or done him some other kindness. Once he sent me an orchid which I was of course not allowed to wear, but I kept it in a vase in my room and was the envy of my friends. Perhaps it was because he was a Californian that flowers were a natural expression of his sentiments on all occasions. In any event, he was ever a great one for send-ing them or bringing them.

It was long afterward that I picked Augie apart, trying to dis-cover what made him so charming, so easy to be with and to like. On that Sunday it was his appearance that made an impres-sion on me. He was the first man I had ever seen who matched Esther in beauty. I was amazed to find myself thinking a man was beautiful. The proper word for a man was handsome, but Augie was more than that. He had the same shining quality that Esther had, though they were not alike, he was as dark as she was fair. He was, I decided, like someone from an old time, a Crusader's squire or Saladin or a young Eastern king on a gold coin.

Augie had none of the peacock quality which can destroy a man's attractiveness that in our day made us say of his looks "Arrow collar" and forget him. If Augie was vain, as he probably was, he did not betray it. He wore his good looks as casually as an Englishman wears good clothes.

I must have liked Augie even on that first day. He was gay and friendly and treated me as politely as he did Aunt Lucy, but I don't remember liking him or thinking about him. What I re-member is looking at him and Esther.

It's clear in my mind as a snapshot if a snapshot could have been in color then: the two of them at their first meeting, stand-ing quite still in the Easter parade, face to face, with her hand in his.

We all liked Augie as we got to know him. He came often to the house on Saturdays and Sundays. Esther came too, alone or with Rikki or Mr. Scott, but the latter seemed more Father's friend than ours. I never could quite call Mr. Scott Richmond, nor do I think he would have found it appropriate. We were both satisfied by my addressing him as you.

Having Augie, the girls said, made our family complete. It was as though the brother who was born between Esther and Maud had not died as a baby.

A family perks up I discovered when its intimacy includes a stranger. Augie accompanied us on walks with Mademoiselle. When Augie was along, a walk turned into an adventure. I had never before met a grownup who was willing to explore the Ramble in the park or climb the tower. On rainy days he played councan or Parcheesi with us before he went off to the Racquet Club to play squash.

Father was pleased that Augie was well liked at the clubs. It was an excellent sign, he said, when men liked a man. "Even the older men like him. He's a modest chap for all his good looks and money and I believe he manages the latter intelligently. He's well thought of in California, Richmond tells me."

I was astonished to learn that Father was a little sorry for Augie.

"The lad's lonely," I heard him tell Aunt Lucy. "Misses his sisters. He's the only boy and I imagine they spoil him as our girls do."

Aunt Lucy said she thought that more women than his sisters would spoil Augie.

"He's extraordinarily handsome," she said, "and he's a married man."

Father laughed. "My dear Lucy, Augie can hardly be considered a threat to our girls. They're too young."

"They're growing up, James. Esther is grown up."

"Esther is married and the others are schoolgirls. I'm happy to have the boy feel that this house is his home. I owe that much to his maternal grandfather. Mr. James was exceedingly kind to me when I was a young man starting out, even before I met Eleanor."

Our lovely spring continued with more family excursions than we had ever had, visits to the Aquarium and the zoo and to the Statue of Liberty.

Usually I longed for spring in New York to be over. The park in its pale green with blossoms bursting through was so inviting that I could scarcely bear to look at it on my way to school. It was not a season to be shut up in classrooms. I would think of Southampton, of the cool smell of the air after we passed River-head, of the first noontime on the beach when the ocean was too cold for bathing but the sand was warm when I sifted it through my fingers. June was one of my favorite months in Southampton. I was always a little afraid of the ocean, and I liked the early summer when one could admire but need not go in. I liked my riding lessons with Emmet Cosgrove, the head groom at the livery stable. We went along the back roads beyond the village where the fields were white with potato blossoms. I liked Mecox Bay where Bertie sometimes took me clamming.

People from other summer places refuse to believe that South-ampton, when I was a child, was surrounded by what they call "country," but they're mistaken. We had little hills with a few clumps of trees, and where the Island was wide and the shel-tered fields were flat we had beautiful tall trees. We even had pine woods, though they are scrubbier than I thought then. Best of all, we had salty ponds and dune grass and the sea. The pret-tiest landscape if it is beyond the sound and sight and taste and smell of the sea, is not my idea of country.

Every year by May my sisters and I were impatient to be near the ocean again, but none of us wanted this spring to end.

When at last it was June and we were getting ready to leave the city we were cheered by Augie's announcement that he would be coming to Southampton. He thanked Father for his invitation to stay with us at any time and explained that he need not take advantage of this kindness. He was, he said, going West to settle a business matter and to talk over winter plans with his wife. He had the offer of two good houses in New York and three in Boston, among which he wanted her to choose. He had made arrangements with the Irving House for the month of August in the hope that she would bring the children to Southampton. Though little Sophie was barely two and Sister not yet one, their mother felt that two moves in less than a year would be unsettling for them.

"But I hope," Augie said, "to persuade Sophie to bring them to Southampton."

I thought happily that the pleasures of the spring were not over after all, and I turned my face to the summer and the sea.

One of the nice surprises of the summer was that Aunt Lucy came to stay with us.

Aunt Lucy's husband, the Suffragan Bishop of New York, had died not long after Mother and, at that time, Father asked Aunt Lucy to live with us but she said there was no need for her to give up the ways in which she was set. Father could manage very well with the help of Mademoiselle and of Bridie Smith, who had been Mother's maid; Bridie would make an excellent housekeeper.

"The flat on Fifty-ninth Street is home to me," Aunt Lucy told Father, "and I like to get above sea level in the summer. I'll go to the Profile House as we always did. But whenever the girls need me I'll come."

This she had done. If one of us was ill she came to stay and if at any time we pleaded with her to stay overnight she did.

Aunt Lucy kept a few things in Mother's room and they were transferred to Southampton in the summer, but Mother's room remained her own. Her silver bureau set and her ornaments and the photographs of us and Father as we were in her years remained as she had left them.

Until now Aunt Lucy had paid us only two long visits. She stayed with us during the winter before Esther's wedding and she returned a year later to be with Esther during her confinement.

Father was delighted by Aunt Lucy's decision to spend a summer with us when there was no need for her presence. The winter was another matter, he could understand her keeping the flat in town where she and the bishop had lived for fifteen years and he knew she would never be willing to dismiss her maids.

"Lucy's like her younger sister in that," he said. "Eleanor couldn't stand to give anyone notice. I had to do it for her." He fell silent as he always did when he unexpectedly remembered Mother out loud.

The summer was different from the spring, but when I look back on it by itself it is a lovely time. For me it was a continuation of the last best years of childhood before one slides into the scaring beginning of adolescence. We didn't use the latter term nor did our elders; they took refuge in their quotations and referred to "the maiden of blushing fifteen" and to "where the brook and river meet" or they talked matter-of-factly of a daughter or a friend's daughter who was almost a young lady and something really must be done about her hair or her carriage or that tomboy manner of hers. What had been natural behavior for years must be curbed and altered. My friends and I were still safe from improvement at our parents' hands. We were supervised and corrected but we weren't nagged at to be something new. We understood when and where we were expected to be clean and neat and polite. We knew how to behave at the dining-room table and at church and on other grown-up occasions. On our own occasions we were free.

Looking back and considering pleasure, not happiness, which is rare and can come at any age, I think those years were for most of us as agreeable as any we would ever know.

The years now are somewhat the same. I have learned to think of myself as old, since that is how the young think of us, and middle-aged is not a description attractive enough to be worth hanging on to.

The pleasures of age and childhood are not unalike: food and books and games and embroidery and the theater and one's friends. And we have the unexpected pleasure of grandchildren —at least my delight in them was totally unexpected. They are dear and entertaining and one loves them, but they are at one remove and we haven't the agonizing responsibility. We also can enjoy again the freedom from change and decisions. Now as then, we cannot, unless we are perfect fools, make a decision that will overturn our lives, and our years have a blessed sameness, though they go faster than they once did. I remember Emmet Cosgrove telling me when I was too young to understand him, "In the end the years go by so fast, miss, that they slap you in the face." In their slowness those first years were better, but now we have the satisfaction of knowing that with any luck things will go on more or less as they are.

In that summer, as now, many of my pleasures were vicarious. I enjoyed being an onlooker in my sisters' world.

Maud and Julia were beginning to be young ladies. Though Maud wasn't pretty, she had nice skin and she held herself well and that was a blessing because she was too tall. She was only two inches taller than Esther, but in our generation every inch counted and Maud's height, which would be little more than average for our granddaughters, was an embarrassment to her.

In some way, as can happen with sisters who are near of an

age and alike in coloring, Maud reflected Julia's prettiness and they were spoken of as those attractive Cameron girls.

"Esther is the beauty of the family," the mothers and governesses said, "but the girls are attractive in their own way, especially Julia, and of course they are still at the awkward age."

The awkward age lasted longer then and was in truth awkward for most, which was hard on the young but gave their parents a longer span of hope. No one, however hopeful, could have imagined that summer that any of us would ever equal Esther.

This, I thought must have been how she looked when she came out. I didn't remember, but I had heard from grownups that a girl is at her peak in that first season with all the world and all her years ahead of her. I remembered Esther as a bride which had seemed a peak to me, though a rather solemn one, but when I said this to Pa, he told me a girl had better be serious when she was getting engaged and married and thereby deciding her whole life. That dewy-eyed folderol was all very well in a novel but in real life love was a serious matter, and my sister, he assured me, had decided wisely. Richmond Scott was a solid citizen, a fine man who would look after her, enough older and with the same background.

"She couldn't have done better," Pa said, "if I'd chosen her husband myself."

I don't think it occurred to Pa then or later that in fact he had chosen Mr. Scott himself.

Once in a while Julia talks about that summer. She doesn't know any more about it than I do, perhaps not as much, but once in a while she gets going on it.

"It was a heavenly summer," she'll say, "but it's the last young untroubled Southampton year and that makes it uncomfortable to remember, though I enjoyed it at the time. I was beginning to find my footing in the teens and I was discovering that the awkward age needn't be as awkward as I'd been led to expect. I ought to have seen the danger signals, and I would have if I'd taken a good long look at Esther and Augie, but fourteen doesn't look long at anything but itself. I didn't. Oh well, yes, I kept an eye out for Maud, but mostly I thought about myself from the time I got up in the morning until I went to bed at night. I thought about my hair and more becoming ways to fix it and about how I could talk Aunt Lucy into letting me have more sophisticated clothes. I wondered if it was worth my while to get to be really good at lawn tennis. I knew it was worth while to be good on the dance floor. Dodworth's had been some help in learning the basic steps, but dancing class once a week isn't enough, and I made Maud practice with me by the hour. I can still see the triumphant grin on her face as we attained the proper speed in the Viennese waltz. She caught on to any new fast step sooner than I did. She was a natural born dancer. It was only at our first parties when the boys were too short for her that she stiffened with embarrassment and stumbled over their feet. Later she was all right once she was actually on a ball-room floor, and I never had any real difficulty finding partners for her."

Sometimes it's Maud's prowess in the ocean that is on Julia's mind. I remember that, and it amazed me that anyone as shy as Maud should face the breakers and the treacherous undertow so fearlessly.

"She was a terrific swimmer," Julia will say. "When we were in the water she was the leader, the one who made me brave, I guess reckless is the word. Goodness, we were young and crazy. I shudder when I think of us thumbing our noses at the life-guards and swimming beyond the barrels on a red flag day, but it seemed a lark at the time. It didn't seem a lark to Pa, and Maud and I were in serious trouble I can tell you."

Julia doesn't look serious when she tells me about this or any other escapade. She grins as wickedly as if she was back in her teens with Maud.

"We had a lot of fun in that last absolutely carefree summer," Julia will say, and then sometimes she will stop and frown before she continues (if she continues—she doesn't always). "It makes me mad, makes me feel a fool to remember how many of our good times that year we owed to Augie, and the most infuriating thing is that they were good times, I can't change that. Will you ever forget, Nell, when we were becalmed in Gardiner's Bay and it was almost dark before a motor launch came to our rescue? We dived off the sailboat in our clothes, and it was a fine adventure altogether. And the clambake Augie arranged for us on our beach? Maud and I were certainly innocent lambs where he was concerned. We took him for granted, Pa's dear young protégé from the West. We didn't pay the slightest attention to him and Esther except as two kindly grownups who added to the summer's pleasures. Well, if we were blind as bats so was Pa, but of course he was in town all week. Maybe Aunt Lucy realized but if she didn't you can't blame her, even the dreadnaughts were caught napping for once."

The older ladies who ringed the floor at dances and from under their parasols observed the beach were known as the dreadnaughts. They were, I think, astonished to be surrounded and replaced by the rising generations. From the side lines where they found themselves, unexpectedly quickly it must have seemed, they watched and speculated and deplored and resisted change. The young and even the younger middle-aged were afraid of their sharp eyes and their acid tongues. Yet the dreadnaughts could be merciful. They would cover the retreat to virtue of a young sinner if she hadn't gone too far. I suppose they still do. Self-appointed guardians of society must still exist though the young haven't even a name for them any more and society is an outmoded and meaningless term and it's hard to say what would, today, be considered going too far.

Other times, other customs, I tell myself. I'm too lazy to be a guardian of anyone except Roberta. Not that I'm aware of doing anything, it's just that I'm here. Remembering Aunt Lucy, I know that the older generation is a wall at your back. When the wall is gone and there is no Aunt Lucy and even your doctor and your banker are young, you are old.

At the end of July, Augie moved into the Irving House alone. The expansion of the Wenger Corporation's interests required that he be near New York, he said, but Sophie had remained firm about keeping the children in California for the summer. They would join him in October in the house he had rented in Boston.

Mr. Scott was in Scotland, and Esther and Rikki were staying with us. She and Augie were caught up in the life of the young marrieds. It was not only children who moved in a group. Even the babies with their nurses and the very old ladies had their schedule and their fixed meeting places.

The young marrieds were under thirty and their group included bachelors and girls who had not yet married. Esther and Augie fitted easily into this summer clan. They played doubles at the Meadow Club and in foursomes at Shinnecock. They went to the weekend dances. At the weekend Southampton was full of visitors including extra men and unattached girls, and Esther and Augie were as often as not at separate dinner parties.

During the week Augie was only occasionally in New York. When he was in Southampton he dropped in at the house in the afternoon or for family supper. He and Esther took us out in his motorcar. They came clamming with Bertie and me or they organized expeditions for all of us to Montauk Point or Sag Harbor.

They did not, with us or with their contemporaries, appear to seek each other out. They did not play tennis or swim or dance with each other more than with anyone else. They did not seem driven by a need to be within close reach or sight of one another. They were content to be in the same place at the same hour. It was enough in that beginning to be on the same verandah or the same beach, however crowded. It was enough, I suppose, to be in the same world.

Good looks are an excellent camouflage for the beginning of being in love. A plain girl becomes pretty and one wonders about her. A beautiful girl is safer from prying eyes. I think no one except Aunt Lucy wondered about Esther.

Esther talked to me about that summer long afterward when the truth about it wasn't important and there was no reason to conceal or alter it.

Nothing had happened, she said, except that she and Augie had not so much fallen as drifted into love.

It was the sort of idyll that Esther had imagined before she grew up and then had forgotten in the rush of her popularity. The family was in mourning for Mother in the year before Esther came out. She did not go to dances or to any large or formal gatherings. At seventeen she was not only the most beautiful debutante to be introduced to society, she was a refreshingly unexpected beauty. It was exciting, she said, to be suddenly and simultaneously a grownup and a success, but it was also bewildering. Oh, it was fun to be the belle of her year. She liked the beaux who filled her dance cards, she enjoyed the bouquets and the cotillion favors and the compliments they offered her, but before the year was over, before the Tuxedo Ball came around again, her success seemed like a childhood game too long-drawn-out. What should have been a grown-up world was like the spinning globe in the nursery, not like a real world at all.

Then, Father's friend, Richmond Scott began with Father's approval to pay serious court to her. He was about fifteen years younger than Pa but he seemed, Esther said, to be of the same generation. He was not a boy, but a man who offered a grown-up life; he offered solidity instead of frivolity, he offered wisdom and strength and a safe place.

"It's hard to remember now what Richmond offered me. I think I thought he would give me a lifetime like Mother's with Father, only longer." Esther shook her head. "It's hard to remember and it doesn't matter. Eighteen is too young to decide a lifetime."

Esther told me that Augie had been too young too. He was just over twenty-one when he and Sophie, two years his senior, were married.

"Anyway," Esther said, "on that Easter morning we met and almost without realizing it we were caught in the web of the spring and the summer. Neither of us thought of it as a second chance to be seized secretly or openly, had the latter seemed possible in those days. We didn't really think at all. It was a lovely time that happened to us and we moved in it and with it until just at the end when we tried to hang onto it as you do when you know you are waking up and you try to keep a dream from dissolving."

Esther and Augie moved through the August weeks as a girl and a boy in their teens might move through a summer vacation, living the days one by one without counting them, enjoying a familiar routine in which everything is newly seen because the other is there: the sea on a fair day when the blue flag is flying, the high dune at Flying Point, the lighthouse at the end of the

old Montauk Road, the sun blazing on the lawn tennis courts
. . . For Esther the long-known landscape was a strange and
beautiful country.

This was a new, dimensionless time that had neither direction
nor end until abruptly on a September weekend, it was over.

"And there we were with vacation over. Do you remember,
Nell, the jolt with which summer used to end? Suddenly it was
over and back we must go to school. It was like that for Augie
and me. Back we must go to real life and we discovered how
desperately we didn't want to."

The September weekend was a cold and rainy one until Sunday afternoon when the rain stopped and the wind died and the
sun was warm as summer.

The maids had packed the silver and china for town. Pa had
gone to the South Side Club. He always escaped when we
moved back and forth, and Mademoiselle and Bridie Smith preferred to have him out of the way.

Aunt Lucy agreed to our having the picnic supper at Flying
Point which one of us suggested.

Augie came, and Maud and Julia brought Betty Conway and
her brother Bunny, and Bertie was there. Bertie was considered
family. He lived two blocks from us in New York and his uncle
had married a cousin of Mother's. He was nearer Julia's age than
mine but he was my friend. It was thanks to Bertie that the girls'
informal parties, even evening ones, were comfortable occasions
for me.

By the time we had finished supper it was dark, but the boys
kept the fire going and no one wanted the last hour of the last
summer day to be over.

Someone produced marshmallows and between toasting them
and piling wood on the fire we didn't notice when first Esther
and Augie and then Aunt Lucy wandered beyond the firelight.

Aunt Lucy did not say anything to me nor, as far as I know, to anyone else until after Esther told me.

"We hadn't had half a year," Esther said, "and now it was over and we couldn't bear it."

Augie suggested that they collect more driftwood and Esther followed him out of the light into the deep shadow below the dune.

They did not say a word except their names. In love, the name of the other is more than the fondest endearment.

"Esther," Augie said. "Esther . . ."

They stood still and turning found themselves in each other's arms.

"Neither of us made the first move, Nell. I don't remember either of us moving at all only that there we were holding on to each other. Augie's mouth clung to mine and our bodies were as close as if they were one, no longer two."

If we had all come running and shouting across the sand, they wouldn't have heard. They didn't hear Aunt Lucy. She had to come close to them which she hadn't wanted to do.

"Children," she said, "I'm sorry."

Still they didn't hear or move until Aunt Lucy put her hand on Esther's shoulder. Then they separated slowly as one slowly wakens from sleep and a deep dream.

"Aunt Lucy?" Esther's voice was soft and questioning. Aunt Lucy was, as any intruder would have been, a stranger.

"Yes, dear. You must come back, you know."

"We were saying good-by. We were, weren't we, Augie? There's nothing else we can say."

Esther began to cry, not noisily as one starts to cry but quietly, with tears trickling slowly down her face as if she had been weeping for a long time. She held her hands, palms up, in front of her, astonished at their emptiness.

"There isn't anything else to say, is there, Augie? It was what children call 'a pretend' and now it's over."

"It's over," Augie said, "but it wasn't a pretend. It was real, Esther. We'll know that forever."

"Good-by is hard enough," Aunt Lucy said, "without my moralizing. But I must tell you to be quick. Get some of that driftwood, Augie, and we'll bring it back. Try not to cry, Esther, and keep out of the firelight."

"And that was our good-by," Esther told me. "It was really a good-by to innocence. Oh, I know it wasn't truly innocence. I have no right to use the word." She paused and frowned. After so many years the admission was still painful. "But it seemed a time of innocence in which we had hurt no one, not even ourselves until the end. And it was over. Innocent or not, it was a lovely, young time and it was over."

Later, Aunt Lucy talked to me about that evening.

"Poor Esther meant her good-by and so perhaps did Augie." She sighed. "I hoped. I hoped Sophie would keep her husband on a tight leash. I made up my mind to tell Richmond he shouldn't leave Esther alone so much, and I did do that. I told him she moped when he was away on his business and pleasure trips. I didn't say anything to Esther. Talking would do no good and might do harm. I hoped that she would take a long look at Rikki and realize that it would be possible for her to lose him. It's frightening when one has nothing but hope to count on. I always told your uncle that it was the shakiest and least comforting of the virtues. Love, he would tell me, is the all-encompassing and eternal virtue that will outlast the others. He meant St. Paul's kind of love, of course, but any kind can be all-encompassing while it lasts and violent and dangerous. I was pretty sure this was a first love for Esther and I was afraid of it. I had also seen enough of the world to know that a final romantic good-by can be the first step to a meeting on another level."

3

THE YEAR begins in the autumn, at least when one is of school age it does, and that is the age that sets the pattern.

In that October as in every October, school and the year began together. I was in a new class with new teachers except in elocution and penmanship. There were new girls to meet, even if we looked askance at them at first. There were noisy reunions with old friends who had spent the vacation in places as distant as Maine or Europe. I plunged happily into this year. Last summer and last spring receded and only this autumn, this time now, existed.

Augie was living in Boston. He had vanished from our life as summer friends often did, but I was too busy to miss him or even to mind Esther's being in France with Mr. Scott for two months during the establishment of the Paris branch of the bank.

The autumn is exciting to a child not only because it is a beginning but because it is brief and studded with splendid holidays.

As October ends there is Halloween. In our day well-brought-up children were not allowed to go trick-or-treating. I never heard of it, but we had ducking for apples and no one told ghost stories as well and as terrifyingly as Bridie Smith.

Next came Thanksgiving, a big day in our house. Father admired it for being both Puritan and American. We listened, rapt, to his dramatic account, always with some new and interesting detail, of the landing at Plymouth Rock, of the staunch and high-minded pilgrims and of their dealings with the fierce and colorful Indians, and we enjoyed our rich holiday meal with its unpuritanical trimmings of mottoes and a Jack Horner pie from F. A. O. Schwarz.

Before we could settle down to school again after the long agreeable weekend we were in December with the steadily increasing almost unbearable anticipation of Christmas and finally the arrival of the Eve with stockings and carols and St. Luke and then the great day itself.

That was a fine Christmas for me. I was still young enough for it to seem as if the wealth of the Indies was spread out beneath the tree. A rajah doll with a huge jewel in his feathered turban stood out in the profusion of toys, but I had more lasting pleasure from Sophie Rose, named for my favorite character in my favorite set of French books. Tales like *Sans Famille* depressed me, but the *Bibliothèque Rose* was endlessly entertaining. Sophie Rose had a fur-trimmed coat and jewelry and white kid gloves and a lace-edged pocket handkerchief. Esther had bought her at the Nain Bleu in Paris. Aunt Lucy gave me my most grown-up present, a miniature gold mesh bag just big enough to hold my church dollar if the bill was folded very tight and small.

In the afternoon Esther and Mr. Scott arrived at the house with Rikki who, surfeited with presents at home and tired from the already long and exciting day, ignored the toys we had assembled for him and was content at first to admire from Esther's lap the tall, sweet-smelling, thickly ornamented tree. What was that? he asked over and over until he got the answer straight.

"An angel," he said craning his neck to see the topmost ornament. The angel in her blue robe must have seemed just as real and just as strange as the balls of gold and silver and shining color, frosted and netted and completely unlike any ordinary nursery ball.

"A ball? Is a ball?" he asked uncertainly, and slid from Esther's lap. He tugged her hand until she accompanied him near to the tree which must have been vast as a forest to him. He pointed to the ornaments of his choice. "Give Rikki this one. Give Rikki a fishie, give Rikki a bird." B for Bird, F for Fish, these were recognizable from the pictures in his alphabet book, though the pictures were not so shiningly colored. He clasped the fish too tight and was startled when it broke, fortunately not hurting him, and fell in scattered gold and crimson fragments on the floor. He frowned unhappily at this disintegration of a seemingly solid object and then was distracted and laughed as Esther held out the small turquoise blue bird.

"Mother will hold," Esther said, "Rikki will just pat. Carefully, Rikki." And Rikki stroked the white feathered tail of the glass bird.

It was in the afternoon too that Bertie brought his present to me, a fishing rod of all things. I had a fountain pen for him, expensive to buy with my own money, though saved up for some time, and a more interesting and sensible present, I thought, than his to me.

I might have known that Bertie would guess what I was thinking. Thirteen must be as self-conscious, as self-centered a time for a boy as for a girl, but Bertie's deep-set hazel eyes looked out, not endlessly inward; he watched other people and thought about them. It was an odd thing for someone that age—for someone any age, particularly a male—to care that much about other people.

He smiled at me and said, "It probably seems a queer present for Christmas but it's for next summer. I'm going to teach you surf casting."

"Oh, Bertie, you never would."

A rod for surf casting! It was a great Christmas present, I realized, and not only because Bertie's allowance wasn't much bigger than mine. Surf casting would be a lovely thing to think about when, in January, the year stretched out into the long flatness of winter.

The best of that Christmas was not yet. Father brought me the best of my presents when the last guests had gone and the day was quieting into evening.

"Couldn't introduce this little mite into all that hullabaloo," he said.

I stared puzzled at the L. P. Hollander hat box that he had placed on the nursery floor. A hat box was more like Easter than Christmas, I thought, and then I heard a small rustling, bumping sound. I lifted the lid, and there, climbing out of the tissue paper was a small, white fluffy puppy, a Pomeranian, Father said. It was, he told me, a present planned for me long before by Mother. She said one couldn't fill a town house with dogs and if they gave Esther a puppy, every other child must have one in its turn. Esther had been consoled first with a doll and later with a horse of her own in Southampton.

"And now," Pa said, "she has Rikki and no need of any other pet and neither Maud nor Julia ever really seemed to want a dog."

"I did. I wanted a dog called Fluffy and now I have her."

"It was your mother's idea. She said one day toward the end 'Let the little one have a puppy when the girls are big and have no time for animals. Being the youngest by so much she'll need a dog more.'"

Father was knowledgeable about sporting dogs but not about toys, and Fluffy grew up to be a spitz, but she was handsome and good-tempered and I loved her. It's hard to remember the quality of the affection a child pours out on a dog. One remembers it better than one remembers why and how one loved a doll but still one doesn't, I think, remember accurately.

I do remember—and I suddenly realize I never told Pa this. I wish I had. Oh dear, those vain wishes for the beloved dead: if one had only not left undone, unsaid, this particular, small thing. Well, anyway, I do remember that, aside from my dear companion Fluffy herself, I was always glad that Father gave her to me on that best of Christmases. She was the crowning glory of the last of the enormous, overflowing, completely magical Christmases I was to know.

"In secular terms," Maud would add sternly when we reminisced. She was wrong, but there's no arguing with acquired bigotry. In those early years there was a nostalgia, when surely one was too young for nostalgia, and a softly glowing brightness in our carols and in the Nativity story which Aunt Lucy, continuing Mother's custom, read aloud on Christmas Eve that no later songs or stories ever held for me.

However, our Christmas was in the main an extravagant and merry family festival. Pa spoiled us outrageously on this day because, I think, he was trying to make up to us for Mother. Perhaps he was also trying to make up for the meager, puritanical Christmases that he, as a boy, had known in Delaware County.

The winter moved at its accustomed, creeping pace. January, February, and March used to be not only the long part but the real part of the year. To this day the phrase real life takes me back to those slow, frostbound months. The patterns of school and the park were set. We were enclosed in a cold, orderly time. There were none of the variations of the softer seasons. We were on the narrow track of the school year, as unalterable and familiar as a commuter's daily journey.

I was aware of the grown-up world, the family world, but it receded into the background.

The day after New Year's Mr. Scott went to Chicago for his railroad board meetings and then on to California. Esther stayed in New York with Rikki, but she came only rarely to the house. I complained about this to Pa.

"Well, my dear," he said, "your sister has grown up. She was young when she married, but sooner or later a woman must cease to be a daughter of her father's house and become the mistress of her own."

It seemed to me that Esther's house was not hers, could never be her own in the way that ours had been Mother's.

The house on Murray Hill had been Mr. Scott's before his marriage. It was a tall, narrow, deep house and a silent one. Rooms and halls were thickly carpeted almost to the walls so that feet, even Rikki's and mine, never clumped or clattered. There were Tiffany glass lamps and chandeliers. Roberta tells me that Tiffany glass is coming back, but it sheds a dismal light. The Scott house faced north and in the reception room and the parlor what cold daylight there was was blacked by full, heavy plush curtains. The long, high-ceilinged dining room was at the back facing south but it too was dark. It was above the half-basement kitchen in a two story extension that reached to within a few feet of the opposite houses and three layers of curtains shut out the neighbors' windows.

The only cheerful places in the house were the spare bathroom on the third floor landing and Rikki's room. The bathroom window was large and uncurtained; it was grainy opaque glass with a border and inserts of stained glass. The bathroom, like the nursery above it, faced south and the sunlight fell in multi-colored circles and curlicues and heraldic designs on the floor and on the lining of the mahogany encased tub. The coffinlike tub was to my mind one of the few interesting objects in the house. The others were the peacock feather screen in the dining room, the pale-faced marble lady, draped in bronze, who held a torch at the foot of the front stairs, and the polar bear rug in Esther and Mr. Scott's bedroom. The last was not only splendidly fierce to look at but a pleasure to recline on, which was more than I could say for the rest of the furniture.

Rikki's was the only pretty room. The curtains, patterned with sheep and shepherds, were blue toile de Jouy. They could be drawn far apart to let the sunlight stream through the net glass curtains. The furniture was painted spotless white except for the drummer boys at the head and foot of the crib and the clowns on the wardrobe doors. On the blue-papered walls hung pictures of puppies and kittens and Mother Goose characters. The lamps were not ordinary uninteresting shapes: two were bronze trees with yellow porcelain birds perched on their branches, one was a gilded cherub, and the fourth was a Dresden china shepherd. Esther had brought them from her room at home. Like Mother, Esther knew that a child's room, the place where it sleeps and wakes, should be full of pleasant company.

At a family luncheon during the Christmas holidays, Mr. Scott had told Father that the nursery would do for now but in a year or two his son would have a more manly room.

Next to me, Esther spoke barely above a breath.

"At least he has it for now."

She added in a comforting voice, "It's all right, Nell. No one has anything for much longer than that."

Remembering Esther's words, I wished that she might have Mr. Scott's house only for now and not much longer.

I told Pa that it wasn't a pretty enough house for Esther. He bade me be patient and assured me that Esther would gradually make the house over to her own taste.

I wished that in the meanwhile Esther would come to our house more often, but she continued to stay away and during her rare visits she was different: remote and preoccupied—this isn't true. Oh, it's true, I'm sure, that Esther was remote and preoccupied, but it's not true that I was aware of it. Even in memories, particularly in close family memories, there is vanity. One wants to have known, to have been in on everything, not to have come last to any family happening, however painful. Perhaps it's not entirely vanity. I love Esther and love wants to reach back, to make over the past, to have helped. I wish I might have helped Esther in whatever way a child could, but I wasn't paying attention to her. I was absorbed in my own activities.

It was early in March that I heard Julia talking to Esther, pounding her with the awful voice. It was the same voice I had heard her use once to a new maid who had broken some cherished possession.

Quick as a flash Bridie Smith had pounced, "Don't you dare, Julia! Don't you ever dare talk to anyone in your father's house like that, as if she wasn't a person, as if she was dust. You apologize to Mary this minute before she walks out on us and who would blame her? But you would have some explaining to do to your father, miss!"

When I heard Julia going at Esther there was no Bridie at hand. I was in the conservatory with the lights out. It was dark enough for me to have a satisfactory game of jungle exploring and still there was enough light from the hall for me not to be too scared if the sharp, dry feeler of a palm branch touched me unexpectedly.

The girls' voices came from the hall. Probably Esther had fled from the parlor or the library to escape the battering voice.

"How could you? How could you, you Esther Cameron, like any common slut in a dingy hotel room? How . . . ?"

"Please don't. Please, Julia." Esther's voice came in gasps as if she were running hard or were being whipped.

"Mary Ames and her mother saw you with him. Mrs. Ames swears by a veterinary in that part of town and they were coming out of his office with Mary's dog and there you were coming out of the Ivanhoe Arms or whatever it's called with yours. And dog is too good a name, too clean a name for him, the dirty, sneaking—"

Esther was running down the stairs.

"I'll tell Father," Julia screamed after her. "It's my duty. I tell you I'll tell Father."

The front door slammed and Julia was silent. I heard Aunt Lucy's step and her voice.

"You'll tell your father what?"

"I'm going to tell him about Esther."

"Hush, Julia, or you'll tell the whole household. Come upstairs with me where we can talk quietly and calmly."

I stood still after they were gone. I was frightened with the unreasoning fear that makes it impossible to move a muscle when one wakes from a nightmare in the dark.

I had heard Maud and Julia quarrel and sometimes they screamed at each other. This was different and I was afraid. This was what Bridie had called talking to a person as if she was dust. I didn't understand what Julia had said. All that about a dog. Esther had no dog. This was some nonsense of Julia's. Angry, wicked nonsense, but only nonsense I told myself.

Bridie found me shivering in the conservatory.

"Do you want to scare yourself silly, you and your jungle games?"

She shooed me upstairs and I said nothing.

There are a number of half-magic rules that one learns or invents and adheres to when one is a child. I have forgotten them except the obvious, generally known ones like: "Never step upon a crack . . ." But the one I used that night I have not forgotten: "If you do not tell it to a single soul it is not true."

With the help of my rule I pushed the memory down and out of sight. When occasionally it troubled the surface of my mind, I muttered fiercely, "Just some of Julia's nonsense, everybody knows fifteen-year-old girls are silly." Quite soon it seemed as if nothing bad had happened.

Despite my determined ignorance, something had happened. Mrs. Ames and her daughter had seen Esther and Augie coming out of a West Side hotel. Other people had seen them in other places. There was a whisper of talk, not yet loud, not yet in print. It was a closely guarded whisper that did not spread beyond a small inner circle of society. The dreadnaughts held their fire. Perhaps—though even now it's hard to believe such a thing of those firm-bosomed, marcelled ladies—perhaps they had mistakes of their own to remember or perhaps—a little easier to credit—they had reached the age when the young, even the young married, seem pitiful and one hasn't the heart to bar their avenue of retreat from folly. Also, fortunately, those who knew or guessed about Esther and Augie belonged to a group of which our family was a part, a group that was linked by school days and intermarriages and husbands' and fathers' clubs and business partnerships.

Mrs. Ames was a connection of ours by marriage, and she and Aunt Lucy devised a story that Mary and Julia appeared to accept: Esther had visited a dependent in reduced circumstances and Augie had been kind enough to accompany her to this unfamiliar and shabby part of town.

She had been a fool, Mrs. Ames told Aunt Lucy, to let Mary see her shocked astonishment. I can hear Aunt Lucy's answer as if I'd been there. "Oh, my dear, can't we all be fools sometimes and at any age? But at least we can try to protect the poor young in their folly."

Aunt Lucy must have frightened Julia into holding her tongue. Aunt Lucy was almost never angry, never angry at all when she pointed out small errors in our ways, but on rare occasions her face and her voice would freeze as, with her lips scarcely moving, she spoke her mind. I think that on this occasion she terrified Julia into temporary silence. Julia did not reveal until long afterward that Mary Ames had seen Esther and Augie coming out of the hotel. She has never mentioned the scene in the hall to me, nor, I think, to anyone. Perhaps she was frightened and shamed by her own violence. Also I know, if she doesn't, that in her queer, unforgiving way and in spite of James Henderson, Julia never stopped loving Esther.

I do not know whether Aunt Lucy said anything to Father. Perhaps he had heard. The whisper must have reached the men's clubs and there is always a well- or ill-meaning friend to tell even a father. My guess is that neither Aunt Lucy nor Pa were anxious to bring the truth into the dangerous open ground of speech.

Mr. Scott returned at the beginning of April and Esther came to the house only with him, and she avoided every circumstance in which she might find herself alone with a member of the family.

Father or Aunt Lucy would certainly have made an occasion for a private talk with Esther, but before they were able to do so, the situation was altered. In May, Mr. Scott announced that Esther was expecting a baby in January. He called on Father at the office to tell him the news and Father told us.

"Richmond is not one to show his feelings," Pa said, "but I could see how pleased he is. Furthermore he has decided to sell the Murray Hill house and to buy the Davis place in Westbury.

He has, he said, made up his mind that it is healthier for children to grow up in the country."

Aunt Lucy told me much later that the move to Long Island, more than the news of the impending baby, silenced the whispering. Even if there had been a little something, the ladies said, a smart young couple like the Richmond Scotts would never bury themselves in the country the year round if they were not devoted to one another.

The baby was born in mid-November. Fortunately, Aunt Lucy had insisted that Esther move to our house early in October, before the winter set in and made travel from Westbury slow and difficult if not impossible.

Esther was gravely ill after her daughter's birth, and Christmas was an anxious time which none of us had the heart to celebrate. There were no stockings and no tree and no carol singing.

The baby was doing remarkably well, Aunt Lucy assured us, though naturally she was very tiny. No matter how many one has seen, a newborn infant is always tinier and lighter to hold than one remembers, and family and friends accepted the doctor's and Aunt Lucy's pronouncement that this premature little one must have special care and few visits even from relations. To my astonishment Mr. Scott listened to Aunt Lucy. I had never known him to be much of a listener but he obeyed the rules and did not come often to see his wife and the baby.

The baby may have been smaller than average, but what I noticed was that she had a more interesting face than I expected in an infant. Her dark clearly defined eyebrows gave her identity. She wasn't an anonymous blob like most of the young babies I saw in the park.

By January, Esther was convalescent and allowed to sit up and presently to walk around her room.

Since our house was full, Mr. Scott stayed at the Union Club

during the week and spent most weekends with Rikki in Westbury. As soon as Esther was strong enough, he announced, he
would move her and the baby down to Long Island. Aunt Lucy
was concerned about the trip in winter, but she said so only once
and did not argue with Mr. Scott. However, he was obliged to go
West in February and Esther's and the baby's departure was post-
poned to April.

In March the baby still had no name, which worried me. I had
one friend whose parents had taken so long to decide on a name
that by the time they selected Cornelia she was irrevocably
known as Baby Elliot, and when she got to school she hated it,
but by then it was too late to change it. And Baby she has remained to this day.

Aunt Lucy was sitting with Esther and the baby when I decided to speak.

"She has to have a name," I said. "Baby is awful. You can just
ask Baby Elliot if you don't believe me."

"She'll have a name." Esther gently twisted a strand of the
silky, almost black hair into a tiny curl. "A beautiful name. Richmond said he didn't care. Since she's a girl, he's leaving it to me
and I've finally chosen. I've chosen Allegra."

"Like the girl in the poem! I never thought of a real girl being
called Allegra, but it's lovely isn't it, Aunt Lucy?"

"It's very pretty," Aunt Lucy said, "and it's unusual. A little
too unusual, Esther. I wonder . . . Would you think me a vain
old woman if I suggested Lucy Gore Scott?"

"I know you're not vain, Aunt Lucy, and you've always said
there were too many Lucy Gores in our widespread family connection, so why now suddenly do you suggest it?"

Oh dear, I thought, one of those ancestor conversations. Aunt
Lucy will get out the book and they'll go over all the names and
the poor baby will get some family name, maybe even Hannah

Maria with a long i. I shuddered. I had been saved from Hannah Maria after a Baltimore ancestress on the Turner side, only by Father's insistence that I be called after Mother.

I looked up. Aunt Lucy hadn't fetched the book. She and Esther were talking in the guarded tone and phrasing that grownups used in front of servants and children. It always astonished and hurt me a little when Esther joined them beyond my reach. And over a name, I thought crossly. What's in a name? We learned that in elocution class.

" 'What's in a name?' " I quoted proudly, " 'that which we call a rose by any other name would . . .' I don't mean she ought to be called Rose, of course, but Shakespeare names for girls are nice, Hermione, Rosalind, Viola . . ."

"No, Nell, not Shakespeare," Aunt Lucy said firmly, "and not a name with a hidden significance, Esther. I want this child to have a conventional ancestral name."

"The seal of family approval?" Esther asked.

"If you like, my dear. It's not a bad thing for her to have, but why don't we say it would please me to have such a dear little namesake?"

"And would it please you, Aunt Lucy? Would it really, truthfully please you to have this namesake?"

"It would. So do as I ask. Call her Lucy Gore Scott."

In April Lucy Gore went with her mother to Long Island.

I saw her only twice again, once when we stopped in Westbury on our way to Southampton in June and for the last time when we stopped on our way back in September.

By September, she was, I think, the prettiest baby I have ever seen. One couldn't say she looked like a doll, because dolls are usually blue-eyed blondes and Lucy Gore's eyes were a deep, soft brown, almost as dark as the ringlets that framed her face, nor was hers a doll's stolid, immovable face. She had the kind of small, almost heart-shaped face that changes in expression and even in coloring so that it is almost impossible for a painter to catch a likeness, though Sir Joshua Reynolds might have managed it as he very nearly did with the fortunetelling children. Lucy Gore would have been difficult for an artist to capture but she is easy for the memory to hold. She was all those years ago and not my child and I can still see her as she was on that September afternoon. I must have been distracted by the excitement of the return to town and the new year ahead, but I remember Lucy Gore in her mother's arms. I remember that little, laughing Gypsy face as if I'd seen it day before yesterday. I recall Rikki less vividly but if I try I can see him, fair and straight and solemn, standing beside his mother on the front steps of the Westbury house and waving to us with one hand while the other holds tight to Esther's skirt.

I wish I could stop looking at that day.

Mr. Scott had taken Esther with him when he went to Scotland. They had been home for only two days and Esther was radiant. I know perfectly well that there are as many kinds of joy as there are of love, but Esther's joy at being back with her children is something I find painful to remember. I realize that for some, perhaps even for many women, children are not the first joy, the first love, but for most of us, surely for all to whom it comes, certainly for Esther, the sorrow over a lost child, over lost children, is the irreparable one. It is the unimagined, the not foreseen, the heart-piercing sword.

4

THE only unusual event of the early autumn was that Maud entered Barnard as a freshman. None of my friends had sisters at college. The customary thing was for a girl to come out after she graduated from school but Maud said she preferred to wait a year for Julia.

Father did not take kindly to the idea of a daughter at college. To his mind, there was something unfeminine about a college girl. She was, he said, a figure of fun who belonged in the pages of *Life*, not, he added, that Mr. Charles Dana Gibson would ever draw a flattering likeness of her. The suitable way for Maud to spend the winter if she wished to postpone her debutante year was at a European finishing school.

"Please, Pa, no," Maud pleaded. "French, the piano, literature and sew a fine seam. I speak French and there's a better library right in this house than in any finishing school. Bridie has taught me to sew and I haven't more than an average ear for music. I think I have a good mind and I'd like to learn to use it."

I heard bits of the argument which had continued through most of the previous May. Pa hated to say no to his daughters and anger was his natural and immediate reaction when one of us forced him into this unhappy position.

It was Aunt Lucy who one day helped to bring the disagreement to an amicable conclusion.

"Your aunt will tell you," Father said, "that college for a

woman is not only unheard of in our circle of friends but unusual in any circle. You don't have to be unusual, Maud, you're a pretty girl."

Dear Pa. We were all his pretty girls. To him Esther was not lovelier nor Maud plainer than the others.

"It's unusual, James," Aunt Lucy said, "but not unheard of even among the families we know. The youngest and prettiest of Mr. and Mrs. James Duer's daughters graduated from Barnard."

"That's true. I had forgotten."

Pa sighed. I know now, being a parent myself, that it was a sigh of relief. Before permissiveness was heard of, it must have been a joy to give in, to see a beloved young face light up as one said yes.

"Very well, Maud. Since your heart is set on it, I'll send you to Barnard, but on one condition."

"Any condition, Pa. I'll do anything. I'll give up coming out next year."

"Indeed you won't. It may be hard work but you can manage to combine being a debutante and a college sophomore. After all, I managed to work part of my way through Columbia. That is my condition: You will come out with Julia, you will do all the conventional and appropriate things. You will wear your higher learning as Alice Duer Miller wears hers, unostentatiously and with grace."

"I will, Pa. I promise. I won't be new rich about it."

"That's my girl."

I realized that they were both happy that their disagreement was ended, but Maud's desire to go to college remained a puzzle to me. Everyone had to go to school and I liked Spence because of the company and the pattern of our days. I didn't mind lessons, but I couldn't imagine wanting to prolong them for four additional and unnecessary years.

My opinion that college was merely a continuation of school was confirmed as the weeks went uneventfully by.

The only difference I could see was that Maud's college day was longer than our school one. Her room had always been piled with books. The piles were higher now and the heavy volumes made hard work of dusting, Bridie said. Mademoiselle shook her head and gently complained about some of the books though many were borrowed from Father's study. Certain things, even certain philosophies, were fit for Monsieur to read, she said, but were not suitable for a jeune fille.

Unlike other French governesses I knew, Mademoiselle was cheerful and calm and blue-eyed. She was Swiss, not French. Mother had selected her because, since she came from Geneva, her accent was impeccable and she had neither the Gallic temperament nor the Gallic religion. She was Protestant.

The one slightly peculiar thing that occurred at the beginning of Maud's college career was of a denominational character. At luncheon on a Saturday in November she startled us by announcing that she had that morning attended a service in a nearby Catholic church.

"You did what?" Pa roared, and then, glancing at the waitress who like all our servants, was an Irish Catholic, he added in as restrained a voice as he could manage, "How did you happen to do that?"

It was an assignment, Maud explained, for her course in medieval history.

"So your professor sent you all off to the medieval church, eh? An interesting idea. You must tell us about it later."

When we were alone in the parlor after luncheon, Maud said the students had not been sent to Catholic churches, the assignment was only indirectly sectarian. The professor had been talking of miracle plays and their origin in the church and had suggested that the young ladies, on Sunday, attend churches other than their own and see if they could place themselves outside their accustomed concept of worship and recognize the drama, the myth acted out, that was inherent in all Christian ritual.

The idea of suddenly appearing on Sunday at a Presbyterian church had embarrassed Maud. "A wedding or a funeral is different, but I didn't want to explain if I met friends that I was, so to speak, sightseeing in their church."

"Also," Pa pointed out, "you would have found less not more myth and drama in a Presbyterian church than in your own."

"Well, I decided it would be less conspicuous to go on a weekday and I know Bridie sometimes does so I asked her and she told me they have services every day."

"I hope, my dear, you didn't embarrass her, didn't make her feel that you were a curiosity seeker."

"Oh no, Pa. Besides, none of us could embarrass Bridie. She's put up with us for too long."

"And did you think the Mass, as they call it, was like a play?"

"In a way it was, the gaudy vestments and the theatrical gestures, genuflecting and crossing themselves and all that. Of course, I couldn't understand a word the priest was saying, it was all in Latin . . ."

"But, Maud," I interrupted, "you took Latin at Spence."

"He went very fast and his accent was completely incorrect, not the tongue of Cicero I can assure you."

"It doesn't sound very interesting," I said.

"It oughtn't to have been." Maud frowned. "It oughtn't to have been interesting at all. They, the priest and the little boy he had with him, mumbled so and went about everything so matter-of-factly and yet, in some queer way, it was impressive. I can see what our professor meant. In the parts of the service that were quiet except for the boy ringing a bell there was something dramatic. I think dramatic is the right word . . ." She hesitated. "It was queer, Pa. The people who were there weren't taking part as we do, they were more like an audience than a congregation but not like an audience at a play. They knelt almost all the time and straight up, not comfortably, like Episcopalians. They were more like an audience at an event. I watched them as much as I watched what was happening at the altar— that was the queer thing. It was as though they believed something was really happening."

"They do indeed believe," Pa said. "Poor souls, they believe anything their priests tell them. Well, Maud, it may have been an educational experience at that."

"It was an experience, rather a strange one, but I suppose if a Catholic or a Jewish girl, we have some of both, goes to St. Thomas' tomorrow, she'll find that a peculiar and fascinating experience."

Sunday at St. Thomas' was nice, especially the singing, but I couldn't imagine a visitor finding it fascinating. It was just Morning Prayer and in spite of what Pa said not all that different from what the Presbyterians had. I'd gone to their church once when I was visiting Baby Elliot.

I also thought that Pa, though he spoke quietly, was not pleased at Maud's excursion and if she was wise she would not report at the family table any other extracurricular experiences the college offered. I don't suppose I actually thought like that then, certainly not in those words, but I could see that Pa was holding himself in. I think now that one of the grownups' quotations must have been trembling on his lips. "He that toucheth pitch . . ."

Lucy Gore died of pneumonia three weeks after her first birthday. I remember the date because through *Hans Brinker or the Silver Skates* I knew that the sixth of December was the feast of St. Nicholas, a holiday for children, not a day on which one of them should die.

It was hard to think of Lucy Gore as dead. She was different from the little brother whom I had never known except as dead in heaven and in Woodlawn. Now Lucy Gore would be in Woodlawn and the thought made me sick. I still believed in heaven then but it was far away, years away, and I had only a vague picture of it, harps and angels, Jerusalem the golden with milk and honey blessed. It was a place for old people, or anyway, grownups, not for children, not for Lucy Gore.

I had never been to a funeral and under different circumstances, even sorrowful ones, I'd have wanted to attend one. A few years before, a great-aunt on the Gore side had died and I was disappointed to be the only member of the family who was left at home. I had seen funeral processions and had watched them pass with what my elders would have called morbid curiosity though I think it was part of the normal interest a child takes in all the grown-up activities from which it is excluded. In conversation funerals and weddings were often bracketed.

I didn't want to go to this funeral. I didn't want to believe that Lucy Gore was lying by herself in the white hearse that preceded the line of carriages as we drove to the cemetery. I didn't want to look about me at Woodlawn at the heavy slabs and monuments and at the oblong hole, into which they were going to put Lucy Gore.

While our family grouped themselves behind Esther and Mr. Scott at the graveside I clung to Aunt Lucy as I hadn't clung to a grownup in a long time. I stared down at my high shoes and the shiny, black buttons stared back at me like dead eyes. I closed mine not to see them, not to see anything in this place.

As the service was ending I heard shocked gasps behind me and I opened my eyes. I couldn't see very well because of being blinded by tears of cold and misery. The minister's stole, flapping in the wind, was a purple blur. I wiped my eyes and turned my head away from him in the direction in which all heads, including his, were turning. Walking towards us with his arms filled with white roses, was Augie.

The minister began, I think, to read a final prayer as the coffin was lowered into the grave but I can hear only Esther's crying, I can see only the roses falling from Augie's hands onto the small white coffin.

Aunt Lucy went to Esther's side, and I followed her. Then there was silence except for the noise of the dirt being shoveled into the grave. Father moved toward Esther, but neither he nor Aunt Lucy could persuade her to leave until the men had finished their work to the last spadeful. Then Mr. Scott turned. He walked over to Augie who was standing beside me.

Mr. Scott stood still and solid as one of the granite monuments. He did not raise his voice, but I could hear every cold syllable:

"You dirty son of a bitch."

I recognized the sound of hate, but I did not understand the words. Such words were not used lightly in those days and I had never before heard them.

The minister who was related to half of New York heard and so did the undertakers who sooner or later entered all the best houses.

Mr. Scott strode down the path. Father put his arm around Esther and led her past the silent group of friends and relatives. Aunt Lucy and Maud and Julia and I followed.

Mr. Scott was waiting beside his carriage. He looked at none of us, spoke to none of us, except Esther.

"For my boy's sake I covered up for you. Now I'm through. You can go home with your father or your lover, whichever you prefer."

Father helped Esther into our carriage and she drove home with us.

Within forty-eight hours of the funeral the gossip that had been whispered nearly two years ago was recalled, but this time the talk was not a whisper limited to a small circle. The Scott-Wenger scandal was the subject of general conversation in which it was deplored and enjoyed and mocked. It was the basis for the most popular jokes of the winter on the floor of the Stock Exchange and at the men's clubs. References to it found their way into the sensational press. The fullest and most detailed information was made available by *Town Topics*, a journal that was known as the backstairs bible and was read in nearly every drawing room. Pa had never looked at *Town Topics* and Bridie Smith now banned it from our kitchen, but my sisters heard what was in it as they heard most of what was said and printed. Even I heard small, mean scraps of the grown-up talk about our family.

I know all the events of that winter but I learned them slowly by piecing them together from my own scanty recollections and from accounts that others gave me bit by bit as I grew older.

My one immediate, still hurtful memory is of the weight of the scandal as it fell on me.

There is no use trying to tell Roberta or any young person what scandal was like when I was a child. The young cannot even imagine the heavy burden as children endured it then. There aren't scandals any more. There is gossip of course and gossip columnists, but the latter announce an adultery as matter-of-factly as an engagement, which it frequently turns out to be, and a divorce causes no more stir than a wedding.

It was different in our time. A house involved in scandal was an unhappy place to be. It became, at least ours did, a place of whispers and a place of ghosts. Maud and Julia said later that Esther, pale and listless and restlessly walking from one room to another, was like a ghost, but we were the ones who seemed like ghosts to me. Esther was real, real as Rachel weeping for her children. And Pa was real. He was, I thought, admiringly, a sort of Samson in reverse, holding up the shaky pillars of our house. He talked in his accustomed voice. The rest whispered: Bridie and Mademoiselle, Maud and Julia, the maids below stairs. When Aunt Lucy came she made things more comfortable, more as they used to be. I did not understand why she wasn't staying with us in these bad days. Later I learned that Father had decided we were not to do anything which would make us seem a family beleaguered.

I prayed and I had Fluffy. Julia would tell me that to put the two together is irreverent, but I think it's a credit to Aunt Lucy's religious teaching that during my childhood God was as real as one of His creatures and that both were a comfort to me.

"Oh, Fluffy," I can remember crying into her thick, furry coat, "oh, Fluffy, this is a terrible house now, but I'm scared when I have to go out of it."

When we went to school in the morning, Julia walked with Mademoiselle and Fluffy and me not, as had been her custom, a few paces ahead of us with her friends. It was as hard for her as for me to face school, but she must have had a Baby Elliot too, so I think it was kindness that kept her at my side.

When I got to school it was Baby Elliot who stood staunchly by. It may be that a ridiculous name gives a child practice in courage. At all events, Baby was brave. She was a frizzy-haired, nearsighted, skinny little girl with the heart of a small, fierce lion. It's hard for a child to break a drawn-out, embarrassing silence, but Baby managed it at Spence and in the park.

Classmates, not noticing that I was in the room, would bring reports from home: "My mother was saying to Father that after all poor Mr. Scott had no choice except to . . ." "Listen, they left *Town Topics* in the library and it said that Mrs. Wenger won't divorce him and . . ." "My Aunt Harriet was at the funeral and she said that never in all her born days . . ."

In the park the governesses had their say: "So American, so vulgar, this public exposure of marital difficulties! Now in England . . ." "We Germans are a people too family-loving, too orderly for such indelicate . . ." "I'm afraid I can say only that in France we are more practical than the Scotts and Monsieur Wenger about these matters . . ."

Worse than the talk was the self-conscious silence that interrupted it when my presence was observed. I can still hear Baby's chirping voice as, with some commonplace remark, she started us talking again. I suppose I remember it so clearly because Baby has never lost that soft, high-pitched, schoolgirl voice.

After we grew up our paths gradually diverged. Baby has moved since her second and very rich marriage in gayer circles than I, first Café Society and now she is the dowager queen of the Jet Set, but when she alights in New York or the Hamptons we lunch and talk late into the afternoon and are at home together as if there were no years or places between us. I have not forgotten her kindness in that bad patch of time but I never mention it. She would only say, "Oh, don't be sill!" and break the painful remembrance off short as in the park and at school she broke the silence.

I don't like to think about that sad winter, but memories are wayward and once they start one can't stop them even if one wants to.

Julia would stop them for me quickly enough. She would tell me to let the dead past bury the dead and for goodness sake why remember unpleasant things? James Henderson, she would remind me, always said that one's memory should, like a sun dial, record only the sunny hours. But Julia has gone off to take her bath and dress and then she will hurry off to church and on to lunch at the Colony Club. I had my bath before breakfast but I must get dressed, it's late in the morning for a member of my generation to be sitting around in her wrapper.

My memories don't leave me. They are still with me in my bedroom. While I brush my hair I look at the photograph of Father on the bureau. It startles me by seeming younger than I ever remember him to have been though when it was taken he must have been well into his fifties. Of course the fifties no longer seem really old, but even so Pa looks younger and stronger than his age. Partly it's because of his thick, unruly brown hair. It's flecked with gray, but not even for a photograph will it lie flat. His youthful appearance is due also to his being clean-shaven. Unlike many of his contemporaries he has no mustache, and one can see the curve of his mouth which seems more Greek than Scotch or Puritan to me, but that may be because I'm remembering how he looked when he smiled. It's odd to be thinking about how Pa looked. He was lean and tall and a little bit leathery. He was, I realize, good-looking in a craggy sort of way, but I never thought of Pa as good-looking any more than I thought of Aunt Lucy as pretty, though she was. One can see it in some of her photographs and I can remember the bright blue of her eyes and her fair, faintly pink complexion to which her light and, later, gray hair was becoming. She dressed it high, with an encircling pompadour in the mode of her girlhood. She

held her well-shaped little head proudly and never allowed her
neck to sink into her shoulders as so many elderly ladies do.
There was nothing soft about Aunt Lucy's prettiness, but it had
the innocence as well as the elegance of another era. She had
the small hands and feet of her generation, and she spoke with
the crisp, old-fashioned, now forgotten New York accent.

When I was young I never thought about Pa's or Aunt Lucy's
looks. Whether they were handsome or plain, old for their years
or young, didn't matter a pin. All that mattered was that they
were there and even this I took for granted most of the time.

In that winter I was more steadily aware of what they meant
to us. Our house was a safer place when Pa came home from the
office and a more natural one when Aunt Lucy appeared.

At Woodlawn Father had put his arm around Esther and he
was determined to keep it there. Much could still be salvaged
from the wreckage, he stubbornly insisted to Aunt Lucy. Divorce
was possible nowadays if it was handled right. Mrs. O. H. P.
Belmont, for one, had carried it off and that was some years ago.
Both she and William K. Senior had been received almost immediately, though separately, by practically all the best families.
For the present, Esther was in mourning for her infant daughter
so there could be no question of her sending or getting invitations. There would be a year, even two years if necessary, before
her position would need to be put to the test.

On the day after Lucy Gore's funeral, Augie telephoned Father and asked to see him. Father told him that the only way in
which he could be helpful was to go back to his family in Boston
and stay there. Since Pa, even for a local call, always shouted
into the telephone, Maud and Julia overheard his part of the
conversation.

"Get out of New York and stay out . . . No, I don't want to
listen to anything you have to say . . . No, you listen to me.

Make your peace with your wife, if you can . . . It's too late to talk about being fair to Esther, all you can do for her now is to leave her alone . . . No, leave her alone. You've done enough damage and, so help me God, if you do anything to make her situation worse than it is I'll break every bone in your body . . . All right, for her sake then. I don't care how you put it as long as you never come near her . . . Yes, I mean never. You are never to come near this house or my daughter again."

Father told Aunt Lucy that though Richmond had everyone on his side, he was bound in his pain and anger to make a mistake.

As Father had foreseen, Mr. Scott did make a mistake which slightly chilled the ardor of his supporters. He refused to allow his name on Lucy Gore's tombstone. This was not well thought of. Children should not pay for their parent's misdeeds. They always do of course, but it makes people uncomfortable.

Father ordered a stone on which was carved: "Lucy Gore aged one year and twenty-one days, granddaughter of James A. Cameron."

This was known and approved. The protection of one's own was what was expected of a gentleman.

Father's efforts to protect Esther were also viewed, I believe, with a certain amount of sympathy (sympathy for him, not for her), but it was not considered likely that he would be successful. The betting at the clubs, James Henderson later told Julia, was twenty to one with few takers that Richmond Scott would divorce his wife in New York and that she would never again be received in good society.

Esther was indifferent to the outcome of Father's battle on her behalf. She asked only one question: Would she ever see Rikki again? There was no hope of that, Father told her. Richmond cared deeply for his son as, to give credit where credit was due, he had proved. He would certainly demand and obtain the complete custody of Rikki.

Pa was gentle with Esther. "What's done is done," he said, "and there's no use to cry over it. Vain regret is the most useless thing in the world. You'll have to go on from here."

"Without Rikki?"

"Without Rikki. I'm sorry to say it, but that's the fact and it's better for you to face it now."

When Esther talked to me about that winter, she said, "Pa was good, you know. He never once told me I should have thought of Rikki sooner."

It was through Rikki that Father persuaded Mr. Scott not to sue Esther in New York. He pointed out that the newspapers, even the most respectable, would print every word of the proceedings, and would forever after rake up the story to enliven a Sunday supplement. The case would never be forgotten and Rikki would suffer not only from his mother's irretrievable loss of reputation, but also through his father's loss of prestige in the financial world. Bankers, Father said, and even Mr. Scott's less fastidious railroad friends were afraid of the effect of scandal on their depositors and stockholders and they did not consider anyone an innocent party from a business point of view where a notorious divorce was concerned.

Mr. Scott finally consented to let Esther get the divorce in a western state where milder grounds than adultery were accepted. A separation agreement was signed; it gave the custody of Rikki to his father and stated that Esther, being well provided for by her father, waived any right to a monetary settlement.

Father then offered one more piece of advice on which Mr. Scott acted within less than a year.

"Move out to Chicago, over half your business interests are there anyway. Give Rikki as well as yourself a fresh start. People here will take your side. Bound to, I know that, but they won't like doing it. You and Esther have too many family connections here, neither her relations nor yours will thank you for involving them in an ugly and uncomfortable situation. I hope that eventually Esther will live in some other city, possibly abroad, but for the present she needs the protection of my house. You're lucky, Richmond, you can get out now and leave the whole mess behind."

In July Esther and Aunt Lucy went to Nevada. Esther had protested that Aunt Lucy, not only for her own sake but out of consideration for the bishop's memory, should not go on this journey. Bishop Greer would certainly disapprove and might say something.

It wouldn't matter to her if he did, Aunt Lucy said. "I don't think he would. Bishop Greer is a kind and tolerant man. However, the only bishop whose opinion has ever mattered to me is your uncle, and he preached love. He always used the word love he said because too many of his flock and of his colleagues had given Christian charity a cold and empty sound."

Esther continued to argue. Her uncle, she was sure, would not like her aunt to be countenancing divorce. Countenancing, Aunt Lucy said, was another of her husband's least favorite words. He would want her to do this small, easy kindness for her niece. There was to be no further discussion. Aunt Lucy was going with Esther, and, never having been west of Philadelphia, she was looking forward to the trip.

I don't like to remember that I was relieved that Esther stayed so long in Nevada. That state's requirement for residence was six months in those days and Father insisted that Esther wait an extra month before filing her suit and remain in Reno for a little while after the divorce was granted. There must, he told Aunt Lucy, be no possible ground for questioning the validity of

Esther's intention to become a Nevada resident. One couldn't tell how the New York courts would rule on out-of-state divorces, and caution now might prove useful later.

Maud and Julia could not help being glad that there was no shadow on their debutante year. This may have been in Pa's mind but more likely he was playing for time for Esther, time for people to stop discussing her, time for a new scandal to catch their interest.

In November, Cousin Maud Bronson, a contemporary of Aunt Lucy's, gave a tea for Maud and Julia and the Philip Sheldons had a large dinner party for them before the Assemblies. Mr. Sheldon was Bertie's uncle and Mrs. Sheldon was our second cousin once removed.

Maud and Julia would have liked their coming-out dance to be in the spacious ballroom of the Waldorf Astoria, but Pa said no, not a hotel, it was more fitting to present one's daughters in one's own house. They were not to worry, he could limit the older people to relations and intimate friends since Cousin Maud would have room for the entire Old Guard in her mansion on Washington Square. Our house was large enough for the girls to include all their young friends, not excepting the newer ones.

They weren't all that new, Julia said indignantly, even if Pa didn't happen to know their parents.

Pa reminded her that in his youth, he had been new to New York himself so he was not inclined to bar more recent arrivals, though one must pick and choose among them.

"And let me tell you this," he said, "if society doesn't take in new people and new money it will wither away and be supplanted by a livelier, richer group. I trust your judgment Julia. Invite all the young people whom you consider attractive."

Julia still recalls proudly that the Cameron party was one of the best of the year. She has a right to be proud; even then she was a good hostess. That particular gift is perhaps most clearly recognizable in the young. This was so in my day and again in Roberta's. Parents provided practically identical food and drink and for dancing the orchestra was almost always the same, it was either Markel or Miss Byrne at our parties, either Meyer Davis or Lester Lanin at Roberta's, but some houses were fun to go to, one was in good spirits on the doorstep, and some were a little dreary, a little stiff, and one was nervous for and with the hostess. Julia could have managed to make the ballroom of the Colony Club as gay as the Stork Club in Roberta's time or the discotheques I read about now.

In Washington, in Brussels, even in Berne, which I think of as a rather stuffy city, Julia's parties were a success. One reason was her guest list which always and everywhere included the unexpected newcomers as well as the scarcely-to-be-hoped-for figures of established national and international importance. Julia herself however was the source of the lightheartedness, the anticipation of enjoyment that filled any room in which she was the hostess. How could a plump debutante feel nervous or a stranger lost or a shy royalty conspicuous, when the hostess was so completely at her ease, so delighted to be giving this party of all possible parties, so happy that you, her dear friend, have come, so certain that there never was a finer merry-go-round than the one we are all riding on this evening?

I had no standard of comparison as I sat with Mademoiselle in the curve of the stairs above the second floor hall and watched the arrival of the earliest guests. I supposed that young ladies always came to a ball with faces as bright and eager as Cinderella's. It did not seem unusual that a grown-up party should start immediately without an uncomfortable interval of waiting, that the musicians should be playing and the first arrivals be laughing and talking and dancing and pleased to have come in time for the beginning of this lovely evening.

Pa was a good host and a generous one. The food and wine he offered were excellent though never ostentatiously so. He would, for a shy daughter, have unobtrusively taken over the party but on this occasion there was no need for him to do more than make the handful of older people welcome. Looking back at him, I can see that he was proud to be able to leave the evening and the young guests and her sister Maud to Julia.

Maud was apt to turn silent and awkward at a large gathering, but she felt safe with Julia. Together they were the attractive Cameron sisters, and Maud never needed to worry about partners for dances or for supper. I wonder if Julia realizes that it was through watching out for Maud that she learned to watch out for every guest. At Julia's most formidable receptions no one was allowed to feel left out. An obscure freshman congressman felt no less comfortable than the Chairman of the Senate Foreign Relations Committee. Of course Julia realizes where she learned every trick of her trade as hostess for James Henderson in his various posts. She had a natural talent for it but like any talent hers grew with practice and discipline.

Practice and discipline came later. In that first carefree winter Julia simply enjoyed herself and carried Maud along. Certainly it was an easier time for them because Esther was far away. I can understand that. What I don't understand, at least what I mind having to remember is that it was easier for me, too. I didn't mind then, didn't feel disloyal, I just enjoyed the return to normal of my life at school and in the park.

It was not until spring that Aunt Lucy and Esther came home. Aunt Lucy decided they ought to see the orange groves of Southern California and the Grand Canyon before returning to the East.

Esther slipped quietly back into our house but not completely into our lives. In the pale sad colors of her half mourning she did at that time seem rather like a ghost to me, a shy family ghost who vanished when guests came. She would say to Julia, "I won't come down to dinner since you're having people. You can explain that I'm still in mourning."

I wonder if Julia ever had to explain, if anyone ever asked for Esther.

I don't remember much about Esther's return. It was before the *Titanic*, I know, because I saw her crying for a friend who was lost. Esther's return is overshadowed in my memory, as is that whole spring, by the disaster. It frightened me: the great, lighted ship suddenly gone down in the dark, so many people dead, people our families knew, not long ago ones in a history book or faraway foreign ones in a volcanic eruption or a massacre. The sinking of the *Titanic* was the first outside event that shook me, that was as actual to me as a family happening.

In the following winters I used to look with interest at Colonel Astor's young widow. It was strange to have a neighbor, even one I had never met, who had survived a catastrophe. Her house on the corner of Fifth Avenue and Sixty-fifth Street was not far from ours and I quite often saw her on the Avenue. She was pretty and blond in her flowing white weeds and, because she might so easily have been dead, a mysterious and romantic figure.

In the park in those same winters there was Colonel Astor's daughter Alice. She was four or five years younger than I, and I didn't usually notice anybody that age, but I haven't forgotten her. I can still see her: a thin, tall little girl, dressed all in black, with her slender, black-stockinged legs flying along below her short black skirts and her black hair streaming behind her. A child might have seemed absurd in such deep, almost royal mourning, but she didn't. Alice Astor reminded me of Sara

Crewe, and when I saw Alice I knew that Sara could truly have looked like a princess. Alice had more elegance, was more like a du Maurier drawing than the pictures that illustrated my copy of Mrs. Burnett's book, but she looked exactly the way I had always wanted to imagine Sara, and from then on the child in the book whom I knew so well and the child in the park whom I didn't know at all became one in my mind.

We moved to Southampton, as we always did, before Esther's birthday, which was in June.

The rest of us had city birthdays, Julia's in February, Maud's in March and mine on the fourth of April. A birthday celebration made an agreeable break in the school year, but Esther said she liked her summer birthdays and our big, gray, shingled house was a perfect setting for a party.

Mother had spent her childhood summers in Morristown, but she told Father that she had always longed for the seashore and he agreed to her choice of Southampton. In her day the fashionable place to be was on Lake Agawam, but she persuaded Father first to rent and then to buy a house on the very brink of the ocean. It was a tall rectangular house with large, wide-windowed rooms. On my first trip to Europe I was disappointed that I could see less of the ocean from my cabin than from my room in Southampton, and no place on the big liner seemed as much like a ship as the round piazza. The round piazza had been added to our house by Mother. It was built out over the beach beyond the dune. It was roofed and securely railed in and held up by strong posts and crisscrossing beams, and from it one could see nothing but sea and sky. It could be reached officially only through a door from the dining room but we had all learned to climb up and down the outside supports. Mother had meant her addition to be an outdoor dining room, but the top of a dune is a windier place than she had imagined, and the round piazza became for all of us an outdoor playroom. There was matting on the floor and the sturdy wooden furniture was comfortably padded with cushions covered in faded sailcloth.

I am too old now to want to live right on top of the ocean and, besides, since the hurricanes it hasn't seemed a prudent thing to do, but I have a friend who has a house on stilts in Bridgehampton. Her living room is oblong, not round, but its windows open wide on ocean and sky and it reminds me of the round piazza. I enjoy sitting there on summer afternoons.

The year Esther returned from Reno her birthday fell on a Saturday, so Father was in Southampton. There was to be no party, but we all had presents for Esther. Probably they were specially nice ones but I can't remember anything she received that morning except the sprays of small yellow flowers that looked like butterflies. I was not in the house when they were delivered. I was down on the beach. The sky was gray and what little breeze there was came from the north and the ocean was flat and all one dull color so I didn't stay long but climbed up to the round piazza, where I found Julia. She gestured to me to be quiet and mouthed something I couldn't hear. I couldn't hear anything but Pa's voice through the screen door. He was shouting.

"I don't need to see the card, I know from your face who sent them."

I tiptoed close to Julia and whispered that we better climb down to the beach. She pointed to her georgette crepe dress and her high-heeled pumps. She was arrayed for Saturday at the Meadow Club, not for climbing. She seized my wrist and held it firmly. I understood. She wanted me to stay because if we were caught, two would seem less like eavesdropping than one.

I stayed, and it wasn't because Julia made me. I wanted to

know what was going on. When we heard Augie's name we both wanted to know and we sat still and listened to the voices in the dining room.

"If I wasn't sure from your face I'd know that nobody but Augie Wenger would send those newfangled orchids."

"They're pretty, I've never seen any like them."

"Stop fiddling with the damn things and look at me, better yet, look at yourself in the mirror over the sideboard. Suddenly you look alive. But it's no good, Esther. It's no good looking like this for that feller. He'll spoil everything for you."

"What have I got to spoil? No, listen to me, Pa. What honestly have I got? There isn't a chance of my seeing Rikki again now that Richmond's taken him to Chicago. What have I got to spoil?"

"Only the rest of your life, that's all. You think you're very old, but believe me, my dear, you're young."

"In three years I'll be thirty."

"Don't talk like a child. You're not a child, but you are young and you still have all the time in the world to make a good life for yourself. Some one will come along, some fine man . . ."

"But I don't want anyone but Augie. I love him. Surely you realize that."

"And do you think he loves you? Do you think women leave him alone or that he wants them to? Oh, he won't get himself into another scandal. He's sitting pretty with Sophie backing him up, and he knows it. Because of her he's received everywhere in Boston. Likely to be elected to the Somerset I hear. Do you think he wants to give all that up? Do you think he loves you or just wants to have you on the side? For God's sake, Esther, think straight."

"I'm trying to, but first I must write Augie and arrange to see him as he asks and hear from him what his situation is."

"I'll tell you what you must do. You must listen to your father."

"I'm listening, Pa. I owe you that much. You've been good to me. Not many fathers would have stood by as you've done."

"Nothing I've done is any good if you're going to throw it all out the window. Now listen to me. I know the world and you don't. Augie Wenger is poison for you. And if Sophie were to divorce him, which doesn't seem probable, he'd still be no good to you. Even married to each other, you and Augie could never be anything to the world but a scandal. You've got to forget him. I know, I know, you're thinking easy enough to say, hard to do. But it can be done. In time . . ."

"You talk as if I were a girl Julia's age."

"You're a young woman your age. You're a pretty young woman and, to be blunt, you're a rich young woman who will some day be considerably richer. If you'll just have patience, in a few years you'll see—"

"Do you really think that in a few years I'll be visible again, that people will stop looking through me unless I'm with you or Aunt Lucy?"

"It's hard now but if you continue to behave with dignity as you have so far—"

"It was for Rikki's sake. I kept hoping . . ."

"There never was a hope of your having Rikki. But for your own sake go on as you've begun. With the family standing by, just your aunt and myself for the present, but you watch, your mother's relations will rally, not many for a while, but in the end, all of them. And other people will forget, won't care any more. People do forget if you give them half a chance. And give yourself a chance, Esther. Forget Wenger. You can. You will if you don't see him. If you won't do it for your own sake, do it for mine and your sisters'. After all, they deserve a little consideration. Give me your promise to keep Wenger where he belongs, right outside your life."

There was a silence. It seemed endless as I waited for Esther to answer Pa, but probably it was only a minute or two before she spoke. She was crying, and her words were stumbling and indistinct.

"I promise, Pa. After all you've done, of course I promise, and I'll keep my promise."

"I know you will. I trust you."

"But it's hard, Pa, it's very hard to . . . to . . ." Esther's voice was muffled and we couldn't hear. Pa must have taken her in his arms, not to see her cry. He hated to see us cry.

"I know, dear," he said. "I know, but you'll see. It'll get easier. There's that much to be said for time, it does make things easier. And try to believe this, everything will work out for you if you let it . . . Here, take my handkerchief."

Esther blew her nose a few times and then she gave an unsteady laugh to mark the end of her crying.

"You're awfully patient with me, Pa. I have no right to cry or be sorry for myself when this is all my own fault."

"That makes it no easier for you, makes it harder, but try not to cry or look back. Try to go on from here . . . Well, we've talked enough. I think I'll get a breath of air."

We heard the distant slam of the front door and then Esther, with Augie's orchids in her hands, came out to the round piazza. She stood still, startled at seeing us. Against the gray of the shingles and of her handkerchief linen dress, Esther's hair and the orchids shone like gold. The flowers were almost as pale as silver gilt but her hair was the color of red gold, a lovely warm gold that one never sees in jewelry any more.

She must have realized that we had heard every word. She held the flowers toward us. I can't then have thought she held them as a shield against us, but that's how it seems as I look back at her.

"I must put these in water," she said, and turned, and was gone.

Julia sat silent and unsmiling.

"What are you looking so glum about?" I asked. "Aren't you glad everything's going to be all right for Esther? Pretty soon, from what Pa said."

"Pa, the incurable optimist. He won't see. He just won't recognize that promises are easier to make than to keep."

"That sounds like a grown-up quotation."

It was not a grown-up quotation, Julia told me. It was a grown-up fact that I was too young to understand. I was too young to understand anything and there was no use talking to me.

I was relieved when she left me alone. I understood her and I didn't want her to talk to me. She didn't believe Esther would keep her promise. I believed Esther and I think subsequent events proved me right, but Julia thinks they proved her right.

Sitting here now, looking back uncertainly, I wonder how I or Julia or any one can be sure that her memory mirrors the truth of the past without distortion. Some of what I remember most clearly, most fondly, may be only what I wish had happened. I think one can't help rearranging the past a little.

5

THIRTEEN is a peculiar age. It was called awkward in my day and difficult in Roberta's, but no adjective describes it exactly. I think it was easier in my time than it became later because we were still treated like children. Thirteen and fourteen were in our elders' opinion only the negligible beginning of the teens. They kept after us and tried to improve our appearance and our deportment but we were not yet considered young ladies and our station in life was unaltered except in the minds of the more precocious among us.

For most of us it was not a becoming age. Some, having shot up too rapidly, were uncomfortably tall, some were too fat, and many were afflicted with pimples. The biggest change was noticeable in feminine behavior at dancing class. The boys behaved in their accustomed dogged, surly way but almost all the girls were different. They giggled and whispered and fluffed out their skirts while they waited on the dump heap (our name, not Miss Robinson's, for the row of gilt chairs to which girls retired between dances). On the ballroom floor they chattered at their partners when the latter had all they could do to concentrate on the steps, forward side close or slide and slide and one two three. Ragtime tunes and dances were not permitted at Miss Robinson's, though we did later in the winter move on to the hesitation waltz and the one-step.

"They simper," Baby Elliott said scornfully of the girls, "and toss their hair around and talk in a mincing way."

Baby remained as dour as any of the boys. She made no effort to charm, but she was light on her feet and dancing came as easily to her as skating or running. Boys sought her out as a partner because she made dancing seem less of a drudgery. They were also grateful because she did not insist on talking to them. One of them told her so. "You've got sense, Baby," he said. "You know how to shut up."

Baby repeated this tribute to me. "As if there was anything to say to them," she snorted. "They may be thirteen, but they're as bratty as they were at ten."

Baby still looked like a little girl and I think that in the main she felt like one. She enjoyed the pleasures of childhood and did not reach ahead, and this has remained true of her. Baby has never looked wistfully forward or back. To her, now has always been good enough. Today, as long ago, she is a cheerful and contented companion at the age at which we happen to find ourselves. She also has the luck to have the kind of looks that adapt themselves becomingly to any age. At thirteen she was small and neatly made and agile (she still is) and she was cute-looking. (She's still cute-looking in a Meissen china way if one can picture a Meissen lady dressed by Mainbocher and Chanel and Pucci.) At thirteen she didn't bother about her appearance. "Clean and neat is all my mother asks," she said, "and it's all I'm willing to give. Time enough to discard my Peter Thompson and get myself up as the queen of the May when there's a king in sight."

I suppose that Baby, like myself, had dreams of a royal knight on a white charger or in a high-powered motorcar. She must also have had some far more disquieting imaginings, but she had the grace to keep her secret thoughts to herself and she managed, thank goodness, to impart that grace to me.

"Listen," she would say, "it'll probably be great to be grown up. It was great being little and playing with dolls and we've outgrown that. So let's enjoy what's great now before we outgrow it." And off she would tear on her roller skates, with me at her heels, down one of the steep walks that adjoin the Mall. Or she would whistle through her teeth and fingers (Baby could whistle as well as any boy) and summon a group of whispering, idling friends to a game of crack the whip.

I've always been glad that Baby kept me sensible. I think adolescent yearnings and confidences might haunt one's memory more embarrassingly than a few inhibitions. I was thankful even then because of Bertie. When he came down from St. Mark's for the Christmas vacation he praised me. Compliments from him were rare, and I was pleased when he said he was proud of me. "Most girls get silly at your age and want to be grown up and can't and fall flat on their faces. You're the same nice little girl you always were."

Bertie made it sound all right to be a little girl, and, as Baby pointed out, I might as well enjoy it, it wouldn't last forever.

"And who knows," she once asked, "that what comes next will be as great as this?"

I knew Baby was brave so it was consoling to learn that she too had occasional qualms at the thought of being grown up. That's one of the ways in which parents made life easier for us than it is for older children now; they let us be scared, didn't relentlessly drive us on to the social and romantic battlefield before we were ready for it.

At home things seemed to me much as they had been last year with the added pleasure of having Esther there and knowing that all was well with her. I believed that what Pa had predicted would happen was happening. I think I'd have noticed if Esther had never been invited anywhere or had never appeared when there were guests. The fact that she did not go out much and did not always appear did not disturb me, or perhaps I was not aware of this then but learned it later.

Maud and Julia were the young ladies of the house, and it was only proper that entertainments should revolve around them. They gave a New Year's Eve party, and I was allowed to watch and to dance once with Bertie (fortunately it was a plain waltz in which I had been thoroughly drilled) and I stood between him and Pa in the circle for "Auld Lang Syne." After the front door was opened to let in the New Year, Pa gave me a sip of his champagne to toast it and then sent me off to bed.

Esther came up to my room when I was in bed. It was hard to go to sleep to dance music, she said, particularly the modern kind. Ragtime violins were fun to dance to but they were a little too lively to be a lullaby. She closed the door into the hall to shut out the noise of the band and said she would sit with me until I fell asleep.

"And then you'll go downstairs again?" I asked.

"No, I don't think so. This is a young party."

"But you're young, Esther. Pa said so."

"Not that young. Not the kind of young Maud and Julia are."

"But all their boys danced with you, so you must be some kind of young."

"Oh yes, I'm some kind of young—don't worry about it, Nell. It's nice for me to be safe home again. It's good to be sitting here with you."

It was good, I thought happily, to have Esther back. Of my three sisters, she was the kindest to me, the first to notice a small discomfort or worry and, as was natural, I loved her best. This was not, I realize, entirely fair to Maud and Julia. Because of the years between us, it was easier for Esther to be patient with me. Maud and Julia were children with me and big children don't find a little one as enchanting as grownups do. Then, when they were young ladies, I was a big child tagging after them.

Well, fair or not, Esther was always the sister of my heart. However, I was fond of the others and they of me and as the age gap between us narrowed and finally disappeared we became equals and contemporaries, friends as well as sisters. Now—and this is the bond between sisters that is stronger than affection or congeniality or anything—now Julia and I remember a family lifetime together. Even if we remember it differently, no one else remembers it at all. I'd be lonely without Julia.

Our house was a merry, rackety place that winter. It was filled with the girls' friends. The front door banged as they came and went. They rushed up and down the stairs. They gathered in the parlor and laughed and talked to the accompaniment of the Victrola, which was silent only when it was being wound up or when it was abandoned for the piano. There was always someone present who could play the piano, and the rest of them would sing. Sometimes they would harmonize college songs or other old favorites, but usually they sang the latest songs.

Then and until long after I was married there were new songs for every season of every year. The new songs were played and played and then were discarded and replaced by new hits. Even now a song from my youth recalls the year and the season when it was new. Just the other morning I turned on the radio and heard "A Pretty Girl Is Like a Melody" and I was back in June in 1919, while the ship's orchestra played the score of the new *Ziegfeld Follies*.

One of the odd things to me about Roberta's generation was how much they danced to old tunes. When Bertie and I took her to her first Junior Assembly, the orchestra, as we walked in, was playing "Soft Lights and Sweet Music," a song I had first heard the year before she was born.

The songs of my own time are the ones I can date with precision. I'm not sure what songs the young danced and fell in love to in 1913, but if Julia were here, she could tell me in a minute. Of course she and Maud and their friends weren't the young to me then, they were grownups. The girls, as they arrived at our house, were richly elegant in their furs and their heavy velvet hats, and they moved with grace and assurance on their high heels. All the girls and young men who came to our house can't have been handsome and happy, but that's how I remember them.

Julia had more beaux than Maud, but Maud had two whom I remember. Bunny Conway was attentive to her. They had always been friends, and it was natural at this stage in their lives for him to behave like a beau, though not a serious one. There was a boy from Boston who was, I think, truly devoted to Maud. He came down from Harvard to New York almost every weekend and he was constantly at our house. He had a bony, ruddy New England face and he played the ukulele and I liked him, but I don't remember his name, not Thayer, not Cabot, I can't think what it was but it was an outlandish name even for Boston. Anyway, he later became a Unitarian minister so he wouldn't have done for Maud.

Julia had lots of admirers. She told me once that in Lent that year, when parties were few and Alfred Sampson was in Aiken, she was almost engaged to two of them, "which meant," she said gleefully, "that they were committed and I was free. Isn't it awful, Nell? I can scarcely remember them. Tony Draper was one. Poor Tony, he married a rich frump and lives in Milwaukee, of all impossible places. And there was the one from Maryland who was with the Guaranty. His family had a manor house on land that was originally theirs by royal grant and that seemed romantic to me. The young can be awfully silly. It's lucky for me that James was attractive and hard enough to get to make it interesting for me to go after him. Don't think I didn't maneuver Martha into inviting me to Washington that spring. I ought to thank my stars that I didn't marry someone who was never going to bother to get anywhere or be anybody. I might have and it might have been nice, might have been lovely, but I'm certainly glad now that I didn't wait around to find out—well, good heavens, I don't need to tell you about Alfred, you know how impossible it was for any girl to hook him. Love them and leave them was his motto."

If Alfred had asked Julia to marry him, she'd have had a fight on her hands with Pa. He would not have approved of the match.

The Sampsons were attractive, particularly this third generation, Pa admitted, and Alfred was the most attractive of the lot, but they weren't solid people. They were well-to-do, very well-to-do indeed, but theirs was sudden money and it was spread thin in a variety of enterprises. It could melt away as fast as it had been accumulated. Young Alfred had been brought up to be nothing but a rich man's son, always a terrible mistake and the more so if a fortune was not firmly established. If wealth was to be preserved, let alone grow, the heirs to it should have some financial training, should know more about money than how to spend it.

Julia insisted that she was not serious about Alfred, but she wouldn't let her father be unfair to him, he was a fine horseman, a fine shot.

"Yes, yes," Pa said impatiently, "I know that, and polo takes nerve as well as skill. He's good at all the things that cost money—polo, hunting, shooting, and fast motorcars, and if he found himself without any money, there he'd be with his occupation gone. He'd be lost, and his wife would be miserable."

A girl, Julia said, would never be miserable with anyone as much fun as Alfred, but she didn't intend to marry him, so Pa need not worry.

Pa did worry, I think, but he was wise enough not to pursue the subject.

I thought at the time that Julia was in love with Alfred, but very likely it was the idea of Alfred rather than Alfred himself that attracted her. He was an eligible young man, but he was a gay and dashing eligible young man, not the slow, steady sort that parents wanted for their daughters, he was one the daughters wanted for themselves. Alfred, however, was elusive. He was not long out of Yale and he showed no sign of wishing to settle down into domesticity. He singled Julia out and was obviously taken with her, but he didn't make her conspicuous, didn't put her in the position of looking foolish when his attentions came to nothing. Besides, by then there was James Henderson.

Julia enjoyed her admirers and her friends. She enjoyed her popularity and her prettiness. She was always a pretty girl and later and for a long time a pretty woman, but in the year after she came out she reached the height of her young grown-up looks. She had, by then, learned how to dress and how to manage her thick, wavy hair. Her model was Irene Castle, not one of Mr. Gibson's ladies. Julia had the slim, pert, unstatuesque kind of looks that were becoming stylish. Someone, probably Alfred, said she looked like a motorcar girl, not like one left over from the horse and carriage days.

Julia was having the time of her life, and if it hadn't been for Maud, I think she might easily have spent a year or more being almost engaged to this one and that and not have settled down to marriage with anyone.

It was on a Sunday afternoon in April that Maud astounded us all and upset Pa as I had never seen him upset, not even during his battle for Esther. We were all home and there were no guests. Pa came into the library where we were sitting and put three books on the desk. He scowled first at the books and then at Maud.

"I went to your room," he told her, "to retrieve my copy of *The Age of Reason*. It's valuable and I was afraid it would be mislaid, and I found Tom Paine keeping some strange company. I don't mean Darwin or Bob Ingersoll, he'd have been at home with them and with James Frazer."

I recognized the last name. I'd seen it on some volumes in Maud's room. They were called *The Golden Bough*, which sounded like a lovely collection of fairy tales or legends and I tried to read one of the volumes. It was hard going, but I did find one beautiful bit about a king and a tree and a sword which promised well and turned out horribly . . .

The silence interrupted my train of thought. Pa was staring angrily at Maud and that seemed unfair to me since the authors he was talking about came right from his own bookshelves. He picked up *The Age of Reason* and slipped it into his pocket. Then he pointed to the other two.

"I don't think," he said, "that Tom Paine would care for the company of those two prelates, nor do I understand why Cardinal Newman's Apologia or Cardinal Gibbons' work on the faith of his fathers should be in my house. I see from the fly leaves that they are the property of one Agnes Ryan and I assume she lent them to you, proselytizing as they always try to do."

"Not really," Maud's voice was low. "She didn't want them any more. She—she was going to throw them in a trash bin at Barnard."

"Ah, so she learned to reason at Barnard. I congratulate her and the college."

"Oh, Pa, don't." Maud's face was flushed and her forehead and her nose were shiny with perspiration. "It's sad for Agnes to have lost her faith, and Catholics aren't necessarily stupid. There are some brilliant ones. Take Chief Justice White—"

"Yes, yes, R.C.s always bring him up. They conveniently forget Taney. Poor Taney, he was a fine jurist but the Dred Scott decision is held against him, though speaking strictly as a lawyer —well, never mind that. Why did you bring these books home?"

"Because to begin with you've taught me to respect books, any books, and I couldn't bear to watch Agnes break their spines and covers and throw them out as she intended, so I asked her to let me have them. I was going to give them to Bridie, but . . ."

"But?"

"But then I was curious and I decided to read them."

"I can understand that," Pa said, but his voice was still harsh. "Intellectual curiosity is a healthy thing, not that the Romans have much to offer to the modern intellect. They'll not give you the answers to Ingersoll or Darwin. Well, now you've looked the books over, you can give them to Bridie. How long have you had them, by the way?"

"Since October."

"And they were still on your bedside table! What's this all about, Maud?"

"I'm trying to tell you, Pa. I've been trying for ages but I keep putting it off." Maud stood up and dabbed at her eyes. "I'm not crying, I'm just nervous. You may as well know. I'm going to become a Catholic."

"Good God, you can't do that! That's the servants' religion."

I was shocked, not by what Pa said, which was just a statement of fact, but by the sound of his voice when he pronounced the word "servants" as if they were dust. I felt like crying. Perhaps I did start to cry, because Pa said sharply, "Now, Nell, let's not have tears. Your sister doesn't mean this."

"But I do. I hope to be received into the Church sometime in May, it's the month of our Lady and . . ."

"Please, Maud, spare me their superstitious jargon."

Angry words like these reverberated through our house for the rest of April and into May. Superstition, idolatry, the Spanish Inquisition, the Scarlet Woman, the dark ages, the Irish. Over and over, the ignorant Irish who, according to Father, ran the Catholic Church in America.

I knew that Bridie couldn't help hearing some of what was said and I wanted to comfort her and tell her Pa didn't mean her, but it was a queer turn around for me to be comforting Bridie Smith, and I felt shy when I tried to speak to her. As I might have known would happen, Bridie was the one who comforted me.

"Now don't you be worried about me and the others, Nell dear," she said. "We know your father, and a finer, kinder gentleman there never was, but, you see, he's upset, more upset than most would be. Where he was born and raised they're frightened of the Church, and it's in his blood."

"Pa? Frightened?"

He was brought up to be frightened of Catholicism, Bridie explained. She had a cousin who grew up next door to Delaware County in Sullivan. In all that neck of the woods, Sullivan, Ulster, Delaware, they were afraid of Catholics. Bridie's cousin remembered when she was a child hiding with her mother in the cellar with no lamps lit in the house on the nights when they were out gunning for the Catholics.

"My cousin said to me, 'There weren't many of us and we

hid and there were hundreds of them, the blowhards, and they had the guns, but they were afraid of us.'"

Bridie sat me down beside her in the coziness of the house-keeper's room and gave me a cup of tea. I was not to mind on her account, she said. I should mind for my father. This was a bitter thing for him. A fear a man has grown up with since before he can remember isn't one he easily gets over. Fear, Bridie told me, is a great breeder of hate.

"But Father doesn't hate you, Bridie."

"Of course he doesn't. He just hates having his girl turn Catholic. It's a blessing from Almighty God that Maud should have come to believe in the true faith and something I never thought to see happen to any of you, but it's hard on your father, the poor gentleman."

"Oh, Bridie, you don't hate anyone, do you?"

"Dear me, no! That would be a mortal sin. I hope I don't hate anyone. Except of course the English. And Cromwell above all. May he never rest."

Now that I was no longer worried about Bridie, I had time to realize that I didn't like the idea of one of my sisters becoming a Catholic. It was such a queer thing for a person to do, and it was making the whole family miserable. Even Aunt Lucy was unhappy. She spoke gently, but her voice was sad as she begged Maud to consider the gravity of the step she was contemplating.

"It's hard, I know," Aunt Lucy said, "not to react stubbornly to opposition, but don't rush into this, dear. Wait until you're sure."

"I am sure," Maud said and was silent. She talked very little to any of us. She did not even try to answer Julia.

"I'm not angry, Maud," Julia said. "I can leave that to Pa. I'm just plain embarrassed. My Lord, what a family to be trapped in! We've just barely survived a scandal and a divorce, and whatever Pa says, we're only hanging on by our fingernails and now you decide to make us a laughingstock. Can you see yourself in Southampton going to church with everybody's maids? And then the friends you'll make for us, all those lovely lace curtain Irish who hover hopefully on the fringes of society!"

Pa also pointed out that Maud would find herself associating with some pretty impossible people.

Aunt Lucy disputed this. "Now, James, you know perfectly well that there are some charming Catholic families in New York, a little clannish, but charming. I've heard you yourself say of old Mrs. Noel that—"

"That I consider her a great lady of the old school and I do. What I'm talking about are the run of the mill R.C.s, the great majority. I don't mean the Noels or the Hoguets or the Couderts," Pa said as in another connection, another fear I suppose, but one he did not share, people said "I don't mean the Belmonts or the Pulitzers or the Speyers."

Esther puzzled over Father. "It's queer, Nell, he's angrier at Maud than he ever was at me. He never was angry at me at all, only sorry for me."

I told her what Bridie had said about fear.

"Maybe that's part of it," Esther said. "He certainly has no love for the Catholic Church, not in its role in history and philosophy and not in local politics. We've all heard him lash out at the Power House. Then, of course, Pa is something of a snob, like all his generation. At least he's a snob for the four of us, and a Catholic is certainly not the thing to be. But I think that what's put him beside himself is that he can't fight the Catholic Church, can't save Maud from it as he thinks he could save her from an undesirable suitor. Poor Pa, he's determined to save us all from everything and this time he knows he's licked."

Maud was received into the Catholic Church early in May.

Tim Farrell hopes it was on a feast of St. Michael that they have then. "She'd have needed an archangel," he says, "to defend her in your wasps' nest."

The unexpected thing and the great relief was that she needed no defender. She had left a note for Pa telling him what she had done and had gone to supper with Aunt Lucy in order to avoid the final explosion, and there was no final explosion.

I persuaded Bridie to give me my breakfast early with her the next morning so as not to be with Father and Maud in the dining room. I needn't have been nervous, Bridie told me when I came home from school. She served breakfast herself, explaining to Father that the waitress was off. Bridie had given the girl an extra day, not wishing any one but herself to hear Father have his final say.

"And, of course, your father saw through that. He smiled at me like his old self and said, 'I have fought a good fight, Bridie, if you'll allow a heretic to quote St. Paul, and I used some harsh words in the battle which I hope you'll forgive; they were never intended for you. Now, as I told this girl of ours when we met on our way to breakfast, that's all water over the dam and we'll go on peaceably from here."

Whatever his feelings, however long it took him to be reconciled, if he ever was, to Maud's conversion, Pa was as good as his word, and Esther and I rejoiced.

Julia was a little snippy about Pa, saying he was trying as he had with Esther to make the best of a bad bargain, but I think that she too must have admired his self control.

We were grateful to Father because peace reigned again in our house, but it was an uneasy peace. Our family had been affected by Maud's action. It was unsettling to us and peculiar to the rest of our world that one of us should turn Roman Catholic.

I used to look at Maud and wonder what she believed, what

she thought. I knew that what she had done was wrong, of course, but in a way it was romantic, like eloping, and I was curious.

I expected Maud to come home from her church, smelling of incense. I expected some change in her and there was none, except that she went off by herself on Sunday mornings and skipped the meat course at dinner on Fridays. I expected her room to become a shrine with statues and possibly candles. I'm afraid I thought a little idolatry would be interesting, but Maud's room remained the same except for a softly colored statue of the Virgin and Child and one of those could be seen in any house where the family went in for Italian art.

I didn't realize that Maud was showing as much restraint as Pa. It must have been hard for her not to make a display of the outward signs of her religion.

Maud seemed grown up to me, but girls her age were sheltered in families like ours and she was not by nature self-assured. She must have worried about what this Catholic life she had chosen would hold for her.

Both the boy from Boston and Bunny Conway stopped coming to see her. Julia went to Washington to spend the last two weeks of May with Martha Henderson, and Maud was not invited. Our house, suddenly quiet after the winter's gaiety must have been gloomy for her.

Later Maud often had more to say than any of us cared to hear about her religion but she never referred to the early days when it was new to her and she was alone with it in our family. I think they must have been hard days and I think she was brave.

6

THE HENDERSONS were what Father considered solid people, not showy, not vastly rich, but firmly established in wealth and influence.

The first James Henderson left what is now Westchester about a hundred and fifty years ago with the intention of going out to Ohio to settle. Like many others, he stopped on the way, attracted by the potentially rich farming country in the northwestern part of New York State. He obtained a land grant and prospered and added to it and founded the village of Henderson. His descendants continued to increase their holdings until these included not only large tracts of farmland but also a substantial amount of urban property. Valuable sections of Syracuse are still held by the Hendersons. They have never been a parochially minded family limited in ambition to one corner of the state or of the Union. The sons and grandsons of the original James married well and widely into New York City real estate and Boston trusts, into Philadelphia clothing and Pittsburgh steel and Chicago meat packing.

"It's an intricate and interesting financial genealogy," Father said, "if money counted as quarterings they'd have nearly as many as the Hohenzollerns."

It was not Father, however, who found the fourth James for Julia. She found him for herself.

The Hendersons have traveled far, but their home base has

remained the village of Henderson. It is still a Victorian town in the American Victorian styles of Polk and Buchanan, of Hayes and McKinley. It is not an inhabited museum like Cooperstown or a resurrected and preserved one like Williamsburg, but the Hendersons from their hilltop overlooking the lake have kept an eye on the village. They have discreetly lent a helping hand to descendants of early settlers and to desirable newcomers, and as the family interests and power grew they did not withdraw from local business or local politics.

Henderson is smaller than Auburn or Seneca Falls or Geneva. It has the same variety of nineteenth- and early-twentieth-century architecture, the same broad, tree-lined streets, but no numbered highway bisects or encircles it. Thanks to the watchfulness of the founding family, there are no unsightly modern innovations. There are two drugstores and a tearoom, but no diner. There is an attractively appointed, well-run inn, but no motel, and while the interior of the moving-picture theater is comfortable and air-conditioned, its plain wooden façade is stubbornly 1912. On the outskirts of the town are a bowling alley, a Little League baseball field and a community golf links as fine as any club on the eastern seaboard can offer its members. Each generation of Hendersons has donated amenities as perfectly equipped and as unostentatious as money can buy (young James has just completed a modern marina which is known as the new dock), but Henderson itself remains an old-fashioned York State town with a breath of western air blowing through it.

The Hendersons are too astute to suggest to any outsider such a politically inept description as Lords of the Manor (Julia is the only one who calls her small, white-columned, Greek revival residence on the estate the Dower House; it is spoken of locally as the yellow house on the Henderson place), but Lords of the Manor are what the Hendersons have been and what young

THE BEST OF FAMILIES

James intends them to continue to be. "After all, Aunt Nell," he said to me, "indigenous leadership is the democratic word today and that's what the family has always given our village."

The Hendersons have interested themselves tirelessly and effectively in state politics, mostly behind the scenes, but they have on occasion sat in the legislature, and one of them was lieutenant governor. Just after the turn of the century James's father was appointed to complete the term of a United States senator from New York who died in office. When Senator Henderson's term ended, he decided not to seek election by the legislature but he saw to it that he was succeeded by the candidate of his choice. At the time of his appointment he bought a house on Dupont Circle, and the Hendersons continued to spend the winters in Washington so that Martha and her younger brother Norman need not change schools nor their mother endure the icy, snowbound months in northern New York. She had had enough, Mrs. Henderson said, of blizzards and bitter lake winds in her youth in Chicago. Senator Henderson did not object, since he was involved on the national level in Republican party affairs which were in a rather disordered condition. Father always admired Theodore Roosevelt but the latter made many Republicans, including Senator Henderson and Mark Hanna, nervous.

Once Martha was grown up she would have liked to spend the summers in Newport or Southampton, but the senator would not hear of it. "We have had to be in Washington in the winter in recent years and now, since James is going in for the Diplomatic Service, it is practical for us to continue to have a house here, but it's not our home. We don't live anywhere except in Henderson."

James agreed with his father. "You can visit anywhere you like, Martha, and Norman, too, if he . . ."

"I wouldn't give you a nickel for a summer anywhere but on the lake," Norman said.

"Good boy, Normie. Look, Martha, it would be a mistake for the family not to spend as much as we can of the year at home. Our roots are not in the national scene but in York State, and that's where what position and influence we have began and continues. Besides, Henderson is the place we belong in, that we've known since we can remember and I love it . . ."

"I do too," Martha said, "I just like to get to gay places once in a while. And you needn't be so sanctimonious, James, you leaped like a trout at Julia's invitation to go to Southampton with me for the Fourth of July. You could easily get to Henderson for the Independence Day celebration if you wanted to."

"No, since Julia has been kind enough to ask me, I'll go along and keep an eye on you, miss. Southampton is a pretty gay place."

"Not really," Julia said. "Oh, on weekends, yes, but our house on the dunes is peaceful and you can spend as much time as you like just relaxing. I promise you on the round piazza you'll feel a thousand miles from anywhere."

Martha Henderson had quite often stayed in New York with cousins of hers who were connections of ours through the bishop. She and Maud and Julia were about the same age and they became friends. Until now they had not visited each other, but Martha had come up from Washington for my sisters' coming-out party and for the New Year's Eve party this past winter.

I did not realize that I had ever seen James, but when he came to Southampton I recognized him. He had been at our house on New Year's Eve and again on a Saturday in the early spring.

He was as tall as Father but less rugged. His cheekbones were high and his light brown eyes were set with the suggestion of a slant. He had something of an Indian look, especially in the summer, when his face was as tan as his flat straight hair. A wooden Indian with the paint rather faded, I thought at our first meeting, until he smiled. He had a sudden boyish smile which always made him appear younger than his years and saved him from seeming unbearably pompous even when he was uttering platitudes. I gradually learned that James used platitudes as a mask for his thoughts as our elders used quotations. He had a single-track mind and a quick one, quicker and sharper than his speech. His career was his first concern, and he didn't care if he was sometimes a bore as long as he was never indiscreet.

During the weekend I thought of James as Martha's older brother, not as a beau for Julia. I was more interested on her behalf in Alfred Sampson, and I was disappointed that he had sailed for England at the end of April.

My own summer was pleasant except that I saw less of Bertie than I used to. He was to enter Harvard in the autumn and was considered practically a college man and was invited to debutante parties and weddings and other festivities beyond my reach. I minded this as I minded when he went to St. Mark's and was no longer in New York in the winter except for vacations, but I accepted it. There was a pattern to growing up and Bertie was in a different part of it from me as he always had been. The difference was more marked than when we were nine and twelve but there was nothing I could do about it. Besides, we still shared some daytime activities. At the beach, at least in the ocean itself, there were no age barriers and Bertie kept an eye on me in the surf and bossed me around, especially on red flag days, in his old friendly way.

We still went clamming, but Aunt Lucy, before she left for the White Mountains, made a new rule about it. She would rather, she said, we took one of the girls with us. Honestly! I thought, it was a wonder she hadn't said she would rather we took Mademoiselle. We sometimes had taken Esther or anyone who wanted to go, but to make a rule about it!

After Bertie had gone to get the rakes and pails and borrow his family's car, I complained.

"Well, you see, dear," Aunt Lucy said, "you're beginning to be a young lady."

"No one treats me like one. Bertie certainly doesn't."

"I know, but then you aren't quite. Poor Nell, it's hard to be in between, but that's where you are for the time being and there are rules for young ladies, even for ones as young as you."

"I call them silly. And you're never silly and Pa isn't either. And Mademoiselle is the most sensible governess in the park or in Southampton."

"We didn't make the rules, Nell, but I'm not sure they're silly. Anyway, like them or not, we have to live with them. You're too old to go unchaperoned to Mecox Bay with a boy without being criticized, not only you but your father and Bertie. You don't want that for them, do you?"

"I guess not, but I think all these rules are a lot of silly nonsense."

"Some of them are, I suppose, but it would be harder to live in a society with no rules at all."

"Could that ever be, do you think?" I asked, entranced by the possibility of a Utopia in which my own way would be the only rule.

"I shouldn't imagine so. I sincerely hope not. Now find one of your sisters."

I found Maud on the round piazza, and she agreed to go clamming. Surf casting was, I realized, over for me. I was the only girl I knew who had ever tried it. The three of us had a nice afternoon but I made up my mind to accept Baby Elliot's invita-

tion to spend the last two weeks of July with her in Bernards-
ville. It was a more spread-out community than Southampton,
and the limitations of our age would be less apparent.

Baby and I and her friends had fun. We rode and roamed on
foot over their places. We played wolf and had paper chases up
and down the hills. Our parents allowed us to stretch the two
weeks to four, and August was half over before I returned to
Southampton.

James Henderson was again visiting us. He had spent three
weekends on Ox Pasture Road with cousins of his mother's,
Bridie Smith told me, and something was certainly up.

"It's lovely to watch," she said, "just like a play."

Julia said nothing except to Maud, to whom she talked endlessly. She needed a confidante and that, I thought as I watched
them go off together was like a play, like an old-fashioned, grand-
style French one. It was nice too that last spring's coolness between them had melted. They had not so much made up their
quarrel as skipped it, which is, except between lovers, the only
way in which a quarrel is ever satisfactorily ended.

In September, Julia went to Henderson for a week's visit, and
in October James spoke to Father. The engagement would not
be announced until December, but Aunt Lucy and Esther and I
were told, as were Mademoiselle and Bridie. Maud had known
as soon as James proposed.

I was pleased to be included at the grown-up level and to
know all that was happening. When Julia received her marquise
diamond solitaire I saw it as soon as Maud or Mademoiselle or
anyone. When Mrs. Henderson came to New York, ostensibly
for a few days of shopping but actually to call formally on Aunt
Lucy, I heard about it.

It was customary for a girl to send notes to a long list of relatives and friends telling them of her engagement before it was

announced in the newspapers. While Maud and I helped by
sealing and stamping the envelopes, I imagined myself in my
turn someday writing "I want you to be among the first to know"
and I felt a pang for Maud. She had missed her turn. An older
sister must mind being left on the shelf by a younger one. Maud
must be worried and I worried for her and decided to consult
Aunt Lucy. She reassured me.

"A religious conversion is an emotional experience," she said,
"and I think Maud, though she doesn't talk about it to us, is
absorbed in it still and isn't thinking about marriage for herself
just now."

"You don't think," I blurted out, "that Julia's first because
she's prettier?"

Then Aunt Lucy told me something which I wish every plain
girl could hear: a young girl, a young woman is pretty just because she is young, youth is pretty, is physically appealing in
itself. Maud's skin was as smooth and fair as Julia's and mine.
It was a pity that her hair was straight and so unmanageably
long and heavy, but it was a lovely pale color.

"It's no use pretending that Maud isn't plain-featured," Aunt
Lucy said, "but the young, even the not very pretty young are
agreeable to look at. They have a clean untouched freshness that
never comes again. And let me tell you something else, Nell,
just as many plain women as pretty ones marry well and, what
is more important and not necessarily the same thing, just as
many marry happily."

I was to stop worrying, Aunt Lucy told me. An engagement in
a family was a happy event and I should enjoy it as Maud was
enjoying it. Once Julia was married it would be hard for Maud
to be a separate sister after being one of a pair for so long, but
her turn would come. In all her acquaintance, Aunt Lucy had
never known an old maid who couldn't have married if she'd had

a mind to. Some women, whether or not they were consciously aware of it, preferred the single state, but she did not believe Maud was one of them.

It seems to me looking back that Aunt Lucy was abruptly silent and that her smile was forced. She may have realized that Maud's Church offered a woman a dignified and, I suppose, in its peculiar way, a romantic alternative to marriage. Very likely, I am imagining this. At any rate, thanks to Aunt Lucy, there was no shadow over my enjoyment of Julia's engagement.

The wedding was planned for May at St. Thomas' but in February James was appointed second secretary to the American Embassy in Paris. It was a post he had hoped for but he had not thought it would come so soon. He could not expect to get home leave for six months or more probably a year.

It was decided that the marriage would take place in Paris.

Paris in the spring was my first foreign city. That encounter remains by itself in my memory and is never confused with subsequent visits. Later I learned to know the city as one knows an old friend but the recollection of that first visit is like the sudden recollection, unblurred by time, of how an old friend looked when one first knew her and she was young. Only it was I, not the city, who was young when we first met.

La ville lumière, Mademoiselle had said, but I had had no idea of what to expect, and besides, I was looking forward with more interest to Julia's wedding than to the capital in which it was to be held.

Paris was indeed a city of light by night as well as by day and that is how I remember it in a series of small, bright impressions, separate one from another, like the bright square pictures that the magic lantern used to throw on the sheet on the nursery wall when we were children.

The wideness was all I could see at first. Instead of a tall, close-together city, narrowly bounded by its rivers, here was one whose bridges spanned the great central river, a city that spread out beyond both banks in broad avenues and circles and parks. I felt as though my eyes were stretched beyond my capacity to see. Perhaps they were, for all I have kept are separate squares from a magic lantern which I might later have judged differently but which were of equal value to me then and therefore to my memory now. The overwhelming majesty of Notre-Dame that blotted out of my mind every palace, temple, edifice I had ever before seen or imagined. The blinding chalk whiteness of the Sacré Coeur on the top of Montmartre. The cool dimness, patterned with light, under the arching trees in the long, grass-carpeted allées of St. Cloud. The Place Vendôme, with its elegantly matching buildings curving around the column on which the carving spiraled upward to the figure of the Emperor. In the colonnades of the rue de Rivoli the little shops crammed with treasures which were not too dear for my allowance to buy and as the colonnades came to an end, across the street, shutting out the sun, the long, somber walls of the Louvre, where Catherine de Medici had wickedly held sway, as incredible actually to see as the Snow Queen's ice palace would have been. On the Champs Elysées the creamy heaviness of the chestnut blossoms leading me and leading me toward the solid, arrogant Arch of Triumph. The strange shape of the Trocadero rising up like a fabulous beast against the evening sky, I could not remember where I had seen its like but somewhere in some illustrated volume of fairy tales or myths. The shining black patent leather brightness of the Place de l'Opéra on a rainy night when all the lights were doubled by their wet reflections. The morning when, looking across the Seine at the ungainly grace of the Eiffel Tower, I saw an aeroplane circling above it. The tower was the most modern building I had ever seen. Our tall buildings at home were after all just tall buildings, but this queer, tapering, open-work metal structure seemed as if it had not yet been invented, it was a fantasy from the future. I thought it eminently suitable that I should have seen my first aeroplane in the sky above the tower.

It was in Paris that I had my first glimpse of my grown-up self. I was allowed for the wedding and the festivities that preceded it to put my hair up. It did not feel secure; it kept sliding as if I had a soufflé on my head, and for another year except on rare occasions I was glad to wear it down my back again, held firmly and comfortably by a barrette or a flat bow on the nape of my neck. I remember my astonishment at the sight of the stranger in the mirror better than I remember the reflection itself, but I came across a picture of me in Julia's wedding album at Henderson some years ago and the odd and surprising thing was not the old-fashioned, matronly arrangement of my hair but the roundness of my face. That is the unfamiliar thing in old photographs, the apple-firm roundness of our faces. In her lace and satin dress, looking out from a cloud of tulle that floats from a diamond crescent above her forehead, Julia is as pretty as I remember, but her little round face, full and unlined as a child's, is young in a way I didn't notice then, didn't see at all.

Julia was at her attractive best on her wedding day. Her eyes were as bright as the diamonds that held her veil and the veil, absurdly bulky in photographs, was light as a cloud then and as becoming as spun sugar to an angel on a Christmas cake. Julia was as pretty and rosy and sparkling as any Christmas angel, but I don't remember her as clearly as I do Maud. At the reception at the Crillon in the enormous salon and on the high-roofed, columned terrace overlooking the Place de la Concorde, the one I can see is Maud.

Maud and Martha Henderson were the only bridesmaids.

Julia had ordered their dresses in New York. They were of wheat-colored taffeta as pale as Maud's hair. At her fitting Martha had seemed pleased, as she should be, Julia said; any shade of yellow was well known to be becoming to brunettes. Still it was foolish to risk putting a foot wrong with the in-laws and to make sure Martha and Mrs. Henderson were satisfied Julia decided to let them have the final word on the hats which were to be made by Reboux.

When we arrived in Paris, Martha and her mother had already picked out a shepherdess model which was not only the latest style, Mrs. Henderson said, but so right for young girls. Maud was pleased with their choice and when she unpacked it at the hotel and twirled it on her hand for me to see, so was I. It was of the finest, palest Milan straw and was flowered and beribboned. It dipped in the front and turned up at the back. It was too sophisticated for Bo Peep; it was meant for one of Watteau's ladies in pastoral fancy dress. It was the kind of Paris hat I had dreamed of when Pa promised me one. What I got, under Mrs. Henderson's supervision, was an almost plain Panama with just a twist of pale blue moiré ribbon to match my dress. The shape was becoming and I looked all right in it, but it was not my idea of a French hat.

The shepherdess hat was disastrously unbecoming to Maud. I did not see her in it until the day of the wedding, but Julia warned me. "It's awful to laugh," she said as she went into gales of mirth, "but I can't help it. It's hard to find the right hat for Maud, but this one is the limit! On her it looks like the hats peddlers' horses wear in the summer. Poor Maud, but I don't think she realizes how comical she looks."

Perhaps Maud didn't realize or perhaps she was used to clothes looking wrong on her. I felt sad for her at the church (although I had a wild desire to laugh which I controlled with difficulty) but not afterward, and this is what I remember. I was used to seeing her look plain and, even without the hat, rather like a horse; the startling and unforgettable thing was to see her almost pretty.

When the dancing began at the reception I escaped to the terrace and there I found Maud and a slight, fair-haired man. They were standing beside the balustrade that overlooks the Place de la Concorde. Maud had taken off her hat and her hair was blowing a little untidily in the breeze. She beckoned to me and introduced me to Louis Martin. "Mr. Martin is an artist, a graduate of the Beaux-Arts, and he has been telling me about his idea for a painting of the Place."

"I couldn't have told Miss Cameron if she hadn't seen for herself. She has a painter's eye."

Maud blushed, not as she often did when embarrassed with a painful perspiring wave of scarlet from her neck to her forehead, but with a gradual, glowing increase of color in her cheeks. In the soft light and with her hair blowing, she looked almost as pretty as Julia and she wasn't stiff as she usually was with strangers; her hands were relaxed as they rested on the top of the balustrade and her voice had a lilt to it as she said, "Mr. Martin is flattering me. It's only that I always see the black draped statues of Strasbourg and Lille more sharply than I see anything else in all this wide expanse."

"Most people never see anything once they're a little older than this young sister of yours," Louis Martin said. "They don't look at anything the way children do. As one gets older one gets in one's own way, one becomes oneself the—the—"

"Figure in the foreground?" Maud asked.

"Exactly. You haven't reached that stage yet, have you, young lady? You see the black-draped statues?" He smiled at me. It was a friendly smile. I could understand why Maud wasn't shy with him.

I couldn't help it, I explained. The obelisk and the fountains ought to be more interesting, but the statues in mourning were what I looked at the most.

"They draw your eyes off center. That's what my painting will be. Off center. The lost cities, the lost provinces negating the entire proud display of peace and victory."

"Are you really a painter?" I asked. I had never met one before. "I mean is that what you do?"

"Yes, it's what I do, but no ambitious canvases yet. However, if you'd like to come with your father and sister to my studio, I'd be happy to show you . . ."

"Portraits and like that?" I asked.

"No, I paint models who don't care how I make them look. I'm trying to learn to paint as I see."

"Your own private reality?" Maud asked.

"I suppose that's the only reality anyone has. I try to paint what I see. An apple on a dish, the fold of a cloth pushed back on the wood of a table. A dead bird, knowing how it is made down to the last bone so I can paint the deadness. The human figure in slow detail until one knows the whole moving, living body. Perhaps painting day after day for a week, a hand like yours resting on the gray stone."

"But not yet the Place off center?"

"No, not yet, Miss Cameron. I've still a long time of nothing but discipline and drudgery."

He sounded cheerful as he answered Maud though his words reminded me drearily of the most boring aspects of school.

His cheerfulness is what I best remember about Louis when, during our remaining fortnight in Paris, he took Maud and Pa and me sightseeing and on the afternoon on which we visited his studio. It was big and rather bare but a good deal airier and brighter and neater than I expected. Because of *La Bohème* I had thought of artists as a sad as well as an untidy lot. Musetta was the only one whose gaiety did not seem forced to me.

Louis' gaiety was not forced; it rippled gently and naturally, and with him Maud was natural too. The excursions he suggested were pleasant, easy ones—breakfast on the island in the Bois, a picnic at St. Cloud, a boat trip on the Seine, tea at Rumpelmayer's. After the formality of the embassy dinner and the other entertainments for Julia and James, it was fun to do simple and really entertaining things, to watch a Punch and Judy show on the Champs Elysées and buy a balloon. I even rolled a hoop, decorated with ribbons and clusters of tinkling bells. It was so pretty it tempted me but I explained out loud that I was too old for such a childish diversion.

Louis insisted on buying me a hoop. "It'll be nice for you to remember," he said, "as if you'd been a child in Paris instead of a young lady. Come along, I'll roll one too."

He bought another hoop and without a trace of self-consciousness, raced it down the path beside mine.

I was sorry to say good-by to Louis at the boat train on the day we left and I knew Maud must be too, but he was coming to the States some time in August to visit his parents in Smithtown, and he accepted Maud's invitation to stay part of the time with us at our end of the Island. It had always been Julia who invited boys to stay. I couldn't remember Maud ever before asking one of her own. I was pleased that she had found Louis and he her. That was one of the things I noticed about them, each had found the other as easily and unself-consciously as a child on a beach or some other playground finds a friend at first sight.

On the ship and after we got home, Maud returned to her old stiff ways, but I no longer worried about her. When Louis came he would once again transform her. She would be the hatless, gloveless Maud who had picnicked on the grass at St. Cloud, the Maud who had picked up her skirts and raced after Louis and me and our musical hoops on the Champs Elysées.

In the seven days on the *Provence,* Paris and the wedding receded with unexpected swiftness into the past. This was my first experience of the queer timelessness of a return sea voyage. No matter what gay and pleasant company is on board, no matter how quickly any single hour or day goes by the entire duration of the trip is time drawn out, suspended in another dimension. Even now when time goes faster every year I notice and enjoy the fact that it slows down, comes almost to a stop when Bertie and I return from Europe by ship as we prefer to do.

At fifteen I didn't think about time; one doesn't when there is so much of it. What I did notice was the slowness with which the ship appeared to move. In my cabin, especially in my berth at night, I was aware of the sound and feeling of motion, the throbbing of the engines and the straining and creaking of wood, but when I looked through the brassbound porthole in the morning and when I went up on deck the ship seemed always poised at the same spot exactly opposite the center of the unchanging horizon. Her progress was imperceptible except on the map outside the smoking room where our westward course was recorded.

I played shuffleboard with Maud and walked the deck with Pa. Best of all I liked to stand at the rail and look down at the water pulling and springing away from the side of the ship. These waves were not like the ones on the shore. They rose in jets of spray and foam without losing their glassy roundness and fought the suction of the ship without breaking as the surf did on the beach at Southampton. This was the same old Atlantic, but the churning water revealed colors I had not imagined in a northern sea, blues and greens and a whiteness so crystal-clear that it didn't seem possible that it contained even one grain of salt. I found no place on the *Provence* where I could see a great curve of ocean and sky as we could from the round piazza, but this narrow turbulent channel was a new and mesmerizing sight.

Aunt Lucy and Esther were in Southampton. They would come to New York to meet us, but not until we were back in Southampton would I have a chance to tell them about Paris and the wedding. I would tell Mademoiselle too and Bridie Smith and Bertie and my friends and in the telling I would recapture the immediacy of my recollection which I had lost on the voyage home.

I wanted to tell about the city and the wedding, but as I imagined myself telling Esther, a nagging anxiety which had not troubled me since before we left New York returned. I looked down at the swirling water beside the ship and hoped it would suck the anxiety down and drown it. When, on our walk, Pa and I made the turn on to the open deck at the bow of the ship, I hoped the wind would blow every thought in my head out to sea. I had discovered that strong outside things can put an end to inner disquiet. It was not possible to worry when you ran or skated at top speed until your breath was gone or when you fought your way against the wind in blinding, stinging snow.

Nothing on the placid June crossing was enough to keep me from wondering unhappily about Esther's absence from the wedding. Before we sailed for France I had been given the reason and I had accepted it because, I suppose, I had wanted to. In April, Aunt Lucy had been laid up with a heavy chest cold and she had not recovered sufficiently to sail with us. At the last minute Esther had decided to cancel her passage and to remain with Aunt Lucy in New York.

"For so many years when one of us was sick," Esther said, "Aunt Lucy stayed with us. I think it's beginning to be our turn now." And neither Pa nor Aunt Lucy could persuade her to change her mind.

On shipboard the questions I hadn't wanted to ask kept repeating themselves in my head. Was this really the reason Esther hadn't come with us or did Julia say something? Oh, not Julia, please not Julia, but did someone? Did Martha or Mrs. Henderson? Did one of them have a few private words with Esther at the stiff little tea party at our house in April? I remembered their talking to Cousin Maud Bronson and to Mrs. Sheldon, but I didn't remember either of them addressing a word to Esther. Had they? Did one of them say something to her then or on some other occasion?

I had been home almost a week before I had a chance to talk to Esther alone and in satisfactory detail. The first thing I told her was that I thought Louis Martin was going to be a beau for Maud. Father had said in passing at the luncheon table that we had met the Harry Martins' younger son in Paris.

"The one who paints but he's not a dabbler, takes his work seriously which is all one can ask of a man whatever his profession may be. We had some pleasant outings with him after the strenuous wedding festivities." And Pa went on to speak of other matters: the party for Julia and James at the American Embassy, the Poniatowski ball, and his agreeable afternoon with Aunt Lucy's friend Mrs. Wharton.

"Louis Martin really likes Maud," I said to Esther. "And Maud likes him. I don't suppose Pa noticed."

"There's very little Pa doesn't notice. He'd never embarrass Maud by saying too much about a possible suitor. Just a casual approving reference and he's off on some other topic. But he must be delighted."

"Pa didn't seem delighted. He seemed to take Louis Martin for granted."

"For so bluntly outspoken a man he can be extraordinarily tactful. Think how some parents embarrass their children. Pa never. Of course he's delighted at the idea of one of Mr. Harry Martin's boys for Maud. Especially for Maud. Mrs. Martin was a Guarrigue so the boys are Catholics."

"But Louis Martin didn't seem . . . he never said . . ."

"Nell, dear, that New York French Catholic lot don't seem and they practically never say. This would be absolutely perfect for Maud."

"I wish you could have seen them in Paris. They were so natural together, not a bit as if they'd just met."

"I wish so too, but I couldn't leave Aunt Lucy."

"Was that the reason?" The questions that had been troubling me burst out before I could stop them. "Did you really not go to the wedding because of Aunt Lucy or did Julia or anyone say anything? Oh, Esther, did someone say something that made you not . . . that stopped you?"

"No, Nell. Nobody said anything. Julia was in a whirl of excitement. And no outsider would dare. Pa stands firm between me and the brutal spoken word."

"Good! I was just afraid. Still I'm sad you couldn't come."

"Don't be, I'm not. I truly did stay home for Aunt Lucy. It was only right after all she has done for us. But don't be sorry for me, I was glad of an honest excuse not to go. The Embassy crowd, to say nothing of the Hendersons, are a pretty stiff, strait-laced group. I face people like that when I have to, but I hate it and I only do it for Pa's sake. He fights hard for me and I can't let him down."

"But he said everything was going to be all right. Ages ago he said everything was going to be all right for you."

"Perhaps it will be some day. Some improbable day."

I must have shown my distress. Esther touched my cheek gently. It was a comforting gesture of hers that a long time ago had reminded me of Mother. I looked at Esther's left hand, on which she wore a sapphire ring in place of Mr. Scott's diamond. I stared at the deep flawless cabochon set in the circle of brilliants and I remembered a stone blazing in lamplight, a stone as burningly deeply blue as one of the little flames when the gas logs were turned low in the nursery fireplace.

"That's Mother's ring, isn't it?" I asked and for a moment remembered and then the ring was Esther's again.

"Yes, it was hers. You weren't three years old but you remember. A small child remembers more than anyone believes possible. You do remember Mother, don't you, Nell?"

"Not very much," I admitted reluctantly. "It sort of comes and goes."

"That's better than nothing. Nothing at all wouldn't be fair."

Esther's eyes darkened with tears, and I looked away not to embarrass her. It slowly dawned on me that she was not crying for Mother and me but for herself and Rikki.

I wanted to break the silence but I didn't know how. Then Esther said, "It'll be all right for me, you'll see." She spoke in the cheerful, reassuring voice that as a rule made everything all right for me, but for a minute I felt like crying. I felt like crying not for me or my sister or my mother but for Rikki because he didn't have Esther.

"Come along, Nell." Esther stood up. "We're both getting weepy for no good reason except that a wedding in a family seems to make people cry more easily."

We were on the round piazza and she walked over to the railing. "Let's climb down and take a run up the beach. Pa always recommends exercise as a cure for the doldrums."

"Climb down? I haven't seen you do that in a long time!"

"I still can. Don't forget, Pa said I was young."

"And he said you had all the time in the world."

"So he did. And somewhere in all that time some lovely thing must be waiting for me."

"Maybe tomorrow, Esther! Who knows?"

"Who knows? Anyway, on some fine future day."

We climbed down the posts, discarded our shoes and stockings, and tucked up our skirts and ran along the hard, damp strip of sand between the dry beach and the breakers until we couldn't breathe.

I lagged behind, waiting for Fluffy to catch up. She no longer outdistanced me or circled wildly around me as I ran. I was growing up but Fluffy was growing old. Not really old, I told myself, only middle-aged and staid. Still, I wished my dog's years could go at the same pace as mine.

My barrette had held firm but Esther's slippery pins had not, and her hair had come down. I can see her standing, a few yards ahead of me, as still and straight as one of Edmond Dulac's ladies with her red hair falling around her in a shining cloak. Esther's hair is more untidy than theirs, more alive as it is ruffled by the breeze from the ocean, but she has the same tall, small-boned body, the same satin white skin, and, even with her nile green linen skirt tucked up like a goose girl's, she has the royal look of one of Dulac's magic princesses. I remember thinking that Esther could make the old, everyday Southampton beach seem like an enchanted shore.

I didn't need Pa to tell me that Esther was young. As we started up the beach again she ran like a girl who has only lately grown up.

When we were completely out of breath we stopped and staggered toward a dune and collapsed on the soft, powdery sand at its base. We didn't talk, we just sat and looked at the ocean and the sky and the colors changing as the afternoon ended and we breathed the damp, salt air and listened to the waves pounding.

After a while Esther stood up and shaded her eyes with her hand and watched the breakers.

"The tide's turned," she said, "we better go back while we still have firm sand to walk on."

As we walked slowly home I told Esther about Paris and the wedding. I told her about putting my hair up and about my French Panama hat.

Esther laughed. "Trust Mrs. Henderson to find you the nearest thing to an L. P. Hollander hat in Paris."

I told her about the shepherdess hat which, she said, sounded like a silly hat.

"I don't believe Martha looked very well in hers either."

"She looked all right," I said.

"A hat that makes a girl look just all right is a very silly hat indeed."

Then we both laughed happily because Mrs. Henderson, that worldly and imposing lady, was after all nothing but a silly hat chooser.

The shepherdess hat reminded us of the enormous plumed picture hat that Julia had bought with her first dress allowance. She wore it proudly to church and on the way home it flew off her head and sailed high in the wind like a majestic Chinese kite until it fell to destruction beneath the wheels of a coupé on Fifth Avenue.

Esther and I, walking along the beach, laughed because we remembered old, funny times and because we had run so fast that Esther's hair had come down. We laughed because the sun was still warm against our faces though the sand was chilly under our feet. We laughed at anything at all because it was nice to be walking together on our beach.

7

IN REMEMBERING a lifetime, one's own or one's family's, the turning points are marked. Personal history readily divides itself into chapters. Then and afterward and now are plainly and separately to be seen. For me, for us, on that day or in that season, a chapter began, a time began or ended.

For my generation an August day in 1914 ended the time we had known up to then and I can't even remember the date. I feel stupid standing here and trying to think of the date on which the world I grew up in began to come to an end. Not the world, just a part of it, just the setting that I believed was permanent. I suppose in every generation a child's world, happy or unhappy, seems a lasting city. This is how things are, will be, a child thinks, and then they're not. One's grown-up life, however peaceful and agreeable, has an unsettled quality, and one looks back. I have been happy and yet I have sometimes been homesick for the unchangeable, lost time. I remember, with nostalgia, absurdly unimportant things like East Side streets with houses all the same height. I look from my terrace at the Chrysler spire sharp as an icicle and I remember the rows of low, mostly narrow houses and, on Fifth Avenue the French castles that have been replaced by rectangles of steel and concrete and glass, 660 and 666 and old Mrs. Cornelius Vanderbilt's cream and rose brick mansion on the corner of Fifty-eighth Street, overlooking the plaza and the Pulitzer fountain. I must have been nearly grown up when the fountain was new, but I have long known it and it pleases me that every year at Christmas it is lit with garlands of bulbs as delicate and brilliant as the ones that gleamed in the chandeliers in the dowager's ballroom.

Every generation must have a golden age to remember but looking back on the one my generation had, I think it was more golden than most. I realize—I've read it and been told it often enough—that all sorts of things were wrong with the prewar world and I can't argue. Still, growing up in America then was more tranquil; it was something we knew how to do. The rules were fixed, the setting was firmly there and would not be removed by the stagehands. The curtain was never going to come down. This year was like last year and next year would be the same. We knew where we were today and nothing could change tomorrow. If I reminisce about that time, not just with my friends but with Americans whose childhood—however different and distant from ours—was in the same epoch, we share a time and a place where things were as they ought to be, as we wish they could in some fashion, some day, be again. Any slight, shared recollection will start us on the road back, will make an acquaintance or a stranger met on a ship or train seem like a friend or relation: trolley cars and the ferry to New Jersey and the wonderful, fast, rattling ride on the Elevated; Little Nemo and Buster Brown and his faithful dog, Tige; Sundays or other formal occasions with high-button shoes and white kid gloves so tight that each finger must be laboriously worked into its separate, stiff compartment, and the wooden stick on which even naturally wavy hair was harshly twisted into sausage curls; the discomfort of long clammy stockings and water-logged slippers and a ballooning mohair dress when going in bathing—just to say "going in bathing" is enough or to mention the side stroke. Any forgotten phrase is enough to remind us that we who lived in prewar

America are of one vintage. We may have lived far apart but we grew up together.

I remember my sisters and my friends and me in the war years but I don't really remember the war. (It was a long time later that it became World War I and I still think of it as The War.) There have been too many books and plays and movies, too much discussion and propaganda. The symbols and the facts have been interpreted and manipulated this way and that too often—Edith Cavell, for instance, and the *Lusitania*. The *Athenia* reminded me a little bit though she was only a pale reflection of the shock of the *Lusitania*, but Edith Stein with the yellow star of David on her Carmelite habit put Edith Cavell back into focus as she was when I first heard her name and wept for her before clever people explained and excused her execution.

When it began, the war was still remote, still like a war in a history book or in a novel. Like everyone I knew, I was passionately on the side of the English. The English were not only the ancestors of most of us, but the heroes of our books, and I had always been for them except—and in spite of Henry V— during the Hundred Years' War and, of course, during the Revolution and the War of 1812. It was nice to be able to be unreservedly for the English and the French at the same time.

Very little was changed in our way of life before 1917 and not much after that. I remember small things. It's odd how one remembers first the symbol and then the fact. I remember the small starred service flags in the windows. The blue stars for sons and husbands in the Army, some perhaps already over there, were a patriotic display that I admired, wishing that I, like some of my friends, had a brother old enough to go. Then gold stars began to appear and I looked away. I remember the casualty lists printed as matter-of-factly as names of contributors to the Fresh Air Fund. I know, knew then, that the lists were shorter than those of the French and the English, but they were our own. What happens to one's own really happens. I think I was made aware by our casualty lists of the years of dead young men since 1914. I didn't recognize many names in the local lists but they were names from here, from New York and Brooklyn and Newark and Long Island City. They were names from here, and here, wherever it might be in the United States, had always been, was always supposed to be safe between its oceans.

Some of the names we knew. It's not pleasant to realize how many I have forgotten. Someone says, "Oh yes, she had another brother but he was killed in the First World War," and the rest of us at the luncheon or bridge table say, "I had forgotten," and we fall silent, trying to remember a boy we must have known when we were growing up.

I have never for a minute forgotten Bunny Conway. He called on Maud before he was shipped out and gave her a pair of second lieutenant's bars. Bunny had no serious girl, and Maud was pleased. It was a long time since May in Paris and her meeting with Louis Martin. Louis had not visited America in the summer of 1914. He had joined the American Motor Ambulance Corps with the Second French Army. When we came in he enlisted in the American Army and was assigned to the camouflage people.

In 1917, Maud was delighted to have Bunny's insignia. Every girl wanted to have a beau in the Army or Navy or, most romantic of all, in the Air Corps. We didn't really believe or imagine the reality of the war yet and I was glad that Maud had someone in it and proud that Bunny was going. I can hear my eighteen-year-old voice as I gaily said, "How marvelous for you, Bunny. Soon you'll be over there." I don't like to remember my last words to him. I knew him when he was quite young. He was a year older than Maud, but he must have been quite young when he let a snake loose at supper in our house in Southampton. It was only a grass snake which I recognized because Bertie had kept one as a pet for a time, but Maud and Julia and Betty Conway screamed, and Bunny's joke was a success. He was funny. Perhaps I wouldn't think so now but he gave me many a hearty laugh then and I liked him and I wish I had said something else. Looking back, it seems callous and stupid to have congratulated a boy who was on his way to France (where this boy's body would be blown into unrecognizable fragments) as if he had just made the Yale football squad. It was callous, I guess, and stupid, but more than that it was not knowing. We none of us knew then what war was like. The bands were still playing; the agonizing books and the photographs came later.

Our world and our ways seemed little altered by our being in the war. There were dances, though the big balls were usually for the Red Cross or some other worthy cause. There was a lot of easy patriotism, but we were earnest about it. I remember a Red Cross course and all of us wearing becoming veiled headdresses while we rolled bandages. I remember us on the round piazza knitting skein after skein of khaki-colored wool. I remember small things like meatless days and semaphoring for preparedness and amateur spy scares. I had forgotten some of them until I read *Bab: A Sub Deb* to my oldest granddaughter when she had measles last spring.

"It can't have been like that," Nellie said to me, as her mother has often said of the past I knew, "it sounds silly. Not Bab, I like her and I like the story, Granny, but it sounds like another world. I can't believe it was like that."

I told her that it was indeed another world, but it was like that. Mrs. Rinehart had an impeccable ear and eye for the people of her time, particularly for young girls and elderly ladies, even if Nellie couldn't believe it.

"After all," I added, "I don't believe a word of John O'Hara though I'm told it's all exactly how life is today."

I remember small scenes of the war both before and after we were in it.

Fluffy and I watched the parade for Marshal Joffre from the James Speyers' drawing room. Mrs. Speyer was the bishop's second cousin, a childless old lady who loved children and animals and was kind and welcoming to both. I can still remember the filmy softness and the faint violet scent of the handkerchief she gave me when I cried at the sight of the legendary figure in horizon blue. He reminded me of short, chunky, stubborn Frenchmen whom I had encountered in Paris. So many of them, I thought, must now be dead, taxi drivers, policemen, railway porters.

Bridie and I stood wedged in the crowd on the sidewalk and waved and cheered ourselves hoarse when the Fighting Sixtyninth, home from the Mexican border, marched down Fifth Avenue. After America entered the war Colonel Bill Donovan and Father Duffy became Bridie's heroes and they reconciled her to being allied with the English.

I remember Bruce Bairnsfather's Old Bill and Edward Streeter's "Dere Mabel." I remember a song, "Keep Your 'ead Down, Fritzie Boy," which we thought hilarious, I hope because of its cockney dialect and not because Fritzie Boy was trapped in No Man's Land, but I can't be sure.

A curious thing about the wartime popular songs is that all of them, the comic ones, the wistful ones, the absurd ones and the ones too distinguished for oblivion are equally poignant in retrospect. I have been told that in England "Tipperary" was never sung or played after the war and in this country, at least to my generation, a song like "There's A Long, Long Trail," which once was agreeably sentimental, is now sad to hear.

However, in their own time the songs of 1917 and 1918 were fine and I was gay as a lark as I danced and flirted to their accompaniment.

Being eighteen was not as I had long imagined it. Oh, I was a full-fledged young lady, I was out, but in wartime the fact was marked only by an informal midsummer dance at our house in Southampton. It was a queer coming-out party, with the boys who should have been there in distant camps. It did seem to me that the Army went out of its way to transfer officers and men from one end of the country to the other. Almost all the familiar masculine faces at the weekend parties were those of boys sixteen and seventeen and even fifteen. The older ones were mostly officers from Upton and other Long Island camps. However, the strangers were handsome and dashing in their uniforms, and they were not aloof as I had thought older men might be toward a debutante. Most of them were far from home and they must have been lonely and grateful for my party and for all the parties that were like peacetime Saturday nights, with girls in summer evening dresses and elderly ladies keeping an eye on the dance floor and making occasional forays into the darkness beyond the verandahs of the Meadow Club and Shinnecock. I suppose the dreadnaughts were a comfortable and homely sight rather than a fearsome one. Ladies like that were to be found in every American town then and, seeing them, the strangers must have been reminded of the dowagers of Wichita or Memphis or San Diego.

In the first years after the Armistice when I looked back on the wartime parties in Southampton and New York I was a little critical, a little ashamed of the round of gaiety as usual. Now I'm glad we had the parties. I don't remember the faces or the names of the young strangers, but now I realize that they were young. In any picture of that time the face between the jaunty cap and the high, stiff, military collar is a boy's face. Even Father Duffy and Colonel Donovan in their wartime photographs look young and defenseless to my eyes today. Most of the officers I proudly danced with were in their early twenties and of no higher rank than first lieutenant. They seemed mature and sure of themselves but they must have been shy, and probably every last one of them was scared some of the time. I'm glad they had the parties which were, I realize, more valuable than the things we gravely thought of as war work: the wool we knitted, the bandages we rolled, the tin foil we collected, the meat we went without on Tuesdays. I think Tuesday was the meatless day, but I'm not sure I remember accurately.

I do remember the dances and the heady feeling of being grown up and a success in Southampton and, in the winter, in the larger world of New York. I enjoyed it, though it was rather like being a success in an unknown city. I was glad in the Christmas holidays to see boys from St. Mark's and St. Paul's and Groton. "Mere infants" we said of sixth-formers, but we danced with them happily enough.

In New York there were Allied officers as well as American ones. There were old friends too sometimes, on furlough or on their way to another camp or to France, and there were ones in the Navy on leave, but never Bertie. I wished he could see me in my glory, a grownup at last. Finally I was his equal, and where was he?

The day after he graduated from Harvard, Bertie went into the Army, and he had been sent to a camp in Texas. It was over two years since we had spent any time together. In the summer of 1916, he had been at Plattsburg.

It was queer to have caught up with Bertie and then to have him not there. I think I minded, I think I missed him, but this may be only in retrospect. I remember that I knitted him a khaki muffler. In spite of Bridie's efforts, socks and sweaters were beyond me. Bertie probably realized this and he wrote me an appreciative thank you note. Later he sent me a postcard of the Texas town where he was stationed and I thanked him. I had never had occasion to write to Bertie before and I hoped he would be impressed by the grown-up wording of my signature: "As ever, Nell." I added a flourish below my name.

What I most clearly remember of the summer of 1917 and of the winter in which 1918 began is that I had a lovely time. I was pleased with myself and my popularity which was greater than I had expected. I was sorry Bertie could not see and admire me, Nell Cameron, one of the belles of the year.

I didn't have Bertie but I had plenty of admirers although because of the war they came and went rather rapidly.

Then in late December, Alfred Sampson came and stayed. In 1916 he had joined the Lafayette Escadrille and now, having been wounded, he was home.

Soon after he returned he appeared at our house.

"This is one of the places where I had fun a hundred years ago. It's good to be back," he said. "Your having grown up so pretty, Nell, is an agreeable little dividend."

In his Air Corps uniform he was a gallant figure. He limped slightly and that seemed romantic to me. The wounded warrior home from the field of battle.

"Sorry about the gimpy leg," he said, "but they tell me it'll soon be as good as new. Even as it is I can manage to take you and your sisters dancing. Altogether, they've patched me up pretty well, but they've grounded me for the duration. At least, let's hope the year they mentioned will prove to be the duration."

"In the meanwhile what will you do?" I asked.

"They'll give me a long furlough and then small jobs, Liberty bonds, escort service. I'll be a patriotic set piece I suppose, but I'll have plenty of time on my hands and you girls have an obvious duty to make the hero's homecoming a happy one."

Lots of girls would have been delighted to add to the joys of Alfred's homecoming, but he seemed to prefer our house and our invitations.

At first I wondered whether he had after all been in love with Julia, whether he liked to be with Maud and me because we reminded him of old, happy days. I felt embarrassed when I first mentioned Julia and told him that she and little James had come home from Paris and had settled down at Henderson with her in-laws and were in Washington with them for the winter.

"Now that Martha's married," I said, "Julia has taken her place as the daughter of the house."

Alfred listened cheerfully. "That's good," he said, "that's correct. Julia always was a correct girl in spite of her flirtatious, sophisticated ways. And a pretty girl. She sure was pretty."

"She still is. You talk as if she was old."

"I didn't mean to. It's just that Julia and I and everything before 1914 seem a hundred years ago. However, you and I are now and we're going to have fun. Maud too. And Esther. What's she up to? I haven't laid eyes on her since that first evening at dinner. She's a dazzler isn't she? Always will be is my guess."

Esther was the one of us who worked hard, though hers was not war work. I think perhaps she had tried to find something with the Red Cross or the Y and that the committee ladies made it impossible. She worked all day long five days a week at the Babies' Hospital.

"It's difficult," I explained to Alfred, "for the peacetime things to get people. Everyone wants to do war work though it's not easy to do anything much unless you're trained which we none of us are. I guess Maud will be some day. She's taking courses at Columbia toward an M.A."

"Good for her, I like Maud. I like you all, the beauty, the brain and the baby. Maybe I like the baby best."

"If you mean me, Alfred Sampson, I'll thank you to notice I'm no longer a baby. I've grown up while you've been away."

"I do notice, and very nice too."

On any occasion that he organized Alfred invited Maud and Esther as well as me. He took us tea dancing and provided escorts, sometimes foreign officers, sometimes Americans. He accompanied us to charity balls and to the play, and for about two weeks I thought the three of us were equal in his eyes. Esther came with us rarely, but Maud almost always. I was as pleased for Maud's sake as for my own that Alfred had adopted our family.

Alfred's sisters were married. Gladys lived in St. Louis and Muriel in Philadelphia. His older brother, Lucius, unlikely as it seemed for a Sampson, was a mathematics professor at the University of California. The other Sampsons, his Uncle Cecil's children, lived in New York but they were ten to fifteen years older than Alfred and it was natural enough, I thought, that he should adopt us as sisters. I didn't think this for long. He quickly made it clear in small, subtle ways that I was his girl. I remembered from the old days that Alfred wasn't the marrying kind. Perhaps the war had changed that, though he appeared unchanged by it in every other way.

I didn't worry about his intentions. It seemed to me that wartime was a temporary time. War brides were romantic and occasionally I envied them, but still this seemed a time between, not one in which to decide anything as permanent as marriage, should Alfred astonish me by suggesting it.

I liked having him as a beau. He had the Sampson charm and their pale, long-nosed good looks. The Old Guard spoke scornfully of their being a family of no more than three generations, but in Alfred's generation and his father's, the Sampsons were

as distinguished in appearance and manner as any of the Old
Guard's most cherished ancestors. The New York Historical Society has a portrait of a nineteenth-century Livingston who
might be Alfred's twin.

I liked Alfred and I was attracted by him. Eighteen, however
uncertain the time in which one reaches it, is an age for falling
in love and I enjoyed falling a little in love with Alfred. As far
as he fell, I told myself, I would fall and no further. I liked Alfred for himself and I also relished the small, secret triumph,
which only a younger sister can know, of capturing my older
sister's beau.

I thought only a younger sister can know, but it turned out
that Pa was observant.

"Look here, Nell," he said to me, "try to realize that it was
Julia's good luck that Alfred didn't want to get married. Don't
be beguiled by a small sisterly triumph."

"I don't know what you mean, Pa."

"Yes, you do. I mean don't marry Alfred if he asks you because
he didn't ask Julia."

"Honestly, Pa . . ."

"Sometimes it's as well to speak honestly. As I said to Julia five
years ago, I like Alfred but I wouldn't want to see you marry him.
For the reasons I gave her which I'm sure you remember and for
one more. He's been hurt, maybe crippled by the war—and I
don't mean his leg or the other wounds the doctors have patched
up."

"Honestly, Pa," I said again, and was maddened to hear myself
sounding as if I was still thirteen years old, "Alfred hasn't been
one bit affected by the war except his poor leg which is practically as good as new. Why he never so much as mentions the
war."

"Exactly," Pa said. "Go slow, Nell, I beg you."

"Oh, Pa, please . . ." I wanted to beg him not to look old which for a frightening moment he did and then the look was gone and I said, "Please don't worry. Alfred and I aren't going very fast or very seriously. Even if he wanted to, I don't think I'd want to get married now with the war. I'd rather wait till things go back to the way they used to be."

"Things never go back to that, my dear. But you're right, war years are more unsettled than most and not a time for lasting decisions."

"I'm not going to decide anything and neither, I'm pretty sure, will Alfred."

"I don't know about him, but you're my girl. I know you. You weren't christened Eleanor for nothing. You're as pretty and good-tempered as your mother. Try to be as sensible."

"You know," I felt at my ease with him again, "to a girl my age sensible sounds a dull thing to be."

"Eleanor was never dull. She was full of fun, but she was wise. And she was young. She was always as young and gentle and lighthearted as a bride."

He was silent and so was I, not knowing what to say.

After a minute or two, he stood up and paused beside my chair. "Let's hope you have your mother's wisdom," he said, "as well as the pure oval of her face and her fair, silky hair."

He patted my head. That was a gesture from a long time ago and I remembered nursery evenings and Father towering above me while I finished my supper.

In February, Julia came to New York to spend a week with us. A day or two after she arrived, she and Father and I were alone at tea. We talked, or rather Father and I listened while Julia talked about wartime life in Washington.

Presently Pa asked, "Ever see anything of Harry Martin's boy,

Louis? I believe he's stationed in Washington. With the camouflage people, if that will help you to identify him."

"It's difficult," Julia said. "In their uniforms they all look alike."

"It would be a nice thing if you looked him up. His father's an old friend of mine and his mother . . ."

"Is an old snob as you know very well, Pa."

"A bit *collet monté* as she would put it, but Louis is a nice lad. Your sisters and I saw quite a lot of him in Paris after your wedding."

"Oh-h-h." Julia drew a deep breath. "I know who he is now. The one with Maud at the Crillon. Do you mean anything came of that? Now don't be devious, Pa. Tell me or I'll ask Maud. Or maybe Nell would be better."

"Much better. You don't want to embarrass Maud. There may have been the beginning of something between her and Louis. Nell would know better than I. In any event I'd like you to get hold of the boy, he may not have many friends in Washington."

Then Pa went on to speak of his pleasure over James's promotion to first secretary and Julia told us that Ambassador Herrick, in a letter to Senator Henderson, had spoken highly of James.

Louis Martin's name was not mentioned again until Julia and I were alone.

"Now tell me," she said. "Was there anything between Maud and Louis Martin?"

"I was pretty young myself, so I could be wrong, but I still think there was a little something, though I guess not enough to survive the wartime separation."

"That was a real separation. I mean it was as though all of you over here were in a world as far away as Mars. If we felt it in the Embassy how much more Louis must have. Ambulance service is no joke. It's natural that nothing came of their budding ro-

mance then but now—only, look, Nell, what about Bunny
Conway?"

"Poor Bunny, wasn't it terrible? Betty told Maud they
couldn't find a single . . . they didn't know . . . Betty looks awful. Maud says Bunny being a year younger than Betty makes it
worse for her. She tries to talk about him and she can't."

"What about Maud? Someone in Washington told me that
Maud got engaged to Bunny before he was killed. She hasn't
said anything and I haven't asked. I will say she seems all right."

"But, Julia, there wasn't anything. He wasn't even a heavy
beau. He gave her his lieutenant's bars and it was nice for her
to have someone to write to and knit for. That's all it was. Of
course, she feels awful but no more than I do or anyone who
grew up with him in Southampton summers. And then at the
end of last summer—"

"Oh well, then," Julia said, and got briskly to her feet. "The
thing for me to do is to spy out the land. You remember Dotty
Morris?"

I shook my head.

"She was in my class at Spence. She married a Guarrigue.
Her brother's in the Navy. James wrote me that he'd seen him
when he was on leave in Paris. That gives me a perfect excuse to
ring Dotty up and ask her to lunch."

Julia arranged the luncheon and returned from it with a report
and a plan.

"Old snob," she said, "old witch, too. Dotty's husband is a fairly
distant cousin, so she didn't mind telling me about it. It wasn't a
bit embarrassing because Dotty's not a Catholic and she thinks
Maud was engaged to Bunny and doesn't care two pins about
Louis Martin. Dotty told me that when Louis got home he told
his mother that he had met a young Miss Cameron before the
war and hoped to see her again. Mrs. Martin must have thought

he meant you. She wouldn't remember our exact ages. Anyway she seemed quite pleased and murmured about our dear father and our dear Aunt Lucy and all the dear Turners and Gores. Then Louis said he knew she would be even more pleased to learn that Maud was a Catholic. And at that point Mrs. Martin hit the ceiling."

"Because Maud's a Catholic? But Mrs. Martin is a Catholic."

"It seems peculiar to us, but then we hardly ever have to contend with converts. Anyhow according to Mrs. Martin's account to her friends and relations she turned pale, though how you can see yourself turn pale I can't imagine and said, 'My God, Louis, not a convert! I had no idea you meant Maud Cameron.' And she asked Louis and the bon Dieu, simultaneously I gather, why he couldn't have found a French girl, a cradle Catholic, if he wanted to marry one or else a nice Protestant like his brother Paul's wife? Converts were so difficult, they took religion so seriously, the Church was life and death to them. And they filled their houses with bad Catholic art. Particularly for an artist a convert would make an impossible wife and so forth and so forth."

"But, Julia, one of Father's big complaints about R.C.s was that they're always proselytizing."

"Not ones like the Guarrigues, it seems. Dotty says they're forever telling what they consider killingly funny stories about converts. There's one they love about some bishop on his death-bed saying whatever else he had done wrong in his life, at least he had never made a convert. Poor Maud, it's hard on her after all she went through with us, to have Catholics down on her too, but you must admit it's comical."

"I don't call it comical, I call it mean."

"People like the Guarrigues are different from Irish Catholics. They don't force their religion on other people, and I gather from Dotty that they don't want it rammed down their own throats. But Mrs. Martin's views on converts aren't the main difficulty. Here's the real problem, the thing that has scared Louis off. The old girl has heard something about Maud and Bunny, not much I'll bet, but she told Louis that Maud had known Bunny all her life, that they had been childhood sweethearts and had become engaged before he was sent over. Maud, she said, was heartbroken and Louis mustn't think of intruding on her sorrow. Of course, Louis believed her. A mother can get away with anything."

"Then what can we do?"

"I have a plan." Julia grinned and looked exactly as she had years ago when she devised a scheme to outwit Mademoiselle or Aunt Lucy. "I'm going to invite him—"

"Oh, Julia," I interrupted her, "that's no good, you can't invite him to dinner out of the blue and announce that Maud isn't grief-stricken but open to offers. What on earth could you say to him?"

"Nothing." And Julia explained that she intended to give a party in Washington on the last Saturday in February, which fell between her birthday and Maud's. There wasn't much time but enough if she sent telegrams off right away. Wartime parties in Washington were either for a noble cause or informal. This one would be informal, not too big for Louis and Maud to find each other and not small enough for their meeting to seem contrived. I was to come with Maud and we and our men could stay with the Hendersons. We must each bring a man. Maud mustn't appear a maiden all forlorn.

"You can bring Alfred Sampson," Julia said, "and he can get someone for Maud."

I suggested a French captain who was quite attractive. His

English was poor so he enjoyed being with Maud and me to whom he could speak French.

The captain would be fine, Julia said, and Alfred Sampson always made a girl seem attractive.

"And speaking of little somethings, Nell dear, I hear a little something has started between you and Alfred."

"Oh, not really." I hoped I wasn't blushing, but my face felt hot.

"If you're wise you'll keep it that way. At least on your side. Alfred's a wary bird. Set your cap for him if you want to, but not your heart. You might get it back in small pieces."

"Honestly! Don't talk to me as if I was an infant with not enough sense to come in out of the rain."

"Sorry. But I think I know Alfred better than you do. Still, I'll admit it must be annoying for you to have us all keep on thinking of you as our baby sister. Cheer up, some day we'll all seem and look and feel the same age and won't that be dreary?"

Our elders never tired of reminding us that the best-laid schemes of mice and men went aft agley, but I have noticed one thing about well-laid schemes and that is that they quite often turn out to be complicated plans to bring about events that would have happened anyway.

The party itself turned out exactly as Julia had planned. The Hendersons' Washington house was a late-nineteenth-century palace with a huge, heavily gilded ballroom in which I could not imagine a young, informal party. Two hundred people would be lost in it I thought, and only a large-scale orchestra could fill the musicians' balcony; the fashionable ragtime band that Julia had engaged would never be able to make its rhythms heard when it was perched a story and a half above the dancers' heads.

I needn't have worried. The high ceiling and the balcony, the deeply grooved columns and the acrobatic cherubs and full-bosomed mermaids were masked by red and white canvas that transformed the coldly handsome room into a tent as gaily welcoming as a circus. At one end a platform had been built for the musicians and every wild note could be heard and the famous saxophonist was brilliantly illuminated during his solos when all the lights except the largest spotlight were dimmed and he was caught in its changing colors. The sides of the tent were banked with hedges of cheerful little flowers and there were bouquets of red tulips and white freesia on the small candle-lit tables where guests could sit on the edge of the dance floor as at a cabaret.

Julia had not attempted to soften the austerity of the mahogany and dark green satin walls of the dining room, but the buffet table and the professionally manned bar opposite it and, as in the tent, the small, brightly flowered tables, made the dark old room seem unexpectedly festive. There was no grand march and no interval for supper. Food and drink were served continuously and the music played all night long.

The supper march was unnecessary, Julia explained, except at a great ball and it was always an ordeal for the shy and sometimes awkward for anyone. There wasn't a girl living, she said, who hadn't on occasion, in a panic, accepted an unwelcome supper invitation for fear of being stranded on the ballroom floor at the first thundering chords of the march.

"My little tables on the dance floor are a help too," she said, "for the shy or strangers or the not too popular. They solve the wallflower problem and make it easy for me to arrange a change of partners, and besides, it's fun to be able to sit casually at a table with someone instead of deliberately sitting out. Unless, of course, you want to find a nook, there are a few of those in this stone monster of a house."

It was, I thought, a lovely party.

"I suppose it's informal," I said to Alfred, "but it looks lavish to me."

"Looks expensive you mean, but it doesn't hit anyone in the eye. It must have cost plenty but it doesn't scream money at the guests. That's all that's asked for in wartime, the appearance of simplicity, telegrams instead of engraved invitations, canvas, expensively draped of course and strung with hundreds of little lights, but it's canvas, not satin. No potted palms or long-stemmed roses, just unassuming spring flowers which at this season cost a fortune, just a few elderly footmen in dark livery instead of a platoon of them in scarlet velvet court costumes, just the silver service, not the gold . . ."

"Stop being sarcastic, Alfred Sampson, about my sister's party. Julia arranged this to be kind, to give Maud and me a good time."

"Sorry. But the home front is a little staggering to one who has seen the other. However, if this is some intricate plot of Julia's for a worthy end, I'll forgive the means. She didn't have to go to these lengths to give you a good time, so what's she up to for Maud?"

I put a finger to my lips. "A secret. Maybe I'll tell you later."

I didn't have to tell him. He could see, as could I, as could anyone who was watching.

Quite early in the evening Maud and Louis met. She was coming out of the tent with the French captain as Louis came up the stairs. They walked quickly toward each other and stood still for less than a minute, and then as naturally as if they had seen each other four days—not four years—ago they wandered off together. Watching them I realized that no clever plan had been necessary, no exactly right circumstance and setting. We could just have invited Louis to tea or family supper. No matter where they had met, Maud and Louis would have been, as they were tonight, together. The splendid party, so carefully arranged for their benefit, might not have existed for all the notice they took of it. They wandered through it as they had wandered through the allées of St. Cloud. They met again in the palatial house as they had met the first time in the hotel that had once actually been a palace. Now as then, here as anywhere, they met and were unself-consciously, happily together again. This time, I thought, they would not easily be parted.

Sunday was a heavy day at the Hendersons', but none of us except the French captain had the energy to escape any part of it.

Louis had been invited to midday dinner and was staying for supper. The captain was taking the Congressional back to New York. He told me, before he left that he found American Sundays, at least among the old-fashioned rich, difficult to endure and so, since he was not needed . . . He smiled and suddenly looked much younger, which made me realize that he was probably older than I had supposed. It's as difficult to guess a Frenchman's age as an American Indian's or an Indian Indian's for that matter.

It had been, the captain said, a pleasure to watch Mademoiselle, my sister and her young man. *"La jeunesse, le premier amour, ah, mademoiselle, c'est beau quand même."*

He shrugged, bowed and saluted in farewell and added that youth and first love were beautiful to watch but it was restful to have left them both behind one.

Only Maud and Louis seemed to find the long afternoon agreeable. They moved or rather sat through it as happily as they had wandered through Julia's party. They were as quiet as the rest of us and listened as patiently to Senator Henderson's views on the unfortunate aspects of the President's home front policies and on his deplorable tendency toward idealism in world affairs. My face and Alfred's grew stiff with suppressed yawns,

but Maud and Louis smiled as contentedly as if they were listening to each other, though neither of them said more than a few
polite words out loud.

The day seemed endless to me, and I was relieved when it
was finally time for the cold supper which concluded the Sunday
ritual.

Senator and Mrs. Henderson retired early. Little James's
nurse had been given the evening off and Julia was in the nursery. Alfred turned on the Victrola, and Maud and Louis, to the
accompaniment of "For Me and My Gal," started a game of
Russian Bank.

Alfred watched the card players for a few minutes.

"It's a good thing," he said, "that you didn't begin your game
in the presence of the senator and his lady. No Sabbath card
playing, or secular music either, in dear old upper New York
State, I'll wager, and the rules of that community are obviously
the ones that are observed in this house. Come on, Nell, get a
wrap and we'll go out for a quick breath of air. I need to take the
taste of boiled Sunday out of my mouth."

It was a very quick breath of air, around the Circle and back.
When we returned, Alfred dismissed the footman who had let
us in.

"We'll see to the lights," he said. "Let's stay down here, Nell,
and give the young lovers a chance."

"In the front hall?"

"No, my sweet. I prowled the house earlier for one of Julia's
nooks and the best seemed to be a little ground-floor anteroom."

He led the way and I followed.

"A bit stiff," he said, "Alavoine at its most formal, but some
kind soul has laid a fire, so it will do."

He lit the fire and we settled ourselves in two slippery, satin
upholstered chairs.

"Anyone can see that Louis and Maud are in love," I said, and told Alfred how it had begun in Paris and then been interrupted by the war. "Julia planned last night's party to bring them together again but it could have been managed much more simply than she thought. Poor Julia! All her trouble for nothing."

"Not entirely for nothing. Your sister had her eye on James's career as well as on Maud's happiness. Both the Under Secretary and the Assistant Secretary of State were here and the senator from Rhode Island and his beautiful Mathilde. And the Longworths and the Wadsworths and any number of useful guests. Even if Maud didn't need the party, it wasn't entirely wasted."

"You sound as if you didn't like Julia, didn't—"

"But I do like her. I always did, and what's more, I admired the sharp little mind that her soft prettiness concealed from the unwary. Julia knew where she was going. I admired that. Still do. I'm a lazy, directionless chap myself, but I can appreciate the movers and doers." Alfred stood up and poked the fire. "Borrowed time is a strange country to live in. It has no sign posts and no direction for them to point to if they existed."

"I don't understand a word you're saying, but you sound sad. Or maybe you're just tired."

"We're both tired after last night. And how could I be sad? I'm one of the lucky ones. I'm sorry I sounded disagreeable about Julia's party. You know, I think it was nice for Maud, at that. I believe it will be nice for her some day to look back at the sparkle and gaiety that surrounded her when the bells started ringing again for her and Louis Martin."

He took my hand and pulled me to my feet. "You're tired and it's late. Too late for me to get serious but just the same I'd like to ask you if you think the bells will pretty soon start ringing for me and my gal. You are my gal, aren't you, Nell?"

"I'm not sure."

He drew me closer and I let him. I knew he was going to kiss me and he did.

On two occasions I had been kissed good-by by wartime admirers, but theirs had been light and awkward kisses.

Alfred was not awkward. His lips were light on mine for what seemed a long and I think exciting moment. Then he held me much closer and the kiss changed. I knew there was a different way of kissing, girls had told me, but being told about a thing is different from experiencing it. I felt quite queer. It's hard to remember but if I'm honest I think I must remember that I liked it. I liked Alfred holding me and kissing me that way but I didn't want him to. Later while I was getting ready for bed I puzzled over why I hadn't wanted him to go on kissing me and holding me. It wasn't because of Aunt Lucy's guarded warnings, I hadn't even thought of them or of Bridie's more outspoken advice. It wasn't that I was scared—oh well, maybe a little, but what I still remember clearly is that I wanted desperately to be my own again. I freed myself from Alfred's kiss and his embrace and put as much distance between us as the small, cluttered room allowed.

Alfred stood where he was and, to my relief, didn't look annoyed. He smiled and after a minute he spoke in a kind, unembarrassed voice. "Dear Nell," he said, "I didn't mean to scare you. I didn't realize you were such an unsophisticated and correct little girl."

"I may be a prude—"

"That you are, my love. But a pretty prude and a very young one. That's it, isn't it? You're still very young. I had forgotten there are girls like you."

"Everyone's always telling me I'm young and treating me that way." I felt angry though I couldn't think at what or whom, certainly not at Alfred.

"I'm going to treat you that way too, but not always. Some day those bells are going to ring for you and me." He put his arm around me in a friendly fashion and led me to the foot of the stairs. He gave me a quick hug that was not in the least romantic or scaring and told me to go along to bed, he would put out the lights.

Halfway to the first landing I turned. He was watching me and, feeling extremely grown up and daring, I blew him a kiss and ran the rest of the way, as fast as I could to my room.

On Monday I traveled alone to New York. Maud had agreed to cut her classes and stay for another week with Julia. Alfred couldn't leave Washington for a day or two, as he had to see some people at the War Department.

My journey was like the continuation of a dream. I had slept unexpectedly soon and soundly Sunday night and I didn't remember dreaming at all. The evening with Alfred was the dream that continued now.

This morning at breakfast Alfred had been the same as usual and so had I. We drank our coffee and ate our eggs and listened to Senator Henderson, and then Alfred, after a hasty, general farewell went off to an appointment.

Not quite the same, either one of us, I thought, and let the magazine I had not been reading slide from my lap. There was a secret between us, a beginning. The anteroom had been the entrance to another place, as if, like Alice, I had gone through the big, cloudy looking-glass above the mantel and had reached a path that would lead to a garden. I didn't go alone as Alice had done and I wasn't young like Alice, I wasn't a little girl any more. I was like her in not knowing where I was going, but I didn't care. I was content to remember the antiqued glass that reflected nothing and the fire beginning to burn low and the two of us in the quiet room. Alfred, home safe from the war, and I,

barely grown up, had all the time in the world. I let myself slip
back into the gray-paneled room and let the love scene play itself
over, a very small love scene, but my first, and I liked remembering it. It still puzzled me that I had put an end to it so quickly,
had so fiercely pushed Alfred away, wanting not to belong to
anyone but me. It had been like the enormous effort one has to
make in order to wake from a dream, but one doesn't try to escape
from a lovely dream and this one had seemed lovely. In the parlor
car I looked back on the evening with pleasure. I saw myself
moving through it and I wished there had been a mirror, a good
clear one, in the front hall so I could actually have seen myself
when I turned on the stair and put my hand to my lips. However,
I could picture myself quite well in my head. It was an agreeably romantic picture and I enjoyed looking at it for some time.

When I got to our house Bridie opened the front door and
greeted me not as the heroine of romance that I felt myself to be
but as though I were still at Spence and home late from school.

"So here you are at last," she said, "back from your galli-
vanting."

"Honestly, Bridie, I don't call visiting my sister Julia galli-
vanting."

"Call it what you like but it's too bad you didn't come home
yesterday so at least one of you could have been here when
Bertie came. Esther had to take somebody's place at the hospital,
your father was at one of his clubs and there was no one to welcome the lad but myself."

"Bertie's in New York? Oh good!" Now he would see how
grown up I was, I thought, and, oh boy, when I told him . . .
well, no, I guessed I wouldn't tell him that.

"You needn't be so pleased with your 'oh good' and the face on
you of the cat that just swallowed the canary. Bertie's not here.
He came to say good-by and is on his way to France by now.

They're not supposed to say and he didn't, he just said he had only a twelve-hour pass and it was up at six o'clock but he wrote you a note which I have here and gave me a big hug and said, 'See you when the war's over, Bridie.' You can bet he was disappointed that not one of you was here to wish him good luck."

I went up to my room with Bertie's note in my hand and was indeed back in the old Spence days where Bridie had placed me. Romance was all very fine and no girl was readier than I to enjoy it but Bertie was my friend and it was mean I hadn't been here. Oh, he had his mother and father, and Elsie, his married sister, and her brood would have rallied, but Bertie always came to our house for part of a day of celebration like Christmas or when he was leaving for St. Mark's or anything like that. We were as much his family as his own was and we ought to have been here.

I unfolded his note.

"Dear Nell. Sorry to miss you. Ma will give you all my news. Bridie says you are quite the belle and I'd never know you. I'd know you all right but it's hard to believe you've grown up while my back was turned. I'll have to see this for myself when the war is over. It won't be long they say. Out of the trenches by Christmas this year for sure. Say good-by to everybody for me. Love, Bertie."

It was mean, very mean, I thought, that Julia's party should have been this weekend of all weekends. It had been a lovely party and a lovely weekend and I had enjoyed every bit of it. That was the thing. I didn't like to have been having a lovely time while Bertie was embarking on a dark, dirty troopship.

"Come on, Fluffy," I said, "let's take one of Father's brisk walks."

I was too old to talk to her but if I went out with her I wouldn't have to talk to anyone else about Bertie's having gone off to the dark, dirty war that they were always saying would be over by Christmas and then it never was.

"Come on, Fluff." I attached the leash to her collar and hurried her downstairs and out the front door. If we walked fast enough I wouldn't have to think about the war and the ship plowing toward it with my oldest friend on board. Before Baby Elliot, before anyone I knew, Bertie had been my friend.

8

DURING March and April, Maud and Louis became engaged.

From the first evening in Washington they were together, and as far as I could make out, they never hesitated, never stood outside their relationship and looked at it and themselves. One of them never seemed a step ahead of the other as they walked side by side on a road they didn't so much explore as recognize. They knew, knew right away, I suppose, that it was the road home.

Julia has told me that from the beginning Maud spoke of Louis as though he were a permanent part of her life, but she did not report, as Julia had done to her, on the progress of the romance.

"She never even told me when Louis proposed," Julia once said indignantly. "I don't believe he ever did propose. I know he never spoke formally to Father. Maud and Louis just began to talk about what they would do when they were married. There hadn't been one word about an engagement when I was in New York that April and Maud said casually at dinner that Louis wanted to go back to Paris after the war was over and that was where they would live when they were married. They were perfectly agreeable about being engaged, but I was the one who had to remind them that first a girl gets engaged and the families are told and after a proper interval for formal calls and letters to relations and friends, the engagement is announced, and after another decent interval there's the wedding. You must remember how vague they were about the whole thing."

I remember.

Louis came to New York when he could, but it wasn't easy for him to get away even for a Sunday. Maud went far more often to Washington. In our day—and this I think must be true in any day—a girl didn't like to appear to be the pursuer, though, then as now, she often was. I don't believe either Maud or Louis gave a thought to how things looked, they were too absorbed in how, at last for them, things were. They didn't make a complicated charade out of being in love. It's curious and it's nice to remember that Maud who was so easily embarrassed, who shied so awkwardly at society's small, glittering fences, should have fallen in love easily and happily.

Even Mrs. Martin didn't make Maud unhappy, though Maud was puzzled by her future mother-in-law.

After Julia got the engagement on its conventional track, Maud returned from her first official Martin family luncheon in a state of bewilderment.

"They are the queerest people," she told Aunt Lucy and Julia and me. "It was just a small hen party. Mrs. Martin and her sister Mrs. Janvier and two Guarrigue cousins around my age and an old lady they called Tante Nini, a Madame de Something whose name I never disentangled from the rolling Rs. Anyway, nothing but family and will you believe that they never said one word about how glad they were that I was a Catholic? Cornelia Martin, Paul's wife, couldn't be there, so it wasn't as if they were holding back on her account. And another peculiar thing, though they're all Catholics, the Church wasn't so much as mentioned."

"People don't talk about religion," Julia said, "we never do."

"It's different with Catholics. Even Agnes Ryan, who's lost her faith, never seems to want to talk about anything else."

"The one at Barnard who gave you the books?" I asked. "Do you still see her? I wouldn't think you'd approve of her."

"Maybe I shouldn't. I've never asked about the rules on the fallen away, but—"

"My! What strange little technical terms you've acquired!"

"Be quiet, Julia; I'm answering Nell's question. Maybe I shouldn't approve of Agnes, but all I know is that I'm eternally grateful to her and I'm fond of her."

"How does she feel about you?"

"She's curious about me and she's fond of me, Nell."

It was a peculiar friendship, I thought.

I must have spoken my thought aloud because Maud admitted it was an odd relationship. She and Agnes were, she explained, like travelers met in a railway station, one getting on board and the other getting off to change trains. You wouldn't think that journeying in opposite directions would be a bond, but it was. The fact of journeying at all was the bond.

"Anyway," Maud said, "from our opposite directions Agnes and I talk. She's my oldest and best Catholic friend, though I've come to know two or three others in Southampton and I have Bridie."

Maud said that Bridie possessed an inexhaustible store of legends. One didn't believe them exactly, but they were an extension or a kind of parable of a truth in which one did believe.

"Like George Washington and the cherry tree?" I asked.

It was a little like that, Maud said, though fortunately most saints, including the original Bridie, had more gifted chroniclers than Parson Weems, and a legend was not a fabrication, it grew naturally if sometimes rather wildly out of love and hope.

Maud began to illustrate what she meant with the story of St.

Christopher. "The name alone is enough," she said, "the Christ bearer—"

Julia interrupted her, "Please, Maud! Just because you can't talk about your religion at the Martins, don't start on it in this house or at least save it for the servants' hall."

Maud flushed and her voice was sharp. "It wouldn't do this house any harm to have a little religion in it somewhere besides the pantry and the kitchen and the housekeeper's room."

"Really, Maud, you might show some respect for Aunt Lucy's presence if not for Nell's and mine."

"Stop it, both of you," Aunt Lucy said. "You sound like children and not very nice or loving children."

The quarrel ended abruptly as childhood quarrels had ended when Aunt Lucy intervened.

There was an awkward pause. Maud and Julia, as children, had not been embarrassed by their noisy disputes, but now their shrill, angry voices seemed to echo in the uncomfortable silence.

Aunt Lucy smiled and said gently, "Dear children, I know, of course, I know that you are loving sisters, all four of you."

As she spoke I was back, and Maud and Julia too, I think, in the old, simple time when there was always a grownup near at hand, when Aunt Lucy or Bridie or Mademoiselle was there to keep or restore the peace. I was delighted to be grown up at last, but for a moment I thought there was a lot to be said for the more circumscribed and orderly years when our elders were in charge and we didn't have to decide and arrange everything for ourselves.

"Even loving sisters," Aunt Lucy continued, "to say nothing of neighbors and strangers can learn to dislike, even to hate one another over religion. That's why it has been classed, along with politics, as a dangerous subject of conversation. It's sad, Maud, isn't it, that love and hope should come to this? But that's how it

is. I know it's hard not to discuss what one cares about deeply
and it's a disappointment for you not to have the pleasure and
freedom of Catholic conversation with your in-laws. Still, you
can talk about your church with Louis, I imagine."

"Oh, Aunt Lucy, I can talk about anything with Louis."

Maud and Louis' engagement was announced soon after we
moved to Southampton, and the wedding was planned for
September.

This was Maud's year. She was queen of our castle and I was
pleased for her.

It was our year too, Alfred said, and he complained that I was
putting him off.

"It's not putting you off, Alfred." We were sitting on the
round piazza. It was one of those windless, misty days when sky
and sea melt into each other and the horizon is hard to distinguish. I stared out at the grayness. What else was it but putting
him off? a small voice in my head inquired.

"It's just being fair to Maud," I said, answering Alfred and
silencing the small voice.

He did not accept my answer. "You mean we must continue to
mark time until September? That's not good enough, my sweet,
not nearly good enough."

I told him that it had been hard on Maud to have Julia who
was younger be the first one married and it would be just the
limit for me to start treading on her heels now.

"It's hard to explain to a man," I said. "Age doesn't mean the
same thing to you as to us. Even a girl who is hardly old at all
can be frightened or at least embarrassed by her years."

Alfred took my hand. "You seem to be talking a lot of nonsense in order to avoid talking about us."

"It may seem like nonsense to you, but honestly it would be

unfair, would take some of the cream off for Maud if I got engaged now."

His hold on my hand tightened as he said, "I'd like a good deal more than being engaged."

I pulled my hand away and stood up.

"Alfred Sampson, what are you suggesting?"

"Not what you think, though it's a nice idea, a lovely idea."

"Fresh!" I said, and felt myself blush at the childish word.

"Dear Nell, you are such a baby. Don't you know you needn't be afraid of me?" He put his arm around me. "Don't tremble, I can wait, but not forever. I don't want to be engaged to you, I want to be married to you." He pulled me close to him and I ducked my head in order to avoid the kiss that was coming.

"No, please no," I said in a voice that must have been muffled, but he heard me. He relaxed his embrace and held me at arm's length.

"No to everything?" he asked. "No, even to a kiss? Isn't that a little extreme?"

Once again I wearily explained that we must wait until after Maud's wedding and kissing and all that would make it harder for us.

"Kissing and all that is very nice, you know," Alfred said and lifted me off my feet and kissed me briefly but deeply.

He dropped me gently into a cushioned armchair. "Such a dear little girl you look in that big chair, but little girls have to learn to grow up. I'm not going to wait for this one much longer."

"Till after Maud's wedding?" My mouth felt dry and my voice sounded hoarse. I cleared my throat and said I must be getting a little cold.

Alfred laughed and cupped my chin in his right hand. "You are a baby, at that, aren't you? All right. Until after Maud's wedding, but once she's married I'm through waiting. It'll have to be yes or no. It'll be yes, won't it?"

"I think so. Truly I think so. It's just that I'm not sure."

With his left forefinger he slowly traced the outline of my lips. "You'll be sure. I'll see to that."

Mrs. Martin did not make Maud unhappy, but she troubled and distressed her. Maud wanted a small wedding in the little church to which she had gone as a freshman at Barnard and to which she had later returned and she wanted to be married by its pastor who had received her into the Catholic Church.

When Mrs. Martin motored down from Smithtown to spend the night with us and discuss the wedding arrangements she was not pleased.

"Our Lady of what?" she asked. "I never heard of it."

"It's not far from our house," Maud said, "and it's the first Catholic church I was ever in. The old pastor was kind to me when I went back. He could see I was nervous and he made everything easy for me and sent me for my instruction to the nuns in Twenty-ninth Street."

"Ah, yes, the Convent of Marie Réparatrice behind St. Leo's." Mrs. Martin's face brightened. "St. Leo's would do very nicely. Several families we know go there. We ourselves have always gone to the French church on Twenty-third Street and I think Louis would rather like . . . Still, if you prefer St. Leo's . . ."

"I don't want to be married in St. Leo's. I want . . ."

Mrs. Martin seemed not to hear. "Then of course," she said, "there's the Cathedral. There's no lovelier place for a small wedding than the Lady Chapel, and we could have dear Monseigneur Lavelle. I think, really, the Cathedral is the solution. And James, I believe, would prefer it. Protestants take St. Patrick's more or less for granted. Civic and business funerals and weddings have accustomed them." She looked inquiringly at Aunt Lucy. "Don't you think, Lucy, that James . . . ?"

"James will want whatever Maud and Louis want. Louis is coming to us for the weekend. Perhaps, Germaine, you and Harry would come too."

"Oh, my dear, we'd adore it, but this weekend is not possible. However, Louis can stop off and see us on his way to you."

"I want Louis to be pleased," Maud said. "I thought he was. He said he liked my little church when I took him there."

"My dear, naturally he would say so." Mrs. Martin smiled. She had a friendly smile and her voice with its faint echo of her parents' French accent, was low and agreeable, but she was a determined woman, and I did not think that Louis, any more than Maud, would be able to avoid doing exactly as she wanted.

"My dear child," Mrs. Martin continued, "obviously you and Louis want to please each other. My Louis is generous as I'm sure you are. Still I do think perhaps it would be fair for him to be married in the French church or the Cathedral, both of which he has known all his life. Your little church can't mean quite so much to you. You've known it only a short while, would it be very hard to give it up for Louis?"

"No, of course not. It was just that he didn't seem to mind."

On the Thursday before Louis' arrival Maud met Julia in New York where they were to look at sketches and models for the wedding dress. When they reached Southampton on Friday evening Julia was cross and Maud was discouraged.

"I keep telling her," Julia said at dinner, "that in the first place the heat made trying on or even looking a perfect misery and and in the second place she has to use a little imagination."

"No amount of imagination would make me look all right in those lace and tulle and looped satin creations."

"I thought the velvet one at Thurn was lovely and with your height you can carry it."

"You mean the Mary Queen of Scots one? I'd look a pretentious fool in it! I'd look a fool in every last one of them. Why can't I get married in a dressy suit? People do, especially in wartime."

"It's nice to have a wedding gown," Aunt Lucy said.

And, Julia added, it was eccentric not to have one and the last thing this family needed was more eccentricity.

Pa pushed back his chair from the table. "Now don't you two start snapping at each other. You're both tired is the trouble. You settle this, Lucy, dresses are your department. I'm going to get a breath of air."

"Your father's right," Aunt Lucy said. "You're worn out. You can go in town again when it's cooler, Maud, and look around a little more."

"We've been everywhere," Julia said, "Bendel, Thurn, Bergdorf Goodman. They all have pretty things, Aunt Lucy, and if Maud will just settle on a dress, once it's fitted and perhaps modified to suit her, I know it'll be becoming."

"Not one of them is right for me." Maud was near tears. "They're designed for young girls. I'm twenty-five. Those dresses make me look like the Countess Gruffanuff. I want to wear a suit, and if Louis doesn't mind I will. I'm going to ask him."

On the following evening, Maud asked Louis.

"Darling Maud," he said, "every man in the world would like a small, informal wedding with no fuss, no big hurrah. Still, as your aunt points out, a wedding dress is nice and I'd like to see you in yours."

"But, Louis, I'll look silly."

"It's possible for any woman to look silly in the wrong dress but I think we can find the right one."

Louis then explained that he had consulted a fellow officer.

"Chap I knew at the Beaux-Arts, did theatrical costume designing before the war. When I described Maud to him he told me to take her to Herman Tappé. He says Anna, the top model there, is very much Maud's type. Tall, fair-skinned, blond."

Louis did not have to be back in Washington until Tuesday, and he proposed that he and Maud take the early train to New York on Monday and see what Tappé had to suggest.

Aunt Lucy nodded approval but Julia frowned. Never, she said, had she heard of a girl shopping for her wedding dress with her fiancé.

Louis smiled. His smile was like his mother's, and I began to think that he had also inherited her determination.

"I'm a painter, Julia, and we're an unconventional lot. You'll have to get used to it. Now, another thing. Maman spoke to me about the church and that's all settled."

"Does it have to be St. Patrick's?" Maud asked. "I'd rather something smaller. Your mother mentioned a French church you go to. That would be easier for me, but of course if you . . ."

"Stop worrying, Maud, it's settled. I explained my feelings to my mother and we are to be married in your church."

"You don't mind, Louis?"

"On the contrary. I'm delighted. The church reminds me of small southern European ones, no touch of worldliness about it. Nor about its pastor; he and his church are exactly right for us."

Maud was elated when she returned from her visit to Tappé.

Mr. Tappé had studied her for a long time and had sketched on a pad from time to time.

This had not embarrassed her, Maud said, looking back in astonishment.

"And he didn't bother me when he talked about how I should look and walk. He got me so interested in the dress that I forgot

about myself. And since everything he suggested seemed wise I
didn't mind how preciously he put it."

At the end of an hour or so Mr. Tappé had disappeared into
another part of the shop from which he returned with some soft
white and silver material which he draped first on Anna, who
was used to standing patiently, and then on Maud.

The design, Maud told us, was not yet complete in final detail. She could say only that it would be sort of Greek with long
flowing sleeves. Mr. Tappé did not wish her to wear gloves,
white kid gloves, he said, were so dancing-schooly. And she was
to wear ballet slippers. He had made her walk for him in her
stocking feet.

"He said he could tell I had walked barefooted on sandy
beaches and this was the timeless feminine walk that would be
appropriate to the dress he had in mind. It was not a dress for
a mannequin mincing on high heels."

"Good Lord," Julia said, "flat shoes, no gloves. I never heard of
such a thing. What about your veil, or is he going to eliminate
that too?"

"Indeed he's not, but no tulle, thank you, he said, or that
custard-colored abomination, ancestral lace."

The veil was to be of the finest white mousseline de soie. It
would fall softly and naturally over Maud's shoulders and would
be held in place by a wreath of silver leaves.

Maud grinned like a ten-year-old as she reported that Mr.
Tappé had said her hair was a rare shade that was pale enough
to stand silver.

"And I needn't have bridesmaids. He says they're too girly-
girly for words and as *vieux jeu* as the Vassar daisy chain."

Julia insisted that a bride must have at least one attendant to
hold her bouquet during the ceremony.

Maud shook her head. Mr. Tappé had said there was no need

for a bouquet. Wasn't this a Catholic wedding? Then a rosary was the perfect answer. It was simple, it was classic, it was far more becoming than flowers to a woman's hands and during the ceremony it could slip back on her wrist as easily as a bracelet. Surely someone in the family had a pearl and diamond rosary.

Maud had looked anxiously at Louis. The only beads she possessed were black and silver ones Bridie had given her.

Louis assured her that there was no lack of jeweled rosaries in the Guarrigue family connection and he was certain a pearl and diamond one could be found.

Though Maud need not have a bridesmaid, she must have a witness to sign the register, and if Father didn't mind she would like to have Agnes Ryan.

"Mind? Oh, I see. That's thoughtful of you, Maud, but no, I don't mind. As I told you long ago, water over the dam is over the dam and done with." Father smiled and there was no edge to his voice as he added, "But you're certainly a full-fledged R.C. even to proselytizing."

"I suppose it seems like that, Pa, but Irish Catholics almost never get away from the faith even if they lose it. Agnes is engaged to a boy who went to Holy Cross. He's in France with the Sixty-ninth. I don't know how good a Catholic he is, but he's a Catholic and he won't get over it. Neither will Agnes. She'll fight the Church and rail against it to me, but she'd defend it to her last breath against a non-Catholic. I'm sure she'd be happier if she believed again and our Lady's little church might be a doorway for her. Anyway, I love Agnes and I'd like to have her with me on my wedding day."

"Well then!" Pa said, "that's the main thing isn't it? Have her, by all means."

We quickly discovered that Agnes was not related to the Ryan family we knew. Julia asked hopefully, and Maud told us that Agnes' parents lived in Newark and were no connection.

I was disappointed. Old Mr. Thomas Fortune Ryan's sons and their children were an elegant and fashionable clan. They had a family likeness as strong and as patrician and as distinctive as that of the Hapsburgs. Agnes wouldn't have the brilliant, curiously set eyes or the unmistakable Ryan nose. She wouldn't have the Ryan charm or the Ryan voice.

I had never seen Agnes, but I was pretty sure I knew the type: the snub nose always a little pink as if from a perpetual cold in the head, the pale bulging eyes and the almost colorless lashes, the voice that had lost the famous Irish laughter but had retained the underlying mournful cadence.

Agnes had substituted intellectualism for piety, and I was certain there would be no mischief to her, no sparkle as there must have been to Bridie Smith in her youth. Even now, on her day off, Bridie had a snap and a dash to her. She knew how to choose a hat (something that Mademoiselle had never learned), and she wore it with an air. Poor little Agnes would, I feared, be dowdy. There lingered in my mind Pa's college girl whom Charles Dana Gibson would not care to sketch, but Mr. Gibson had sketched bright-eyed Irish girls such as Bridie must have been. Agnes' eyes would be dull from poring over too many heavy volumes. She would be solemn and not quite sure of herself and I was afraid she would not have a very good time at our house at the reception which was to follow the church ceremony. It was to be a comparatively small reception for relatives and intimate friends and this would make it all the more uncomfortable for an outsider.

Just thinking about Agnes Ryan without ever having met her, I began to share Maud's sad and fond anxiety for her. My anxiety had a different basis and, realizing this, I realized I had the cure for it. I decided to ask Alfred to look out for Agnes. He could make a girl feel at her ease anywhere.

I thought I knew the type, but at the church on Maud's wedding day I learned for the first time something that I have since had to learn over and over. There is never a type, there is always only the person.

When we arrived Agnes was waiting for us in the vestibule. As Maud's witness she was to sit with the family.

She was like nothing I had preclassified and imagined.

She was taller and slimmer and younger than I expected. Her small head was poised proud and high above the dark fur that encircled her white throat. Her black hair was brushed sleek as satin in two wings beneath the brim of her hat. Black as ebony. White as snow. I had never thought to see this color combination in real life.

Julia took one look at the cunningly slanted brim of the hat and at the long, slim-waisted cut of the sable-trimmed, powder blue duvetine suit.

"Reboux," she whispered to me as we entered the church, "or I'll eat my own hat, and the suit is unmistakably Paquin. Fancy this vision of chic coming out of Newark! And the church is quite pretty, too, in a gaudy, baroque way."

Except for Notre-Dame in Paris, I had never been inside a Catholic church and I had assumed that Maud's would be Gothic to however cramped and dingy a degree. Out of curiosity, I had walked past it, but I had not been able to tell much from the exterior. Placed between low houses and perched on a steep flight of steps, it appeared narrow from the street.

The interior was surprisingly wide and welcoming. There were no heavy columns, no dark pointed arches. Frescoed walls surrounded the altar in a high, deep, semicircle. The stable at Bethlehem was portrayed on one side and on the other the carpenter

shop at Nazareth. Clouds of painted angels rose toward the roof
and hovered over our heads. The colors were clear but not garish,
mostly sepia and gold with touches of cream and blue and old
rose. I was reminded of painted Italian boxes I had admired on
the rue de Rivoli.

A big, blazingly bright Venetian glass chandelier hung from
the ceiling and the altar was massed with candles. Irregular
clusters of shorter and thinner candles flickered before the shrines
along the walls of the nave. There may have been other, more
practical sources of light that I didn't observe. I was aware of a
general golden glow and I was happy that Maud had chanced
upon and then stubbornly clung to this particular church which
was a warm and becoming setting for a bride.

It was Herman Patrick Tappé who had wrought the miracle
of the day.

I (and everyone, I think, I hope) felt a shock of pleasure and
astonishment when Maud walked up the aisle with Father.

Mr. Tappé had not made her pretty, he had made prettiness
not matter.

The silvery, pleated column of Maud's dress moved with her
as if it were part of her body. (Years later Maud confided to me
that Mr. Tappé had forbidden her to wear a corset but this she
had kept secret from everyone except Bridie, who had helped her
to dress.) She walked slowly and freely, but naturally. Nothing
about her seemed artificial, nor was it, she told me in the same
burst of confidence.

Mr. Tappé had rehearsed her and rehearsed her in what she
naturally did when she was not in a crowd of people or thinking
about herself. He had even left his shop though September was
a busy season and was waiting for her at the back of the church
when she arrived with Pa. He draped her veil over her shoulders
and said, "Remember what I've told you, dear. Walk as you do

on the beach but slowly and with your head well up as if a strong wind was holding you back."

When she was on public display, Maud's hands seemed to get in her way. They never looked right, and before the wedding I had silently regretted that she was to have no bouquet with which to hide them, but on the day, the long sleeves fell back gracefully as Maud placed her left hand lightly on Father's arm and in her right hand held Tante Nini's pearl and diamond rosary.

The Russian hairdresser whom Mr. Tappé had engaged and instructed did something remarkably clever with Maud's unmanageable hair. He braided and twisted the greater part of it on the nape of her neck in a coil that gleamed through the folds of her veil. He piled the rest on the crown of her head. It was not stiffly confined by the wreath but fell softly from beneath it in smooth ringlets that seemed to be as short and as springy as the curls that tumble over a child's forehead. Mr. Tappé had been right to use silver for the wreath. Against it Maud's hair was pale as gilt and the effect was lovely.

Later, at the reception, Maud's curls straggled into long, straight wisps over her eyes, the smooth coil on the back of her neck began to come apart, and the wreath kept slipping to one side. Before she danced with Louis she removed veil and wreath and pulled her hair back and pinned it all in its accustomed untidy bun.

It seemed as though what we had seen in the church had been an illusion, a mirage produced by the light from the candles and from the garlands and sprays of Venetian glass flowers. In the plain, everyday light of our house, Maud was her plain, everyday self again. However, mirage or not, illusion or not, for her half-hour in the church, Maud was The Bride, the traditional, timeless figure of romance that every girl would like to be on her wedding day.

Alfred and I walked from the church to Maud's reception.

He slowed our pace until we were out of earshot of the rest of the younger people who had chosen to go on foot, not in the procession of automobiles.

"I shall have more fun than I anticipated," he said, "you can't possibly any longer think that that ravishing Irish witch needs anyone to look out for her."

"She's pretty, but she might be shy with strangers."

"Not she. She's another of the movers and doers and I will bet you that fashionable strangers are her meat. So, my love, you and I are going to enjoy this day, our day at last."

It was Maud's day I pointed out and we were not going to make ourselves conspicuous and take any of the limelight away from her.

"So it will be tomorrow. Wait, stand still a minute. I want to talk to you. Not about us. I'll leave that to tomorrow and the day after, all the days after. Tell me, what's wrong with Esther? She looks like a marble statue of herself."

I hesitated not knowing what to say.

Julia and I had been in the library at teatime on the day before. We had not yet looked at the *Sun*, but when Esther came in she picked it up.

Julia asked if there was any news. Esther didn't answer. She stood still and dropped the newspaper on the desk and stared down at it while with her left hand she held on to the heavy desk chair as if to steady herself.

Julia and I looked over her shoulder, and there was Augie's picture.

There on that afternoon at tea, as this morning after breakfast, was Augie's picture, but this was a young Augie, an Augie in uniform. The accompanying article was not the final obituary. That has come fifty years too late. Is it wicked to think like this? I don't know. I only know that hateful wishing, like vain regret, is useless. Besides, Esther would not have wanted me now or then or ever to wish or even imagine harm to Augie.

On the eve of Maud's wedding, the *Sun* in a dispatch from France announced that August von L. Wenger was reported missing. Esther must have known, I thought, that the missing were rarely found alive. She knew that Bunny had been reported missing for weeks before the fact of his death was established.

Julia broke the silence. "Well! That's a face from the past, isn't it? I hope from the past."

I angrily told her to shut up and then realized that it didn't matter what either of us said. Esther wasn't listening. She stood still and silent, her head bent over the newspaper.

Julia loosened Esther's grasp and forced her down into the chair and told me to fetch some of Pa's rum from the tea tray.

"Look at me, Esther, listen to me," Julia said. "You can't go to pieces, Maud's wedding is tomorrow."

She would not go to pieces, Esther said slowly. She sounded like someone just learning to talk and she stared at us like the blind man in the Gospel who saw people as trees walking.

Julia took the cupful of rum from me and held it to Esther's lips and watched her take several sips and then removed the cup, saying that would do for now and Esther must sit still and try to relax.

Esther started to reach for the newspaper and then let her hand fall heavily to her lap. "I don't understand how it happened so soon." She spoke in the same flat, dragging monotone. "I don't understand, I don't believe, I don't . . ."

Julia attempted to turn the eerie monologue into a normal conversation.

"I heard that Augie was in the Air Corps, but I didn't know he was over there." She raised her voice. "When was he shipped over, Esther? In the summer?"

Esther shook her head slowly and painfully. "It was before that but suddenly the time is short. Suddenly all the time in the world is gone."

While Esther was speaking, Bridie ran into the room, just as she had run to us long ago when we hurt ourselves.

"Is Esther . . . ?" she cried, "Ah, here you are, my darling. Now you come with Bridie."

Esther allowed Bridie to lead her away. At the door she paused and looked blindly over her shoulder at us. "It was the last Sunday in February," she said. "It was the last day and now there are no days left."

I remember that late afternoon and all that was said and the blue flame under the kettle and the skin stretched tight on Esther's knuckles as she held on to Father's chair. I remember it now because I later had occasion to think about it, but on the way to Maud's reception I did not go over the scene in my mind. I was conscious only of the old fear and shame of scandal and the need to protect Esther.

Roberta is always telling me that I have a transparent face and should never attempt deception and I probably neither looked nor sounded natural as I told Alfred that Esther had had sad news of a friend but it would be better not to mention it to her or anyone.

"Oh." Alfred's eyes met mine in comprehension. "What an ass I am! I never thought of Esther when I read that Augie Wenger was missing. I'd forgotten that old story."

I felt my skin pricking hotly as it had done in the park and at school. "Stop it, don't talk about it."

"Of course not. Shock isn't good to talk about or to see. Worst place to see it is in a mirror, but there you can't do anything about it. I can do something about Esther. Come on, Nell, hurry. We've got to help her through this day."

I had trouble keeping up with his long strides and when we reached our house I paused to catch my breath.

Alfred grinned at me. "Nothing to it," he said, "I'd rather face a saber-toothed tiger than some of the members of the closed inner circle into which you were born, but we'll handle them. I'm sure your father and your aunt are standing by with guns at the ready."

Alfred and Pa and Aunt Lucy steadily and unobtrusively stood guard over Esther until the last guest departed. A few of the guests joined the quietly protective conspiracy. I was glad to note that the Sheldons and Bertie's parents as well as Cousin Maud Bronson were among them. They raised their glasses of champagne toward Esther so that she appeared to be the center of a merry congratulatory group, they covered her silences with light chatter, they made her seem her usual self to a casual on-looker and they stood between her and the persistently curious.

It was a bad day for Esther, no matter what anyone tried to do for her, but at least she was spared the indignity of amused and malicious pity.

On the morning after Maud's wedding Alfred came to our house. Morning hours, he said, were good ones in which to decide a lifetime.

I looked around the parlor, a room I had known since I could remember. With Alfred I would have a different life. I would spend it in different rooms. Well, I told myself crossly, I'd always expected to spend it somewhere else with some stranger. Why was I undecided and apprehensive? I looked inquiringly at Mother in the sunlight of her portrait and wondered what answer I thought she could give me.

Alfred took my hand and drew me close to him.

"I want to know, Nell," he said, "I've waited long enough. I want to know now, today. Are you going to marry me?"

I freed my hand from his and stepped back. "Please, Alfred, don't. It mixes me up when you touch me."

Was I still afraid, he asked. Still unsure?

"O promise me, Nell, as the old song has it. But, of course, you're too young to remember 'O Promise Me.' Nell, Nell, are you still too young for everything?"

I did remember the song, snatches of it. I looked at Mother again. She had sung it. It ran uncertainly in my head. "O promise me that some day you and I will take . . ." I didn't want to be anybody's. Not yet, not even some day, not for good, not for a lifetime.

"Aren't you sure yet, Nell? I could teach you to be if you'd let me."

"I have to think." My lips were dry and I licked them.

"Don't be nervous, love. I suppose all girls are over taking the big step, but don't be."

"Wait, Alfred." I drew further away, fending him off with my hands. "I guess I am nervous." And I was, but not for me, for him.

Julia and other girls had been triumphant over the number of proposals they had received and they were lighthearted as they counted their rejected suitors on their fingers. I hated the thought of saying no to Alfred, but I couldn't say anything else. I liked him and I was attracted to him, but not enough, not enough to say yes to a lifetime.

Miserable, not looking at him, I shook my head. Never again, I silently vowed, would I let a man propose to me before I was sure of myself.

"I can't, Alfred, I'm not sure."

"If you aren't sure by now, you never will be. If all you can do is stand there not letting me near you, digging in your heels, I may as well give up."

"I'm sorry." And I was sorry and embarrassed and I didn't understand myself. I'd go a long way before I'd find anyone as attractive, anyone who charmed me and made me feel important and desirable as Alfred did.

"Don't be sorry, Nell. These one-sided things happen, as I ought to know. Finally the biter bit, which is fair enough. Don't be sorry or sad for me. I'll find other girls or they'll find me. But I want this one pretty badly. So? This is the last call, my love."

There was silence. He didn't move. He was waiting. I could still say the word. It was no use. I couldn't say it. I couldn't even look up and face him.

After what must have been a short interval, though it seemed long and painful to me, he spoke.

"You are sure after all, aren't you? You're sure it's not me you want to grow up with. I guess I always knew it in my prematurely aged bones. So long, Nell, and good luck to you when you do grow up. I think I'll drop by San Francisco and visit brother Lucius for a while. I can talk the dear old War Department into finding me a spot of work out there."

"Good-by, Alfred," I managed to say in a low voice, but he was gone.

I felt flat and dismal. I liked Alfred and I would miss him. Even more, I admitted to myself, I would miss his patent devotedness of which I had been proud and other girls envious. It had been fun to have Alfred Sampson as my heavy beau but this wasn't good enough for him and anything more wasn't . . . wasn't right for me. I couldn't explain it any more clearly to myself than that.

I decided I would tell Aunt Lucy. She would make me feel

better. She always did. True, she had said to me, just before I came out, "Don't be one of those girls who collect proposals like scalps. If you don't intend to marry a man, keep him from asking you. It can usually be done if you want to, but if you can't manage to keep him from speaking, remember he has offered you the best he has. Respect that, don't make a boast or a confidence of it to friends."

Telling Aunt Lucy wouldn't count. A confidence was as safe with her as at the bottom of the sea. Safer than if I kept it to myself. Sooner or later Julia and others would notice Alfred's disappearance from my life and would commiserate with me. It would be easier, then, to hold my tongue if I had told Aunt Lucy. She, at least, would know I hadn't been jilted.

The last of 1918 was a strange time and a frightening one.

The war was going well. Any day, any day now, the military experts predicted, it would end in victory.

In our minds, in my recollection, it ended twice, on two separate days. The first premature report on the seventh of November lifted our hearts with hope and relief. For a few hours we rejoiced. Now it was finished. Now over there they were safe and the guns were silenced. The false armistice has forever blurred the true one in my recollection.

Over here we were not safe. I wondered if Alfred, in California, was, not glad, but in some way grimly satisfied that in the final months of the war, fear and sudden death had come to the home front which had thought itself comfortably remote from danger. No, of course not, he couldn't be. No one could feel anything but unmixed sadness at the death of the young. And it was in the main the young who died of the Spanish influenza: the boys in the camps (they said that at Upton alone there were more deaths in one day than on the western front) and in cities younger boys and girls and young parents. And children. I remember the white hearses, I remember the names of Spence girls younger than I. They had been little girls when I was at school. And Betty Conway. She had minded so much being safer than Bunny and after all she wasn't. She caught the influenza and died of it ten days after Maud's wedding.

It was strange to be alive in that autumn in a city, three thousand safe miles from the war, that was swept by a death against which the Atlantic had been no defense. It was queer to be so piercingly aware of the reality of death, of its imminent possibility for anyone.

Even children knew. A family with four little boys had just lately moved into a house next door to ours. I can still hear the oldest boy (he must have been about ten), calling out to a small companion at his front door, "Been measured for your wooden overcoat yet?"

Two weeks later the boy and one of his brothers and his mother were dead. I don't know his name but I can still hear the shrill bravado in his voice as he tried to arm himself with a joke against the first shocking awareness of his own mortality.

It was in December when the epidemic had almost run its course that it reached our house.

It must have been a Saturday because Father was home for lunch.

I had taken Fluffy for a walk and when I came in I felt rather queer and sickish. It must be the heat of the house after the cold outside, I thought, the house is terribly hot, Bridie never lets it get as hot as this . . .

I started into the dining room with the others, Pa and I suppose Esther and Mademoiselle, but Pa's presence is all I remember.

I felt very queer indeed and the room and the light began to waver and slip away from me. I heard a voice a long way off, my own voice, "Pa, I'm sick. I'm very sick, Pa. I'm frightened."

Then in the sliding, darkening room I felt Pa holding me and I heard him say, "You're all right, Nell. I've got you safe, dear. I've got you. I'll keep you safe."

Pa's voice was the last thing I heard before I slid into complete and silent blackness.

That illness was a long time ago and I don't remember any of it clearly any more. The acute part of it I have entirely forgotten. Not entirely . . . at the edge of my mind, almost within my reach is the memory of a memory. As I slid into the dark I was not frightened because I could hear Pa's voice as long as I could hear anything at all.

9

It was Esther who told me about Father, but I knew before she said a word.

Esther and Bridie had nursed me and their nursing had saved me. At least it was said that it was good nursing that—sometimes, not always—brought anyone through the Spanish influenza. Nursing and luck. I was one of the lucky ones. It was a little like being safe home from the war, but only a little, only remotely like it. I had shared the general fear of the epidemic to which we somehow grew accustomed, but when the influenza struck me, Pa had been there and his voice had gone down into it with me. At the moment of terror, which may be something like the moment before battle, because of his presence I had not been afraid. There were fever nightmares, I suppose, but I don't remember them because it was not the I I know, the conscious I who endured them. All I now remember, all I probably remembered in the first lucid days was that I had been very sick and Esther and Bridie, though not plainly seen or heard, had been with me. At last I was out of the misery and confusion and was myself again and Esther and Bridie came and went in the usual three-dimensional and undistorted way.

I remember clearly a day—the second? the third?—one of the first of the convalescent days, in which Esther told me about Father. It was a January day and the morning was a remarkably bright one for winter or possibly my eyes were not yet accustomed to unshaded light.

I knew—not wanting to know—what she was trying to tell me.

Perhaps through the noise of delirium I had heard something, but I think not. Esther once said that a trained nurse at the Babies' Hospital had warned her that one must assume that any patient, child or adult, in high fever or unconscious, might be able to hear, to understand. Esther would have been careful and so would Bridie. Bridie was instinctively wise with a child, sick or well, and none of us ever entirely grew up in her eyes.

Esther had thrown something light-colored, a scarf or a sweater, over her black dress but the crape-trimmed dress may have betrayed the truth. In those days we wore mourning that was too deep to be easily disguised. More likely it was the fact that Pa had not come near me, was not now in my room.

I think Esther started to tell me in the manner that was called gentle then. We were taught to break bad news gradually, though in my opinion this method must have broken the listener's courage bit by bit.

I didn't want Esther to tell me. I didn't want to be sure.

"Tell me quickly, Esther. I know, so tell me quickly." This is what Esther later said I had said.

She told me that Father had come down with the influenza a few hours after me and that he was dead.

He died and was buried while I was ill and recovered. It was a strange sensation to hear this as an irrevocable, flat truth. I remember the strangeness better than I remember the sorrow. We knew, naturally we knew and accepted but did not yet imagine that some day our elders would die, as would we in our turn. Some day, not now. I was still young enough for now to be as lasting as forever. I remember the strangeness and emptiness of now being broken off short. At some point the emptiness was filled with sorrow and I cried.

It was the first sorrow, the first death. Lucy Gore's death had been sad and shocking, but it was not part of a sequence. It was something apart, like an accident that need not inevitably be repeated. And the fact of Mother's death was for me always in the past, always part of my recollection of her.

I did not on that January morning think: this is the first of our deaths. Only in looking back do I think this. At the time Father's death was an ending but I did not realize it was the beginning of our own.

Looking back I can be grateful that it was quickly and, they told me, easily over for him, and I think too that he would not have liked old age, would have been impatient and angry with it.

Pa was sixty-six when he died, but he did not seem old, did not I'm sure feel old. Perhaps one never does though this the young refuse to believe and they may be right. In many ways I am aware of the half-century that separates me from the Nell who lay in her bed crying for her father, but as Baby Elliot would tell me, old is what we are and we may as well enjoy what's good about it. I do or at least I've grown used to it. Pa might not have grown used to it and he was alone. Oh, he had all of us, but in the latter years, more than in any, one needs someone of one's own time, one's own generation. Pa had friends, but a friend is not quite enough.

On that January day I didn't think about Pa growing old or dying a harder death. In the midst of sorrow one neither finds nor wants to find consolation and the comforters who point out alleviating or merciful or even fortunate aspects of your sorrow, your loss, are worse than the ones with whom Job was afflicted.

Only now can I look back and think maybe this was the right time for my father to die. I don't think this (maybe is the operative word) I just wonder and hope. You can never think it is the right time for someone you love, he always should have died hereafter.

When then was now I didn't think or wonder or hope. I cried because Pa was dead and because I hadn't known, hadn't grieved for him, right away. Esther sat beside my bed and didn't try to talk. She knew more about sorrow than I did, and she must have realized that the only person who could have given me strength and comfort was Pa himself.

My convalescence was slow and it was some time before I felt able to go downstairs. There were family conferences; lawyers and trust officers came and went and I signed the papers that were brought to my room, but I didn't want to be part of the discussions nor did I think that the opinion of an "infant over fourteen" would carry much weight. I didn't yet want to be part of our family life with Pa not there. The dining-room table without him at its head was an outward and visible sign which I was reluctant to see and I was grateful to be allowed a tray in my room or in the old day nursery.

James had come from Paris, and he and Julia were staying with us. They were my guardians and the executors of the will. Julia explained that the bulk of Father's fortune was left in various trusts for us and our children and grandchildren. The trust department of Father's firm was in charge of all that but, she said, there were also our houses and family possessions and cash balances and insurance and readily negotiable securities. The disposal of these was left to the judgment of the executors and guardians.

"It seems funny to me for you and James to be my guardians," I said, "doesn't it to you?"

"Well, you see, I was the only one married when Father drew

up this will. If he'd had time he might have appointed Maud and Louis, too."

"And not Esther? She's the eldest."

"Oh, Nell, you know Pa! There's a good deal of money involved in the houses and everything. He would always think financial matters were safer with a man and naturally he realized that James, like all the Hendersons, has a sound business head."

I wished Pa had chosen Aunt Lucy for my guardian, since I had to have one, but he couldn't have thought it sensible. Pa was always sensible where law and finance were concerned. And he was kind. He would have considered it unkind to ask Aunt Lucy to change her way of life at this late date. With Julia and James as guardians, things would go on more or less as they had in the past. We were Pa's dear girls and he trusted us. He didn't trust our business heads but he trusted our hearts. We were his dear and loving girls who loved one another and we would with Aunt Lucy's help and guidance keep the family together until my marriage whenever that might be and until Esther's. Pa never lost hope of the latter. A fine future day for Esther was a reality to him.

I was obviously strong enough to attend the final family conference. It would be just family, Julia said, and I ought to be there. I was too young and inexperienced to understand all James's decisions but I ought to hear them and take part in any discussion.

"You don't need me," I said, "you and James and Aunt Lucy can decide everything. And Esther and Maud and Louis, of course."

"Louis can't get away from Washington. He won't be mustered out until the end of the month, but Maud will be here."

"And Aunt Lucy. She's the one who will really know how we

should arrange everything. She'll probably spend the summer with us in Southampton and—"

"No, Nell, we're not going to burden Aunt Lucy. It wouldn't be fair to her at her age and Father wouldn't want us to. It was to spare her any responsibility that he appointed James and me. James has, as he says, broad shoulders, and he is able and willing to carry the load Father has placed on them."

We gathered in the parlor for the final conference. James, with Julia beside him, sat on the sofa beneath Mother's portrait. Our group was a contrast to the sunlit painting. As I look back at us I am reminded of another much smaller painting which I can't place, a picture of black-clad ladies posed formally in a bright summer setting, a morning room I think. Had Louis been with us, he might eventually have made one painting of the two: our smiling, lightfooted mother in her yellow striped skirt and white shirtwaist and her daughters stiff and silent in our heavy black dresses in the room where the Victrola had played unceasingly when the girls were young, where they had danced on the parquet floor, where my friends and I had played hunt the thimble and a trick man had entertained us at a birthday party. It was a room filled with ghosts, I start to think, but the past did not seem in the least ghostlike as the memories crowded around me. We were the ghosts, ghosts from a future which should not yet have arrived. Mother—never imprisoned by the massive carved and gilded frame, always ready to leave it and join some cheerful company beyond our sight—seemed more alive than any of us.

We were for the most part solemn and attentive as James outlined his plans, though I didn't listen closely as he talked about securities and bank accounts and insurance. When he mentioned our houses I paid attention. He had decided, he said, to put both of them on the market.

"But where will we go?" I asked. I was frightened by a sense of the past dissolving around me, this room and Mother's where Aunt Lucy stayed when she came, the library and Father's desk and chair, my room on the fourth floor and the one in Southampton where I had slept and waked since I could remember, the round piazza and the sight of sky and sea, the houses Mother and Father had made for us gone in a minute, discarded like dolls' houses because James had decided. I glared at him.

"They're our houses," I said. "You have no right to sell them."

"There's no need to look like that, Nell," he said. "You're not an orphan of the storm and I have, not a right, but a responsibility both as executor and guardian. Julia, I may add, is in complete agreement with me, aren't you, dear?"

"Of course, James." But Julia didn't look at me.

"It's not possible, Nell," James continued, "for you to live here or in Southampton without your father. Among other reasons I cannot ask your aunt at her advanced age to assume the burden of running such large establishments."

"Esther and I and Mademoiselle and Bridie could easily manage. I know Mademoiselle has been planning to retire to Switzerland but she'd stay."

"That would hardly be fair to Mademoiselle," Julia said, "or to Bridie who is no longer young, but we'll get to Bridie presently. Let James finish about the houses."

"Finish them for us you mean."

It was not his purpose to finish the houses for us, James explained, but to turn them into assets for me and my sisters instead of the white elephants which from every point of view except a sentimental one they were bound to become for our family. I was not to worry, there was no hurry, this was not a fire sale. The house in Southampton would be let furnished for the summer, probably for several summers. Ocean-front property would continue to increase in value and it would be wise to hold it for some time. Our city property, he told us, was worth far more than perhaps we realized. Did we know that our father had bought and the estate owned not only this house but the two small houses between it and Fifth Avenue as well as the corner one and its neighbor, which gave us considerable frontage on the Avenue?

We didn't know. This was not the sort of thing Pa discussed with us.

"It's potentially an extremely valuable holding," James said, "and I am in consultation with real estate experts in your father's firm. We may decide to develop the property ourselves, but more likely we'll hold it for sale at the proper time and price. The rentals from the other houses will more than cover the carrying charges. In the next few months we'll close this house and divide the contents among the four of you. One thing you must get through your head, Nell, is that you cannot continue to live here without your father."

"Where will Esther and I live?"

"You're too pretty, my dear, to have to live with any of the family for very long." James gave me one of his boyish smiles, but I didn't smile back, and he continued, "Julia and I feel, and I'm certain Esther is woman of the world enough to agree, that you should divide your time here or abroad between the Martins and ourselves."

"But I don't understand. Why can't Esther and I—"

"Please take our word for it. I'd rather not be more explicit."

Esther spoke for the first time. "You may as well be as explicit with Nell, James, as you have been with me, and since Julia and Maud are in agreement with you . . ." She glanced at Maud who flushed and said, "Let's not talk about it."

"I think we must." Esther turned to me. "Our sisters and our brothers-in-law, this one anyway and he's in charge, do not think it would be proper for you, now that Father is gone, to live with a divorced woman."

"That's ridiculous," I said, "Pa kept us together and Aunt Lucy would. We can live with her. There are two guest rooms in her apartment."

"That won't do," Julia said. "I don't think even you, Esther, would try to put Aunt Lucy in such an impossible position."

"It's you and James who are making the position impossible."

"It's not of our making," Julia said, "as you very well know. You gave yourself away when Augie was reported missing and when you came to life again when we got the news that he had been found, hale and hearty, in a German prisoner of war camp. He's with our Army on the Rhine, I understand?"

Esther didn't answer and Julia continued, "Well, he'll be home eventually and then you'll probably pick up where you left off on the last Sunday of last February."

"That's not true." Esther turned away from Julia and looked at me. "What Julia is saying is not true."

"It's not what I'm saying, it's what you said: 'It was the last Sunday in February. It was the last day.'"

"Please, Julia, don't . . ."

Listening to them, I was back in the dark of the conservatory, listening to their voices in the hall.

"Oh, I know your story is that you were at the hospital on the Sunday Augie was shipped out, but I don't for one second believe you. And there were lots of other days when I'll bet you weren't at the hospital but meeting . . ."

"Julia, you shut up," I said and, to my fury, burst into strangling tears. Much help that was to Esther.

Esther drew her chair closer to mine. "I'll be all right, Nell.

Even without Pa I'll manage. I won't be a scandal, but since the Hendersons think I am and even the Martins . . ."

"No, we don't," Maud said in a low unhappy voice, "but as Mrs. Martin says, we can't be too careful about what she calls *les convenances* where a young girl is concerned. Can't you see, Esther? It was different when Pa was here."

"Very different," James said. "This whole subject is a painful one, but since Esther has opened it up, let us calmly consider the facts. Mr. Cameron was a powerful figure downtown and in society, and he was able to battle fairly successfully for his daughter. With his death the situation is altered. Your aunt will soon be approaching threescore years and ten and her age will take an ever increasing toll, so that in effect, Nell, Esther would in the eyes of the world be your chaperone, and this simply will not do."

Esther was pale but her voice was steady as she said to James, "Nell would be happier in New York than in Paris or Washington or wherever you and the Martins are. If I take a house or a flat of my own will you let her live with Aunt Lucy?"

"You know perfectly well that your aunt would not think of offering Nell a home and not you."

Esther shook her head. "You've seen fit, James, to picture Aunt Lucy as a frail old lady on the edge of senility or the grave, I'm not sure which, but you mustn't believe in this figment of your imagination. Aunt Lucy is getting old, though only in years, and in this situation she's powerless, but she's sensible and can face facts. She wants to have Nell and me, she told me so. When I tell her that unless I remove myself from the scene she can't even have Nell and that you'll start the winds of scandal blowing she'll agree to the arrangement I suggest. Not that she'll like it, but she'll agree."

"You probably would prefer a place of your own where you can—"

James interrupted Julia. "Now, my dear, I'm sure Esther will behave with discretion. Her position outside her father's house will be a little more difficult but I'm confident she can handle it with dignity and we must all be grateful for her suggestion. Certainly, Esther, if your aunt agrees to this arrangement Julia and I will give our consent."

"She will," Esther said. "She's a practical woman and she knows, though she would phrase it more elegantly, that you can't fight City Hall. I assume that this is the last decision with which I'm concerned, so if you'll excuse me, James?"

"We've still Bridie Smith's future to settle. Although she was handsomely remembered in the will, we ought—"

"Dear me, what have you in mind for her? Not that it matters, Bridie has a mind of her own and can take care of herself. I'll send her to you."

After a few minutes Bridie joined us, and James asked her to be seated. "This is a family conference," he said, "and you are very much a part of the Cameron family."

"Thank you, sir."

"Too much a part of the family for us to fail to be concerned for your future and we have a suggestion which we hope will be agreeable to you. We are closing this house and Southampton. Miss Nell will live with her aunt, and Mrs. Scott has decided to take a flat or house of her own. Mr. and Mrs. Martin are moving to Paris and they would like you to go with them."

"We'd love to have you," Maud said. "And you'd be happy in France, Bridie. It's a Catholic country, you'd like that."

"As for religion, I don't know that I'd like a place where all the Catholics are French. Their ways are not my ways. And as far as you're concerned, Maud, you'll be better off with French servants. It's lovely of you to want me, but since you don't really need me, I'd rather not go so far away."

Maud could not persuade Bridie to change her mind.

"I know what," I said, "you could come to Aunt Lucy."

"I know I could, Nell, but your aunt has three good steady girls. I found them for her myself and they're all the help she needs."

James cleared his throat. "It's not that we want you to keep on working, Bridie, it's that we want to find a home for you with the family. After your years of faithful service it's the least we can do. If you wish to retire, and this seems a sensible decision to me, you will be welcome at Henderson. We have a big establishment and there will always be a room for you."

"Thank you, sir. I know my young ladies would never see me want for anything, but there's no fear of that. I have my savings, and Mr. Cameron was more than generous in the will. Still, it's not in my mind to retire yet, I've quite a few working years left."

"But, Bridie, where will you work?" Maud asked. "You've said no to every plan we could think of."

"Don't fret, Maud, I've a plan of my own."

Bridie stood up and said to James, "It's my desire to go with Mrs. Scott—if she'll have me, and I believe she will—as housekeeper or lady's maid." She looked over James's head at the portrait. "I came to this house as lady's maid to Mrs. Cameron and I'll be happy to leave it with her eldest daughter. If you'll excuse me, sir, I'll go along and speak to Mrs. Scott."

Early in March, Esther found a house that pleased her, and she and Bridie would soon move into it. In Aunt Lucy's apartment the guest rooms were being got ready for me. One was to remain a bedroom and the other was to be turned into a small sitting room of my own.

Our house was waiting to be turned inside out and left empty. In my mind it was already empty and deserted, but to a visitor it would appear unchanged.

On a cold, windy day I came in from an early afternoon walk with Fluffy. She had disappeared into the kitchen, but I was in the front hall when the bell rang. I opened the door and for a minute or a second, for a small space of time which I can not now measure, I thought that a visitor, a stranger in uniform was standing on the threshold. Then he took off his visored cap and I recognized him. He was sturdier, broader, more solid than I remembered. I remembered a boy, a college boy too old for me but nevertheless a boy and Bertie wasn't a boy any longer, he was a man.

"You're back," I said, "finally you're back."

"And you're here and everything is the same."

He looked at me and then past me at the double doors of the dining room and at the red carpeted curve of the stairway. He tossed his cap on the hall table and slung his trench coat over one of the high-backed tapestried chairs.

"Everything is the same," he repeated. "Not quite everything. You're different."

"Not really."

"Of course not really, you're Nell. But you're Nell grown up. You're taller too, aren't you?"

"I don't know."

"I don't know either and that's a funny thing, for me not to know how tall you are."

He took a quick long stride towards me and put his hands on my shoulders and stood looking down at me. Then he bent his head and kissed me on the forehead.

"Now I know," he said and moved a little away and smiled at me. "Now I know how tall my Nellie has grown."

We stood looking at each other. He was still smiling but his thick, dark brows almost met in a questioning, searching frown, and I, smiling back at him, must have had a surprised expression on my face.

We had known each other for all the years we could recall. We weren't strangers, couldn't feel like strangers, and yet this was a first meeting, a first sight, a first time. This was a new time for us and we were astonished but, as we told each other later, not entirely astonished. In some hidden corner of mind and heart this encounter was not unexpected. As we stood there, as we looked gravely at one another, I knew, I was sure. This was what I had been waiting for.

Bertie took my hands gently in his and turned them over and looked at them as though he had never seen them sticky with sand and fish scales and tanned by the sun until they matched my leather sandals. Still holding my hands, he looked up slowly from them to my face. He looked at me as if he had never seen me before and I looked wonderingly at him, at the cowlick which, though better controlled than it used to be, had not entirely disappeared, at his deep-set hazel eyes. (Their color changes with the light from gray to amber to almost gold. Hazel, I suppose describes them and anyway Bertie says no man wants to be told he has golden eyes. "Mine," he says firmly, "are plain mud color, but hazel will do if you want to be fancy." Hazel will do, but gray to amber to gold is how I think of them.) In the dull afternoon light in the front hall his eyes were gray with just flecks of the amber I remembered. I pulled my eyes away from his and smiled so he would smile back. His smile still turned up a little more on the right side of his mouth than on the left. His shoulders were wider than I remembered and he held himself straight and tall. The gangling, slightly round-shouldered look was gone. This was Bertie whom I had always known and never known until today.

We didn't say anything, we just looked and held each other's hands.

The silence wasn't strained. Bertie and I had often been, are often, quiet together and there has never been a strain, never an embarrassment between us, not now, not in the years when I wasn't able to catch up with him, not in all our time together.

"Been a long while," he said.

I nodded, not wanting to interrupt this beginning, this meeting, this first sight, first kiss. I could still feel his kiss on my forehead. And I still can now, this minute. It's curious that so light a touch of his lips should be so deeply remembered. I suppose it's because it was the first.

Fluffy interrupted us. She returned from the kitchen and in spite of her rheumatism jumped joyfully, if awkwardly, on Bertie and then collected herself and sat up like a lady and held out her right front paw for him to take, which he did. He was the one who had taught her that trick in her first Southampton summer.

"Good old Fluff. She remembers me."

"She ought to, she's known you all her life. Just like me."

"All your life, Nell, and all mine that I remember clearly. Come on, let's go up to the day nursery where we can talk. We've got lots to catch up on. I'll see the others later. Who's here?"

"Just Esther and James and Julia."

"And not your father . . . that's so hard to realize. You don't want to talk about it yet and anyway you know how I feel. It just doesn't seem possible that he's gone. Oh, Nellie, I am sorry. And Ma says there are going to be all sorts of changes."

"Everything's changed."

As we climbed the stairs and passed the familiar rooms, I could see the dreary transformation of our house as if already it was dismantled with curtainless windows staring blankly, but probably they wouldn't stare for long, they would be boarded over. The red carpet and the oriental rug would be rolled up. The vans would come and tables and chairs and everything would look tired and worn as even well-cared-for furniture does when it is piled together and dispossessed.

"Oh, Bertie, everything's changed, everything's sort of awful. But you know what?" The unexpected cheerfulness of my voice took me by surprise. "You know what, Bertie," and as I spoke I realized that what I was saying was not so much an expression of love and trust as a plain statement of fact, "I don't mind so much now that you're back. Even things I mind will be all right now."

"What I'm here for. I'll do my best. Always, Nell. Long as I live I'll do my best to make everything all right for you, even things you mind. Bound to be a few of those along the way, but we'll get through them together."

We sat on the old cretonne-covered canework sofa in the day nursery and tried to fill in the years that had separated us. I told him how bad I felt that I wasn't home on the Sunday he was shipped out.

"I felt bad too, Nell."

"It was on account of Julia's party." And I told him how Maud and Louis had come together at the party Julia had arranged for them. "It was a lovely party, Bertie." Then I remembered the Sunday evening and felt my face grow hot and knew I was blushing.

"Were you the belle of the ball? Others besides Bridie have told me that you've been quite the belle. Plenty of beaux, I expect."

"Well . . ." I hesitated.

"You don't have to tell me about them."

"If I don't someone will. The only at all serious one was Alfred Sampson."

"Poor Alfred. He had a really bad time. I heard about it from friends of his in France. He got his machine back over the Allied lines but not one in a hundred would have walked away alive from that fiery crash. He didn't walk, dragged himself, poor fellow. He was weeks, months, I guess, in a hospital."

"He never said."

"He wouldn't. The ones who had it the worst don't. So he was your beau, was he? Well, I couldn't expect you not to have any."

"I wish now I hadn't but it was fun to have Alfred as an admirer. Partly because of Julia. You remember?"

"I remember."

"But without his having been her beau it would have been fun for me to have someone that attractive at my beck and call and other girls envying me. What was bad about it was having to refuse him in the end."

"So long as you did is all I care. I'm not going to pity Alfred Sampson where girls are concerned, he'll never lack for them."

"And now—and this makes me so mad, Julia makes me so mad!"

"Maybe you made her mad landing Alfred when she couldn't and then letting him go."

"That's what she doesn't know and I can't tell her, though I'd like to, but Aunt Lucy says that's a mean thing to do. Julia probably wouldn't believe me anyway and she keeps being sorry for me and Maud too and I suppose the Hendersons and Martins and Guarrigues are all saying, 'Poor Nell.'"

"What the dickens does it matter what people say? You know it wouldn't really have mattered except to your female vanity if Alfred had been the one to walk out."

"Of course it wouldn't, once you came, but I didn't know you ever would. There was I grown up and where were you? Never here."

"Well, I'm here now and I don't intend to leave. Ever."

And then he kissed me, kissed me on the mouth this time and it was nice and I wasn't scared or troubled. I just felt lightheaded and not in the least shy.

After a while we started talking again. My head was on his shoulder, as naturally as it might be now, when I suddenly blurted out, "I never could have married anyone but you, Bertie, I'd have been embarrassed."

"Don't let it worry you. You aren't going to marry anyone but me." He laughed in the old friendly way and kissed the tip of my nose. "Did I ever tell you that you have the prettiest nose I ever saw?"

"Oh dear, a nose is such a boring good feature, although Aunt Lucy says I'll be grateful for it when I'm old. As if it matters what you look like when you're old. Can you imagine us, Bertie?"

"No, I can't, but I expect we'll look okay to each other. We did when I had a mouthful of gold braces and when you bit your nails. And the Christmas vacation you cut a bang and by the time you gave up trying to get it even—"

"I had only about an inch of hair sticking over my forehead. Even normally I didn't look so great, nor you either. The way they dressed us! You in your droopy knickerbockers buckled below your knees and me in my Peter Thompson and our ribbed wool stockings and high shoes. We must have been sights."

We laughed and looked back and looked forward. We talked and were silent and talked again.

It was a dark day and when we had come upstairs the lamps were already lit on the fourth floor and the curtains drawn. We didn't realize that the afternoon had gone and the evening begun until Bridie came to tell us that tea was long over and dinner would be ready in twenty minutes.

I meant to keep Bertie's and my discovery of one another a secret between us for at least a little while but I was not successful. On that first evening at dinner Esther and Julia guessed, I suppose from the way Bertie and I looked at each other or didn't look at each other.

Bertie told me that when they sat together over cigars and brandy, James didn't say anything to indicate his awareness of the situation, but he opened a box of Pa's most expensive cigars and sent the waitress to ask Bridie for the Napoleon brandy. He made it clear that he was prepared to welcome Bertie not only home from France but into the family.

"And, of course, Ma and Pops guessed right away. It seems that everyone but us expected this."

"It's not very romantic to do the expected thing."

"Now, Nell, we don't need to be romantic in anybody's eyes but our own. It's nobody else's business."

"I guess you're right."

"You bet I'm right. And this makes it easier for us. You watch, they'll let us be married by June. They'd never do that if I was some young Lochinvar of a stranger, if our first meeting had in their view been a first meeting. It doesn't matter why they're pleased so long as they are. Ma and Pops are almost as fond of you as they are of Elsie, and your sisters like me even if Julia thinks me a bit unexciting compared to Alfred Sampson."

"No she doesn't. She thinks I'm lucky that it's you, not Alfred." (Even if I didn't yet realize it, Julia had told me, I was lucky; the Alfred Sampsons of this world were often responsible for girls marrying sensibly and well on the rebound. Anyway, she added, I had always been fond of Bertie.) "And I am lucky,

Bertie, and I want them all to know that finally, finally, I have my heart's desire that I was waiting for."

"I know. Isn't that enough?"

I nodded and he put his arm around me and held me for a moment.

"Now, my girl, let's talk sensibly and make plans. We'll aim for June so we can have the whole summer before I start at Columbia Law School."

Bertie was sensible about many things in that time which should have been a sad time. It was sad. Always, underneath the planning and looking forward it was sad not to have Father there. Sometimes, waking up and realizing all over again that he was dead, I thought I couldn't bear it, but because Bertie was there and shared the sadness I was able to bear it. Bertie minded about my father as I would some day mind about Ma and Pops. It's good to have in-laws who seem as much your family as your own. It must be hard in a marriage to have to be careful not to put a foot wrong with the other side. Bertie and I never had to be careful. We took each other's families as comfortably for granted as they took us.

Bertie had always called Pa, Mr. Cameron or sir, but I, like all the young in Southampton, called Bertie's parents Ma and Pops, though such informality toward our elders was unusual in our day.

Ma was a friendly, large-boned, clumsy woman with a booming voice. She was graceful only in the ocean and on the golf links. Her skin was weatherbeaten from years of summer mornings at the beach and afternoons at Shinnecock. Outwardly she was not what we thought of as a motherly type. She was not in the least like the soft-lapped, gentle-voiced mothers who were to be found in the novels my generation grew up with. No one could have been more different from Marmee March or Lord

Fauntleroy's Dearest, but we felt at our ease with Ma. We were as welcome in her house as in our own. Even when she had ladies for tea in the living room or was expecting twenty guests for dinner there was room for us and our refreshments in the library and on the vine-covered porch that overlooked Lake Agawam. In Ma's house there was always food enough for Bertie's friends to stay for lunch or supper.

I had taken this generous, casual hospitality for granted partly because it appeared effortless and partly because Pa and Mademoiselle and Bridie had run our house in much the same way, but now that I was on the verge of having a home of my own I made up my mind that when Bertie and I had children any house we lived in would be as much theirs as ours. This was not the case in most of the houses I knew, but Bertie and I would do as Father and Ma and Pops had done for us.

Pops was a quiet, rather stringy-looking man. His pale high forehead and his drooping mustache reminded me of the White Knight. Pops was shy, but he did not make my friends and me feel shy. We talked about our pleasures and difficulties and presented small problems for his consideration as I can not remember our doing with any other grownup except one of our own. That, Father once told me, was not astonishing: Pops was an experienced listener. He probably knew as many family secrets and had settled as many family quarrels as any lawyer in New York. His clients hardly ever found themselves in court and no will that Pops had drawn was, as far as Father could recall, ever broken or even contested. Furthermore, under Pops' careful but not unimaginative supervision, estates grew and prospered.

"In spite of his gentle manner and kindly ways," Pa said, "and kind heart up to a point, Pops is a shrewd old bird, and make no mistake about it there isn't a smarter family and trust lawyer in the city."

It was Bertie who persuaded me to move to Aunt Lucy's before our house was touched. Even though Esther had bought a house of her own, I didn't want to leave her until she moved into it; but Bertie told me I was wrong. "Esther will be busy getting her new house ready," he said, "and it will distract her from watching your old house gradually being dismantled, but if you're there, your sad little face will remind her. Move to your aunt's."

I did, and probably Bertie was right and it was better for Esther not to have me around to worry over. It was certainly better for me and it has left me able to remember our house intact. I can close my eyes and walk through every room.

Before James left for Paris, he arranged for the division of our furniture and other possessions. Appraisers would make the final, exactly even division, but if there were some particular objects that any of us wanted, we should mention them now. I told Bertie I couldn't easily think of our things separately. All that I knew I wanted was Mother's bureau set.

"And maybe you'd like something from our house, Bertie, and I could ask for that too."

"I would. I'd like to have your father's desk and chair from the library."

Eventually the contents of our house were scattered in many houses. Most of my share has lost its identity as Bertie and I have mixed my family things and his and have added purchases of our own, but wherever we've lived, Bertie has sat in Father's chair and worked at his desk and Mother's silver-backed brushes and silver and tortoise-shell combs and her velvet pin cushion with its ring of dancing silver cupids and the pair of silver-mounted crystal vases have been on my bureau and her rose-garlanded oval mirror, easel-backed like a picture frame, has reflected my face.

On Bertie's advice I stayed away from the final businesslike parcelling out of our belongings.

Julia brought my list to me at Aunt Lucy's. Near the top was an item that startled me: "Portrait of Mrs. James A. Cameron by John Singer Sargent."

I ought to have it, Julia said, because of my not remembering Mother and being named for her. Naturally everyone of us would like it, but Julia and James had decided that it would be fair for it to go to me, and Esther and Maud had not questioned the decision.

After Julia left I told Aunt Lucy that I thought one of the older ones who remembered Mother better should have her portrait. "By rights Esther ought to have it. She can remember Mother when she was as young as she is in the painting, and anyway Esther is the eldest."

"I believe Eleanor would want Esther to have it," Aunt Lucy said, "there's something special, I imagine, about a first child and yourself young when she was born. Mind you, I know there's something special about every child and of course, my dear, about the baby of the family. You were a delightful surprise to your mother. And Maud and Julia so near of an age that she loved them together. And the boy. She never forgot him nor the joy of having had him. The grief of loss she never mentioned except, I suppose, to your father. They understood each other and thought alike about most of the daily things that count. Neither of them, for instance, had a favorite among their daughters. Still, in the existing circumstances, I think they would like Esther to have her mother's portrait. Why don't you give it to her?"

"Could I, do you think? Or would James?"

"It no longer has anything to do with James. The portrait is your property and you can do what you like with it."

"I'd like to give it to Esther and if it makes James mad all the better."

"Don't give it to make James mad, give it because you love Esther. And remember, James acts according to his lights. You might not care to live by them, I'm sure I couldn't, but you can't change him. And he's Julia's husband. She's your sister, you can't change that either. You can't ever divorce a sister, Nell. In a sense all sisters are Siamese twins and must manage to live with each other. It's easier if they love each other. It's hard for Julia, even though she's not aware of it, to be hard on Esther. Poor Julia . . . But give the portrait to Esther."

Julia sailed with Maud and Louis for France in April. Before she left, she agreed, as did James by cable, that Bertie and I could become officially engaged. Our relations and friends were told, but because of my family being in mourning there was no formal celebration nor any announcement in the newspapers. No wedding date was set but it was accepted that we would be married quietly early in the summer.

By May, Esther moved into her new house. It was east of Park Avenue in a block where many houses, including hers, had gardens.

I had hoped that Esther would some day have a house as pretty as Mr. Scott's was ugly, and this house, I noted with pleasure on my first visit, was exactly that. It was as pretty and frivolous and airy as the Murray Hill house had been ugly and solemn and shut in on itself. The exterior was pale coral, and on the south wall wrought-iron balconies, painted white, overlooked the garden. The effect was Mediterranean, I thought, not that I had ever been in southern Europe but that was how I imagined the houses there, washed inside and out in pale colors, with flowering trees beyond tall french windows.

"It's perfect," I said, as Esther and I settled ourselves in the high-ceilinged second-floor living room. "Those straight, plain curtains are like a frame for the garden."

The curtains were of cotton or linen in the same oyster white as the walls of the room. Chairs and sofas were covered in blue glazed chintz that was pale as ice against Mother's fruitwood tables. These were her spring and summer curtains and slip-covers, Esther told me. In the autumn there would be bolder, warmer colors and heavy cut velvet curtains to shut out the cold. "Bridie has warned me that there'll be a terrible floor draft from my beautiful windows."

"I'm glad you have Bridie," I said, "but I wish everything was the way Pa said it would be for you some day."

"Dear Pa. He always believed in that future day on which a fine man would come along."

"Pa was usually right, Esther, and I bet he will be yet."

"He was right, though I never thought he would be. I've had more propositions than proposals and most of the latter came from some of our gallant Allies, who were willing to marry money at any price. Then in the autumn of 1917, Pa was proved right, though I never told him. A doctor from Cleveland came to the hospital to do postgraduate work in pediatrics."

Esther said that Father would have liked the doctor for his calm, solid self and also because his mother had been a member of a New York family we knew, so he wouldn't have seemed a completely middle-western stranger.

He wasn't for long a stranger to Esther. On their first meeting at the hospital, he said, "You must be my sister's Esther Cameron. She has a picture of you that she cut out of a magazine the year you both came out. Grace came out in Cleveland but that didn't count as far as our Mamma was concerned, and she took Grace to New York. A relative of yours arranged for Grace to go to a dinner your father gave for you before a very grand party. She was timid about going to it and you were kind to her."

Esther shook her head regretfully, and then, as she looked at the doctor a faint recollection stirred. Aunt Lucy had asked her to invite an out-of-town girl before the Assemblies.

"Yes, I think— Is your sister a little like you but smaller? And her hair was curlier, a nut brown maid except for her blue eyes."

"That's Grace. You do remember her."

"She's a little vague in my mind after so many years but one thing I remember distinctly, she danced like an angel. My aunt asked me to help her get started, but it took only the least little push, no more effort than blowing a feather off my hand, and once she had partners, she lost her shyness. Yes, I do remember her now. I can see her beaming face as her card was entirely filled up and an extra if there were enough was all she could promise the young men who flocked around her."

Because of Grace, the doctor and Esther became friends at the hospital as, with this sort of link, strangers quickly do on a ship or in a foreign city. There was not much time for friendship let alone falling in love at the hospital, but the doctor managed.

His way of loving her was new to Esther. He fell in love with her, with Esther herself. He seemed to consider her looks to be no more than a becoming garment in which she, Esther Cameron, was clothed.

He called her Esther Cameron, as if it were one word. That was how his sister affectionately and gratefully pronounced her name. He knew that Esther was now Mrs. Scott. He knew her story and it was important to him only because it had happened to her.

"I wasn't a scandal to him," Esther said, "any more than I was a beauty. I was Esther Cameron, all one word, whom he intended to marry and take care of."

It was early in February of 1918 that Esther agreed to marry him in the spring and return to Cleveland with him. It seemed to her that she was fond enough of him for them to build a life together. And she could not, she said, describe the relief, the lightness of heart with which she looked forward to leaving New York with someone kind and dependable.

"Someone who loved me, Esther Cameron, not my red hair or my white skin or any separate thing, not my mother's family or my father's money. He didn't know about the last two attributes and if he had he wouldn't have cared. He just cared about me, not about anything I happened to be or have. I thought we would be happy. I thought there could at last be for me a peaceful happiness, improbable and undeserved as heaven, and I looked forward. For the first time in years, for that little while, I looked forward."

"Then why? What happened?" I asked.

"The last Sunday in February happened," Esther said. "Augie happened."

I had been so sure Julia had been wrong. I looked miserably away.

"Don't look like that, Nell. Julia was wrong. Though she might not have been. A promise, even to Pa, wasn't much to hold on to when I heard from Augie."

Augie had written her that he would be in New York that Sunday on a twelve-hour pass before he was shipped out. He named a time and a meeting place and said he would be waiting. It could, he wrote, be the last day on which they would ever meet.

Esther found the strength to sign up for the hospital for the twelve hours. Once she had signed, she had to report. Once there she couldn't leave.

She hadn't expected the doctor to be at the hospital, but he had been summoned at five in the morning to a patient who was dangerously ill. They met at the little boy's bedside. He was a clever doctor, she told me.

"Clever is too slight a word, he's better than that, he's a wise and skilled physician. One of the few who see clearly and act decisively. He has a medical sixth sense I guess. If it hadn't been for him, the boy would be dead."

The doctor and the nurses, with Esther to fetch and carry, worked all day. It was eight o'clock in the evening before the boy was out of danger and the doctor took Esther to a nearby Child's for coffee and a sandwich.

All she could think of was that Augie's pass was up and the last day was over.

She looked across the table at the doctor and saw, not his thin, tired face but Augie's.

"It was as though I had seen Augie the day before. It's always like that when, unprepared, I am reminded of him. I can see his dark eyes and the way they are set in his head, and the curve of his lips. I can see his hands and the way his body moves. When I suddenly, deeply think of Augie, I am with him and I can't see another man, can't bear to have another man near me."

The doctor talked about their plans. He spoke of the suburb where they would live, the house they would build, the family and friends who would welcome her and none of it, Esther said, was of any more interest to her than a story in the *Delineator*. He was a kind man, a good man and, she thought detachedly, he meant no more to her than the stranger sitting at the next table. The doctor looked close to exhaustion after fifteen hours at the hospital and she hadn't the heart to say that she couldn't marry him. A few days later she told him.

"But, Esther, if you were fond of him and he loved you."

"Not a fair enough exchange for him if I could have done it. I knew that evening I couldn't. I should have known from the beginning. And you must know how it is for me, you were there when I thought Augie was dead. Augie would have been with me in the house I built with another man. He'd have been in bed with us. It wouldn't have been any good. Be glad I realized it before I got into another sorry mess."

Esther walked to a window and straightened a fold in a curtain and stood looking out.

Presently, she turned her back on the garden and said, "Before I show you the rest of my pretty house, give me your advice about this room. Shall I find a big baroque mirror to go on that wall and reflect the garden, or would it be too much?"

"It would be pretty, but I think Mother's portrait would look nice there. That's my house present to you."

"Nell! That's an awfully big present. You better think it over."

"I have thought and what I think and Aunt Lucy and Bertie too is that by rights the portrait ought to be yours, you're the eldest. All my life you've made things right for me and it's nice for me to be able to make one thing right for you."

A week later the portrait was in its place facing the garden, and Esther was pleased. She was more than pleased, she was happy to have Mother there. And looking at them, I thought—as when I was little I sometimes thought, half believing, about a picture or a china figure or a beloved doll—that Mother looked pleased, was smiling more contentedly than usual. I was too old for such a childish fantasy to have more than a second's reality, but it wasn't fantasy to think the light-colored, uncluttered room a perfect setting for the summer portrait and to believe that Mother and Father would be happy to have it there, to have Mother there, standing by.

Bertie and I were married in the chapel of St. Thomas' on the seventeenth of June. Only the members of our immediate families were present: Aunt Lucy and Esther, Bertie's parents, Elsie and her husband and their three boys, and the Sheldons. And Mademoiselle and Bridie Smith, of course.

We could not, Aunt Lucy decided, have anyone else at the chapel and at her apartment afterward. Once we started with cousins and dear friends and connections we would, before we knew it, have a full-scale formal wedding on our hands, and that, on account of Pa, would not be right. Fortunately, there was no problem, as Cousin Maud Bronson was in England visiting her only child, a daughter married to one of the Cecils, whom she hadn't seen since before the war. It would have been impossible not to invite Cousin Maud, Aunt Lucy said, and then it would have become difficult not to invite the Ameses and the Gore cousins and the Speyers and the Martins and Hendersons and the whole of the Turner connection and, in the end, most of the Old Guard.

Aunt Lucy also decided that on my wedding day I was to come out of mourning and stay out. Pa would not want me to go on my honeymoon in black or even in the dismal grays and lavenders of half-mourning. My trousseau was to be as bright-colored as Julia's and Maud's, and, though so few people were to be present, I must have a proper wedding dress. I thought an elaborate wedding gown might look out of place, but Esther helped me to find the perfect dress. It was a cross between a summer evening dress and a graduation dress but prettier and more romantic than either. It was made of organdy circled with inserts of embroidery and it had a tiny, fitted, short-sleeved bodice with a narrow, satin-sashed waist and a skirt as full and wide as a bell. My tulle veil was short but not bunchy. It was held smooth and close to my head by a wreath of orange blossoms from which it fell just to my shoulders like a gay little mantilla. I looked nice, I think, but I don't really remember. I remember my sisters' weddings better than my own. I wasn't frightened. I couldn't be frightened in any adventure with Bertie. Still, this was a pretty big adventure, and as the day drew near, I felt a tightening of excitement, an almost unbearable breathlessness. It was, I told Bertie on the evening before, like the painful, tightening anticipation of Christmas when I was little. I can say anything to Bertie and never worry that I'll sound foolish to him.

On that evening—it's long ago but not far away—Bertie took my hands and held them. While he held them they grew quiet and I realized they had been trembling and so had the rest of me. Now I was quiet.

Bertie smiled and asked, "Okay now?"

I nodded and he said, "Sure it's exciting and if we're lucky it'll be better than Christmas but nothing to be scared of, Nell."

"I am a little I think. If it wasn't you . . ."

"But it is me. It's us, Nell. So, okay?"

"Oh, Bertie, oh, Bertie," I remember repeating his name and starting to shake again and he gave me a big friendly hug that carried me to the door of my room. He didn't kiss me, just held me tight and then let go and told me to go to bed and put my mind on looking my best tomorrow.

I think I slept quite soon and did not wake until well after it was light, but that night and the next day and evening I remember only in bits and pieces. I remember myself in my veil in Mother's mirror. I remember the antlered mirror in Aunt Lucy's hall when we came back from St. Thomas'. The accidental sight of my reflection startled me. I thought I might be looking pale, whiter than tulle and orange blossoms, but what I saw was a rosy-cheeked, shining-eyed Nell. All brides are nervous, I told myself then and Bertie later, but nervousness seems to agree with me.

I remember bits and pieces.

I remember Elsie's curly-haired, brown-eyed, matronly prettiness. It was an unself-conscious prettiness. Elsie didn't usually bother about her appearance—she was like Ma in that—but for the wedding she had taken trouble. I can't think what her dress was like, but I can see her pale blue picture hat. The thin straw bent beneath the heavy clusters of grapes or were they currants? Some kind of round, glossy fruit beneath which the brim curved becomingly. Elsie looked lovely and I was glad. I hoped Bertie and I would have a daughter as well as sons and it was nice to have prettiness in both families for a girl to inherit.

I remember the white bow and the spray of lilies of the valley on Fluffy's collar. She was going blind and usually she moved stiffly, with an old dog's walk, but she was very perky on that day.

I remember the candles with bead-fringed shades on the table and the gray mist that shrouded the Hudson below the windows of the restaurant where we dined on our way to Cousin Maud's country place which she had lent us for the beginning of our honeymoon, but what we ate or what we said I can't recall.

I hardly remember the ceremony except for a kind of flash of it in the middle. I don't think I had stage fright but perhaps something related to it. An actress once told me that in a play she would sometimes find herself in the middle of a scene and would know what lines came next but of how she had got there she would have no idea. It was like that for me: suddenly I was in the middle of the ceremony and I repeated I Eleanor take thee Robert and Bertie must have said I Robert take thee Eleanor and my wedding dress was a costume, and, oh, I meant every word, for better for worse (as if anything could ever be hopelessly worse with Bertie there), but they were like words said in a play by actors, by strangers called Eleanor and Robert. Till death us do part—that was easily said then, but now it gives me a shiver. I'll think of something else quickly. I'll think of Cousin Maud's Victorian house looming above the porte-cochere in the dark and of Bertie and me trying to behave naturally in front of the prim, elderly housekeeper who opened the front door for us in a blaze of yellow light.

Cousin Maud's room with its two adjoining dressing rooms and baths was more like a sitting room than a bedroom. There were comfortable chairs and a sofa. There were vases of garden flowers on a pair of consoles and on the low table in front of the sofa were two silver wine coolers that held a quart of champagne and a quart of milk and between the coolers a bowl of fruit and a platter of chicken sandwiches covered with a damp cloth.

We looked at each other and were silent and beyond the wide silled, open windows the sounds of the summer night were suddenly loud in the room.

We left the food and drink untouched. It's queer the little things that the body remembers. I remember how terribly hungry we were later and how greedily we ate every sandwich and drank all the milk before we went back to bed.

We had known each other always but we were young and shy. The two dressing rooms were a blessing. One of us said something about its being late and I vaguely remember taking my overnight bag into Cousin Maud's dressing room while Bertie disappeared into the one that had belonged to her long deceased husband.

Our wrappers were so obviously brand new, as was my nightgown and I'm sure Bertie's pajamas, that we still seemed fully clothed when we returned and stood awkwardly beside Cousin Maud's broad, high, canopied bed.

Bertie took my hand and moved my wedding ring up and down on my finger.

I thought of the ceremony but I didn't remember it any more clearly than I do now.

"It was like a play," I said.

"What was?"

"The ceremony. It sounded so queer, I Eleanor take thee, Robert. Eleanor and Robert sounded so formal as if they were strangers, not us at all."

Bertie moved the ring almost to the tip of my finger and then slid it slowly back into place. "Ah, Nell," he said, "with this ring I thee wed. With my body I thee worship. I Bertie take thee, Nell."

He took me in his arms and that's all I remember in words. The rest my body remembers.

10

Looking back at the beginning of our marriage the week at Cousin Maud's seems long, longer than a week. It went quickly, but it goes slowly as I remember it. It's a queer thing about a happy time that it slips so quickly by while it's happening and is sweet and slow in retrospect.

We've never been back to Cousin Maud's Hudson River house but it's clear in my mind. I can see the river though the wide, high windows of the big room downstairs.

The big room was crammed with massive furniture, its walls were thick with paintings, family portraits and Italian masters of uncertain provenance and four beautiful English landscapes. Every flat surface was crowded with ornaments and souvenirs collected over a lifetime. The cabinets and bric-a-brac stands were inlaid with mother-of-pearl and the stiff, high-backed chairs and sofas were upholstered in tufted bronze satin. It was an overwhelming room on first acquaintance but not a gloomy one. In the daytime there were magnificent views from the windows and after dark every corner was cheerfully illuminated by the brass and flowered glass chandeliers and wall brackets and lamps. The tallest lamp with a huge bubble of a yellow glass shade stood on the large round table which was in the exact center of the rose-and-gold-patterned French carpet. The table was covered with a tasseled gold plush cloth and on it was an array of ornately framed photographs flanked by a collection of curious objects, some of which I can still recall: an elephant's tusk, its entire curved length minutely and deeply carved with delicate figures that we could distinguish in detail only with the help of an ivory-handled magnifying glass; a silver and tortoise-shell box shaped like an Eastern palace and a pair of bronze baby shoes; a brass telescope and a jeweled music box from which a tiny gold bird rose like a phoenix.

I suppose the room was ugly. Certainly it should have seemed absurd to our young and modern eyes, but I don't think it did even at first sight. It had a self-possessed Victorian dignity: there it was and a visitor could take it or leave it. We took to it and were at home in it. We liked the clutter of unrelated ornaments and the velvet-bound photograph and postcard albums and the outdated globe of the world which stood on one of the glass-fronted bookcases. Most of all we admired the upright piano with its movable brass brackets that held fat white candles. We lit them and the flames were reflected in the smooth, polished wood as in a dark mirror. We turned out the electric lights and played a duet by candlelight. All we could manage by ear was "Chopsticks."

I remember fiery sunsets from our bedroom windows while we were dressing for dinner and I remember the morning light which wasn't strong enough to wake us because the windows faced west on the river and south on the garden. When we did wake we saw the east light reflected from the shiny leaves of a thick, tall tree whose branches reached up beyond the top of the south window. The leaves may not have been shiny but only have seemed so as they fluttered in the morning sun. However, that is how I remember them, that is how I remember all of Cousin Maud's house, inside and out. Floors and furniture and silver and brass were shiny with polish, the wooden railings of the south porch and the wicker furniture gleamed with white paint. The under-gardeners set up the sprinklers and played the hose on flower beds and lawn and the spray arched and sparkled in rainbow-colored fountains.

It was a lovely house and garden and river bank, a lovely beginning for Bertie and me. Every once in a while we remember it aloud when something reminds us, a painting of the Hudson River School or someone's old-fashioned family house; not long ago it was a doll's house on loan to the Museum of the City of New York. We remember Cousin Maud's house with affection but on the morning of the day we were to sail, we left it without regret. We looked forward to the crossing and to being together in Paris and to motoring south in France, perhaps as far as Italy. Bertie, like Pa, is an automobile man, and it's always been a pleasure to motor with him even on foreign roads.

In Paris, Bertie and I were not alone as we had been at Cousin Maud's house. Our days and evenings were spent with the Hendersons and the Martins and their friends. Only our nights were our own. I remember Julia's Avenue Gabrielle apartment with its string of formal salons, and Maud's square, white, modern house in Neuilly better than our suite on the Boissy d'Anglas side of the Crillon.

Though the Paris fortnight was crowded with other people Bertie and I continued to learn to know each other in all the ways of knowing including the Biblical one. We were at the start of the never-ending process of making one life out of two which is marriage. I don't so much remember this or any part of my life with Bertie as move back and forth in it easily, without puzzlement. I puzzle over my sisters, wondering how it really was with them. Bertie is the only person I never puzzle over any more than I puzzle over myself. We remember together. We look at then and now as if we had one pair of eyes between us. Where Maud and Julia, and even Esther are concerned, I'm not sure that what I remember is what actually was. Where Bertie is concerned, I know.

I don't suppose I understood the quarrels which Maud and Julia never outgrew. Just yesterday Julia and I were talking about Maud and she told me I didn't.

"You couldn't understand, you didn't have a contemporary sister," she said. "Oh, I know you loved Esther best. And why not? She was always a grownup to you, a beautiful, romantic, star-crossed grownup that any little sister would make an idol of."

It was different, Julia continued, for Maud and her. They had been equals all their lives. They had been confederates and adversaries and friends. They had been children at the exact same time and then girls and women, neither one ever a rung of the ladder above the other. And if they had had the luck to be old ladies together they would still have quarreled and not bothered to make up, just have gone on amicably from there as they did when they were nine and ten or nineteen and twenty.

"If Maud was here now"—Julia's eyes filled with tears and she wiped them impatiently away—"we might quarrel over that painting of Louis' we've got on our hands but it wouldn't matter. Our quarrel in Paris when you were there on your honeymoon didn't matter. I bet you remember though you're too polite to mention it. Or maybe too kind."

Julia, her eyes still wet, smiled at me and I remembered how pretty she was when she smiled when she was young. I also remembered the quarrel.

Julia and Maud and Bertie and I were in Maud's living room. It really was a living room, not a salon, though more modern and more austere than any I had known in New York and it was flooded with sunlight. Both light and comfort were rare in Paris houses and apartments. Even on the Avenue du Bois, the deep windows and all those curtains darkened the brightest day.

Louis had not appeared for lunch and Julia said that on account of Bertie and me he might have made the effort, James would have been with us if he hadn't been tied up at Versailles.

"Does Louis lunch with his model?" Julia asked.

"They don't really have lunch," Maud said, "just a salad or something and not at any fixed hour."

"I hope she dresses for the meal."

"Now don't start that again, I've had enough of your insinuations." Maud's face was scarlet and there were beads of perspiration on her forehead. I thought, oh dear, here we go and looked imploringly at Bertie, but he was already on his feet and did not glance in my direction.

"My insinuations, as you call them, never seem to have any effect, so for once I'll speak frankly. I'm glad Bertie is here—Bertie where do you think you're going?"

"Just out for a breath of air." Before Julia could stop him he stepped through the open door into the garden and disappeared from our sight.

"Men!" Julia exclaimed, and as she returned to the subject of Louis and his models, I thought of how Pa used to escape for a breath of air from feminine quarrels and tears. In many small ways Bertie reminded me of Pa. I was lovingly contemplating this, making a list of resemblances: Pa and Bertie as escape artists, Pa and Bertie and motorcars, Pa and Bertie—but my sisters' voices grew too loud for me to do anything but listen to them.

"No wonder artists aren't *bien vu*," Julia said, "and don't think because he's one of the Smithtown Martins that Louis can get away with this any more than those left-bank Bohemians."

"Get away with what, Julia Cameron?"

"With spending his days painting naked women who are no better than they should be."

"You think every model is a tart, well let me tell you—"

"Shut up, Maud, we're off the track. The point isn't the models and their morals as much as Louis and his future."

"Louis is quite capable of looking after his own future."

"My dear sister, be sensible, no man is and an artist least of all. Naturally when he was at the Beaux-Arts, Louis had to paint nudes, that was part of learning his profession, but by now he ought to be specializing. You know, like doctors after they finish medical school."

"I don't know."

"You know what I mean well enough. And it's not as if Louis painted pretty nudes or even complete ones. The only word for his work is anatomical. There's practically never a head even sketched, usually there's just a part of a body in embarrassing detail. When I'm in that studio I don't know where to look, honestly, I don't."

"You don't even know how to use words, Louis paints honestly. Just because you have an absolutely filthy mind you—"

"Please, Maud, let's not quarrel. All right, all right it's partly my fault, but listen to me. There really is no future in what Louis is doing. As far as I can see he hasn't got anywhere and people don't think much of an amateur dabbler who has nothing to show he's an artist except a lot of naked women running in and out of his studio."

"They're not naked when they run in and out."

"Don't try to be funny. I'm trying to give you some sensible advice. You ought to encourage Louis to make something solid of his talent and his training. Why don't you at least suggest that he try his hand at portrait painting? It pays well and it would get rid of those awful girls and—oh, Louis, I didn't hear you come in."

Louis was standing inside the doorway. "Sorry to sneak up on you, it's the fault of my espadrilles."

Julia looked with distaste at the paint-stained canvas shoes on Louis' otherwise bare feet.

"Almost as disreputable in your eyes as my models, aren't they, Julia? Listen, my dear," he spoke in a low relaxed voice, "these girls are hard-working, disciplined and for the most part, not promiscuous. But tell me, whatever makes you think that amateur sitters are all that better behaved than the professionals?"

"Oh, of course one hears stories. There are even historical instances but these are exceptions. Anyway, why not try a portrait? You could do Maud. Portrait of the Artist's Wife. Those always go well at exhibitions."

"I wouldn't do a portrait of Maud for the sake of having it go well at an exhibition. Besides, I haven't thought of myself as a portrait painter. I haven't really thought yet of any category, landscapist, animal painter, or whatever. I've thought only of learning my craft until I can paint anything that is in my mind."

"Good Lord, Louis, not animals! Though at that—"

"Yes, at that, some have made a good thing of it, haven't they, Julia? And I must admit that the horses and dogs of the rich are on the average better looking than their women."

"There! You see it's because those girls of yours are pretty that you're spending so much time learning your craft as you call it. And don't get angry and try to shut me up. You can't do it. Of course, you don't want to paint portraits, not even Maud's. That wouldn't be as much fun for you as—"

Louis moved quickly and, it must have seemed to Julia, menacingly. She stopped in mid-sentence. Louis took the hand with which she had been gesticulating and held it firmly.

"Calm yourself," he said, "and listen to me. I'm not angry, but I must, as courteously as possible, ask you to shut up. I think in your peculiar way you're trying to protect Maud. You really don't need to, does she, darling?"

Maud shook her head. She and Louis looked at each other as if Julia and I weren't there.

Louis turned to Julia. "Don't worry about the Martins' respectability," he said. "Painters and their models are quite respectable unless they choose to be otherwise and Tout Paris is sophisticated enough to realize this. And don't worry about what genre of painting I shall choose. If I'm lucky I won't choose it, it will choose me."

"I'm sorry I lost my temper and was rude. It's because I want not to protect Maud exactly but to have everything right for her."

Louis was smiling again. "And you don't think," he said, "that anything at all unconventional can be right."

"I suppose with James in the diplomatic I do tend to take the conventional view. And perhaps I'm worrying a little about my family being an embarrassment to James in his career." Julia smiled uncertainly and blushed. Unlike Maud, she blushed very prettily. "Now can I say just one more thing?" she asked.

"Oh dear, maybe you better not," Maud whispered.

"No, Maud, this is all right to say. Look, Louis, even if you think I should mind my own business, think about portrait painting. That likeness you did in pastels of Aunt Lucy for Maud is charming."

"A sketch, my dear girl, done in haste with affection, not a professional piece of work."

"It's like her and a likeness is the main thing in a portrait."

"A flattering likeness."

"Not when you get famous enough. Then your sitters will accept any way you make them look. Please think about it. It's a lucrative field and it has enormous prestige. Portrait painters are received everywhere, even in the most exalted circles."

Toward the middle of July, Bertie and I motored south by way of Evian and Grenoble and Avignon. It was nice finally to see the bridge of Avignon and to walk on it. We even danced a few steps, pleased to be actually a *belle dame* and a *beau monsieur*, not children pretending. We didn't get to Italy after all. Louis had recommended a *pension* in a hill town high above Cannes and we liked it so well that there we remained, making only short excursions to a beach or a casino, until it was time to go home.

Aunt Lucy met us at the pier. We were to stay with her until our apartment was ready. I had thought a house would be better, but Bridie Smith had advised an apartment to begin with. It would be a simpler way to start housekeeping, she said. I'd learn faster and more thoroughly if I began on a small scale and there would be plenty of time to settle into something permanent after the first baby arrived.

At Aunt Lucy's Fluffy greeted us. She couldn't see at all any more and her welcome was a subdued one. She wasn't in any pain, Aunt Lucy assured me, but her heart wasn't good and the veterinarian said she could go any day.

We had been home only a few days when the morning came on which Fluffy did not wake up.

"It's as though she just waited for me to come home again," I said through tears to Bertie, "but that's a stupid thing to say and it's stupid to cry like this."

"No, it's not. Remember my spaniel bitch, Gypsy? I tell you when I got the word my first term at St. Mark's that she was dead I cried."

"You were only a boy. I'm a grownup. I shouldn't mind this much about a dog."

People, Bertie said, grown up or not, couldn't help what they minded, and small sorrows could hurt just as much as big ones while they lasted.

"Cry all you like," he said, "you don't have to be grown up with me."

I cried a lot but not for long. Common sense told me that Fluffy had had a long life for a dog and her death had been one that anybody would choose, just going to sleep and not waking up. Dear me, I was still very young to be able calmly to pick and choose among the ways of dying.

Bertie and I didn't seem young to ourselves or to one another, we seemed as grown up as we would ever be. Bertie was older than I was, older, because of the war, than the three and a half years between us. He had come through without a wound and without being destroyed inside. Plenty were and took to the bottle or other methods of escaping themselves. Bertie had come back unharmed but he had come back older.

Bertie didn't talk at any length about the war in that summer and winter, but gradually then and through the years I discovered something of what his war was like for him. He never recalled the worst of it out loud. I came nearest to grasping how bad it had been from the way he tried to describe what was good. Good wasn't exactly the word, he said, but in the midst of being tired and being afraid and being dirty and being cold, there were good things, release from strain in a lull or behind the lines, comradeship, laughter. That was the surprising thing, that there were good times to remember. He mentioned this to Pops who said it wasn't surprising, people laughed amazingly easily on the way to and from a funeral. In the presence of death, the smallest joke became twice as large as life, became life itself Pops supposed.

"Look at the Irish and their wakes," Pops said, "we can look down our noses at them all we like but they've got the answer to a basic human need."

THE BEST OF FAMILIES

I remember right after Pearl Harbor, Bertie saying, "God! Those poor trapped astonished bastards. They had no idea. That's how it was when we got to France in 1918. A war had been going on for years, but we had no idea. It's a wonder so many of us got through as well as we did."

In 1919 Pearl Harbor was a long way off and another war was unthinkable. We believed we were safe in a postwar world. It would be a different world, I realized, Pa had told me things never go back to where they were, but it promised to be safer than the old one. We hadn't known that that world and time were prewar. We took it for granted that our time now was postwar once and for all.

I think more about that pleasant false security as I look back on it than I did when I was living in it. I just enjoyed the season in New York and being in the midst of it with Bertie. Even Prohibition, which almost everyone deplored, was a novelty, an adventure. Its sinister aspects were not yet visible, it was a joke that blue-nosed Puritans had played on us under cover of a war, and we enjoyed outwitting them, not that Bertie and I had much outwitting to do. James had insisted that Father's cellar be divided between Esther and me. This was not generosity, he said when Bertie tried to thank him in Paris, it was merely the fair thing to do, since we in America were the ones who had to live with this misguided experiment. Father had seen it coming and had laid in an ample supply of wine and liquor which should last us quite a while.

Neither we nor our friends worried about Prohibition; we didn't worry about anything in that autumn and winter.

Bertie was working hard, harder he said than he ever had in his life. I liked seeing him at Father's desk with his hair rumpled, his jacket off and his tie pulled into a loose string as he pored over his books and papers. It helped me to picture him when he had been far from me at St. Mark's and Harvard.

I enjoyed the weekends and holidays and the zest of the round of peacetime gaiety that filled the last months of the old year and the first of the new. The coming-out parties at the Ritz were unashamedly extravagant. The songs we danced to were not about war any more, they were about Mary and Kitty Kelly and Rose of Washington Square. There were new kinds of musicians, too. It was about then, I think that the Six Brown Brothers first blew loud and clear as they wound triumphantly among the dancers and there was a man who played a ukulele and sang and was a great success at small parties. I must first have danced to Paul Whiteman's orchestra that winter and Emil Coleman's too, but I'm not sure. It's fun to remember Bertie and me making up for the years when he was away as we danced in our friends' houses and in the ballroom and the Crystal Room of the Ritz and in small dimly illuminated cabarets. And at weddings. There were lots of weddings right after the war, lighthearted weddings in a new lighthearted time.

I was matron of honor for Baby Elliot when she married Freddy Ransome. Freddy was a thirteen-year-old girl's dream come true. He had dark gold, crinkly hair and a beautifully modeled, blunt-featured face. Well, well, you never know, I thought when I met him, Baby who was the most matter-of-fact and sensible one of us has found for herself the romantic answer to a maiden's prayer.

"An absolute Greek god, isn't he?" Baby murmured complacently. "How could I resist him?"

How indeed? He was tall and broad-shouldered, he was slow-moving but not clumsy, and he had the palest most expressionless blue eyes I've ever seen.

"He looks at you so straight," Baby said, "none of that sideways, smarmy charm."

Baby was delighted with Freddy and with herself for capturing him. Aside from his looks, though one couldn't possibly think of him aside from them, Freddy was considered a catch. His parents belonged to old, well-to-do families, the father was New York and the mother a Boston Thayer. Freddy was St. Paul's and Yale and, inevitably, Skull and Bones. He had a good war record, which had interrupted but not hindered his business career, and he was spoken of as one of the coming young men downtown. At the wedding his best man told me I'd live to see Freddy president of Bankers' Trust or the Guaranty or wherever it was he worked. And during one of the recent newspaper strikes, when I was reduced to reading Bertie's *Wall Street Journal*, I came across an account of Freddy's career first as president and then as chairman of the board of some big bank with a hyphenated name.

The Ransomes were becoming to each other. Baby always moved like quicksilver, and in contrast to Freddy she seemed quicker and lighter than ever. She danced where he walked and talked a hundred words to his twenty. Freddy seemed more solid, wiser, stronger as Baby looked up at him admiringly.

The Ransomes were at the very center of that dizzy whirling winter season, and this was due to Baby. She has unflagging energy and unlimited curiosity about people. New people, any new people who loom on the social horizon, have always fascinated her. If matters had been left to Freddy their circle of friends would have remained closed and old-fashioned, but Baby's mind was set on enlarging and modernizing it.

It was through Baby that Esther and Bertie and I, early in March, received and accepted a dinner invitation from complete strangers, a Mr. and Mrs. Herbert Thompson, who had lately moved to New York from Houston, Texas. They were fairly young and very attractive, Baby told us, and she liked them and so would we. She added that they had loads of beautiful new money and weren't afraid to spend it.

"They're fun and they're nice," Baby said. "They'll give a great party and you'll know everybody. Please come."

The Thompsons knew how to give a party, and after two East Hampton summers, they knew quite a lot of New York people, but it takes longer than a couple of summers to learn the ins and outs of a community. Aunt Lucy once told me about a hostess, new to New York, who at a formal dinner seated a man next to his married sister. Her little slip caused only mild amusement; the Thompsons' error had more serious consequences.

As Esther and Bertie and I entered the enormous sunken living room of the duplex apartment on Park Avenue a ripple of astonishment crossed the faces of the guests nearest to us. I couldn't imagine what had startled them until we moved further into the room and found Augie chatting with his hostess, who introduced him to us, and mentioned her regret that Mrs. Wenger, whom she had not yet had the pleasure of meeting, had been obliged to remain in Boston.

Esther held out her hand and Augie took it and held it and bowed over it in what I had come to describe to myself as his absurd Blue Danube manner. As I watched them, I was back on Fifth Avenue on an Easter Sunday and Augie was no more absurd now than then, he wasn't the caricature I had managed to make of him in my mind, he was the shiningly good-looking dark young stranger whom we had taken into our house and hearts not quite twelve years ago.

I was angry because he hadn't changed as I had chosen to imagine, and I was frightened because Esther didn't look frightened. In Pa's words, she looked alive again. Galatea, I said grimly to myself. She wore a flowing white chiffon dress and as it floated around her she moved as lightly as if she were walking to music. She greeted acquaintances with her usual composure, but she was different. There was a brilliance, a glow that outshone the wreath of diamonds in her high-piled hair.

To this day I cannot be sure if Augie arranged this meeting or if it was as much a surprise to him as it was to us. The Thompsons told Baby later that they had met Augie at the Somerset Club during an autumn weekend in Boston and had promised to invite him to their first bang-up New York party, but Augie may easily have wangled the invitation. One thing I'd be willing to bet on is that Sophie Wenger never saw it. The only address the Thompsons had was the Somerset.

I heaved a sigh of relief when I saw that Esther and Augie were nowhere near each other in the dining room. I didn't realize that dancing was to follow, the modern informal dancing without cards, just a casual change of partners or, if they so chose, no change at all. I should have guessed from the uncarpeted polished parquet floor and the small amount of furniture in the living room, but I was too preoccupied to pay attention to my surroundings, besides, I didn't feel very well. I had forced myself to come to the party only because I didn't want to break my promise to Baby.

While we were at dinner the living room was transformed into the semblance of a cabaret with little tables and soft rose-shaded lights. The setting and the wild beat of the music reminded me of the party Julia had arranged for another meeting. Oh please, I breathed, don't let this be a lovers' meeting, don't let it be anything.

In the dim light it was hard to see who was dancing with whom, but there was a roving spotlight that caught and held a soloist in the band or a couple on the floor. The last thing I remember of the Thompsons' party was the sight of Esther and Augie caught in the silver beam and dancing in it, not trying to escape it, not even, I think, aware of it. There wasn't a sound in the room except the music. People can't have been so ill-mannered as to draw back and stand in a circle watching as guests at a wedding reception watch the bride and groom, but that's how I remember their behavior, and it needn't have come from vulgar curiosity, it may have been a spontaneous reaction. Esther and Augie were a pretty dazzling pair to watch.

I interrupted the proceedings in an unfortunately dramatic way. I fainted. It was the quick kind of faint that you don't know has happened until you find yourself coming out of it in another place. I found myself on my hostess's bed with Bertie looking anxiously down at me.

"All right now?" he asked. "You scared the hell out of me, but when I saw you were coming to I got Esther to take Mrs. Thompson back to the party. I didn't think you'd want an audience."

I told him I was fine and this only confirmed the suspicions I had had for the last two weeks.

"We were so hopeful that other time when I was late," I said, "I didn't want to disappoint you again so I didn't say anything, but I guess this means that finally the first baby is on its way."

I felt all right though slightly scared—it's horrid to disappear from yourself as you do in that kind of faint—but Bertie said there was to be no nonsense, he was taking me straight home without a good night to anybody.

It might have been better if we had stayed and persuaded Esther to leave with us, but more likely it would have made no difference. Without my fainting and Augie seeing Esther home the story of their meeting would have gone the rounds of Boston and New York and have found its way into print.

The scandal sheets didn't name names, but no one, Sophie included, was left in doubt as to the identity of those involved. The younger sister fainting from shock and the lover seeing the lady home added piquancy to the accounts, and I felt awful, but Bertie said that without these interesting details the fact of Augie and Esther's meeting would have been told, and however the tale was told, the fact was all that mattered and there wasn't a single thing I or anyone else could do about it.

In June I lost the baby. I was far enough along to have a difficult time and I was afraid I had been too badly damaged to be able to have another child. However, my doctor was a friend of the family and he had delivered both Rikki and me, so I trusted him when he told me to stop worrying and get well and leave the rest to Providence. There was no reason on earth as far as he could tell why I shouldn't have a fine healthy infant one of these days.

Months went by and then years and still there was no baby. Bertie and I gradually grew used to the dull, recurring ache of disappointment. After a while we seldom spoke of it.

We minded but we were young and healthy and our days were filled with Bertie's work and my—I can't say work but with my occupations.

I learned to cook and to clean silver and to mend linen. I couldn't tell my servants what to do, Bridie said, if I didn't know how myself.

Aunt Lucy persuaded me to come on the board of the day nursery of which Mother had been founder and president. It was a small, old-fashioned place, but we took care of the children of a good many working mothers and we knew the children and their families and tried to help with problems beyond the limits of the nursery walls. The nursery has been rebuilt and expanded and is part of a big community center. Roberta is on the board of the center and she assures me that it's a hard-working board though larger than ours was and with more varied and impersonal duties. There was, for instance, no fund raising in our day. We supported the nursery ourselves and we engaged and supervised the housekeeper and the kindergarten teacher. It was a completely amateur project and we would today be dismissed as Lady Bountifuls, but we cared about the children and did our best for them.

I occupied myself while Bertie worked hard first at Columbia and then in the firm with Pops. And we had fun. The twenties were carefree years to be young in. Irresponsible is a favorite word for them but present critics have the advantage of knowing what was coming. While we were living in it that decade was not shadowed by the Depression and wars that were waiting and I look back on it with cheerful nostalgia if that isn't an impossible contradiction in terms.

It was a time of innovations large and small. Prohibition was one and women's suffrage was another, and both were received with applause as well as derision. There were more and more aeroplanes flying longer and longer distances, and the air was also invisibly filled with waves that mysteriously brought voices and music to our radios.

In small, frivolous ways, my friends and I were innovators. Make-up that could readily be recognized as such was new and as exciting to discover as a glittering mask for fancy dress. Our clothes were the prettiest and yet the simplest I had ever known and the most daring, as skirts grew shorter and shorter. Our hair was short too, shorter even than Irene Castle's, and smooth and shining and close to our heads. My bob looks rather full and deeply water-waved in photographs, but on the day Mr. Saveli cut it, I felt as sleek and frisky as a shorn lamb.

Everything was newer and younger than it had ever been, fashion and music and the theater. There never was such a decade for new stars and new music and new springs of laughter. There were rising stars in all the lively arts, here and abroad, but American laughter and American music are what still echo in my mind. I remember with pleasure Don Marquis' Mehitabel and scraps of Dorothy Parker's verse and of Ring Lardner's dialogue and a Robert Benchley monologue in a Broadway revue. There were lots of revues, summer ones and winter ones, there were new syncopated rhythms to which everybody stepped and new tunes to sing in every season. It seems to me that there were more memorable songs in the first ten years of my marriage than in all the rest of my years put together.

I had never known New York in summer, at least not for more than a few days at a time, but Bertie and I spent much of our summers in the city, and its summer settings were a delightful novelty to me.

In the Ritz, the Japanese garden really was a green garden of plants and miniature trees with a cool brook winding beneath its bridges. When my friends and I, in our flowered chiffons and our wide-brimmed hats, lunched there, we were arrayed for a garden party and would not have been put to shame at a royal one.

The Central Park Casino was not far from the Mall, and it was odd and as magical as Sir James Barrie's ball in Kensington Gardens to dance through June and July nights next door to my old winter playground.

Nearly everyone, I imagine, has a time when it was very heaven to be young, and mine is my first decade with Bertie.

Roberta used to laugh in astonishment at the idea of its having been a lovely decade and its people pretty to look at.

"I'm sure you were pretty, Mummie," she would say politely,

"but, honestly, those clothes! You can't tell me you really think they were attractive."

I didn't try to tell her but since then, the twenties have been rediscovered and Roberta reads Scott Fitzgerald and listens to early Cole Porter. She looks at my old photographs and asks about the customs of my youth. She makes me feel rather like a period piece as Aunt Lucy must have felt when I asked about the seventies and eighties with interest but as if they were an era as remote as the Renaissance.

"You didn't actually? How sweet and dear of you," Roberta says, not making fun but as if she really thinks it was sweet and dear of us to wear our hats and gloves all day long, to pin orchids on our evening dresses and to have the nerve to wear yards of imitation pearls and diamonds and colored stones if they were put together by Chanel or Lanvin, not by Woolworth. She likes to hear about tea dancing and party calls and Fifth Avenue mansions.

"The Roaring Twenties," she says, and shakes her head. "You make them sound quaintly innocent and not wild at all. I don't expect you and Daddy to have been, but after all, Mummie, the Jazz Age, flappers, bathtub gin, you must have known some pretty wild parties and people."

Some were wild, I tell her, some always are.

"Your father and I weren't stuffy," I add indignantly, "but neither were we idiots. For one thing we managed to avoid wood alcohol. Your father always carried a flask of my father's scotch in case the liquid refreshment should prove to be of doubtful quality. But we went to speakeasies and we danced at the Montmartre and the Lido, and not Viennese waltzes either, we were as expert as anybody at the toddle and the Charleston. We drove or were driven to football games and to roadhouses and to balls as far away as Philadelphia. Your father had a raccoon coat down to his ankles for winter excursions and he looked wonderful in it. And the motorcars were cars to remember. There were town cars that were like elegant little rooms with silk shades at the windows and gold and crystal fittings including a vase for flowers, and there were smart runabouts and high-powered roadsters that raced along the macadam highways. And you could tell one car from another, they weren't the humpbacked look-alikes of nowadays."

Not long ago I stopped myself in the middle of some such outburst and Roberta smiled and said, "Don't stop, I like to hear."

So I told her a little more of what it was like when the century and I were young.

What is impossible to describe to Roberta or anyone who wasn't there is our sense of freedom, of living in a wider, less rigidly conventional world. The Old Guard was still with us to lay down the law, but society's laws and customs were changing at an ever increasing speed. The young were in charge and we were on our way. "To where?" Roberta might ask, and I can only answer that it was a fast ride and a smooth one and seemed, at the time, to have a destination.

11

DURING the summer and autumn that followed the Thompsons' party Sophie Wenger appeared to be moving in the direction of divorce. The general opinion was that she was behaving beautifully.

Augie was living at the Ritz, and in their Beacon Street house, a few blocks from the hotel, Sophie maintained a dignified silence. She didn't say a word against either Augie or Esther, at least none that was reported. She was described by her friends as waiting for the talk to die down before she made a legal move; the recent flare-up of the old scandal was not her fault, poor thing, and for the sake of her two young daughters she would do nothing to fan the flames. It was on her children's account that she had endured an unhappy marriage for so long, the friends said, but no one could blame her if after this latest brazenly public incident, she had had enough.

No one did blame her except, to my surprise, my sister Julia.

In January Julia and James returned to Washington where James was to be attached to the State Department for a while. As soon as they were settled in the Dupont Circle house, Julia came to New York to see if I knew more than what was common gossip.

"What's Sophie up to?" she asked. "She must have been fed to her back teeth with Augie for years. When we were in Paris, James heard from a Boston colleague that during the war, before we were in it, there was a lot of talk about Augie and some girl. Augie is really the limit, the girl was not only young and unmarried, but good family besides. The affair was broken off by her parents and she was packed off to a finishing school in the South somewhere, but Sophie must have known. I wonder if Esther does."

I said I hoped Julia wasn't planning to tell her.

"I would if I thought it would be the slightest use, but it wouldn't be, nothing would, she's been too long and too deeply involved with Augie for anything to—"

"Oh please, oh please," I said, unable to think of any more effective words with which to keep Julia from starting in on Esther.

"Calm down, Nell, I won't say any more. You know what I think and I know you don't agree. Anyway, it's not what we think that matters, it's what the world thinks. And this long-drawn-out martyr act of Sophie's is stirring everything up again. If she intends to get a divorce she should have had the sense and, I may say, the grace to go quickly and quietly to Reno. If she didn't want to spare Esther, she might have given a thought to the rest of us. This is a touchy thing for James. I can see a decent European post going right out the window. I don't understand why Sophie chooses to behave in this antediluvian prewar fashion. It's no good for her children if she cares so much about them. You want to know what I think? I think there's another man and she's laying the groundwork for future Back Bay respectability. I may be wrong, perhaps she's just holding out for a record-breaking settlement. One thing I'll bet you isn't broken and that's that self-righteous, practical, little New England heart of hers."

I told Julia that as far as I could make out, Sophie had done nothing we could fault her for.

"Nothing except sit on display in her Beacon Street mausoleum like patience on a monument, the brave, long-suffering wife smiling at grief and sucking up sympathy and turning everybody against Esther all over again." Julia added that I obviously couldn't tell her anything and Esther wouldn't so she might as well go back to Washington and sit tight.

"Without seeing Esther?"

"I can't, it wouldn't do any good. Besides, I promised James I wouldn't get mixed up in this unfortunate situation. Don't look like that, Nell, it's easy enough for you with Bertie's future wrapped up for him like a Christmas package by Pops. It's different in the foreign service, even a Henderson can be penalized according to the rules of the game and believe me the rules are strict. As James says, the faintest breath of scandal is poison gas to the State Department."

I had not deceived Julia; there was nothing I could tell her. Esther and I had not mentioned Augie's name nor spoken of the party where they met.

The first time we talked about him was on a spring day when Julia was back in Washington. It was still February, but on that afternoon the air was mild and windless and the sun was warm on my face. It felt like April as I walked down Park Avenue to the street where Esther lived. Dressmaker weather is what we called days like this one that anticipated a future season and sent us hurrying to the shops. Bendel and Bergdorf Goodman were probably already showing advance Paris models, and visions of new spring clothes danced in my head as I entered Esther's living room.

I stood still and couldn't say a word. The thought of spring clothes must have reminded me of the May afternoons when I shopped for my trousseau. On one of those afternoons I had first seen Esther's house. The two spring days—though one, according to the calendar, was a day in winter—are paired in my memory. On the first, the room was dressed for summer, and beyond the windows the garden was in bloom and Esther spoke in a dead voice of Pa's future day. Presently she stopped talking and walked to a window. When she turned back to me and spoke of her pretty house her voice seemed as light and youthful as usual. Now as Esther greeted me, I stared at her and listened and wondered how all of us, even I who loved her so dearly could have managed to grow used to the way she sounded, the way she looked during the years in which she came to realize that Pa was right when he told her she was a young woman with all the time in the world, the years in which she slowly discovered that in that entire expanse of time no fine day was waiting for her.

Today Esther looked and sounded young again, younger than Mother smiling at us across the sunlit grass.

I stood with my mouth open. I didn't realize I was gaping like a fish until Esther gently pushed my jaw into place and laughed and said, "I must be transparent as a pane of glass for my good news to show so plainly."

I had forgotten that Esther could laugh quite like that. Suddenly I remembered her playing with Rikki and me on the floor of his nursery and the three of us laughing and laughing. And I remembered, not wanting to, the way she looked and sounded in the Southampton summer with Augie.

"Don't you want to hear my news?" she asked. "Or have you guessed?"

"I've guessed, but I want to hear." And I made myself look pleased as Esther told me she had had a long-distance call from Augie an hour ago and everything was settled. The separation agreement was signed and Sophie would leave for Nevada with her daughters in June after their school closed.

"June! That means a long wait. Oh, Esther, I'm sorry."

"Don't be, don't be. Or be sorry for me if you like. I don't need to arm myself against pity any more. Yes, it'll be quite a long wait, but don't you know, can't I make you see how good it is to have something to wait for? Waiting isn't bad, Nell, waiting is hope. I had pretty well forgotten about hope, it's lovely to have it back."

It was a pleasure to be with Esther in that springtime. She was at her ease, not on guard any more. Perhaps it was I who was no longer on guard against saying the accidentally hurtful word or asking a question she could not answer, but she was different too. Because she could see the future plain, she was able to talk freely about the present and the past, even about unhappy things.

"I mind about Rikki," she said. "I mind his having grown into a stranger whom I've never seen, even in a photograph. My Rikki is still playing in his nursery on Murray Hill, he doesn't exist at all except in my memory." Her eyes filled with tears and she didn't try to keep them from falling. "I thought when he came East to prep school I might have a chance to see him, but apparently Richmond thought so too and he sent him to a school in California. I mind terribly, Nell. I'll mind until I die, but I'll be able to bear it, I'll be able to bear anything now that I have someone to love, now that I have Augie."

Esther knew that Aunt Lucy was uneasy about the attitude the world would take toward her and Augie after they were married, but I told her not to worry.

"I don't mean to sound like James," I said, "but Aunt Lucy is no longer young, she belongs to another generation and has no idea how the world has changed since the war."

"Even if Aunt Lucy's anxiety should be justified it wouldn't matter to me and I don't believe it would to Augie. He loves me, you know."

I agreed in what I hoped was a confident voice but I wasn't in the least sure of Augie.

They had decided, Esther told me, to do nothing to jeopardize their situation now that Sophie had consented to the divorce. Augie would not come to New York even on business.

"I don't think," Esther said, "that Sophie can back out at this stage but I won't feel safe until she gets her decree. Father always said that any legal situation can be treacherous until it's finally settled. Besides, as I told Augie, I owe it to Father to behave in this interval in what he would consider a proper manner."

Esther also consented to go abroad with Aunt Lucy, once Sophie was in Nevada, and to remain there until after the divorce was granted.

In May, Maud learned about the proposed trip from Julia, and she and Louis asked Esther and Aunt Lucy to stay with them in Neuilly.

Esther was so astonished and delighted when she showed me the cabled invitation that I wanted to cry.

"Don't you know we all love you?" I asked. "Even Julia in her peculiar way."

"Peculiar is the word," Esther said, "and it seems very peculiar to me to have my younger sister sitting in judgment on me, but I've grown used to it. Perhaps now she will relent, if James will let her, that is. It will be simpler for all of you once Augie and I are married. Even you feel awkward about seeing him, Nell."

When I uncomfortably denied this, she pointed out that in the past year I had never dropped in on her unannounced, thus avoiding any possibility of running into him.

"He's coming to say good-by. I couldn't refuse us that. He'll be here on the afternoon of the day before Aunt Lucy and I sail. Won't you come in for a little while to say hello to him?"

I was worried about my ability to meet Augie in friendly fashion, but I knew that however difficult that meeting in June proved to be I must get through it and get through it well.

The day of the meeting turned out to be one of Mr. Lowell's rare ones, not too hot, with a soft cool breeze, but when I turned into Esther's block, my hands were wet with perspiration as I nervously buttoned and unbuttoned my suede gloves and finally pulled them off and dried my hands with them. The gloves would be ruined but I didn't want to start off by giving Augie a clammy handshake.

Bridie opened the door to me and before I could say more than two words to her, Augie came running down the stairs.

For a moment I held back, arming myself against this smiling damned villain, but as he spoke and I answered and we went up to Esther together, he wasn't a villain, or if he was he was a person too. He wasn't a walking prototype of evil, he wasn't an actor to hiss across the footlights, he was just Augie Wenger who had played Parcheesi with me long ago and given me an orchid. I had been determined, for Esther's sake, to act as if nothing had happened in the intervening years to make me hate Augie and it turned out to be astonishingly easy.

At a deep level of feeling I still hated Augie, hated what he had done to Esther, messing up her life and leaving his own safe and tidy. And it was perfectly clear in my mind that Father's judgment of him and his behavior was correct. Nevertheless, I found myself liking him. Poets have told us that love and hate can exist side by side, but liking? It was odd, I thought, as we sat at Esther's tea table, but apparently liking as well as love could co-exist with hate.

The fact was, of course, that Augie was a charmer and like

every true charmer, he didn't behave like one. I was the one who seemed a charmer as we talked. I realized that this was one of Augie's secrets of pleasing, it was always the other person who became more attractive: an old lady seemed younger and prettier and a child, as I well remembered, felt older and more important.

Today, what should have been an embarrassing occasion for me was a comfortable one. I didn't know how Augie had managed it and except for the realization that he had managed it, I didn't think about myself or my unconventional situation in being with Esther and Augie, I was too busy observing them.

Our conversation was general, pleasantly skimming surfaces, and our spoons rattled lightly against china as we talked and sipped our tea and ate paper-thin bread and butter, and all the time I was aware of a blaze of love that should have lit up the room like a Fourth of July sky. People use a variety of words nowadays, fixation, obsession, compulsion, commitment, but the one I am accustomed to is love, and since it has been defined in a thousand different ways it seems as good as any.

I had been unsure of Augie where Esther was concerned, had remembered Father asking if Augie loved her or did he just want to have her on the side? Watching Augie now as he looked at Esther, hearing the hoarse little break in his voice when he pronounced her name, I had the answer to half Father's question. Whether or not this was what Father meant by love, whether or not Augie loved Esther as Father had loved Mother —and what two people love in the same way?—Augie didn't want to have Esther on the side. She was at the center of things for him. Julia had said Esther was deeply involved with Augie. Well, if she was, so was he with her.

The first time I ever saw them together I was startled by the way they matched each other in beauty, not alike in coloring or features, but equal. On this June day I saw that they matched each other in love. Whatever one chose to call the love that held them, it was plain to me that both were bound by it, not in like manner perhaps, but equally.

I was happy for Esther and I tried to explain to Bertie why I felt this unexpected happiness and hope for her.

"This is what she wants, Bertie, what she's wanted and done without all these years and now she has it. Whether it's right or wrong or however it turns out, she has it for now. She has Augie as completely as he has her."

"Maybe so. You're usually an accurate reporter, Nell, but in this case you want so desperately to believe things can be made right for Esther."

"It's not what I want to believe, honestly it isn't, it's what I saw. When you're with them, you'll see. Even a blind man would. All he'd have to do would be to listen to the sound of their voices. I won't try to tell you any more. Except this surprising thing: in spite of everything that has happened one can't help liking Augie."

"I can. I always could."

Bertie wore his rigid granite-faced look with which it is hopeless to argue. Sometimes, I said crossly, but only to myself, Bertie is too much like Pa for comfort.

"Don't be cross, Nell." (With Bertie it's no use not to say a thing out loud.) "And don't worry, I won't let him see how I feel. Matter of fact, I don't suppose the thought that he could be disliked ever crosses Augie's mind."

"You think he's vain? He never seems so."

"Probably he is, but it doesn't matter. The fact is that people usually do like him, even your father to begin with, and he was a shrewd judge of men."

"It's easy to like Augie. I don't know why."

"He makes it easy, he responds so naturally, with such pleasure and always just the right touch of shyness. I had plenty of chances to study Augie and his ways during that summer in Southampton and a twelve-year-old boy is pretty hard to charm. I made up my mind about him then and I've found no reason to change it since. Maybe I will after he and Esther are married. I hope so for her sake, hope he'll change is what I mean, but I doubt it."

Esther and Augie were married in Paris in December. Aunt Lucy and Maud and Louis were present at the civil ceremony after which they returned to the Martins' house where a reception was held. The marriage was formally announced in the *Paris Herald* by Maud and Louis.

This pleased me, but it surprised me, and I said so to Aunt Lucy when she returned to New York.

"Catholics feel so strongly about divorce, I'd have thought Maud and Louis would have boggled at . . ."

"Not Louis, not for a minute," Aunt Lucy said. "He's the nearest to a Quaker Catholic I've ever known. There's nothing rigid about him."

"I still wouldn't have believed that Maud would ever condone anything her church is as strict about as divorce. You know how she can carry on, even to you, about the Apostolic Succession and Anglican Orders."

"My dear child, you should have heard her, a first-class casuist was lost to the Jesuits when Maud was born a woman. She spoke briskly about invincible ignorance and an erroneously formed conscience. Then having made her position clear, at least to herself, she grinned at me, you know that ten-year-old grin of hers, and said of course Esther wasn't going to be married from anywhere but her sister's house."

Aunt Lucy told me that the reception was admirably planned. Julia couldn't have got up a better guest list or one more ap-

propriate for what might have been a difficult occasion instead
of the lovely one Maud and Louis made of it. Most of those
present were French, but there were a few members of the American colony as well.

"I wouldn't have expected the French to be there," I said,
"they're Catholics. But perhaps artists are different."

"French society was as well represented as the arts. Maud's
real triumph was in getting any Americans to come."

Aunt Lucy added that Louis had explained the French to her.
Society and the arts he told her, were more interested in each
other than in an old New York scandal they never heard of.
"Mind you," he said, "the Faubourg St. Germain is a bit *collet
monté,* even the ones our age won't receive a remarried European divorcée, but Americans are different, we're not quite people to them. In their eyes we're all red Indians, and divorce is
just one more of our queer tribal customs which must be accepted
if we are to be accepted. And they want to accept us; we're rich
and we amuse them and some of them even like us."

It was a charming and a festive gathering, Aunt Lucy said, and
Esther looked radiant. She also looked radiant at the Mairie,
which was neither a charming nor a festive place. "Here you can
see for yourself, dear, though the newspaper picture is a little
blurred."

As I looked at the photograph in the *Paris Herald* of Esther
and Augie leaving the Mairie, I could see. As I listened to Aunt
Lucy, I could hear. At last for Esther the future day had arrived,
not as Pa had imagined it, but a fine day all the same.

The twenties held fine days for all of us.

Not long after Esther's marriage, while Julia and James were
in Washington their daughter Judy was born.

Julia was delighted. "One of each," she said, "now I don't
have to have any more. A girl is fun for a man and she takes

some of the pressure off the boy. Actually, for young James's sake I might try to have another boy someday. James says Norman is sharp as a tack in business matters, not that James is any slouch, but now he can concentrate on his career and leave the financial end of things to his brother."

James did not have to wait long to get one of the foreign posts on which his heart was set. Let me think, there was Berne and Copenhagen but I can't remember which came first or whether he was chargé in Rome before them or between them. Vienna and Brussels were in Mr. Roosevelt's time, I'm almost sure.

By the mid-twenties James's career was well launched, and he continued to be successful during the Roosevelt administrations. As a career diplomat, James was politically neutral but his father was a rock-ribbed upper New York State Republican until his death in 1937. However, as Bertie pointed out to me, Senator Henderson was no damn fool either, and he undoubtedly found a means, after the national tide turned in 1932, to contribute quietly but generously to the Democratic party as well as to his own.

Louis Guarrigue Martin, Junior, was born in 1925. I can't always pinpoint a year in the twenties, but I cannot forget the date of his birth.

Louis vainly protested Maud's choice of a name for their son. There was no such thing as Junior in French, he said, and the boy would be known as *le p'tit Louis* and would hate it. However, Maud had her way and the child was registered at the United States Consulate as Louis Guarrigue Martin, Junior. Since his father did not use his middle name it would serve to identify le p'tit Louis to French friends.

"A mouthful of a name for someone so small," Louis said to me at the christening, "but it's what Maud wants and I think I'm pleased. Let me be frank, I know I'm pleased."

Le p'tit Louis left that name behind when he went to school and was known from then on as Gar Martin. Maud learned to call him Gar, but sometimes to me and, I imagine, to Julia and Esther she referred to him as le p'tit Louis. It was much later and only for a short time that Gar used the nickname of his early childhood.

I don't want to think about later. I want to think about our lighthearted young years.

I realize, looking back at those years, that what seemed to be a journey from here to somewhere else had in fact no more direction that a smooth fast spin on Mr. Willie K. Vanderbilt's motor parkway to Lake Ronkonkoma and back.

It's difficult to remember in accurate sequence that brief fantastic period. It was a minor interlude rather than an era of importance, but a minor interlude is agreeable to live in, is delicious to be young in. For me it was a plateau of time in which I was always the same age. Before that I was growing up and each year as I changed with it is easily identifiable. I was a small child, I was a big child, I was almost a young lady, I was out. I was five, I was ten, I was thirteen, sixteen, eighteen. In the twenties, mine and the century's, things around me changed but I didn't, I was young forever. My thirtieth birthday, that bleak landmark for the women of my generation, was as far away and as improbable as my fiftieth.

I once said to Bertie, as I had said of us at our wedding, that we were like actors. "We're like actors on a treadmill in an elaborate stage production. We seem to be moving but actually we're standing happily still while the pretty scenery of our time goes by."

"Enjoy it," Bertie said. "I think we'll enjoy all our years one way or another but let's enjoy these while we can, they look darn near unbeatable to me."

For Bertie there was more change—more progress and purpose I mean—than for me. He graduated from law school and went to work for the firm where Pops had already begun to delegate some authority to his younger partner, Uncle Phil Sheldon. Bertie was not made a partner until the early thirties, but from the beginning, his father and uncle treated him as if he were part of the firm and gave him a certain amount of responsibility and, it seemed to me, a good deal of hard work. On most weekday evenings he brought home a stack of papers, but he didn't mind.

"I'm lucky," he said. "The firm's just right for me. I like the investment end, trusts and real estate and such. I was good at puzzles when I was a kid, the cannibals and the missionaries and all the tricky logical and arithmetical ones. High finance is a bit like that, takes the same sort of ingenuity, though I won't make our rich clients uneasy by telling them so. And I like people, like working out their problems. People trust us and bring us all sorts of personal and family problems; seems to me we've inherited much of the work that ministers and doctors used to do. Pops is a whiz at money matters, but his unique quality is that for these New York families he takes the place of a country doctor or clergyman."

Bertie explained to me before he went to the firm that he could not discuss its clients with me. "No more," he said, "than a doctor can discuss his patients."

"But they do. You know they do, Bertie. Doctors can be awful gossips."

"Some of them talk, I guess. Some lawyers, too, but we don't."

I would get used to this, Ma told me, and it was good for our husbands to get away from the firm and its concerns when they were with us.

"Nice for us, too, my dear," she added. "In many professions and indeed in many law firms, men must go in for client hunting and client coddling after hours and their wives have to help. It's agreeable to be free, as you and I are, to have people to dine or to stay because one likes them, not because it's financially advantageous to entertain them."

As a rule we spent Bertie's two-week summer vacation and our weekends with Ma and Pops. Since there were just the two of us there was no point to our having a Southampton place of our own. When Bertie was in town so was I.

The year Gar was born Pops decided that Bertie had been working hard and deserved a proper vacation, and we went abroad for May and June and most of July.

We got to Paris the day before Gar's christening and we were also in time to see Louis' painting *La Biche Dorée* exhibited. Julia had written me about its success and art-minded friends in New York had mentioned it respectfully.

It was a sunlit painting of the small Trianon, though the light was not quite usual. I always think of the scene as having an edge of wind and darkness but when I see it the air is still and bright. There are no shadows, that's the queer thing about the light. It's high noon, a higher, more vertical noon than one has ever seen. The elegant little building, drained of color, is like an architectural drawing of itself, but grass and trees and flowers are brilliant and lush, one can almost see them growing. They are strong and living; the little Trianon holds itself apart, stiff and silent, and one can imagine it overgrown and deserted. At first there seems, even now, not to be a human being in sight. There are no Boucher or Watteau ladies and attendant gentlemen, there is only the white deer asleep on the lawn at the foot of the stone steps. Then one looks again and, yes, there is a figure, half seen, standing in the embrasure of a partly opened window, a girl or a woman, one can't tell which. All that can be clearly seen is a slender, white, jeweled hand that holds back a gleaming brocade curtain. The deer is young, scarcely more than a fawn, and its hoofs are gilded. Its neck is encircled by a gold and diamond necklace from which hangs a pendant of large, flawless rubies that shine darkly in the bright, motionless light. Slowly—or perhaps quickly if one's eye is quicker than mine—one sees that they aren't rubies, but drops and clots of blood and the deer is not sleeping but dead.

When we went to visit James and Julia, Julia said to me, "Louis found his genre, after all, didn't he? Rather a peculiar one, if you ask me, but he's having success and I'm glad for Maud. It's just as well he didn't go in for portraits, he'd have to do Maud. I know he's devoted to her and she must somehow seem pretty to him, but his painter's eye would see her honestly and that would be hard on her, crueler than a mirror—a woman gets used to her mirror. Anyway fashionable portrait painters are getting to be a dime a dozen. Louis has taken a queer tack, but people who know tell me it's an interesting one and that we have a good chance of having a distinguished artist in the family."

We arrived at Julia's in time for her summer party. Wherever Julia's parties were held, they were the same. They weren't monotonously alike, but they all were done in her unmistakable style. It was a gay style and a warm and welcoming one. The dining room and the ballroom and garden or terrace were decorated for the occasion in Julia's special manner, formal enough to please the Europeans but never oppressively so. The dinner music was furnished by a local string orchestra, but the dance band was imported from Paris or London or New York. Bertie once said to me that one can't explain what makes a successful party any more than what makes a hit show; on stage or in a ballroom, the production either jells or it doesn't. Julia's parties always jelled, and wherever James was posted illustrious and

amusing guests made their way to the Hendersons' summer
party.

Julia gave dinners and receptions in every season, but it was
her summer dance that was considered the party of the year by
the international set. The cosmopolitan flavor makes it difficult
to recall which party was held in which capital. Statesmen and
royalties—and not only minor ones by any means—traveled halfway across Europe to Julia's party so their presence gives no
clue to the date or the place, but, of course, it was Berne in 1925,
because the year Gar was born was the year in which I saw
Mademoiselle for the last time.

I had never thought of Mademoiselle as young but neither
had I thought of her as old, she just seemed the usual age for a
grownup. She told me when I was a child that she was older
than Bridie but the difference between them was imperceptible
to me. When Mademoiselle greeted us at the door of her house
in Geneva her hair was white, and I saw with a shock that she
was old.

She was, she said, delighted to see us, seeing was better than
hearing but she did hear all our news from that dear Bridie
Smith who wrote regularly. I felt a pang of guilt which Mademoiselle must have seen in my face because she quickly said
there was no need for any of us to write letters. Our Christmas
and birthday cards were enough. They told her that she was
affectionately remembered by her girls. *"Mes petites filles
modèles.* You remember I used to call you that?"

I remembered. I remembered when she started me on the
Bibliothèque Rose and then at the exact wise moment let me go
on by myself.

I'm glad we went to Geneva and saw the neat and cheerful
house she shared with her younger widowed sister. I remember
the shock of seeing her old, with white hair and with her straight

back bent and her hands swollen with rheumatism. I remember this as a fact, but it's not how I remember Mademoiselle.

I see Mademoiselle as she looked when she read me *Les Malheurs de Sophie,* I see her quick competent little hands as she taught me how to do gros point. My hands were not as deft as hers and petit point was too much for me. Gros point was more practical in any case, she said, it was a longer-lasting occupation. One could not always count on the strength of the eyes as one grew older.

Gros point is a nice memento of Mademoiselle, a nice legacy to keep. I often think of her as I work at it, as I'm working now on Bertie's Christmas slippers. This year they're black with a scarlet monogram. They'll go well with his smart new wrapper from Sulka that I gave him for his birthday. If I can ever get him to wear his new wrapper, that is.

I hear Annie in the kitchen; she must be back from Mass. Annie is my legacy from Bridie. It was in the late thirties that Bridie brought her to me and told me to start her off as an in-between maid.

"Like that she'll learn from the ground up. Margaret will train her for you," Bridie said. "Annie's inexperienced and a bit young, but she's a widow, poor little soul, so if you're lucky she'll have got marriage out of her system and will last your time. She'll keep your house running smoothly and find good girls to help her. Annie will be a comfort to you when you're old."

Annie has lasted my time, will last it out, I hope, and she is a comfort to me.

As she brings in my tray, I smile at her with the affection which, being old-fashioned in our ways, we rarely express, though we both know it's there.

"You didn't ring," Annie says, "you didn't even see me when I looked in a while ago. You've a trick of forgetting lunch when the Mister's not here and that's bad for you. I've fixed you an egg Benedict, you always like that."

"I was thinking and I forgot the time."

"If you can think while you do that French sewing, you can think while you eat. Now don't let your food get cold."

While I start to eat my lunch I go on thinking of old times and of some of the small frivolous things that made them good times. There was vanity for instance, it comes naturally to the young, to anyone of any age, I guess, but when one was young vanity was more becoming and less painful. At any rate it was so natural that I was scarcely aware of it in myself or my contemporaries. We were pretty to look at face to face or in a mirror. The plainest of us was prettier than any of us are now, and I enjoy looking back at us.

I remember a Newport wedding sometime in the early twenties. The bride was an heiress and quite lovely, beautiful really, in a laughing, dark-eyed way. The sensational press wrote her up at length as "The Golden Girl" and I thought proudly to myself: Muriel's awfully pretty with that mass of black curls and her enormous eyes but she's not exactly a golden girl, my sisters and I are the golden girls with our hair that has kept its fairness long past childhood, even Esther, especially Esther, her hair is bright as spun gold, red gold.

Golden girls. At quite a few levels of meaning the name would have suited us. *Golden lads and girls all must . . .* Oh dear, sometimes I regret the ease with which a quotation can pop into my head. Our generation doesn't quote out loud as much as our elders did but all the same we're walking Bartletts. *Golden lads and girls all must as chimney sweepers . . .* A quotation can run around your brain just as persistently as a tune, and I wish this one would stop. *Golden lads and girls all must as chimney sweepers come to dust.* Well, so they must, and I push back my tray and pick up my gros point again. So they must and so they have, but better on the whole, and more fun while it lasted, to have been golden girls, as we were, than drab and dreary ones.

12

I THINK I'll have this slipper finished before Julia gets back from
the Colony Club. She'll bring all the current New York news
with her and sort it out for me.

"You want to know what I think?" I can hear her crisp amused
voice and I can see her biting that rosy, bee-stung lower lip of
hers as she unravels a thread of gossip for our entertainment.
It's Julia's young voice that I hear in my head and the curve of
her full young lips that I see, but she hasn't changed all that
much, at least not to my eyes and ears. Her voice still sounds
light as a girl's as she gives an outrageous interpretation to some
bit of gossip. "My dear, you won't believe it at their age, but
my guess is . . ."

Julia can add two and two and get any number that suits her,
but she's interested in people and curious about them and often
enough to satisfy her, her wild guess turns out to be an accurate
prediction.

I remember how triumphant she was that she had guessed
right about Sophie Wenger.

Within six months of Esther and Augie's marriage, Sophie
married a recently widowed friend of her youth. I never met
Bradford Howell, but from all accounts he was personable in a
stately Boston way.

Sophie's friends said that Brad, God bless him, had been a

tower of strength to her all through her marital difficulties, and they rejoiced over her well-deserved happiness.

"Tower of strength, my foot," Julia said. "Bostonians are as human as the rest of us. I'll hand it to Sophie, though, she's past mistress of the art of having one's cake and eating it. She has her settlement from Augie, which I hear was no mean sum, she has Brad and his comfortable inheritance, and in the eyes of the world she's entitled to all the cake she can lay her hands on." Julia frowned and bit her lower lip. "Oh well, oh dear," she said, "poor Esther, poor girl."

"Honestly, Julia, you're the limit," I said with some asperity, "you never said poor Esther when you should have, and now when she's happy, you're sorry for her."

"I hope she's happy. Augie was a pretty costly piece of cake for her."

It was natural for Julia to be dubious about Esther and Augie. They didn't lead the kind of life she could understand. They traveled a lot but not necessarily to the fashionable place at the fashionable moment. They might be in Venice in August but they were just as likely to be there in May. They went to the Riviera in winter as often as in the newly fashionable summer season. They went where they pleased when they pleased. When they came to New York they stayed in Esther's house. It was curious, I thought, that they didn't seem to live anywhere; they stayed here and there and returned and went off again, moving through the world as timelessly as they had once moved through a Southampton summer.

Every good marriage was, I realized, good in its own way. Esther and Augie's way was not like Bertie's and mine, and I wouldn't have exchanged ours for theirs, but theirs seemed romantic, seemed suited to them.

The event that astonished and disturbed me in the early twenties was Baby's divorce. She had been married to Freddy Ransome less than four years when she told me she was leaving him.

"I'm going to Colorado Springs next week, not as obvious as Reno, but Maury Paul's bound to get the story sooner or later, and I don't want you to read my news in his column, though he'll be kind, he's rather a pal of mine. Don't get upset, sweetie, divorce isn't a scandal any more."

"What about Cynthia?" I asked.

"I have custody with no strings. Freddy doesn't mind, I'll let him see her whenever he likes. Anyway he never wanted a girl, and now he can marry a den mother type and have all the boys he wants. A daughter is what I wanted and I'm keeping her. I wouldn't give Cynthia up for all the money or all the love in the world, not for Harry Parker or any man."

I looked up, startled.

I had met the Parkers at Baby's. They were friends of the Thompsons, though Harry Parker was less parochially Texan than Herbert Thompson. The Parker Ranch had been famous for two generations, and it symbolized wealth far beyond its wide boundaries.

Freddy Ransome preferred the Parkers to the Thompsons, not because of their vast fortune, he had assured me, but because they were more our sort than the Thompsons. Harry's mother was good family, Philadelphia Main Line, and his wife came from Chicago and was related to old Mrs. Henderson.

"What has Harry Parker got to do with this?" I asked.

"Nothing except that I'm going to marry him. I hadn't meant to tell you yet, his name slipped out. Don't worry, their divorce has gone through. Janie got it in Texas. Since Harry owns half the state, it wasn't hard for him to arrange matters quietly."

I stared at Baby in bewilderment. She was too sensible to get into this kind of mess. I told her that she didn't know what she was letting herself in for.

"Nothing embarrassing, Nell, I promise you. Harry had nothing to do with Freddy and me splitting up—whatever people may think, and they don't think long about anything nowadays. Harry's just the man who was there. There's always someone there to give a shaky marriage the final push. Freddy and I are fond of each other, or would be if we weren't married, but we get on each other's nerves."

Baby sighed and pushed her glasses to the top of her head. Her words came in a rush. "My friends and my parties bore Freddy, and his bank and the way he walks on eggs for its holy sake bore me. And the old New York inner circle that's a cozy nest to him is a tight little cage as far as I'm concerned. Oh, I like the people we grew up with, but what is the sense of living in the biggest city in the biggest country in the world and limiting oneself to the brownstone set? Their point of view gets tiresome. Aren't you irritated by those questions that put people on a par with race horses? Who are they? Who was she before she was married? Who was his grandfather? Never: Are they attractive? Are they talented? Are they fun? I felt that if Freddy asked me once more: But who are they, Baby? I'd scream at him: Who are we for God's sake? If I had, he'd have told me: he'd have climbed our family trees branch by branch to the signer, to Washington's aide, to the eminent New England divine, to the Mayflower Company. Poor Freddy, there must be things he wanted to scream at me, not that he ever did or would. Controlled is the word for that boy. We'd have ended up hating each other and that wouldn't have been good for Cynthia. She's better off this way. And Freddy will find a nice girl; girls die over his looks."

When she paused to catch her breath, I tried to point out that

someone was bound to be hurt. She ought to realize, it seemed
to me, that I knew a good deal more about divorce than she did.

"Please stop and think, Baby," I said. "Go slow. A divorce
always hurts someone."

"Not in this case, not even Janie Parker. She doesn't like
Harry's wider world, doesn't like him much, I've often thought.
She'll stay in Texas and finish bringing up their two boys and
be happy as a clam. She might even remarry."

Baby put her glasses on her nose and studied me.

"You are upset," she said. "I guess I sound heartless and
frivolous, but I'm not really, at least that's not all I am."

"I know, Baby, I know."

"I've been miserable with Freddy, and it hasn't been much fun
for him either."

"Divorce isn't fun," I said. "I've seen it and I'm afraid for you."

"Of course, you are. What a tactless idiot I am!" Baby jumped
lightly to her feet. "But you needn't be scared for me. Honestly,
you needn't. Divorce and marriage aren't taken as seriously as
they used to be, the good old until death us do part is just something you say in church. Times have changed, Nell, maybe the
change is for the better, maybe for the worse, who can tell? All
I know is, it's a lucky break for me and I'm on my merry way."

I worried about Baby. I knew divorce wasn't frowned on as it
had been, but it was accepted only for some good reason. If a
husband drank to excess or was flagrantly unfaithful, the wife's
wish to be free was understood, and if she remarried, that was
thought natural enough. The rule was that someone must be in
the wrong. A man in the wrong was usually quickly forgiven,
but it was essential for a woman to be or to appear to be in the
right. Baby would never get away with divorcing a perfectly nice
husband in order to marry a man who had just been divorced
from a longtime wife for her sake.

I couldn't escape the subject of divorce.

Bertie became involved in picking up the untidy pieces after an outwardly calm and unmessy divorce. I knew about it because the wife was the daughter of a friend of Aunt Lucy's, and Aunt Lucy brought her to dine with us and asked Bertie to straighten out the matters, financial and personal, that the divorce lawyers had left in disorder.

There were questions of wills and estates which Bertie didn't discuss with me in any detail. They were, he said, complicated but not impossible to resolve. What troubled him was the carelessly drawn custody agreement. The parents were on the verge of a legal battle for their son and daughter, and this he was determined to prevent. Children, he said, had a bad time in this sort of litigation; they were friendless little hostages who paid for their parents' war.

This was the first case Bertie won by himself for the firm and he won it without taking it into court. He skillfully disentangled the financial snarls and found the way to a clear and equitable settlement which he persuaded his client and her ex-husband's lawyer to accept.

Pops was pleased with Bertie's handling of the case. He had, I suspect, been a little anxious as three fairly large estates were involved. Bertie was proud of having won Pops' approval but he was more deeply satisfied at having obtained a peaceful compromise on the custody agreement.

"At least the kids won't be scarred by a bitter court fight," he said. "Poor little souls; the smoothest divorce is hard enough. I tell you, Nell, we may see divorce taken for granted and made easy for any couple who want it, but it'll never be anything but a misery for children."

Poor little Cynthia Ransome, I thought, though she's very

young and that may help. Rikki had been young. I wondered how it had been for him, if it had been a misery.

I continued to worry about Baby. The day might come, as Bertie said, when divorce would be taken for granted, but that day wasn't here yet, and I could not imagine that the day would ever come when society would accept without protest a double divorce and remarriage such as Baby was embarked on.

I was wrong. My imagination was moving less rapidly than the times. Baby was mildly criticized. There were a few unpleasant, hurtful remarks, but no doors were closed to her for long even among the brownstones.

Freddy's remarriage within a year helped to silence the critics. He chose as his bride a girl from an old New York family. She was not quite a girl any more, she was close to thirty and her friends and relations who had given up hope of her marrying, were delighted that she was not to be left on the shelf. They must have been grateful to Baby for making the happy event possible, and the unkind talk died down and was heard no more.

Baby didn't say, I told you so; no one who remembered being a child would use that maddening grown-up expression to a friend. Just once when she was describing a Tuxedo ball weekend, she giggled and said, "So you see, Harry and I are on our merry way, not that Harry, any more than I, finds Tuxedo Park particularly merry. At all events, my lamb, you needn't worry about me any more."

I was relieved for Baby, and, as I told Aunt Lucy, I was relieved for Esther.

"Divorce and remarriage are all right now, Aunt Lucy," I said. "Even divorce for the sake of remarriage. I've sometimes been afraid that Esther and Augie lead a wandering life because they have to, not because they want to, but actually they aren't any different from Baby and Harry. Times have changed more than I realized. I'm certain now that Esther is all right."

"I hope so, I pray so—thank goodness your uncle taught me not to be hesitant about prayers of petition for anything close to my heart. But I am concerned for Esther. Times change but landmarks remain. Edith Wharton said it all in her story about the unhappy lady she chose to call Mrs. Lidcote. Society may change its laws but it's much too busy to revise its judgments."

"That's just a clever theme for a short story," I protested. "It hasn't anything to do with how things are now."

Both Aunt Lucy and her friend Mrs. Wharton were old, I told myself, and they saw things in the pattern of their own youth.

I looked about me at the high-ceilinged room. I was used to it and fond of it, but it was a setting from another era. Above the mantel was a heavily framed portrait of Colonel William Gore in his Continental uniform; a coal fire burned in the high, old-fashioned grate; on a side table a maroon velvet easel held a collection of family miniatures; Aunt Lucy's slender feet, shod in beaded bronze slippers, rested on a foot stool that was covered in worn black sateen, embroidered with the Turner crest. The pattern of Aunt Lucy's youth was the pattern of all the American generations that had preceded hers. How could she recognize the changes of our time? Still I would try to make her see.

"There's a new freedom in the air," I said.

"I am aware of that. The world you hankered after when you were fourteen, the wonderful world without rules, is closer at hand than I anticipated."

"Not no rules at all, Aunt Lucy, just easier rules. Is that so bad?"

"I don't know, I merely speculate. However, as far as Esther is concerned, I hope the new freedom is making her life easier. Things have been too hard for her for too long."

Aunt Lucy's eyes filled with tears and I remembered her crying on Esther's first wedding day. She had not been happy about that marriage and she had been right. I wished she would sound more confident of this one.

"You are hopeful for Esther, aren't you?" I asked.

Aunt Lucy paused and dried her eyes before she answered me. "Well, my dear," she said, "as far as I can tell, Esther and Augie are happy together. Whether things are easy for them I don't know, but then nobody knows about a marriage except the two people involved. Marriage is the one entirely secret relationship." She turned up the flame under the hot water kettle. "I'll make us some fresh tea and we'll both feel better. And, Nell, try not to worry about your sister. Anxiety is of no more use than hope and both in my view are sad as well as useless emotions."

It was through little Grace Graham's wedding to Norman Henderson that I learned that Aunt Lucy and Mrs. Wharton were more perceptive observers of the social scene than I had been willing to acknowledge.

That year, 1926 or 1927, somewhere in there, Esther and Augie arrived in New York from Bermuda in July, and I persuaded them to spend the coming weekend in Southampton with Bertie and me. It had to be a quiet weekend, I explained, as Bertie wouldn't get back from Chicago until Friday morning and he would be dog tired. One of the firm's clients had moved his headquarters to Chicago and some corporate complications had set in. Pops had sent Bertie to deal with them.

"We don't have to be gay," Augie said, "and it would be nice to be in Southampton again. It would be lovely." He looked at Esther and she at him and I watched them and thought, all is well, all is well.

"Do you still go clamming?" Esther asked. "And can we picnic at Montauk? I'd like to swim from that wide empty beach again and I'd like to drive out to the lighthouse."

That was the kind of peaceful, untroubled weekend that, until the end, it turned out to be.

We drove to Southampton early in the afternoon instead of taking the Cannonball, and our arrival went unobserved. We swam at Flying Point and Montauk rather than at the Beach Club. Ma and Pops were spending the weekend in Lenox, and we had the house to ourselves.

Our only visitor was Mrs. Conway, who called on us on her way to church on Sunday morning. Bertie and Augie were playing golf, and Esther and I were alone.

"Esther, my dear, it's been so long." As Esther held out her hand in greeting, Mrs. Conway took it in both of hers and kissed her.

Seeing one of us after a prolonged interval had cracked the shell of Mrs. Conway's reserve, had, I thought, brought back the old days when Betty and Bunny had spent as much time in our house as in their own. She turned to me and said, "I heard last evening that Esther and Augie were here and I didn't want to miss her. I was afraid you might be driving up to New York this afternoon so you must forgive my calling informally like this in the morning."

When I was young Mrs. Conway had been one of the most imposing of the dreadnaughts, and I had been scared of her. After Bunny and Betty's deaths I wasn't scared any more, only sorry.

There was little outward change in her. She was still formal in speech and manner, but she was less sharp-eyed, less observant of the doings of the young, less interested, it seemed to me, in the deeds or misdeeds of anyone young or old. She joined the ladies at the beach and at the Meadow Club and Shinnecock. I would hear her voice as they talked over the latest gossip, the latest newcomer, the latest deplorable infraction of long standing rules of dress and behavior, but there was a certain absent-mindedness about her as though her mind was literally far away from the present time and circumstance, as though she did not hear any of the conversation, not even her own contribution to it.

Now, having asked for and received the latest news of Maud and Julia and their children, she said she couldn't stay long or she would be late for church.

I was slightly embarrassed that Esther and I, casually dressed, were obviously not prepared for churchgoing, and I explained apologetically that when one had only the weekend in South-ampton it was hard to make an effort on Sunday morning.

That was perfectly natural, Mrs. Conway said, indeed it was sensible, but for her it was a pleasure to go to St. Andrew's where Morning Prayer was exactly that, no more, no less. "This is not the case everywhere I am sorry to say. In many churches, even the ones we've all gone to for years, High Church practices are creeping in. I prefer old-fashioned, undiluted Protestantism. Your uncle was my idea of what a Protestant Episcopal church-man should be." She paused to inquire for Aunt Lucy, and hav-ing learned that the latter was as usual in the White Mountains, she said, "I've always considered the White Mountains rather dull but perhaps they have the advantage of having changed less than other places. I must say it's a comfort here to have one part of Sunday morning as one remembers it. The dune church is still an unchanged little stronghold which is more than I can say for its new neighbor. The Beach Club is a radical change and not in my opinion a change for the better. I fear that eventually our dear old Southampton will become indistinguishable from East Hampton or even Quogue. The Beach Club is the opening wedge. I don't believe you would like it, Esther. I don't think you'd at all enjoy going there. It's quite different from the beach as it once was. But then nothing any more is what it was in the old days."

"I know, Mrs. Conway, I know."

They looked at each other.

To Mrs. Conway, Esther was special I thought. She was the oldest of us and therefore remembered Betty and Bunny clearly and uninterruptedly from the time when they were very small children. And Esther had had a son and a daughter and no longer had them. This was the bond. It need not, could not, be spoken of but it was there and it had brought Mrs. Conway to Ma and Pops' house on this Sunday morning.

I didn't ponder at any length over Mrs. Conway's visit, it seemed natural enough that she should call. Nor did it occur to me to wonder why no one else seemed to be aware that we were down. I was just grateful that nobody dropped in on us, that the telephone didn't ring, that nothing disturbed the quiet weekend I had promised Bertie.

Late in the afternoon, when the four of us were sitting on the porch, I watched the swans on the lake and looked back with lazy satisfaction on the peaceful days. Esther was almost as much at home as I was in Ma and Pops' house and I was content. We all were, I think.

"It's been a heavenly weekend," Esther said. "Being at Ma and Pops' is the next best thing to being in our old house."

Impatient with myself, I said, "I should have taken you there while Bertie and Augie were at the National. Grace and Harold

Graham have our house again this year. They'll probably buy it, which, as Julia says, will keep it sort of in the family. I tell you what, come down for little Grace and Norman's wedding. It's the first Saturday in August."

Big Grace and Esther had been at school together and had been each other's bridesmaids.

"I'd like to see Grace again," Esther said, "but I don't know about a hectic Southampton weekend. Besides we're booked for Austria in August."

"Austria can wait," Augie said, "let's stay over for the wedding."

"We haven't been invited. No reason we should be, I haven't seen Grace in years."

"She probably had no idea you were in this part of the world. She'll be thrilled when she hears. I'll call her right away."

Before Esther could speak, if she meant to speak, Augie said, "Do that, Nell. A gala Southampton wedding sounds fun."

I went into the house and telephoned Grace Graham.

"My sister will be here for the wedding," I told her.

"But Julia wrote that they couldn't possibly . . . oh, you mean Maud. How divine! I haven't seen Maud in ages. I'll whip off an invitation right away. What's the address?"

"Not Maud, Esther. She and Augie will be staying with us."

"Esther! Oh Lord, that's rather awkward, but I'm sure you'll understand—"

"Understand what?"

"Oh dear, this is so difficult and I'm terribly sorry, but Harold is Sophie's second cousin, you can understand how really impossible, I mean . . ."

Naturally, I understood. Grace needn't burble on like this. Of course, Esther wouldn't want to go to the wedding if Sophie was to be there, but maybe Sophie wasn't coming.

"Have the Howells accepted?" I asked.

"Oh no, they regretted. They're in Burlingame for the summer."

"Then that disposes of that difficulty," I said, sounding more cheerful than I was beginning to feel.

"Actually, Nell, I'm afraid it doesn't solve anything. And there's not only the wedding, and I know what Harold's stand would be on that, there's the Hastings' dinner dance at the Beach Club. Mrs. Hastings would call that off in a minute if I told her you were bringing Esther and her husband. You don't seem to realize how people feel."

"I think I do." With a considerable effort I managed to keep my voice low and pleasant. "But I don't believe you do. Suppose you stop and think. Baby and Harry Parker have been invited to the wedding and all the festivities. Harry's first wife is a cousin of Mrs. Henderson's just as much as Sophie is of Harold's. Did the senator or Mrs. Henderson raise the slightest objection to the Parkers' presence? Did anybody?"

"Of course not. Baby Parker is in a completely different position than poor Esther. I hate to say this . . ."

"Then don't."

"I have to, since you insist on playing the innocent out of loyalty. It simply isn't possible for us to invite your sister and her husband."

I could have killed her, but I tried to sound friendly as I made one more appeal. "Look, Grace, you and Esther were bridesmaids for each other, haven't you a little loyalty to the old days?"

"Those days were pretty long ago, and a lot of dirty water has gone over the dam since. Still I'd never be unkind, you know me well enough for that. If Esther would like to see your house again, by all means bring her over some time, and wait, don't hang up, listen to me. Believe me it would be no kindness to

Esther to have her at the wedding, she'd be very uncomfortable. She didn't ask you to ask me to invite her, did she?"

"No, it was my idea." I must protect Esther's pride, all over again I must try to protect—if only Pa were here, he'd fix this damn woman.

"Oh well, then," Grace said, "it's not awkward at all. And if the wedding should come up, you can say the Howells are invited, that gives you the perfect out."

"I don't need an out, my sister and her husband are planning to spend Aug in Austria with Prince and Princess Achtenbergen." I grabbed wildly at a name Augie had dropped, it might give Grace a small, snobbish jolt. "I was just hoping I might be able to persuade them to change their minds."

"Then there's no situation, is there? See you around, dear. See you on the seventh of August for sure."

That was one day, I decided, that I would not be in Southampton, and Bertie would back me up.

"We may not be able to make the wedding," I said. "Bertie has an important client in Chicago and we may have to be out there."

"I see."

Our receivers clicked simultaneously, and I went back to the porch.

No one moved. I stood still, near the screen door. We were all still as living statues in a children's game long ago.

Augie was the first to speak. "That was rather a lengthy conversation," he said.

"You can't have a short conversation with the mother of a bride." I was glad the porch was in shadow as I added, "But, about the wedding, there's a catch. The Howells are invited, she's a cousin of Harold's, stupid of me to forget that."

"In that case, of course, we can't . . ."

Augie interrupted Esther. "The Howells are in Burlingame for the summer, visiting my dear sisters."

"But they might decide to come East for the wedding."

"Don't be absurd, Esther. Sophie wouldn't dream of it. She hasn't to my knowledge laid eyes on Harold or any of the Grahams since she was a girl. Listen, my darling, this wedding is just one more thing, one more door slammed. We ought to be used to the sound of slamming doors by now, ought not to care, and I don't really, I love our life together, you know that, but let's not pretend it's something it isn't."

Bertie stood up and stretched. "Must be getting late," he said, and turned on the porch lights. "How about our making ourselves a drink, Augie? And I want to show you a pair of guns I just got over from England. We can try them out at South Side this fall."

As Augie passed me to follow Bertie into the house, I noticed how boyish he still managed to look. He was a sulky boy at the moment, but a handsome one. He would, I thought, remain a boy all his life, and I was thankful that Bertie, at a much younger age, had become a man.

I walked over to Esther and sat beside her.

"Poor Augie feels badly about his sisters," she said. "He hasn't seen them since the divorce. Even though I purposely didn't go with him last year when he had to be in California, they wouldn't receive him."

"Bitches," I said, to my astonishment. I wasn't used to hearing myself use such language.

"Maybe they are, but also they're probably fond of their nieces, and unless they took her side completely, Sophie wouldn't let them see the girls. That's how Sophie operates."

"I've heard."

Esther continued in a tired voice. "It's hard on Augie and the social snubs are hard on him. I've had more time to get used to them than he has. Then, too, he's more naturally gregarious than I am. But listen, Nell, he meant what he said about our life, he loves it, is in love with me anyway. And I manage pretty well for us. We have a lot of friends in Europe. Funny, isn't it, that Catholic countries like Austria and Italy are easier on us than our own? Still we never stay too long in New York and we have some friends there, mostly new people, but they're attractive and their parties are fun for Augie. One staunch friend from the old days is your Baby Elliot. Even when she was having her difficulties, she never failed to rally."

"That's what I don't understand. If everything's fine for Baby and Harry, why isn't it for you and Augie? It doesn't make sense."

"Whether it makes sense or not this is how it is, this is how Pa warned me it would be, and there's nothing I can do about it, nor you either, so don't try. Remember how Bridie used to tell us, what can't be cured must be endured?"

I took her hand and held it tight. I couldn't think of anything to say.

Presently she said, "I love Augie, Nell, love his good points, love his weaknesses, love him. So I'm all right. However it goes, whatever happens, it's all right with me." She shivered and drew her sweater closer around her shoulders. "It's a bit damp and chilly out here, let's go and find our men."

I looked at the pure line of her cheek and throat. In the hard light of the unshaded bulbs Esther's skin was smooth and unblurred as ivory. I watched her walk across the porch and into the living room; if a girl on the Grecian urn could move this is how she would walk. Of course, Augie was still in love with Esther, how could he help it? And if that was all she had, well, it seemed to be all she wanted. I sent up a quick prayer to Aunt

Lucy's kind and merciful God to let it be enough, to let Esther be happy, and I followed her into the house.

It was several years before I met any of Esther's new friends. When she was in New York, we preferred small evenings with our husbands at her house or ours. Her visits were too short to waste them with other people.

Bertie and I didn't run into any of the group that Baby's friend Maury Paul christened Café Society until after the crash of 1929. From 1930 on they were to be found in almost any house, at almost any party. As much of the old money melted away, as many of the old rich, the old well-to-do, became the new poor, the brand-new rich came into their own.

When Roberta asks me about the frightening crash with which the twenties ended I find it difficult to answer.

"What was it like when the rug was pulled out from under you, even for the people who didn't fall down? I've seen the wonderful *Variety* headline and I know about the suicides and the awful sick jokes. I've heard a lot of details, mostly from Tim's father who got really going in the financial world then, but I never get the whole picture. What was it like, Mummie?"

It's hard to remember a public disaster privately, and this one came upon us with such shocking unexpectedness that it flashes into my mind and out again like a summer thunderstorm. My recollection is also confused by what I have read, by what other people remember. The best way I can describe the crash to Roberta is to tell her it was like a fireworks display gone wrong, with pinwheels flying apart in all directions and blazing rockets and Roman candles falling into the crowd of spectators instead of going swiftly and safely up and up as one expects.

"Even those who weren't hurt were stunned," I say. "We were in a sort of excited state of shock. I think the shock explains the tasteless jokes. Funny, the things that stick in your mind. I remember the joke, maybe it was a cartoon, about the clerk asking the hotel guest if he wants a room for sleeping or for jumping. There were lots of horrid, unfunny jokes like that, but, as Pops used to say, people will laugh at almost anything on their way to and from a funeral. I guess the crash was like that too, like an enormous public funeral that one watches, fascinated, forgetting to mourn."

"No one makes it seem real," Roberta says. "Even you make it sound like a grand opera finale tacked on to the end of a musical comedy. The Depression is much more soberly documented and reported."

"Well, for one thing the Depression lasted longer."

At the time it seemed to last forever as it ground on with no end in sight.

Bertie and I were safe enough, but people we knew were hurt.

The Thompsons were among the first casualties. Early in 1930 they went back to Texas, where Harry Parker found a job in one of his companies for Herbert Thompson.

Cecil Sampson III died of an overdose of veronal sometime in 1931. In two years the Sampson millions had dwindled to nothing. I asked Bertie how a fortune like that could possibly disappear in so short a time.

"This Cecil was no businessman," Bertie said, "but he looked the part and wanted to play it. The rest of them let him. He was the oldest of this generation of Sampsons and the others weren't interested in the making and conserving of money, only in the spending."

"Even if he wasn't a businessman, I still don't see how in less than two years when they had millions . . ."

It wasn't in these last years, Bertie explained. The bad management, the overexpansion, and the carelessness had begun in the mid-twenties, and then, in trying to salvage what was left, Cecil panicked and lost everything, lost more than they had.

"But, Bertie, to kill himself and over money, even that much money."

"There were rumors downtown of an investigation by the grand jury, and I believe there would have been an indictment if Cecil had lived and he couldn't face it. Indictment or not, I guess the poor guy couldn't face himself in the mirror."

I remembered Alfred saying something about seeing shock in a mirror. "Poor Alfred said once . . ."

"Alfred and his lot are all right. Their mother never trusted high finance, and she set up a sizable, unbreakable trust for each of them. I don't know that it will run to polo ponies and fast cars, but Alfred will always be a long way from starving."

There were people who were not a long way from starving, and some of them were among those that I thought were as secure as Bertie and I were.

I still feel shaken when I remember Bertie telling me about Mrs. Conway.

She was one of many, but she was one of the first of the helpless, frightened new poor, and I was fond of her. While Bertie told me what had happened I listened to him and at the same time remembered Mrs. Conway coming to call when Esther and Augie were staying with us at Ma and Pops' house. I could see her white kid gloves and her stiff, flowered hat; I could see the smile that softened her severe, almost immobile face as she affectionately welcomed Esther to Southampton; I could see her smoothing the skirt of her black and white foulard dress, and fingering her jet necklace as she tried to warn Esther against the Beach Club where there would be no welcome.

After Betty's death, Mr. and Mrs. Conway had always stayed

in Southampton until Thanksgiving. When Mr. Conway died in 1928, Mrs. Conway did not alter her yearly schedule.

In the twenties, the summer people closed their houses soon after Labor Day and in the autumn of 1929 none of Mrs. Conway's friends were in Southampton. That November she did not move to New York. She left her apartment closed and tried, unsuccessfully, to sublet it. She had trusted the executors of her husband's will, and after the estate was settled she had allowed them to continue to invest her husband's fortune as well as her more modest inheritance from her own family. She was now alarmingly short of funds, but her financial advisers assured her that this was a temporary situation. Both Wall Street and the White House, they pointed out, were confident of an upturn.

"As if an upturn could have done her any good," Bertie said, "those damn fools had been buying on margin for her and she was almost wiped out in October. Then, trying to recoup, they played the long side of the market while smart traders were selling short."

"Wasn't that a crooked thing for them to do?" I asked.

"I'd say so, though I'm not certain the law could have touched them. It's some satisfaction that they ruined themselves as well as their client. One of them was a broker, a college friend of poor Conway's, and he went bankrupt, the other was the head of an old private banking house, and the bank failed last December."

No one who knew about Mrs. Conway's financial predicament had time to worry about her, and when she was afraid that she would not much longer be able to pay her telephone bill, she requested that her number be temporarily disconnected with the result that anybody who tried to reach her assumed that she was away on a visit or a trip.

In January she was unable to pay her gas and electric bill, and by then she must have been panicky and too confused to ask for an extension of credit. If she had, the company's local representative might have spread the word in the village that Mrs. Conway was in difficulties. As it was, when the bill became overdue the company apparently concluded that their customer had forgotten to notify them before leaving Southampton; no doubt their records showed that the Conway house was usually closed before December first. Mrs. Conway's heat and electricity were turned off.

The stationmaster and Mr. Hildreth and Mr. Corwith came to the rescue but they were nearly too late.

The stationmaster thought it queer that Mrs. Conway should stay down on the Island this long. She hadn't gone up on any of his trains so she presumably was still in Southampton. It seemed to him the maids had gone up, and he didn't remember a new lot coming down, but the summer people's servants came and went too rapidly for him to keep track of them. He was troubled about Mrs. Conway, and he mentioned his anxiety to Mr. Hildreth. They were in Corwith's at the time and the owner of the drugstore told them that he hadn't seen Mrs. Conway in quite a while.

"When she's down she comes in fairly often to buy something and have a little chat," Mr. Corwith said. "Poor soul, she's lonely with the husband dead as well as the children. That house of hers is pretty isolated with everything around it closed up for the winter. I think, gentlemen, we better go along and make sure she's all right."

They went to Mrs. Conway's house and found her and drove her to the hospital. From there Mr. Hildreth telephoned Bertie at the office. Bertie has always had friends in the village with no condescension on either side even in the days when such mutual condescension was taken for granted by both the summer people and their predecessors, the local people who lived the year round in Southampton and its environs as their forefathers had done since the seventeen or eighteen hundreds.

"Mrs. Conway's been found near dead from pneumonia," Mr. Hildreth told Bertie. "The doctor thinks she'll pull through, but she's had a damn close call. There wasn't a scrap of food in the house and the place was cold as the grave. She must have been too sick and too bewildered to do anything but stay there and wait to die."

I asked Bertie how we could help.

"We can't," he said. "It would humiliate her to accept anything from us. Financial help from friends of her own generation will be easier on her pride. I called Mrs. Livingston. She's the one of the dreadnaughts I was sure I could count on. I've known her to rally when you'd least expect it, financially and other ways too, and she rallies quietly not with a flourish of trumpets."

"What can she do?"

"She's done it. She drove to the Southampton Hospital at once. To reassure dear Mrs. Conway, she told me. And you can bet that by now Mrs. Conway is in a private room. 'Several of us can afford to come to Mrs. Conway's assistance,' Mrs. Livingston said, 'and we will.' They sure can and they will."

"You think, Bertie?"

"Probably not all who could, but enough. People are endlessly surprising, and the dreadnaughts are people. Remember what you've said yourself, Nell, there's never a type, there's only the person."

It was hard for Mrs. Conway at her age to become a pensioner even of old friends. It was hard on all the Mrs. Conways.

It was worse for the men in a similar situation, particularly for the middle-aged, Bertie said. "It's hard for a man who hasn't thought of himself as old to discover that it's too late for him to start over, that all he can do is depend on the kindness of more fortunate friends or relations."

I remember Aunt Lucy saying of one of Pa's younger friends, a man in his fifties, "To dig he is not able, to beg he is ashamed, but he's not like the unjust steward, for him there's no other possible alternative, he's an honorable man, a gentleman in the best sense of that much abused word. Unfortunately, he has lived all his life on the income of an inheritance he didn't know how to take care of. He was like a child on an allowance and now he's helpless."

Our world was an uneasy, anxious place in that time. The Depression reminded me of the Spanish influenza epidemic, one didn't know who would be next.

Because of the day nursery I had glimpses of another world where insecurity was becoming a way of life, where there were no rich friends or relations to help, where there was only the bread of charity that to the poor must have seemed not only bitter but uncertain.

I'm not a Democrat. Bertie and I have always voted Republican, but I honestly believe that if it hadn't been for Franklin Roosevelt the people who lived in that despairing world of spiraling poverty would have exploded into violence. If they had who could have blamed them?

I remember when Bertie came back from a trip to Chicago in 1932. It was just after the Democratic convention, and the hotels were dismissing employees by the hundreds.

Bertie told me about the bellboy who came for his bags.

"We're getting our notices now that the delegates have left," he said. "Got mine this morning."

"What are you going to do?" Bertie asked.

"I don't know." The man dropped the bags and stood straight

and looked at Bertie, "I don't know. But I'll tell you this, mister. If I have to get a gun, my family's going to eat."

It was terrible, Bertie said, to have nothing to offer him except a tip. "Maybe if Roosevelt's elected he can do something about the mess we're in, though I don't see how he can do more than Mr. Hoover is trying to do, but I'll tell you this, Nell, somebody's got to do something or this country's going to hell in a handbasket."

I remember a luncheon, a hen party, at one of the new cooperative apartments on the East River. One of my childhood friends from Spence was the hostess, and I was mildly astonished to find one of the new people among the guests. She wasn't arrogant or strident. Some of them in those days seemed to me like Goths dining out in a conquered Roman city. This one had an agreeable low-pitched voice. She said very little, and seemed ill at ease in a roomful of strangers all of whom knew each other well.

When we were seated in the dining room the talk turned to the whereabouts of old friends and the newcomer tried to take part.

"I wonder when Esther and Augie Wenger will be back in town," she said, smiling and obviously pleased to let us know that she was not unacquainted with members of New York's inner circle. "My husband and I are crazy about them, they're such an attractive couple."

This contribution to the discussion fell flat. There was an uncomfortable silence in which I could hear myself breathing. Before I could answer in a natural voice, the hostess said in the too hurried, too high-pitched voice of embarrassment, "Oh yes, Esther's a dear, we've all known her forever." Then searching for a less awkward subject of conversation she hit on the threatened strike of the apartment house employees.

"Imagine in times like these," she said, "their trying to get more money. It really is unforgivable."

I can still see the spotless gray uniforms and white aprons of the waitress and parlor maid who were serving us. I can see the table set with brilliantly polished Georgian silver and Minton china, with heavy crystal goblets and fragile long-stemmed white wine glasses. I remember the centerpiece, a silver bowl filled with hothouse grapes, and I could probably recall the entire four-course menu if I tried.

The conversation continued around me. It veered off to winter plans and the respective merits of Hobe Sound and Palm Beach and then returned to the difficulty of coping with employees who didn't realize when they were well off.

A guest who lived in the building complained about a new elevator man. "He's rather young with an unpleasant, almost insolent manner," she said. "He looked so sullen this morning I actually didn't dare ask him to let my dog out into the garden."

"What does an elevator man get in a building like this?" I asked.

They told me.

I can no longer remember the amount only that it was shockingly small and I said I didn't see how a married man with children could live on so little.

"Well, there are tips at Christmas and anyway a married man shouldn't take a job like this," the hostess said, and the others echoed her opinion.

As if there were jobs to pick and choose among, I thought, for a married man or any other. I helped myself to crême brulée without looking up at the waitress. It would have embarrassed me to meet her eyes.

I wondered what the company at the table would say if I told them about my encounter with one of the mothers at the day nursery that morning. I didn't tell them. It wouldn't have been the slightest use. This was a time of fear. Bridie had pointed out to me years ago, that fear does not breed kindness, and the rich, uncertain of how long riches were going to last for anyone, got angry if one spoke of poverty.

I stirred the smooth, creamy dessert with a silver spoon. I had no appetite for it as I thought about the young mother who had told me this morning that her husband had lost his job. Her words rang so loud in my head that I couldn't hear the conversation that flowed serenely around me.

"It wasn't much of a job, missus, but it was better than nothing. Now we have nothing."

I look back and remember the Depression. I remember its lowest point at the beginning of 1933.

I remember the fear and uncertainty in our own world and I remember the darker anxiety in the larger world beyond our comparatively safe little enclave.

The pity I feel as I look back is real, was real then, but for Bertie and me in our private world, 1933 was a good year. It was the best of years and that's how I remember it.

In 1932 my old obstetrician died and that summer Baby urged me to see a new doctor who was said to be a miracle worker.

I went to see Dr. Damon without telling Bertie. I didn't want to get Bertie's hopes up, in case the new doctor turned out, as seemed likely to me, to be no more of a miracle worker than the old one.

Dr. Damon said in his deep, measured voice, that he was no miracle worker but that often there were things that could be done and he would examine me and then we would talk.

After the examination he told me that in his opinion there was nothing gravely wrong. Probably the whole difficulty lay in the fact that the Fallopian tubes were blocked, and he would recommend insufflation.

I must have appeared nervous, as indeed I was, and Dr. Damon told me not to be. Insufflation, the blowing out of the tubes, was a simple treatment that could be given in his office and in twenty-five per cent of cases it was successful.

I was one of the lucky twenty-five per cent and in 1933, on the fifteenth of July, Roberta was born.

I sit here and see my room in Doctors Hospital and hear the boats whistling for Hell Gate beyond the chintz-curtained windows. I close my eyes and look down at Roberta's little round head. Mostly I look down, but sometimes I hold her up and look into her face and wonder what she will be when she loses the heavy-lidded mask of infancy. I watch Bertie carrying her carefully as if she might break.

I don't know if I was more pleased for Bertie or for me. We were pleased, we were very pleased. When I remember the beginning of having Roberta I use small, matter-of-fact words: the larger words aren't large enough, so small ones are somehow less inadequate.

I can see Roberta as she begins to become a person. I can see her standing triumphantly upright in her pen. I can see her bravely taking three unsteady steps from my chair to Bertie's. As she is about to fall, he catches her and stands up with her in his arms and she looks at the floor far below her and crows with astonishment and pleasure.

The summer she was four, Roberta began to have her own looks and ways, began to be Roberta.

It delighted me to see Bertie's eyes in her face. Gray to amber to gold. Her hair was as straight as Bertie's but not dark brown like his nor was it fair like mine. She wore it then as she wears it now, between experiments in high fashion, in a long, thick, bell-shaped bob that frames her face in bronze.

"Mouse color, Mummie dear, plain mouse," she says, sounding exactly like her father.

Even when she was a child, Roberta's straight hair never straggled limply; it was heavy and smooth and the color of bronze, darker than her eyes and lighter than her brows and lashes. She had a fine-featured, pale little face, and she was not, in the Shirley Temple era, considered pretty except by the discerning.

Louis saw her looks as they were and as they would be. He put her in a painting for us. He was working on sketches for his painting of the Place de la Concorde, and he had started to block out one of the horses of Marly.

"That proud, untamed horse doesn't belong in my picture," he said, "but it will make a fine, imposing background for a little girl."

The painting isn't a portrait of Roberta, though that's how Bertie and I think of it. She is only a small, brightly lit figure in the foreground of the canvas, but she can be clearly seen and recognized. The sky is overcast and the wildly rearing horse seems motionless, in the gray light it casts no shadow. In the west the clouds are breaking apart and Roberta is standing in a strip of afternoon sunshine. Her shadow is tall and it amuses me to look at it nowadays because it suggests Roberta's slim, long-legged elegance in the currently abbreviated skirts. In the picture she is on tiptoe holding a yellow balloon as high as its string will reach. In a moment she will let it fly free. Her hair shines and swings and her feet seem to dance. She is a little girl with the face—still unfinished, not yet as lovely as it will be—of a four-year-old, but she is already Roberta.

She was Roberta in other ways in that Paris summer. She was

her independent self. Even on a crowded street she resisted being what she scornfully termed a by-hander and in Maud's house she stubbornly refused to be taken up stairs or down. "I go by my own self," she would say.

I can hear her thumping down the stairs, step by step. Roberta walks lightly now, but children tread heavily. Their little feet don't patter, they thump. I can hear the four-year-old Roberta on the stairs in Neuilly. From the next to last step she jumps to the parquet floor and slides and runs across it calling to us, "Here I come!"

Perhaps it's because we waited so long for her that from the beginning Roberta has been sure of her welcome. From the beginning, knowing herself to be welcome, she has welcomed any friend, any stranger, any stray, human or animal. She still welcomes strays, even cats, though she doesn't like them much.

"I couldn't leave the poor thing to starve," she says.

The first time I heard her say that was when she found a skinny, glazed-eyed mongrel in the Martins' garden and brought it to Maud. "I couldn't leave the poor thing to starve, Auntie Maud."

By the time Roberta was four, she was Roberta.

13

It's LOVELY to remember Roberta's early years, but I can't keep on. I can't remember the summer she was four without thinking of Esther. In April of that year Esther had a heart attack.

The attack had not been a severe one, she assured me, when I was allowed to see her.

Against the big, square French pillow, her face was smaller than it ought to be, and her eyes seemed larger than ever. Her skin, drawn tight to her bones, was thin as paper.

Esther must have seen my dismay, though I tried to hide it. She lifted her hand in the beginning of her old comforting gesture. She would be all right, she said. Her doctor had told her that with care she could recover completely.

"I'll be practically as good as new, he said, if I'll just go slow for a few months. I hope he'll let me go to the White Mountains with Aunt Lucy. That should be slow enough."

She lay still and flat with her arms at her sides like an obedient child who has been put to bed for a rest.

"Tell me about Roberta. It's easier to listen than to talk."

I talked at some length about Roberta; that's never difficult for me.

"Bridie says you're taking her to visit Maud and Louis."

"We might. We've thought of it, but we'll probably go to Ma and Pops as usual. Roberta's a bit young for foreign travel."

"Don't change your plans on my account. I'll be fine. All I need is rest. The one this is hard on is Augie. It's hard for a man to be cooped up with an invalid."

"Don't fuss about him, for heaven's sake. He'll get plenty of exercise in the mountains, and meanwhile he can come to South-ampton any weekend. Even if we're not there, Ma and Pops will be glad to have him."

For Esther's sake as much as mine, they would rally. It seemed probable to me that, like Bertie, they had made up their minds about Augie long ago, but no one, least of all Augie, would know this. I didn't know, I merely surmised.

"He gets down to South Side fairly often, but a June weekend in Southampton would be nice for him. You're a dear to think of it, Nell. After that there's Cannes, we've booked rooms at the Carlton for July and August."

"Esther, you can't possibly go."

"Not I, Augie."

"He won't want to go abroad."

"He doesn't think he wants to, but he will when the time comes. I refused to let him cancel the hotel suite." She raised her head from the pillow and smiled like her old self. "Can you pic-ture Augie in the rocking chair brigade?" She laughed and her laughter rang true until it was interrupted by a spasm of cough-ing that shook her whole body.

I sat beside her until the coughing subsided.

"I might sleep," she whispered. "Come back tomorrow."

Esther's doctor ruled out any mountain resort but he agreed to Aunt Lucy's suggestion that they go to a hotel on Lake George. When their reservation was made, Bertie confirmed ours on the *Normandie*. I was thankful he needn't give up his Euro-pean vacation. A Southampton one was invariably interrupted.

The time in Neuilly wasn't shadowed by Esther's illness. Aunt Lucy's letters were steadily encouraging as she reported the small daily activities in which Esther was beginning to take part.

On one occasion anxiety took me by surprise. Maud showed me a Book of Hours that Louis had given her, and I came upon a tall angel with flowing red gold hair and a face paler than the parchment on which it was painted. I was sharply reminded of Esther's face, white as the pillow beneath her head, and I told Maud that this was how Esther looked now.

"Oh no, Nell, it can't be. Esther is slim and small-boned for her height, but there's nothing disembodied about her, and that creamy skin of hers never gets a transparent look. It's the red hair that makes you imagine a likeness."

"You haven't seen her. This is how she looks now."

"Not now, when she was ill. By the time you get home she'll be herself again."

"You're sure, Maud?"

"No. How can I be? What I am sure of is that if Esther weren't convalescing as she should Aunt Lucy would tell us. We're not children any more, we're grown up, remember?"

"So we are. Doesn't that seem odd to you sometimes?"

"I can't say it does. What does seem queer is that some day we'll be old, really old like Aunt Lucy. I guess when we get there it will seem natural enough and it won't be too bad if we can be as brisk and up and doing as she is."

One other thing troubled me while we were at the Martins'.

In September, a few days before Bertie and Roberta and I sailed for home, Maud and I were looking at some English magazines we had bought on the rue de Rivoli and there, smiling at us from a month-old *Tatler* was Augie surrounded by a group of rich Americans and titled English.

"A carefree holiday gathering at Antibes," the *Tatler* announced, and listed the names of all who were facing the camera.

"Carefree is the word," Maud said. "I knew Augie was over here, but—"

"It was Esther who insisted that he go."

"She was wise. He'd have been bored stiff at Lake George. It wouldn't have speeded up her convalescence any to have to fuss about keeping laughing boy amused. Just the same it makes me mad to see him with his fancy friends, smiling away without a worry in the world." Maud tossed the magazine to one side. "Oh well, there's no sense in getting angry with Augie at this late date."

I wasn't angry as much as uneasy.

From time to time on the return crossing I remembered the two pictures: Esther as I had seen her in New York, as I had seemed to see her in the illuminated Book of Hours, and Augie, tanned and smiling in the glossy magazine. I was troubled by the disparity between the pictures. It was the first time that I had looked at Esther and Augie together—in reality or in my mind—and thought in sad astonishment that they didn't match each other.

On the afternoon of the day we arrived in New York I went to see Esther. My first reaction was one of overwhelming relief. She didn't look anywhere near as sick as when I had last seen her. I can hear the relief and happiness in my voice as we talked.

Slowly and reluctantly I realized that she was changed. She was no longer an invalid, but she was not the Esther of a year ago or of the years before that. Her eyes were circled in shadow and seemed to be more deeply set in her head. Her face was thin, one could see its structure too clearly, the arch of the brow, the modeling of cheekbones and temples. When Augie came in at about six she got up to greet him, but she moved slowly; the spring had gone out of her body.

All this I see plainly now and I don't want to see it. What I saw then, what I told myself then was that Esther was thin, Esther looked badly, as anyone would after months of illness and convalescence, but she was better, she would be all right.

I can see Augie slowing his naturally quick step to match Esther's pace as he takes her back to the sofa and settles her on it. In contrast to Augie, Esther is not only tired, not only fragile, she is old. She is still lovely, but the last of her youthfulness has drained away.

In the beginning as I watched Augie, I resented his buoyancy and good health. Then, and after that when I was with them, I thought I saw a new gentleness in him, a new strength. Esther had been the strong one, but now in the most loving manner imaginable, Augie took charge.

In November Esther began to talk about their winter plans. Nassau, she said, would be an easy trip for her on the train, and the low-altitude flight from Miami on a sea plane was nothing.

"You like Nassau, Augie."

"I like anywhere you are and for the present your own peaceful house is the best place for you. We're going to stay right here."

As Esther grew stronger they occasionally invited a few friends to dine and they went sometimes to the theater or to a small dinner. Augie, backed up by Esther's doctor, ruled out any large or late parties.

Esther urged Augie to go without her, and once in a while she succeeded in her persuasions, but on most evenings he stayed home with her. He was usually out during the day, and if he came in late from a long meeting at the Wenger Corporation's New York office or from a game of squash and a swim at the Racquet Club, he brought flowers to Esther, long-stemmed Talisman roses or violets or gardenias.

Once when I was there he carried in an enormous, long white box. When he opened it the fragrance of dozens of gardenias filled the room.

"Of all the flowers there are, my darling, these are yours," he said, and took a gardenia from the box and held it against Esther's cheek and kissed her.

When I tried to tell Bertie about the new Augie, he grunted and said, "Could be: a leopard might change its spots."

"Honestly, Bertie, don't be so stubborn. Augie has changed, is trying."

"Sorry, Nellie. Maybe Augie is doing his best, whatever his best may be. And Esther looks more fit, looks happy anyway, which is the main thing. You women! It doesn't take much to make you happy."

"I don't call you not much, I don't call Roberta not much, I don't call what makes me happy not much."

"Ah, Nell, that's nice to hear. After nearly twenty years that's very nice."

It was in January that Baby took me to call on Agnes Fowler.

"She's heaven," Baby said, "luscious-looking and gay and fun. She hasn't had much luck with husbands, the first one drank himself to death. She has one child, a little boy I think, born late in that marriage. Next, she married Matt Fowler. You might remember him. His parents took a house in Southampton for a couple of summers after the war. They came from Pittsburgh and never made the grade with the dreadnaughts."

I shook my head.

"Anyway," Baby continued, "no one could put up with Matt Fowler as a husband for long. It was women with him, not liquor. Agnes divorced him last winter and decided to try her wings in New York, and my bet is that she'll fly high. She's just moved into a Fifth Avenue apartment that she spent a fortune on, and they say it's a dream. We might drop in on her after lunch and have a look."

I reminded Baby that I was less keen on new faces than she was.

"Don't be stuffy, Nell, new people are fun and it wouldn't hurt you to meet a few, so come on."

"If you like," I said, and I went with Baby to Agnes Fowler's.

As Baby introduced me to our hostess, I recognized her. Twenty years had changed her remarkably little.

"You're Agnes Ryan. What fun to see you again," I said, and meant it. It was fun to remember Julia's amazement that a vision of chic could come out of Newark. Agnes was still a vision of chic, and she was startlingly pretty. I thought as I had thought on Maud's wedding day, black as ebony, white as snow . . .

"And you're Maud Cameron's sister Nell. How is Maud? She was good to me in our Barnard days, she tried so hard and so fruitlessly to . . . Well, that's a long time ago, but give her my love. I thought about getting in touch when I went to France last summer, but I was in Paris only a few days before I took off for Antibes. Besides I felt shy about appearing out of the blue after so many years."

Agnes smiled at me, she had a sweet smile, and said to Baby, "Thank you for bringing my old friend's sister to see me."

A vision of chic and, as Alfred had said, one of the movers and doers, but her manner was gentle and her chic hadn't hardened into a stereotype of fashion.

The room in which we were was a stereotype, but it was one of the handsomest modern rooms I have ever seen. It was filled with light from five wide, high windows that overlooked the park. It was painted and furnished in pale, almost colorless colors, off white and beige, but it hadn't a drab, blond look; lamps and tables glittered in glass and chromium and in a corner by the door, a tall gold and crimson lacquer screen reached almost to the ceiling. On the walls were brilliant and complicated canvases; they were angular designs rather than pictures, and I didn't like them, but I found myself looking at them and puzzling over them. Set into the wall above the fireplace was a thick panel of cloudy silvery glass; in its depths one could glimpse small gold and coral fish.

This kind of modern room was already being patronizingly dismissed as *moderne*, but of its kind it was wonderful, wonderful to see, not to live in; there were no photographs, no small cherished ornaments, it had the sweep-it-all-away, start-again-from-scratch look that a modern room of any style nearly always seems to have, and I imagined this suited Agnes. A new start was presumably what she had in mind.

I looked about me, charmed by the sense of light and space. It was more like a stage setting than a real room; even the flowers weren't ordinary. White camellias floated in a jade bowl on a low, mirrored table, and between the windows were frosted glass columns on which were masses of pale yellow flowers. As my eyes grew accustomed to the strong light I saw that the flowers were dozens of sprays of small orchids, and I remembered my first sight of such sprays on Esther's birthday long ago. I remembered—or perhaps I am only now remembering Pa saying, "I don't need to see the card . . ."

In the thirties these orchids weren't a rarity any more, but it was extraordinary to see them in such extravagant profusion.

"I have never seen more lovely flowers," I said, feeling I must say something as one does when one has stared too long at an acquaintance's unusual possession, a handsome but overly ornate piece of jewelry, for instance, or a fashionable but unbecoming hat.

"I have a weakness for orchids," Agnes said, and smiled her sweet, slow smile.

After Agnes had shown us the rest of her apartment she looked at her diamond wrist watch and said, "Forgive me, Baby, if I put you girls out now. It was divine of you to drop by, but I've got this boring appointment with my accountant. He's due here any minute and I must get my checkbooks and stuff together for him. Let's lunch before you go South. I'll phone you. And I hope we'll meet again, Nell. Because of Maud, I may call you by your first name, mayn't I?"

When we reached the lobby Baby said, "That was sort of funny. She could easily have kept an accountant waiting."

"Maybe that expensive apartment has brought on a financial crisis and she's nervous."

"She did seem flustered as she hurried us out, but it couldn't be about money. She's loaded with it and her father before her, and of course Matt Fowler is filthy rich. I'm told she took him for plenty, and who can blame her? He's a complete heel."

I waited with Baby until she decided where to go next.

"Shopping, I guess," she said, "I need a few more things for Palm Beach. Want to come with me?"

I said I thought I'd go home and, as I wanted some fresh air and exercise, I refused Baby's offer of a lift. I waved her off in her Rolls and started uptown to our house.

When I was halfway there I changed my mind and decided to go to Esther's. I headed down the Avenue again, and when I reached Agnes' building a taxi stopped in front of the canopy. I waited, meaning to hail it when it was free, the afternoon had turned unpleasantly cold and windy.

When the passenger jumped out and turned to pay the driver, he didn't glance in my direction, but I looked at him. It was Augie. I don't know how long I stood there after he hurried into the apartment house.

Presently I pulled myself together and walked quickly uptown. Bertie wouldn't be in from the office yet but I wanted to get home and wait for him.

I didn't go up to the nursery, I sat in the living room and waited. It seemed an age before I heard the front door bang and Bertie's step on the stair.

"Nell!" he called. "You there, Nellie?"

"I'm here," I answered, and lit the flame under the hot water kettle.

"Boy, I'm beat," Bertie said as he came into the room. "One of those days when everything piles up at once and . . ." He stood still and looked at me. "What's wrong?" he asked. "Something is. And are you going to give me my tea with your hat on?"

My hands shook as I took off my hat and my voice shook and I talked too fast to be intelligible as I told Bertie about my afternoon.

"Steady, Nell," he said and sat down beside me on the sofa and put his arm around me. "Start over again and tell me slowly from the beginning."

So I began again at the beginning and went on to the end and then stopped. ". . . and Augie got out of the taxi and went into the building."

Bertie held me close for a minute. Then his arm still comfortingly around me, he said, "I thought Augie was up to no good. I didn't like his bringing Esther all those flowers, seemed to me he was overdoing it even for Augie. And when you mentioned late meetings at the Wenger office and late afternoons at the Racquet, I wondered. Augie keeps an eye on the family corporation, and I've heard he's pretty shrewd about it, but I've never heard of his working overtime. And as for the Racquet Club, I stop in once in a while for a workout on my way home and it's months since I've run into Augie there."

"Oh dear, I hoped you'd tell me I was imagining things. Her being in Antibes and the orchids could be coincidence, don't you think? There might even be a perfectly innocent explanation for Augie's turning up. How can I find out?"

"You can't, you mustn't even try. The important thing is that Esther shouldn't find out."

"And let Augie deceive her? The idea makes me sick."

"And let Augie deceive her if he can. If Esther has as little as I suspect, don't take that little away from her, Nell."

"Damn Augie, damn him."

"Damn him all you like to me, but to no one else. Don't let him see, don't let Esther, don't let anyone see the slightest change in your attitude toward him."

"It would be easier if I knew for sure. It'll be hard to act naturally while all the time I'm wondering."

"We can't know for sure. Her being in the South of France could be a coincidence, and the orchids obviously needn't mean anything though they sound like Augie. The pressing appointment with an accountant in mid-afternoon isn't too convincing. But the question I ask myself is, even if Augie wasn't visiting this particular lovely lady, what in hell was he doing at a Fifth Avenue apartment at that hour of the day?"

"Bertie, what'll I do?"

"The hardest thing of all: nothing."

Bertie was right, doing nothing is a hard thing. It was hard to maintain my accustomed friendly relationship with Augie and to hide my uneasiness from Esther, though it was only for a few weeks that I had to keep up appearances and be a relaxed and agreeable guest or hostess in Augie's presence in Esther's house or in ours.

In February Esther suffered a second and massive heart attack.

When she began to recover we knew this wasn't a recovery but a reprieve of unpredictable duration.

The doctor told Augie and Bertie that Esther's heart was too badly damaged for him to be able to give them any real hope. It was only a matter of time, he said, until the end.

When Bertie told me, I asked, "How much time? Didn't he say?"

"I don't think he knows. Esther is not in any pain, Nell, and another comfort is that both the doctor and Augie feel certain that she doesn't realize the seriousness of her condition."

"Augie! How can he have lived this long with Esther and not know her better than that? Esther has always faced hard truths, and you can bet she's facing this one. She was practically grown up when Mother died, and it was her heart with Mother too. Esther must remember and see parallels, but of course, ill as she is, waiting to die like Mother and knowing it, she'll still try to her last breath to protect Augie from any unwelcome reality." I began to cry.

"Don't cry. Not yet. You've got to be strong, Nellie. Whatever Esther guesses or knows, don't let her see that you know, don't burden her with that." Bertie waited until I had control of myself before he spoke again. "There are things you have to do. You must write Maud at once. They're planning a summer visit with Louis' family aren't they?" I nodded. "Then it'll seem natural enough for them to change their plans and come sooner."

"And Julia?"

Bertie frowned and said he would drop a line to James. "His post is a sensitive one these days, and he's been called to Washington a couple of times to report. He may be due in again. If not, Julia can always arrive for a routine visit to her mother-in-law."

"Aunt Lucy. I've got to tell her."

"Not unless she asks point-blank. Your aunt isn't indestructible any more. Her years have caught up with her, and suddenly she's an old, old lady. We've both seen the change in her. I knew you didn't want to talk about it but I guess we better."

I had seen. I had watched Aunt Lucy try to summon her strength and not find it. I had seen the trembling of her hands and heard the tremor in her voice. I had guessed at the effort it cost her to walk without faltering or shuffling and to sit as straight-backed as ever at her tea table.

"Go slow," Bertie said. "Just say as much as Aunt Lucy asks to hear. She knows how much she can bear. Her mind hasn't failed, only her strength."

"She was strong for us all our lives and now it's our turn. Esther said that once. Before Julia's wedding Esther said it was beginning to be our turn, but Aunt Lucy wasn't old then and all of us were young."

One thing that I tried to do was to keep the world from finding out how ill Esther was. As long as she was alive I wanted her to be alive, not be already pronounced dead by the indifferent and the curious. I was determined that she should not be relegated to time past while there was as much as a minute of time present left to her. I knew how ready the living are to banish from their company the nearly dead. "The jig's up with her," they say as they eat and drink with unimpaired appetite. If I could prevent it they would not pick over the details of Esther's illness.

I knew there was bound to be some talk, but I tried to hold it in check. When anyone asked about Esther I answered confidently. We were naturally worried, I said, but my sister was making real progress, and there was every reason to expect her to recover from this attack as she had from the previous one.

Quite soon I was able to report that Esther was allowed to sit up for part of the day. This sounded hopeful to outsiders, though I was pretty sure the doctor permitted it only in order to give a measure of hope to Esther. She probably realized this, but she had her chaise longue moved close to her bedroom windows so she could see her garden beginning to bloom for spring, and I think the doctor was right to allow her this pleasure.

On a Friday morning in May I was in the nursery looking down at our yard and thinking that next year I really must do something about it. I hadn't Esther's green thumb, but I could do better than two crab apple trees and some tulips.

We bought the Ninety-second Street house a year after Roberta was born, and ever since I had been promising myself to do something ambitious with the yard. Well, some day, I thought, when Roberta goes to Spence, and was pleased to be interrupted by the buzzing of the house telephone.

"Madam, a gentleman is calling, I've put him in the living room."

A gentleman at ten o'clock in the morning? I told Margaret she must be mistaken, though as I spoke I knew she couldn't be; my old Margaret didn't make that kind of mistake.

"A gentleman, madam. Mr. Scott he said to tell you, Mr. Scott from Chicago."

I answered mechanically, "Tell him I'll be down in a minute," and I gave Roberta a hug and called her Mademoiselle to come to her as I headed for the stairs.

I wished Bertie were here, but he had taken the midnight to Washington and wouldn't be back until tomorrow.

Mr. Scott after all these years. Why? What for?

Well, no use standing dithering on the landing, get it over with, that's what Bertie would tell me, and I went downstairs and into the living room.

I should have realized that it would not be Mr. Scott. I should not have been astonished when a tall, fair-haired man told me that he was Richmond Scott Junior. "But everyone calls me Scotty."

Rikki had been a fair-haired, tall little boy, and I began to see Rikki in this stranger; I had seen that solemn, questioning look on Rikki's face.

"Forgive my barging in like this, Eleanor, but I think you're the one I used to remember the best, the big girl who played with me sometimes?"

"Not sometimes, every chance I got, and Eleanor is just my

official name. I'm called Nell. Does that help you to remember me?"

"Nell," he repeated. "Nell? No, I'm sorry. I don't really remember much. Except Mother. I remember her, I hung onto remembering her. For a long time I figured she must be dead. Later, Father told me what had happened. And other people talked. Boys at school . . ."

For a moment Rikki's strained young face looked out from the past at me and reminded me of my face in the mirror before school in the bad days at Spence.

He licked his lips and continued, "Well, anyway, I thought when I was older I'd get to see her. Always when I was a kid I promised myself that when I was grown up—"

"You've been grown up quite a while. Why did you never come?"

"I was sixteen when Mother married again. Father showed me a newspaper photograph of her with her . . . with her husband. I could see she was happy. Even in the blurred newsprint she looked blazingly happy, and I decided Father was right when he said there wasn't room in her life for me any more than for him."

"That wasn't true, but you couldn't know, I suppose. How could you? There was no one to tell you. Well, you're here now. Only the thing is, your mother is ill. Very ill."

"I know. I heard. So I came. I guess it was a crazy idea but I wanted . . . I want to see her before she dies again. If I can, Eleanor? I mean Nell."

"I'm sure you can, but I have to think."

I couldn't think clearly. I was afraid of the shock for Esther, but she would want to see Rikki. There must be a safe way to arrange it, if I could only think how to do it.

I made up my mind. Aunt Lucy wasn't strong in body, but she was still the wisest person I knew. I would ask her what to do.

"I'm going to see Aunt Lucy," I said. "She'll arrange every-thing. Is your suitcase downstairs?"

"Yes, I came straight from the station before I lost my nerve. But I wouldn't think of imposing on you; I'll check into a hotel."

"You're not imposing, Scotty dear, you're welcome. Can't you tell how welcome you are? Naturally you're going to stay with us. Margaret will settle you in while I'm at Aunt Lucy's. Do you remember Aunt Lucy?"

He shook his head.

"She remembers you, we all do. Look, Scotty, it's a long time ago but I remember you very well. Maybe if I'm bossy enough you'll begin to remember me more clearly."

I rang for Margaret and told her that my nephew would be staying with us.

"Margaret will take care of you. I won't be long."

Aunt Lucy received the news of Rikki's arrival calmly.

"Why are you so disturbed, Nell?" she asked. "This is a great and unexpected joy for Esther."

"But it could be dangerous for her. With a heart condition that's even a little serious, doctors say that any sudden shock can—"

"I know what they say, but of what they know, even the best of them, I'm not so sure. Besides, in Esther's desperate condition nothing is any longer a threat. It's too late to look for safety for her."

"Then you know?"

"Yes, I'm aware of the gravity, of the—of the finality of Esther's illness. That's why I tell you it's useless to try to keep her safe. Every breath she draws is a danger to her. It would be cruel to deprive her of seeing Rikki again, and it could serve no useful purpose."

"It wasn't to deceive you, Aunt Lucy, that I didn't tell you what the doctor said."

"My dear child, of course it wasn't. You were being kind. I must seem a very shaky old lady and as a matter of fact that's what I am. I suppose I may have had a slight stroke, perhaps more than one. I believe it's possible to have them without realizing it."

"Your doctor would know."

"I haven't time to bother with him. Besides, though he probably could tell me what's wrong, he couldn't do much about it nor do I care to devote the time I have left to being an invalid. Now never mind about me, these manifestations of old age, whatever their cause, are not agreeable, but I manage. Let's get back to Esther and Rikki."

"What'll I do, Aunt Lucy? How should I arrange their meeting?"

"There's nothing to arrange unless. . . . Is Augie around?"

"No. When I talked to Esther early this morning she said he had left for Long Island for the weekend."

"Then there's nothing for you to fuss about. All you have to do is to take Rikki to Esther's house and run up and tell her that he's there. Tell her slowly and clearly, Nell, but don't drag it out, two or three sentences will do. Then bring him up to her room and leave them together."

I followed Aunt Lucy's instructions and took Rikki to Esther's house and told her he was there.

"Rikki is here?" she whispered. I could scarcely hear her and she grew so pale that I was frightened. Then her color began to come back and she said in her normal voice, "Rikki is here! Oh, Nell, go quickly and get him."

When I brought him into her room he went to her and stood looking down at her. He took her hand in his and they looked at each other but neither of them said a word.

I started to leave the room. It would be easier for them if I left.

"Come over here and sit down, Nell, don't leave us," Esther said, and I did as she asked.

She pointed to the low slipper chair beside her chaise longue. "Sit there, Rikki, so I can see you properly. You've grown so tall I have to crane my neck when you're standing."

When he was seated, Rikki said, "You used to call me Rikki. Rikki Tikki Tavi," his voice was unsteady, "that's the name I used to remember."

"You were always going to be Richmond," Esther said, "but it seemed too formal a name for a little boy. Still you've grown up to it now. Would you rather I called you Richmond?"

"No, say Rikki the way you always did, the way I remember."

"It's hard to believe you remember very much."

"Only sometimes. And some things. But I remember you, oh I do remember you."

"Am I changed? Of course I am. That's a silly question."

"Not changed exactly, just more real. I didn't have any photograph of you, but I had a picture in a book of fairy tales. It was lost when we moved from the apartment on the Drive to the house in Lake Forest. It was a book of Irish fairy tales and there was this princess with long, shining, red hair. She looked like you and she helped me to remember you."

"Would you like me to help you to remember how it used to be when you were little and we were together?"

"Yes, tell me about it, Mother, about when we lived on Murray Hill. I've been told we lived there but I've no idea where it was or what it was like."

"It's an old-fashioned section of New York and we lived in a tall, old-fashioned house and almost at the top of it was your room. It was the brightest, sunniest room in the house. It was pretty, maybe too pretty for a boy's nursery, but that's how I fixed it when you were a baby. There were lamps and a clock from my room at home. The lamp beside your crib was a Dresden shepherd."

"With strings of glass beads hanging from the shade; they rattled when the lamp was turned out. I didn't like the lamp going out."

"I should have had a night light for you."

"It wasn't too bad because you used to come back later. I remember that better than I remember anything in the daytime. The door would open and there'd be some light in the room again and you'd be there. I remember that very well."

"All children do I think. I remember my mother coming in to me and Nell has told me she remembers that too when she was little. I guess we've all been afraid of the dark, afraid of falling asleep. Sleep is a small death and probably children are scared of it until they get used to it."

"I don't know about you and Nell. I was just scared of the bear."

"The bear? Dear Lord, the things children imagine, poor little souls."

"There was a bear somewhere in the house. I was afraid of it at night, afraid it would get into my room. It was a big, white, sort of flat bear."

"The polar bear rug in my room. I didn't know you were afraid of it at night, you and Nell used to love to play with it."

"Did we? I don't . . . Yes, I do. It had sharp teeth that hurt if you tripped over them. Was it in your room? I thought I remembered your room, there was pink, silky stuff on the wall by the bed."

"That was my mother's room in my family's house uptown. Her room was paneled in old rose silk and you used to take your rest there when we spent the day. Do you remember that house, Rikki? Do you remember Christmases there? I don't see how you could. You weren't quite four years old on the last merry Christmas in our house."

"I don't remember Christmas, but I'll tell you what I did remember. I remembered a noisy house full of big girls. Is that the house you mean?"

"It must be. It must have seemed noisy compared to the one on Murray Hill."

"It was a fine cheerful noisiness. There was lots of singing and laughing and the big girls all talked at once and their feet clattered when they ran."

"How can you remember them so well?"

"I'll tell you. When you're a kid in a rented house in summer you have to read what books there are. One summer we had this house where the children must all have been girls and there were only girls' books. In some of them there were houses that reminded me of the one you used to take me to. I'd forgotten remembering it but now it comes back to me."

"I don't suppose you remember my family's house on the beach in Southampton?"

"I don't think so. I can remember digging in the sand when I was a kid, but I don't remember where, we had beaches in Chicago, you see. But tell me about your beach."

"It's wide, with high dunes behind it, and the sand is smooth and hard from the surf pounding. Our house was on a dune right on top of the ocean. There was a big wooden piazza, and you used to play there and I used to lift you up so you could look at the ocean stretching around us as far as we could see."

"I don't remember any big house in summer with you. I only remember a small one scarcely wider than its front door. I think I must have dreamed it, the whole picture is so unlikely. There was this little house and you were sitting in front of it with your hair down. There you are all dressed with stockings and slippers and your hair is down around your shoulders as it never was except in your room. You're sitting on the street, leaning against the house with your legs straight out in front of you. I know it's a street because there are people passing by. It's a wooden street, more like a boardwalk. Funny the things a kid thinks he remembers, a Hansel and Gretel size house and you sitting in front of it brushing your hair."

"You didn't dream it, Rikki. You remember me in my bathing suit drying my hair in front of our bath house at the old beach in Southampton."

"But, Mother, you were completely dressed."

"Our bathing suits were dresses in those days, costumes complete with black stockings and slippers. Oh dear, what figures of fun we must have been!"

Esther laughed as I hadn't heard her laugh . . . as I hadn't heard her laugh . . . I couldn't remember when I had heard her laugh with that sudden spurt of delighted amusement. Yes, I could. She used to laugh like that with Rikki when they were young, when Esther was years younger than Rikki now.

"Do you remember what fun we used to have?" she asked. "Of course it's been a long time, but we did have such fun."

"Too long a time. I ought . . . long ago I ought to have . . ."

Esther interrupted his slow, choked words. "Stop that, Rikki, stop that this minute," she said. I remembered this too. Esther could be firm as well as merry with Rikki and me.

She put her hand on his bowed head and said, "It's all right, my dear. We're back together now, and now is all that matters, now is all the time there ever is." She looked at me, "Rikki and I are okay, Nell, we're back together."

I stood up. With her free hand she gestured to me to go and I left her and Rikki together.

Before he took the train on Sunday, Rikki promised to be back in New York on the following Saturday.

In the intervening days Esther talked to me about Rikki, not about their meeting but about the old days. It was lovely she said to be able to talk about them without reluctance and without pain.

On Friday afternoon Esther got a telegram from Rikki saying he would be in on the Century in the morning. Her eyes shone and there was color in her cheeks and I couldn't keep that stubborn deceiver, hope, from springing to life in my heart.

"I didn't think I'd ever be this happy again," Esther said, "for so many years I didn't expect ever to see Rikki again, I didn't even know if he remembered me. I've laid one ghost for him: the ghost of his beautiful romantic young mother. No girl would ever have been able to compete with a princess from a lost fairy tale."

Augie came into the room, "I'm off, dear. I'd like to see Rikki, but . . ."

"Oh, Augie it would . . ."

"I understand, darling, it would be hard for him. For you, too. Maybe he'll gradually get used to the idea of me, but until he does, the most loving thing I can do for you is tactfully to absent myself. I'll be at South Side some time this evening, I've a golf game at Piping Rock tomorrow, and I might stay overnight in Locust Valley. I'll keep in touch." He took her hand and held it to his lips. "There's nothing sweet about any parting between us. It hurts to say *auf wiedersehen* for even this short while."

When the door had closed behind him Esther said, "Poor Augie, he needs a breather, needs to get out in the gay world for a bit. You mustn't hold it against him, as I think you sometimes do."

"No, no, I don't," I said quickly, "and this weekend he couldn't . . ."

"This weekend will be nice for him. He can enjoy it with a carefree mind, feeling he is doing something for me."

"You are happy, Esther?" The question slipped out before I could stop it.

Esther's eyes widened in astonishment. "Of course, you dear ninny, you shouldn't have to ask. Augie has made—makes me happy. And now that I have the only thing he couldn't give me, now that I have Rikki, my cup runneth over." She smiled in a soft, wondering way. "Isn't it queer that Pa's fine future day should be here at last? Not the way he planned it, but here just the same."

I was sitting on the low chair beside her, and she reached out and touched my cheek. "I realize you're sad for me, though you're a good, brave girl and try not to show it. Don't be sad, Nell, I have everything now. I have everything I ever asked. And if now isn't a very long time, well, that's all right too."

We were silent for a minute or so and then Esther said, "It's getting late, dear, you better run along."

I said good-by, "Good-by, I'll see you tomorrow," and I left her.

Bertie and I had finished dinner and we were in the library playing cribbage when Bridie telephoned to tell us that Esther was dead.

"She died between one breath and the next, without waking," Bridie said when we reached Esther's house, "I was sitting beside her with my knitting, and I looked down to count some stitches, and when I looked up again she was gone."

"I'll go to her, Bridie."

"Not now, Nell, the doctor and the nurse are still in her room."

Bertie's arm was around me. "Steady," he said. "You have to keep steady, there are still things to do. We must get hold of Augie before we call your sisters. Esther would want him to be with her when they come."

Augie was not at South Side, and the club was vague as to when he was expected.

"I'll try the Racquet," Bertie said. "Maybe he stopped in for a drink and got caught in a backgammon game."

Augie was not at the Racquet. Bertie tried the Brook Club next and then the Links. Augie was not at either of them.

"Well, that's that for the moment," Bertie said and handed the telephone to me. "You better get through to Smithtown and Washington. After you've talked to your sisters we can call the South Side Club again. God knows what time Augie will show up there."

A hateful idea came into my head, I put down the telephone. "Wait, Bertie, I think we better call Agnes Ryan."

"Maybe we had. Maybe we damn well better had. What's her name now?"

"Fowler. Mrs. Ryan Fowler she'll be listed as."

Bertie opened the telephone book. "Faber . . . Farbstein . . . Farr . . . Fenwick . . . Ford . . . yop, here she is, Fowler, Mrs. Ryan, nine something Fifth, that be it?"

"It must be."

Bertie gave Central a Rhinelander number and held the receiver to his ear for so long that I thought Agnes' apartment was not going to answer.

Finally the receiver crackled.

"Hello," Bertie said. "Is this Mrs. Fowler's apartment? Is Mr. Wenger there? . . . Mr. August Wenger. I want to speak to him . . . There's no mistake. I've been told he can be reached at this number . . . This is his brother-in-law, I'm calling from his house, it's important . . . I haven't time to argue with you, just get him to the phone."

There was a long pause. Then the receiver crackled again.

"Augie? Bertie here . . . Skip the explanations, I'm not interested, I tracked you down to tell you . . . Shut up and listen

to me. Your wife is dead. You hear what I said? Esther is dead
. . . Do that." Bertie slammed down the receiver.

"Come on, Nell," he said, "I'm going to get you away before
he comes. We'll call Maud and Julia from our house. We can
leave Bridie in charge here."

We went up to Esther's room, and Bridie opened the door and
came out to us. She told us that the doctor and the nurse had
gone.

"I'm taking Nell home," Bertie said. "We reached Augie and
he'll be here shortly."

"You're white as a sheet, dearie, go along home with Bertie."

"I can't leave her, Bridie."

"You can leave her with me. Go along with Bertie like a good
girl, you'll need all your strength tomorrow. I'll sit with Esther,
I'll not stir from her side this night."

Saturday morning Bertie stood over me while I ate breakfast.
"You didn't get much sleep last night, so eat, food makes up for
sleep. You have loads of time. The Century isn't due for over an
hour and I called Donoghue early before he could start on his day
off, he's waiting outside with the car."

We were in time and were standing on the platform when
Rikki came down the steps of the Pullman. I thought our greet-
ings sounded natural, but he headed in the opposite direction
from the passengers who were making their way into the station,
and we followed him. When we were out of the crowd he turned
and faced us and asked in a thin, expressionless voice, "She's
gone, isn't she?"

"Yes," Bertie said, "in her sleep, a little after ten last night."

Rikki looked awful. He was pale, and the knuckles of the
hand that held his suitcase were white as if the small piece of
luggage weighed pounds and pounds. I couldn't think of any-

thing to say. Bertie didn't try, he led us to the station restaurant and ordered coffee.

"Take it black, Scotty," he said, "with plenty of sugar."

While Rikki swallowed his second cup of coffee his face began to lose its gray pallor. "Sorry," he said, "it hit me. I knew of course that it could happen any time but I didn't expect—you don't really ever expect, do you?"

"Nope," Bertie said, "you don't."

When we reached Esther's house, Maud and Julia were in the living room. To my relief, Augie was not with them.

"Augie?" I asked.

"He's gone to Wadley and Smythe to see about the flowers," Julia said.

I opened my mouth but anger choked the words and I said nothing.

"I sent him," Julia continued. "Augie's knowledgeable about flowers and it gives him something to do. It's easier when there's something you can do."

That was true, I thought, except now there was nothing to do for Esther. Anything that hadn't been done was left undone forever. I felt sick.

Maud and Julia were talking in low tones to Rikki. Bertie put his arm around me. "Sit in this chair and put your head down," he said, "you'll be all right in a minute."

"I must take Rikki upstairs," I said.

"I'll take him. You stay here for a bit."

Bertie and Rikki left the room and Julia sat down at a card table on which were pads and pencils, the leather-bound address books she had brought from Washington, and the Social Register.

"There's an awful lot to do," she said, "lists of the people to be notified—Esther's friends are pretty scattered here and abroad, Augie can help me on them. Of course, all her old friends will come back now. James has telephoned the notices to the newspapers and he's at St. Thomas' making the arrangements with the rector. We decided on Tuesday afternoon, that will give people a chance to hear and get to town, a lot of people start going away at this time of year. And Louis . . . Where's Louis, Maud?"

"He's with Esther, he sent Bridie off to get some sleep."

"I want to consult with him about ushers but I may as well wait until Louis and James and Bertie can get together on the list. Now about the music, I thought the full choir and—"

"Julia, stop." Maud's voice was shrill. "Stop organizing as if this was one of your diplomatic receptions."

"Someone has to organize any formal occasion, even a funeral, or it's a mess—and I mean to see that every detail of this funeral is as perfect as I can make it. It's the least I can do for Esther."

"The least is right . . . Sorry, Julia, let's not get edgy with each other, though it's what Esther would expect of us and she won't mind. I'll help you all I can, but first I've got an errand . . ."

"Don't go yet, Maud. We've got to round up our entire family connection. Then we must order our black—was that what you were going out for? It'll be simpler if we telephone one shop and let them send everything. Sit down and we'll make a list before we call up."

"I hadn't thought about our mourning." Maud picked up a pencil and put it down again. "But you know what we need, you can make out the list. Veils, stockings, gloves."

"And we'll have to order black-edged note paper," Julia began to write.

"I'll put my mind on all this when I come back. I promise I will, but first I want to arrange to have a Mass said for Esther, St. Vincent Ferrer is the nearest I guess. You needn't look daggers at me, Julia Cameron, it will be a low Mass unannounced. But it will be a Requiem for her all the same."

"Honestly, Maud, of all times to drag in your religion!"

"The Mass won't be announced publicly, it won't be an embarrassment to you."

"Announced or not, it doesn't make sense to have a Catholic service for Esther, there's no point . . . "

"There is to me," Maud said, and left us.

She had been gone only a few minutes when Bertie returned.

"Where's Rikki?" I asked, "I mean Scotty."

"He's with Louis. I came to get you."

"What are we going to do about Rikki? Scotty is he called now? His presence is awkward. Very awkward for him and for us." Julia frowned. "No, on second thought, I believe it's all right. It will look well for Esther's son to be at her funeral."

"It's what he wants to do that matters," I said, "not how it looks."

Bertie put his hand on my shoulder. "Calm down, Nellie, Scotty will decide. I think he'll like to feel there is still something he can do for his mother."

"That's what matters, isn't it, Bertie? To do what you can?" For a moment Julia sounded unsure of herself. "And what I can do is to organize, to make proper arrangements."

"Sure you can," Bertie said, "and it's a darn lucky thing you're here to do it."

I didn't ask what I could do. As far as I could see there was nothing. My sisters were making separate arrangements for Esther according to their separate points of view. I sat silent, wishing I had a point of view, wishing someone would suggest some one thing I could do.

"Come, Nell," Bertie said, "come and say good-by to Esther, and then we'll get Rikki out of here. We can take him to our house. It's up to us to make things as easy as we can for him."

Rikki didn't come home with us. As we left Esther's house, he said he had decided to fly back to Chicago.

"If your man can drive me to Newark, I'll get the first plane I can."

"But, Rikki," I said, "I thought you'd stay until after Tuesday. It's Tuesday that . . ."

"I know. I'll be back. I'll take the Century Monday afternoon. But now I have to get home and tell my father about Mother. I don't want to telephone the news to him or have him read it in the paper. Father's seventy, he'll be seventy-one in September, and this will be a jolt for him. A pretty bad jolt I think. I'm not trying to make a case for him . . ."

"You don't have to," Bertie said, "jump in, we'll drive with you to the airport."

In the car, Rikki seemed unable to stop talking about his father and mother.

"I don't know the whole story. I've only heard his side of it, so I don't know what went wrong between them and gave Wenger his opportunity to move in. Father was bitter, he never got over being bitter. Even now I don't believe he will forgive Mother. But—maybe I'm imagining—but I don't think he ever got over her. He never married again. Plenty of pretty ladies would have been delighted to marry Richmond Scott of Scott Enterprises, but he wasn't having any. I don't mean he didn't have any pretty ladies. Probably he did, he's human. But he didn't marry. Can't you see how Mother would haunt a man even if all he seemed to do was hate her? Maybe this is wishful thinking on my part left over from a long time ago. I used to think a lot about his not marrying, used to read into it the significance I wanted it to have. Sure, he was pretty wrapped up in his business and he had a son to carry it on so he didn't need a wife but I used to think, used to hope—a kid can figure out more ways in which the impossible might happen. Could be I've had my father figured all wrong, but however he feels about my mother, even if he thinks he feels nothing at all, her death is bound to be a shock to him and I've got to go home and tell him and, well, be there with him."

"You don't have to explain to us," Bertie said.

"You see, Nell," Rikki continued, "Father's old. If you remember that maybe you can be a little forgiving even if he can't."

"His keeping you away is the only thing I have the faintest right to forgive."

"It wasn't all his doing. As you said yourself, I've been grown up quite a while. I could have come to see Mother long ago. It was just easier not to. It's true what I told you that I didn't think she cared if I came or not, at least that's what I kept telling myself, but the main thing was that I hated Wenger's guts. The idea of him made me sick. I didn't want to see her with him, that's the real truth. Still I ought to have come. I ought to have come long ago, but I didn't."

"Don't Rikki," I said, "please don't. My father always said that vain regret is the most useless thing in the world."

Rikki looked at me with the solemn, puzzled look I remembered. He looked like that the last time I saw him in Westbury.

"Did your father say that? Well, my father wrote the book. Poor guy. Poor, stubborn guy."

Rikki fumbled in his pocket for a package of cigarettes. He lit one and said, "Sorry. I've talked my head off. I don't know what got me going like this."

"Shock, that's all," Bertie said in a matter-of-fact voice. "We're not our normal selves today, any of us. We'll get some food at the airport and a stiff drink and we'll feel better."

We ate and we drank and we discussed impersonal topics, the fine weather which promised a smooth flight, the relative merits of the leading airlines, and the modern miracle of getting from New York to Chicago in five and a half hours.

"One thing about a train, though," Bertie said, "you know you'll leave and arrive as planned. We'll meet you at Grand

Central Tuesday morning. You can stick with us through the day."

St. Thomas' on Tuesday was packed.

Julia was right; the old friends had come back. The church was banked with their flowers, and they were all here. In the pews they turned to watch us as we followed the coffin up the aisle.

In the old days they had crossed the street to avoid Esther, but today many of them had come quite a distance to be with her when it couldn't matter to her any more, only to them. St. Thomas' was the place to be on this Tuesday in May. I could hear them in Oyster Bay and Far Hills and Tuxedo Park, saying, "I have to go in town tomorrow for Esther Cameron's funeral. It's the least I can do."

The least, I thought, the very least for her, but not for you. This is the funeral of the month, you wouldn't miss it for the world and here you are. Here are the Grahams and here, no doubt, are the rest of Esther's bridesmaids, here are Mr. and Mrs. Hastings, here are the New Yorkers we grew up with, rallying to their own now that she is safely dead and no longer an embarrassment to them. Here you are, wearing the dark clothes and the sad faces of mourners. Here you are staring at us with politely concealed curiosity.

"The son was there," you will report. "I didn't know she ever saw him . . . Everything was done very nicely. I suppose Julia Henderson is responsible for that. Her mother-in-law, the senator's widow, came up from Washington . . . Of course, the Gore-Turner connection was present en masse . . . My dear, simply everyone was there . . ."

There were some who had come to mourn for Esther.

I saw Baby. She was standing next to Mrs. Conway. Their eyes were red and their lips were tight. They weren't trying to look sad, they were trying not to cry. Not far from them was

Alfred Sampson. I had no idea he ever came to New York, but of course if he was in the city he would be here today to stand by Esther. Farther up the aisle was Cousin Maud Bronson's daughter, Alice Cecil. Alice hadn't seen any of us for years, but she had come down from Ottawa where her husband was with an English mission. She had come in her mother's place because Cousin Maud, had she still been alive, would have been with Esther today.

Finally, the walk up the aisle was over and Bertie and I were in the third pew with Bridie and Aunt Lucy and Rikki. In front of us were the Martins and the Hendersons. Beyond them I could see Augie's dark head. He sat alone in the first pew, and I felt almost sorry for him. I think I did feel a little sorry; he sat straight and still, but inside he must have been confused and tormented by guilt and remembered years and Esther young again. Poor Augie, I thought, as I looked at the blanket of small, white spring flowers that lay light as lace, not heavy as a pall, on the coffin. Esther would have wanted me to think poor Augie, but I couldn't think about him much or about Rikki or about any of us who were left. I could think only about Esther who had given her whole life away for nothing.

Then I couldn't think about anything except holding on to myself. I could let tears fall behind the shelter of my veil, but I mustn't make a noise. I held my lips tight shut and listened to the minister.

". . . before the morning watch; I say, before the morning watch. O Israel, trust in the Lord, for with the Lord there is mercy . . ."

Tim Farrell told me once that he wondered how Episcopalians could bear their funeral service. Oh, it was beautiful, he said, he granted us that, but that was the trouble. That torrent of beautiful sixteenth-century English was more than a sorrowing heart should be asked to bear.

I couldn't very well say to him that in our church we are used to hearing beautiful English, but we are. And beautiful words that are familiar are not as painful to hear as an outsider might imagine. Our Psalms and Lessons and our hymns are part of hundreds of Sunday mornings in church and of Sunday evenings at home.

". . . And God shall wipe away all tears from their eyes; and there shall be no more death, neither sorrow, nor crying, neither shall there be any more pain: for the former things are passed away . . ."

Esther used to read aloud to me from Revelation about the city of pure gold transparent as glass. Julia must have asked for a Lesson from this chapter, she must have remembered that it was a favorite with Esther.

". . . I am Alpha and Omega, the beginning and the end. I will give unto him that is athirst of the water of Life . . ."

I remembered my sisters singing after the Bible reading on Sunday night. Pa preferred what he called positive hymns, "Onward Christian Soldiers" and "Fight the Good Fight," but my sisters liked sad, evening ones. I can hear them harmonizing in "Now The Day Is Over":

". . . Comfort every suff'rer watching late in pai-ain, Those who plan some evil from their sins restrain."

We were young enough to enjoy sad songs.

"Now the day is over, Night is drawing nigh, Shadows of the evening . . ."

The only shadows we knew were the ones that literally steal across the sky at evening.

For Esther, Julia had chosen another evening hymn, "Abide with Me."

"Abide with me: fast falls the eventide . . ." and I wept for Esther and remembered her, the oldest of us, not yet twenty, and the four of us singing sad hymns as cheerfully as we sang about Little Buttercup or the bridge of Avignon.

Then I listened to the minister again.

". . . The Lord make his face to shine upon you, and be gracious unto you. The Lord lift up his countenance upon you and give you peace, both now and evermore. Amen."

The service was over.

As we walked down the aisle the choir sang one of Pa's favorites, "Hark, hark my soul! Angelic songs are swelling . . ."

Stronger than the voices of the choir, I could hear his deep voice booming: ". . . Angels of light, Singing to we-elcome the pilgrims of the night."

While we stood outside on the steps, waiting to take our places in the limousines behind the hearse, I could still hear the choir but I no longer wanted to listen to them and their angels of light. We were pilgrims of the night indeed and the end of this pilgrimage would take us to Woodlawn. I couldn't bear to think of it.

I can't bear to think of it now. I would rather remember when we were young, when we were like a family in a book. I would rather remember the good days Esther had. I would rather remember her young and lovely and happy.

14

THE TROUBLE is you can't pick and choose among your recollections, they come uninvited at their own pace, in their own time. They can be summoned only accidentally by whatever may be for you the equivalent of the madeleine dipped in tea: the sound of a forgotten tune, the sight of a photograph in a long unopened album, grandchildren skipping rope to a jingle you used to know. This morning it was Augie's obituary.

Well, if I can't choose as I please among my recollections I can at least pack them all away and put my mind on the immediate present.

I ring for Annie and I ask her what she has for Bertie and me for supper.

"Not supper after one of his shooting weekends, madam. In my opinion gentlemen never eat right when they're on their own. Rose isn't taking her entire day. She'll be back soon and we've planned a proper dinner."

"But it's hard to tell on these weekends what time he'll . . ."

"Dinner will hold. Rose is giving veal casserole, you both like that, and she has fresh pea soup and an apple tart."

I try to keep Annie in conversation. "He'll be starved when he gets in so perhaps with cocktails we could have some of your cheese puffs or would you rather . . ."

"I'm planning on cheese puffs. And there's a few slices of the smoked salmon left from last night if he should fancy them."

"What would I do without you, Annie?"

"You'd do fine."

"I wouldn't like it."

"Neither would I, but we don't have to worry about it. And you don't have to worry about the Mister's dinner, just have a nice visit with your sister, she ought to be along any minute. You didn't make much of a job of your lunch, I see."

She carries out my tray and comes back and lights the lamps. She starts to draw the curtains. "The days are getting so short, it's night before the afternoon is over, but I suppose you want to keep your view?"

Annie knows I'm proud of our view and prefer, except on stormy evenings to keep the curtains open.

"Not this afternoon, Annie, it's gloomy out. Mrs. Henderson and I will be cozier if we have a fire and the curtains drawn."

Annie closes the curtains and plumps the sofa cushions. She lights the fire and gives a quick glance around the room. "If you're through with your newspaper?"

"I am."

"Then I'll take it along. I like to have everything just so when Mrs. Henderson is here. I'll tidy your sewing too and put it away, shall I?"

I nod, and she tells me I ought not to sew by artificial light. "It's murder on the eyes, madam." She collects my gros point and the scattered sections of the *Times* and takes them away.

I'll poke the fire so that it will be blazing cheerfully when Julia comes. The fire doesn't need poking, but I need something to do. I poke the fire. I turn on the wall brackets and turn them off again. I move a vase of roses from one table to another.

I think I'll run in to Bertie's room and borrow the book section of his *Times*.

The doorbell rings. "I've got it, Annie," I call as I let Julia in.

Her face is cold as she presses her cheek against mine in greeting and her perfume eddies faintly around us as she slips out of her pale mink coat and takes off her gloves. I've always envied Julia because perfume doesn't die on her. She never trails a jet stream of scent behind her as some fashionable women do, but the perfume she sprays on her person in the morning is still fragrant in the afternoon.

"How was St. Thomas'? And the Colony Club?"

"The club doesn't change, but St. Thomas' does, though I still see some people we know. Dotty Guarrigue feels the way I do, it's still St. Thomas' for us. It's too late now to start with St. James."

"Was the club crowded?"

"Not too. And, oh, my dear, I had the most gruesome little encounter with Mrs. Hastings. She was lunching with her granddaughter who's getting another divorce I hear. I do find it boring that all the news nowadays is about people's grandchildren. So, anyway, I stopped at Mrs. Hastings' table and she gave me a glassy unblinking doll-eyed look and said, 'Hello Julia, I thought you were dead.' She's older than God and absolutely bats of course, but it was creepy."

"Not a pleasant beginning. How was the rest of your lunch?"

"So-so. What gave me a turn, reminded me for the second time in one day of our old family troubles was Dotty pointing out Sister Wenger to me. Sister whatever her married name is. She was draped in black for her dear father."

Julia pulls off her mink turban and pushes her hair back from her forehead. "I get hot with rage when I think of that setup. Damn Sophie anyway—I suppose it's wicked to say that when she actually has been dead for years, but even now it makes me furious the slick way Augie managed his marriage to Agnes Ryan and Sophie made things easy for them, don't think she

didn't—God, how she must have hated Esther! Agnes Ryan—
you can't tell me there wasn't something going on there before
Esther died."

I haven't told Julia—I haven't told anyone about Augie and
Agnes. This much I can do for Esther. I resented Augie's quick
remarriage. I know, I know: a year is considered correct, not
quick. Probably it's the cold-blooded correctness I mind. And I
mind the smoothness with which from the start it worked for
him. He and Agnes honeymooned in California, where they were
royally entertained by his sisters. And Augie, with Sophie's full
co-operation, was soon on fatherly terms with both his daughters
again. There was even, I remember, talk of a budding romance
between one of either Sister's or little Sophie's girls and Agnes'
son by her first marriage. It never came to anything, and it probably wasn't ever anything more than talk, but the talk was fun
for the world that would have been amused by such an unexpected little postscript to the Wenger story.

"I never thought that marriage would last," I say. "I only met
Agnes to speak to twice in my life but I wouldn't have thought
she was the kind to put up with Augie's nonsense."

"There was a good deal in it for her, and not mainly the
Wenger money, though the rich never object to having more.
It was Augie's social position that was important to her. He
never lost that, you know, it was merely in abeyance while he
was married to Esther. For the last thirty years he has basked in
the smiles of all the best people."

"What I mean is, do you think they were happy?"

"Good Lord, Nell, how many people do you think are happy?
I imagine Augie and Agnes came to an understanding. And they
were neither of them all that young, though I must admit they
remained an attractive pair for a long time. I used to see them
at parties, didn't you?"

"Not often. Bertie and I have never gone in much for café society or the jet set."

"Listen, they went everywhere and knew everyone including the people you and I grew up with."

"We saw them once in a while at the beach when they came to Southampton for a weekend or at a big wedding or a charity ball in town, but we mutually managed to keep our distance."

"They didn't keep their distance from James and me, and that's funny when you think of it. You and Bertie were kinder to Augie in the old days than we were. Probably he was sure he could count on James not to create an awkward situation on a formal occasion. Augie couldn't count on Bertie not to behave exactly as he pleased on any occasion. You always thought James was tough, but sometimes I think Bertie is tougher. Maybe I mean Bertie is his own man. You can't be that in the diplomatic."

Julia sighs and takes a gold-mounted comb from her pocket-book and pulls it through her still thick, still wavy hair. Now that she has let it go completely gray, her hair is almost as soft and becoming a frame for her face as it ever was.

"My hair has always been a bother," she says. "It isn't straight like Maud's, but it's so thick it could be nearly as unmanageable as hers if I let it. Well, better than the pink scalp showing through the scanty white curls." She takes out her diamond monogrammed compact, opens it, and looks at her reflection. "Plenty of hair and good jewelry and the family nose do minimize the ravages of time. At least they distract the eye of the beholder." She puts comb and compact away and says, "Don't think for a minute that I didn't enjoy James's career and his success. It's the one career, the one success in which the wife has a real part to play. Oh, I suppose all wives one way or another, but in the foreign service a woman's qualities as a hostess—and as a guest—make a difference. Not only in the diplomatic, I guess, in any world that takes itself seriously, Hollywood, for instance, or so they tell me. Agnes was probably a big help to Augie in national and international society. She's a terrific hostess, I've always heard, James and I never went so far as to find out at firsthand. But to begin with, it was Augie who was a help to her, let me tell you. Do you think that without him she could have got that mick son of hers into St. Paul's—" Julia stops short.

"Oh, Nell, I'm sorry. I didn't mean . . . I got so mad thinking about Agnes that I forgot, you know I don't mean Tim."

"I know. Please don't fuss, Julia."

"Nobody speaks or even thinks in those terms any more. I sounded like 1910. Nowadays we all know Irish Catholics and lots of people marry them. Believe me, I wish my Judy had found someone like Tim Farrell. He's a darling."

Poor Julia. Judy has been divorced twice and her third marriage to Guy Parsons doesn't seem very stable.

Tim Farrell is a darling. Bertie and I thought so the first time Roberta brought him to the house. It was at the end of the Korean War, and the boy was still in uniform. A stranger in uniform, I thought and my heart melted as I remembered Bertie a long time ago. I discovered later that for this boy the Korean War had not been a small war and that in the course of it he had grown up. "Wars are never small," Bertie said, "for the guys who have to fight them."

We liked Roberta's young man from the moment he very politely and rather shyly entered our house and our life. Tim has got over his shyness, though not his good manners, and I'm grateful to have a well-mannered, gentle-mannered, really, son-in-law. I suppose I can thank the Catholic school I had never heard of for that. Tim was shy to begin with, but also right from the start he has been a little amused by Bertie and me and by Roberta, dearly as he loves her. As he has learned to feel at home with me (you don't call your children's grandmother "Granny" unless you feel at home with her), he has shared his amusement with me. It has astonished me sometimes but it has never hurt my feelings and I think I can say that Bertie and I have never hurt Tim's.

It's queer as I look back that Bertie and I weren't worried by Tim's background and religion. It isn't so much that we didn't worry as that we had the good sense to be pleased. During the Second War and after it the world was changing in frightening ways, and the Irish Catholic establishment seemed a strong fortress, seemed as safe and lasting a city as Roberta could possibly find.

"Nell Cameron, you're not listening to one word I'm saying," Julia says. "You're miles away."

"Years away as a matter of fact. I'm sorry, Julia."

"The past is agreeable to think of sometimes, isn't it? But it's puzzling too. As you said this morning, then was a long time ago. It's queer now with Tim in the family—and even if he wasn't it would be queer to remember how important religion was when we were young. Think how Pa carried on about Maud."

"You carried on quite a bit yourself."

"I was embarrassed. Maud's turning Catholic was the last straw, coming as it did on top of all the mess of Esther's divorce. It was one more upset, one more painful change in how things had always been. When we were children, when we were growing up, when Esther was first grown up, it was pure heaven to me to be one of the Cameron sisters. Esther was the beauty of course, she was queen of our castle. It really seemed like a castle in those days, a lovely safe castle that would last forever, and then the roof fell in on us. Mary Ames was the one who told me about Esther and Augie. I felt sick and angry and frightened. That was the first time in my life I was ever really scared. Then Aunt Lucy calmed me down and smoothed things over, and I didn't say anything even to Maud and naturally not to you. If I don't say anything it will go away, I thought—did you use to think when you were young that if you kept quiet about something, it would go away, wouldn't be true?"

"I did."

"And everything did quiet down until little Lucy Gore's funeral. Then the scandal exploded for fair and everybody knew. Even you."

I wish Julia would shut up. I don't want to go over all that again. But maybe it's been a day of recollections for her too and she has to talk.

"It was an embarrassing time for you, Nell, but not as bad as for me. You were at a better age for it."

"I was?"

"You were. You were what? Ten, eleven? That's the peak of childhood. I remember when Maud and I were there, monarchs of all we surveyed. A hard thing would have been easier to bear then. The teens are different, you're at the bottom of another ladder and it's as difficult and uncertain as if you were little again. Believe me the teens were a miserable place to be when scandal hit our house. I know it was hard for you but you were still safely a child, you weren't aware of everything that was going on, of everything that was being said about our family. It was plain awful for me. That Esther, that my sister Esther Cameron could—I loved Esther in the take-it-for-granted way you love a sister, and I admired her, the oldest of us, the loveliest. Someday I'll get where she is, I told myself and then suddenly . . ."

"You always loved her, you know you did."

"Did I? Oh, I guess I did in a strange, ambivalent way."

"And you had to be sorry for her. After she died you had to be sorry for her, Julia. She gave her whole life away."

Julia hasn't been looking at me. She has been looking back at herself. Now she looks at me and says, "Most women do, some luckily and some not so luckily, but I made up my mind after I saw what happened to Esther that I wouldn't give my life or myself away. It could too easily be for nothing. You were lucky, Nell—you and Maud both. And you didn't have to take second choice. I knew Louis was Maud's first choice, anybody could tell that, but I thought Bertie was your second choice, a sensible second choice but—"

"Julia Cameron will you please not start on that." It doesn't matter to me now what she thinks but it did to the young Nell. "I do think you ought to have got it through your head by this time that there never was anyone for me except Bertie."

"Oh, I've got it through my head. I've had it through my head for thirty years. Alfred told me. I had always assumed that you married Bertie on the rebound and that seemed okay to me. Rebound marriages can work out, a marriage for any reason can work out. It's not how a marriage starts that counts, it's how it goes on. I did think for ages that yours had started on the rebound from Alfred. I thought so till he told me different."

"Alfred told you? When?"

"After Esther's funeral. He was at her funeral, you know."

I nod, but Julia doesn't see me. Once again she's looking at herself long ago. Poor Julia. She must be back at St. Thomas' at Esther's funeral.

"James took his mother back to Washington right after the funeral," Julia says. "He had to check in at the State Department for consultations that would last until some time Friday. We were sailing Saturday and I stayed on at the Plaza. I had no plans when I said I wouldn't dine with you and Bertie, I just couldn't face the evening with Rikki. I was tired, as I told you, and I was in the queer, disjointed frame of mind that a funeral puts you in. It cuts through the present like Aunt Lucy's cone cutting through a paper world."

Fancy Julia remembering that odd mathematical discussion between Aunt Lucy and Maud! One of them mentioned the fourth dimension and Aunt Lucy upheld the theory that time is the fourth dimension.

"Of course, we can't define time," Aunt Lucy said, "nor grasp its essence. Imagine a flat, two-dimensional world and pass a cone through it. All that the inhabitants of that world could see would be an ever widening circle. Of the cone they could have no idea."

"A funeral, especially one that marks a death that breaks off a piece of your own life isn't just sad," Julia says, "it's unsettling. You're not sure where you are any more."

Hoping to change the sad train of Julia's thoughts, I recall the tag line of an old story, "In your grief do you know what you're doing?"

Julia doesn't hear what I say. She's talking to herself, not to me. We'll sometimes do that and when one of us holds forth at too great length on old times or her grandchildren, the other thinks her own thoughts. I've had enough of my own thoughts and I listen to Julia.

She doesn't look sad, she smiles as she gets going on the Plaza, of all irrelevant topics. "Before I went up to the suite I stopped at the entrance to the Palm Court. It was still a setting for Mr. Charles Dana Gibson's girls, and it took me back to the prewar days, to the conservatories in private houses including ours— those were cozy, shadowy little nooks all right—and to the res- taurants of my youth, where string orchestras played semiclassical airs. Later there were ragtime tunes for tea dancing. Do you remember tea dancing?"

She doesn't look at me as she asks the question, doesn't see me. She goes on talking:

"I was standing there listening to the music when I heard a once familiar voice. 'How goes my Julia?' and Alfred touched my arm. 'My poor Julia goes in black silk today. I'm sorry, sorry for the sad day, sorry for Julia, sorry for Esther.'

"I had completely forgotten my black clothes. 'I just stopped for a minute, Alfred,' I said.

"He asked me to stop a little longer and let him buy me a cup of tea. And that was so typical of him, he never gave a thought to appearances. I pointed out that I was in mourning and the Palm Court was not an appropriate place for me to be.

"'Always correct, aren't you, my Julia? Well, where can we go?' he asked.

"I said I could give him tea or a drink or whatever he'd like upstairs, that would be all right, and we went up to the sitting room. When we got there and I asked him what he'd like to drink, he said, 'Nothing this minute.'

"We sat and talked for a while. I was glad he was with me. I didn't want to be alone. I didn't know what I wanted, or so I told myself. Our talk turned to the days when Pa was alive and the family's house was still standing and I felt like crying, I didn't know why. I must have begun to cry a little, I realize, because I remember Alfred giving me his handkerchief and saying, 'Cry if you need to, Julia. Weep all the tears you want for Esther.'

"I dried my eyes and said, 'Oh, Alfred, I don't know what's wrong with me. I feel old and time flying by and I wonder where it's all gone to.'

"'Maybe the years bother you.' Alfred stood up and looked

down at me, 'but they haven't taken much of a toll. You look younger than I ever remember my Julia looking, gentler, more defenseless.'

"He kissed the top of my head. It was a light kiss, light as a feather touching my hair, and I didn't say anything. I remembered all too clearly Alfred's gift for dangerous and persuasive argument, the least unwary word could start him off.

"I didn't say anything, but I knew where we were headed. There was still time to turn back, I told myself. I'd give him one drink and send him on his way."

I can see where Julia and Alfred were headed and I've got to keep her from telling me. If she does, she's bound to wish she hadn't.

"Speaking of drinks," I say, "would you like one?"

"Not right now—funny, that's what Alfred said when I offered him one.

"'Not right now,' he said. 'Perhaps later and a bite to eat. You oughtn't to have room service supper by yourself this evening.'

"He sat down beside me, not touching me, and talked quietly about old times and it seemed as though we were back in them.

"Later he ordered dinner and as we faced each other across the small, round table we were reminded of the other time we had dined alone together. It was after a football game at New Haven in 1912. We succeeded in ditching our chaperoning married couple, whoever they were. Alfred drove his Packard too fast for them to keep up with us. When we were well on our way he pulled into the entrance of a roadhouse. Dinner alone with a man was strictly against the rules, but I hesitated less than a minute before stepping out of the motorcar. I got pretty fed up with the rules sometimes, and besides, I was hungry. We had a delicious dinner and a lovely time. And I was in luck, there wasn't a soul we knew in the place."

I really must interrupt her before she gets back to the Plaza and the end of her story. All I can think of is to remind her that Pa had a Packard once. "Do you remember it, Julia?" I ask. "It was a twin six, and old Gillespie despised it, he said those automobiles ought to be called the sick twins."

Julia gestures to me to be quiet, but her hand is shaking and I take it in mine. She doesn't look young, of course, but I can see what Alfred meant when he said she looked gentler, more defenseless.

"Let me finish," she says. "You may as well know I'm not a plaster saint. Let me finish about Alfred and me. It's a long time since I've thought of that first evening at the Plaza, and I like to remember it. I haven't got all that much to remember about Alfred and me. I like to remember how we laughed as we looked back at the vanished era when dinner à deux was a daring thing for a well-brought-up young lady.

" 'We can laugh now,' Alfred said, 'but that was daring behavior, unusual anyway for my prudent Julia. You were always very correct where public occasions were concerned. Though I remember some private occasions, I remember times in the conservatory in your house.'

"I was pretty correct on private occasions, too. I always managed to keep him from going too far. What I couldn't manage was to keep him from getting under my skin. Apparently I still couldn't manage that, my knees were trembling under the table. My hands weren't too steady either and I folded them in my lap out of his sight.

"Room service took the table away, but Alfred made no move to go. 'It's early,' he said. 'Let me stay a little while.'

"I let him stay. A little while wouldn't hurt, I thought."

Julia shrugs, releases her hand from mine and lights a cigarette.

"Well, you can imagine the rest. But the little while didn't hurt, Nell. The whole three days while James was in Washington didn't hurt. Three days aren't much and I'm glad I had them and they didn't hurt anyone, not even James, if that's what you're thinking. James and I had what is known as an understanding. It consisted of my being supposed to understand him, but he was discreet, he never publicly humiliated me, and I wouldn't have dreamed of hurting his pride. We were fond of each other—I guess I can't expect you to understand James and me. Don't look like that, Nell. Okay, so I misbehaved, but at least it wasn't in Macy's window. I didn't do anybody any harm. You were full enough of sympathy for Esther, who broke everybody's heart including her own. I suppose a small-time sinner who played it safe isn't romantic enough for you."

"That's a nasty thing to say to me, Julia."

"I'm sorry, but honestly sometimes you amaze me. You're a wide-eyed romantic-hearted innocent who refuses to recognize how things really are. You think the straight undeviating life is easy for people. You think what you and Bertie have, what Maud and Louis had, is the norm, you can hardly think it's the norm nowadays, and let me tell you, it never was except for the lucky few. So go ahead and count your blessings but just remember you're a lucky woman to have them to count and don't be too hard on the rest of us, we were only human."

"I know I'm lucky and I guess I sometimes seem smug about it. I don't mean to."

"You're never smug, Nellie dear, but you are rather prim. I'm sorry I shocked you, I forget there's anyone left who's still capable of being shocked." Julia takes a long draw on her cigarette and stubs it out.

"It's queer for me to have told you of all people about Alfred and me," she says. "I've never told another living soul. No, it's not queer, you're the only sister I have left and I trust you. I guess I had to tell someone. My youthful rule works two ways: if you don't keep quiet about a thing, if you tell it to one other person then it's true, then it's now even if it's thirty years ago. Poor Alfred, I didn't know he had so few years left and I'm glad we had those three days—two days to be exact and three nights. I'd have wept a lot more bitterly when he was killed if we hadn't had them."

Poor Alfred indeed. During the Second World War he was given a commission and sent to London where he was some sort of P.R. good-will liaison officer between our Air Command and the British. He'd spent a lot of time in England between the wars and was well liked there.

"It seemed unfair," I say, "for him to have a second war when he'd been so badly hurt in the first one. And then to be killed in that useless, random way. I felt sick when I heard he'd been killed by one of the German buzz bombs."

"Alfred was convinced another war was coming and he had no intention of ducking it," Julia says. "By '38 everyone was pretty sure that Europe was in for it, but a lot of us hoped that the United States would stay out this time. I argued with Alfred. 'Who wants to die for the Czechs?' I asked, and he said 'No one. No one wanted to die for brave little Belgium. No one wants to die period but you're not given a choice.' He even laughed, Nell, and said that in the end, like it or not, everyone died so maybe to die for a reason wasn't the worst way. Then he went on to tell me that if war came he didn't believe this country would have a choice. 'The world's a small place nowadays,' he said, 'countries are involved with each other and they have commitments not choices.' I certainly hoped America would have a choice and I told Alfred so in no uncertain terms. I was already mortally afraid for young James. Well, he came through okay, thank God. Afterward I thought he was one of the guys Alfred was thinking of when he said, 'Everyone hopes that by a miracle there won't be another war and that if there is one that by another miracle his country can stay out but if war does come and we do get into it I wouldn't feel right when our guys are fighting to sit back and do nothing. Anyway I wouldn't enjoy the home front, I didn't think much of it the last time!'"

I remember Alfred's low opinion of the home front in the first war, and looking back at it, it seems selfish or at best not too deeply concerned, but while I was part of it I enjoyed it.

I didn't enjoy it the second time. Bertie and I had been together too long. It wasn't bad while he was stationed in Washington and could come home most weekends, but later the Adjutant General's office sent him to London and to Paris. That was a bad time for me, not only because I was afraid, and when he was in London and bombs were falling I was terribly afraid for him, but also because I felt like half a person.

I had Roberta and I kept busy between the day nursery and my days at the Red Cross. I worked for the blood donor service in the old Tiffany building. Those lofty marble halls reminded me of when Bertie and I were young. We chose my engagement ring there. It wasn't hard on us when we were young and our lives were separated by the difference in our ages, but by the time the second war came we had one life between us. It was a horrid, empty, frightening time and I don't like to think about it.

Julia is still thinking about it.

"Poor Alfred," she says. "It does seem as if some people go out of their way to meet their doom. Look at Maud and Louis. In 1938 James and I begged them to go back to the States, but they loved Paris and their house in Neuilly and Gar was doing well at the Lycée, and they wouldn't leave. Even after war broke out they stayed. All through the phony war they kept putting off their departure. It was absolute folly. Louis' anti-Nazi sentiments were no secret. That damn painting."

"It was quite a painting," I say, and remember seeing it when Bertie took me abroad a few weeks after Esther died.

"I'll say it was, Nell. It created a furor and Louis' name was mud with the Croix de Feu and you can bet the German embassy was taking note. It's a pity he ever painted it. Oh, I realize some people considered it an important work. Lord knows it was talked about enough, pro and con, and I guess it's too bad it was destroyed during the war but it imprinted the name of Louis Martin on the German mind."

"That summer, the summer the painting was exhibited was the last time I saw Maud and Louis together. And the picture reminded me of the first time I saw them on the day they met. Louis talked that day of painting the Place de la Concorde off center, though obviously he couldn't have imagined the darkening shadow of the hooked cross. It was strange to have that dark painting remind me of the cloudless spring day on which you were married."

A l'Ombre de la Croix: the Place off center, and one's eyes focus on the woman of Strasbourg cloaked again in black. She is a woman not a statue though her robes and the heavy rectangular coronet that bows her head are of stone. Her face isn't the face of the woman of Strasbourg, it's the face of Rachel weeping, the face of the woman who would not be comforted. She is not observed from the terrace of the Crillon where Louis stood when he talked to Maud and me. Part of the façade of the hotel slants away from the left foreground, its windows illuminated from within. Jeweled women in pale summer dresses and men with gleaming white shirt fronts are stepping out of their motorcars and through the wide doorway into a blaze of golden light. On the far side of the obelisk the waters of a fountain leap high in the air and reflect the brilliant sunset colors. The shadow of the hooked cross has darkened most of the scene, it has reached the base of the obelisk. It has not yet reached the mourning woman, but she is watching it and it will reach her.

"It can't have been exactly the picture Louis had in mind on your wedding day," I tell Julia, "but when I saw it I remembered that day. I remembered Maud's hands resting on the stone balustrade while she stood beside Louis. She always had nice hands when they were in repose, it was when she was nervous that they got in her way. She was hardly ever nervous after she was married and I remember thinking the last time I was with her that she had beautiful hands."

"The maddening thing," Julia says, "is that after the Germans took Paris James had everything fixed for Maud and Louis to get out. I've never understood why they wouldn't leave."

"It was on account of Gar. He refused to go with them."

"But he was a child, they could have made him go."

"He wasn't a child. He was fifteen in 1940, remember? Louis told Bertie the first time they met after the liberation that Gar wouldn't go. France was his country, the boy said, and he didn't propose to abandon her. Needless to say Maud and Louis couldn't abandon him."

"I never knew that." Tears stream down Julia's cheeks. "I don't understand why I mind not knowing—that's not what I mind, I mind learning one small new fact. It makes the whole thing happen all over again."

Julia mops her eyes and blows her nose. Her lipstick and powder are smeared. She crumples her handkerchief into a wet ball and says, "I'm a mess. I better go pull myself together and put on a new face. Stay where you are, I'll be back."

I wait for Julia and think about Maud and Louis and about Gar who became again le p'tit Louis. That was his name in the resistance.

Louis told us the bare facts. He told them to Bertie when they met in Paris and later he recited them first to Julia and then to me. It was a recitation, an account as dry as the summary at the end of a chapter in one of our history books at school. "This is what happened," he said and licked his lips and spoke in an expressionless voice.

After the United States entered the war the house and studio in Neuilly were occupied by German officers. Maud and Louis were allowed to live in three servants' rooms on the top floor of the house. They had, of course, to report regularly to the German police.

Gar had left the house the day they learned of the attack on Pearl Harbor.

If they received a message from him it would come from le p'tit Louis, he told his parents. He was slight and not very tall, and he looked younger than his sixteen years. "I can pass for a thirteen-year-old," he said, "and that has made me useful as a messenger, but I think I shall not much longer be able to operate from this house." Before Maud and Louis could stop him he was in the garden. They followed, calling to him, but he was gone through the gate into the street. When, later, the Germans asked Louis what had become of his son he told them that although he had not finished at the Lycée he had been sent to friends in the Dordogne. "Gar has never been strong and my wife and I feel he is better off away from the city. He can complete his education when the war is over."

"Nothing worth telling happened for some time," Louis said to me. "We had no news of Gar. The war went on and Maud and

I managed. It was not a good time or a bad time, it was time that passed."

In February 1943 Maud came down with a bronchitis that developed into pneumonia. The servants' rooms were equipped with large radiators, but the German officers had decided to severely limit their use. They regretted the necessity of conserving fuel, they regretted that it would not be possible for Mrs. Martin to be taken to a hospital, since space was not available, they regretted that no doctor seemed willing to accept Mrs. Louis Martin as a patient. Louis did his best for Maud, but she grew steadily worse.

On the nineteenth of February—Louis gave the date in the same flat voice in which he gave all the facts—when he returned from the market he found a note in the pocket of his overcoat. He was allowed to go out to buy food, but he knew he never went unobserved. However, a hand, quicker than a German or collaborationist eye had slipped the folded paper into his pocket. He went up to the top floor bathroom, locked the door, and took the flimsy paper out of his pocket, after he had read what was written on it, he tore it into small pieces and flushed it down the toilet.

The message was brief: "Le p'tit Louis is dead. He was not captured. You will remember he could run like a hare and he was too fast for the Boches. He was shot while running across a field in a direction that led them away from one of our posts. They did not find the post which has since been safely dismantled and abandoned."

Louis said nothing to Maud. This news must wait until she recovered.

Two days later he was taken to Gestapo headquarters and questioned. His interrogators were reasonably correct, he said, and did not further elaborate on their treatment of him.

He and his wife had not heard from their son in some time, he told them. Communications were difficult in these days and they could only trust that all was well with Gar. Yes, his full name was Louis Guarrigue Martin Junior, but he went by the name of Gar.

An old acquaintance of the Martin family had informed the authorities that Herr Martin's son had in early childhood been known as le p'tit Louis. Was this not so? Yes, it was so.

Therefore le p'tit Louis, a member of the resistance, could in fact have been Gar Martin? It was possible.

"It is not possible for us to ask you to identify this Louis. He was shot several days ago and, regrettably, his body was too hastily disposed of. Nevertheless from certain information received we believe it was the body of your son."

"It's possible. Anything is possible."

"Herr Martin appears indifferent to the possibility that his son is dead. The Herr should not be indifferent to the fact that he is responsible for his son's unfortunate sentiments and activities."

After twenty-four hours his interrogators apparently decided that he knew either nothing or too little to be of use to them.

"To the Nazis art was a commodity like any other," Louis said. "They stocked their salt mines with works of assured value, a commercial value permanently established by death and time. A still living, still unassessed, middle-aged painter wasn't worth the trouble of deporting to one of their overcrowded concentration camps, and they let me go home."

When Louis returned to the house in Neuilly, Maud was dead.

Because Louis reported so few details, I couldn't, for a long time, stop trying to fill them in. I would imagine the narrow, top floor room and wonder if its window faced on the garden or on the street, I would put my hand on the cold radiator.

Now once again I see Maud lying alone, dead, with her eyes open until Louis comes to close them for her. At least she never knew about Gar, and I try to see the field across which he runs like a hare. Is it bordered by one of those straight, poplar-lined roads? Is it flat or does it slope uphill until he is trapped against the sky? But surely he will run along the side of the hill? If it's daylight that won't help him.

Julia comes back with her face freshly made up and her composure restored.

She's still thinking about Maud, but it's the first separation between them that is on her mind. She might be starting one of their old quarrels as she says, "I simply don't understand Maud turning Catholic. It embarrassed me, that's true enough, but also it made a wall between us that I hated. There were whole areas of conversation that we either had to skip or else get into a fight. I'll admit her conversion worked out for her. It was much simpler for her and Louis to be of the same religion, though a lot of the time it didn't seem the same. Louis was much more relaxed about their church than she was."

"I suppose to Louis Catholicism was as natural as the air he breathed. To Maud it must have been more like an oxygen tent."

"That's it, Nell, it was natural for Louis to accept without question the whole rigmarole he had been taught as a child, but Maud, after all, was brought up as a good, sensible Protestant. Don't both the Catholic priests and the psychologists say give them a child until it's seven? What you learn at your mother's knee is what sticks. I simply can't understand how one of us could embrace that superstitious, medieval, rigid religion. How could Maud go back on her whole childhood?"

"I'll tell you what I think," and as I say it I realize this is what I think, have thought for a long time. "Because she became a Catholic, Maud was spared the doubts that have infected our generation. Her new religion let her hold on to all the things we used to believe. Certainly there's a lot of Catholic teaching that is complicated and incredible beyond words, but at the heart of her faith Maud remained as staunch and old-fashioned a Christian as Aunt Lucy. And that's more than one can say for most of us."

Julia is frowning. "I don't know what you mean by most of us," she says. "I go to church every Sunday of my life."

"Bertie and I usually go on Sunday to Grace church. That's where Ma and Pops went. I suppose we go for them as much as anything, though I like Morning Prayer. Just the same, Julia, you have to admit that in our time religion has become a pretty lonely do-it-yourself, believe-what-you-choose thing, it's not the way it was when Aunt Lucy read the Bible to us on Sunday evenings and every word was true. And do you remember the second chapter of St. Luke after our carols on Christmas Eve?"

"Of course I do, but we were children then. Naturally as you get older you outgrow some of the things you used to take literally."

"I know. We were only children." And remembering for a quick sharp moment what a child's faith was like, I add, "I think I envy Maud."

"Well, I don't. For one thing her religion made her fantastically strict about ordinary human behavior, puritanical really."

"Oh, come on, Julia. You can't still think Maud was exactly puritanical."

"Because of the painting of her in the garden? What I think about that is that she got carried away, had some kind of brainstorm. She was mad about Louis and anything he wanted was okay with her whether it was those damn models of his or finally herself. Well, I'll bet you one thing, I'll bet you that on the question of the painting being publicly displayed, she'd be on my side not yours."

I'd take Julia's bet if Maud were here to settle it for us. I think I know how she would feel.

"You were shocked," Julia says, "when we first saw the picture two years ago."

I suppose I was. I was certainly startled.

Julia and I were in Paris. We had flown over together for Louis' funeral.

After the services at St. Joseph's in the Avenue Hoche and at the cemetery Julia and I went back to the house in Neuilly where a young man from Coudert Brothers read us Louis' will in which he had left us Maud's silver and china and other personal belongings.

"There is one somewhat delicate matter," the lawyer said. "There is a painting by Mr. Martin entitled, *A Walled Garden Vence 1920.* It isn't mentioned in the document I have just read because final disposition of it has been made to a museum, but it is not to go to the museum during your lifetime unless you both, or the one surviving, authorizes the transfer. Mr. Martin's estate will carry the insurance and other necessary charges until such transfer is made."

"Do you remember that solemn young lawyer, Julia?" I ask.

"Poker-faced, I'd call him. He must have been dying with laughter inside when you said I ought to have the painting because Maud and I were so close and you already had Louis' painting with Roberta in it, and I said, oh no, the fair thing would be for us to share it, you could have it in the winter and when you went to Southampton I'd hang it in the Dower House at Henderson for the summer. I can still see the politely expressionless look on his face when he suggested that we inspect the large canvas before we made plans for it."

He then went on to tell us that in the summer of 1939 Louis had had the foresight to store his paintings secretly in a province that was safely distant from Paris. It was a pity that his well-known painting *In the Shadow of the Cross,* had been sold to a private collector. "A pity," the lawyer said, "from an artistic standpoint, since it resulted in the destruction of the painting by the Vichy Government, but it was fortunate for the owner, whom that government had some reason to distrust. His voluntary surrender of the painting to the authorities created a favorable impression."

"I thought that poor young man was rather long-winded," Julia says. "It didn't occur to me that he felt awkward about showing us Louis' *Walled Garden.* I'll never forget when we went into Louis' bedroom and saw the painting we were being so generous with to each other. There was a garden right enough, and lying in the middle of it was Maud without a stitch. I didn't know where to look and neither did you."

"I was a bit taken aback."

"More than a bit, you went pink to the roots of your hair, Nell."

"I don't doubt it. Louis' death and being in the house in Neuilly with you took me back to the days when we were young. A painting of one of us in the nude would have been unthinkable in those days. But surely by now Maud's youthful self would seem as remote to her as mine most of the time seems to me. And for her to be able to remember herself as beautiful, to know she was beautiful and have the world know it too would make up to her for the years before Louis came, for the years when she was the plain one. When she was young it would have embarrassed her to have the picture exhibited, but I can't believe it would now. It's true as you've pointed out often enough that the picture was not shown even to us until after she and Louis were both dead. Maybe you're right, and Maud, if she had lived to be an old lady, would still be embarrassed. I'll admit it fusses me a little to think of my sister hanging naked in a museum for every Tom, Dick, and Harry to look at."

"You've put it in a nutshell, miss." And Julia glares at me as if we were again very young indeed.

"All right, all right, but what I think is . . ." I'm answering defensively as I used to answer her and Maud when they picked on me, and that's ridiculous. We've been equals for a long time. "Look, Julia, we're old, and what embarrasses us doesn't matter. What I really think is that Maud's young body lying in that garden is too lovely to be locked up indefinitely in the Manhattan Storage."

"I don't want to even discuss it."

"Listen to me, Julia. I don't believe Maud would want Louis' painting hidden away, his best painting, according to the opinion of the experts to whom he showed it and according to the price the Whitney was willing to pay for its eventual possession. It isn't in Louis' usual genre, it isn't in anybody's genre as far as I can tell. It's as simple and unmannered as its title."

Julia makes no comment. She busies herself lighting a cigarette and has trouble with the matches.

I still catch my breath in astonishment when I remember my first sight of Maud in that garden, but the really astonishing thing is that none of us had any idea that Maud's body was as beautiful as her face was plain. Of course in our day we were brought up to be private in our dressing and undressing, and that was easy enough in our big houses where every girl had a room to herself. And heaven knows our clothes weren't revealing. Still we ought to have realized—we almost did on one occasion. Mr. Tappé made us see Maud on her wedding day, made prettiness a trifling matter. For a little while on her wedding day as she moved in that silvery column of a dress, she was the Bride that every woman longs to be and every man desires to possess. I didn't know how entirely this was true of her until I saw Louis' painting. It was just a glimpse that I had had in the glow of the candles in the little church. I particularly noticed Maud's hair, and what I thought about that was that the Russian hairdresser had been remarkably clever.

Maud didn't need a clever hairdresser. In the blazing sunlight of Louis' painting, her hair flows over one shoulder and spreads beside her on the grass in a smooth, straight, widening river of pale gold. Critics have praised Louis for the way in which he used light. He didn't use light in this picture, didn't manipulate it. It's just there shining on the blossoming espaliered fruit trees and on the flower beds that border the wall, shining on Maud's hair, shining on Maud as she lies with one arm flung back beneath her head. I had always been aware that Maud had nice skin, but I had never seen it, not really, not all of it, until Louis showed it to me, fine and supple and flawless as silk. Silk is an inadequate comparison, there isn't any comparison for the warm, living texture. Clothes never did anything for her, she chose them badly, but if she'd been as knowledgeable about them as Julia, they would not have revealed how perfectly Maud's body was made, the firm fullness of her breasts above the narrow cage of her ribs, the gentle curve of her thighs, the long, slender legs.

It's no wonder Louis never wanted to paint another woman's body after Maud's, I think, and don't realize I have thought out loud until Julia says, "For the love of Mike stop talking about the picture. It's one of the things you and I will never agree on. Luckily we're old enough to disagree fairly amiably, but on this I'm adamant, and I'll hand it to Louis, he did consider my feelings—and what ought to be your feelings—in not letting the Whitney have the picture as long as we're alive unless we both say so, and I'm grateful for that small favor. What I do wish is that he'd chosen a museum in Cleveland or Kansas City or somewhere. Why did it have to be New York? And of all New York museums, the Whitney! The Museum of Modern Art would have been better. We know the Whitneys. It's as though Maud had gone to one of their parties in Roslyn or Manhasset without any clothes on."

Julia lights a cigarette, takes three fast puffs and puts it down beside the one that is still burning.

"Look at me," she says, "lighting two cigarettes at once, that ought to show you how the whole idea upsets me."

"The thing is, Julia, that while Louis tried to be fair to us we're not being fair to him and Maud wouldn't like that. We've been told that this is his best painting but the best of paintings can miss its moment unless it's by one of the all time greats. By the time the museum gets Louis' painting its moment may have passed. It might be shown only briefly or even not be hung at all."

"No such luck. They'll hang it but it will be literally over my dead body." In spite of the warmth of the fire, Julia shivers. "Ugh, what a grisly thought."

I feel cold myself. It's amazing how lightly we used to say things like over my dead body or someone must be walking on my grave.

"What time is it getting to be?" Julia looks at her handsome, bold-faced wrist watch, "twenty-five past six, I better get a move on."

She gets slowly and heavily to her feet, which isn't like her, and as I follow her into the guest room I ask her to stay another night.

"I'd love to, but I can't. Young James's plane is picking me up. Besides, I've got to get back, I've a million things to see to before the young start arriving Wednesday. Young James and Gertrude are bringing their gang to me for Thanksgiving dinner—dear me, I suppose Jim is really young James these days but my James will always be young James to me. Have I told you that they're very pleased with Jim at the State Department?"

She has told me, and I know she's delighted. It disappointed her that young James took to finance instead of diplomacy.

Julia is once more her cheerful self as she perches on the edge of one of the beds and says, "Jim and Betsy will be up from Washington. I was afraid they wouldn't make it for Thanksgiving this year with the baby due so soon, but young James said suppose it did arrive early, there was no better place for a Henderson to be born than the Henderson Hospital. Gertrude added her persuasions and it was settled. I'm not sure that Gertrude is overjoyed at the prospect of becoming a grandmother, and I don't blame her; I wasn't. To be a great-grandmother, though, seems rather distinguished. Cameron will be down from Harvard and Pammy has invited her current young man. Gertrude thinks that this one is more than current, that they're getting serious and we're all delighted. I'll tell you who he is, he's a grandson of Liph Brewster. You remember Liph—he was a beau of Maud's a hundred years ago."

Eliphalet Knott Brewster. That was the Boston boy's name. It's strange to remember his earnest young face and his ukulele and to imagine him a grandfather.

"Judy's grown-up two are going to their father, as Judy and Guy have taken off for Mexico City for some film festival. It's hard on Lucy to have them always on the go, but she seems perfectly satisfied to come to me when she's left alone over a holiday."

Julia beams as she mentions her youngest grandchild; she

has a weakness for Lucy Gore Haven and so have I. My fourteen-year-old granddaughter Nellie and Lucy are best friends as well as cousins, and I see the child quite often. She's a cheery little thing most of the time. She and Nellie talk a mile a minute while they dry their long blond hair and brush it as straight as they can. They both have a Cameron look and they remind me of all of us as we used to be, not that we washed our hair every other day as they do, but they have fair coloring and oval faces and straight little noses like ours.

Sometimes Lucy has an anxious look that troubles me. Bertie was right. We have lived to see divorce taken for granted and parents change partners in marriage as casually as on the dance floor, but it's still a misery for children. Once when Lucy was about to spend her Christmas vacation at the Dower House, she said, "I love to go to Grandmamma's, Aunt Nell. It's the only place in the whole world where I'm not a half."

Her older half-brother and sister have been kind to her I think, I hope, but they are brother and sister, Lucy is an extra, a late-comer to a family that was complete without her. Then after Judy and Cass Haven were divorced, Cass remarried and he and his second wife have a girl and a boy. Lucy isn't essential to either of the families she belongs to.

"Lucy loves going to you, Julia," I say.

"It's partly because I spoil her, but in my opinion it does a child less harm to be the favorite than the unfavorite. Now I must dash. Young James's new jet will get me upstate in no time flat and they'll give me dinner on board but I don't want to get home too late."

Julia picks up her suitcase while I take her face bag and she goes into the kitchen to thank Annie and Rose. Annie carries the bags to the elevator and rings for it. When it reaches our floor Julia gives me a quick, absent-minded kiss. She obviously is no longer thinking about me or the old days, she is already at Henderson with the young.

"Bye now," she calls, as the elevator door closes on her, "my love to Bertie."

I better hurry and change before Bertie gets home. I think I'll put on the red and gold kaftan Roberta gave me last Christmas. She says it's the mod thing in tea gowns, but the loops and buttons that reach from my neck almost to the floor remind me of the dresses of my youth. At least this garment doesn't button up the back.

As I get to work on the buttons I look at a color photograph on my desk. It's one Tim took last summer of Roberta and the children running along a high dune. I wonder where he took it; it isn't easy to find an empty stretch of dune in Southampton. The photograph reminds me of how our end of the Island used to be. The year Roberta and Tim were married it was more like the old days than it is now, or perhaps I think that because they were married in Ma and Pops' house and that remains a peaceful unchanged spot. I still think of it as their house, though it's been ours since Ma and Pops died within six months of each other five years before Roberta was married. I liked having her married in their house. It ought to bring her luck, I thought, Ma and Pops' luck as well as Bertie's and mine.

Everything about Roberta's wedding day pleased me. The sun shone and Roberta looked as if she was where she said she was: on cloud nine. I was pleased with Tim; I was already beginning to be fond of him. However, it was not yet Tim who made me confident that Roberta was safe for a lifetime. I was confident not so much because of the boy himself as because of his family, his long and faithfully married parents and his sisters and cousins (including the Holy Child nun and the Paulist father), and his friends. Other groups have changed, I thought, but this one's house is built on a rock, not necessarily in the sense they think—but whatever one's point of view about that may be, the Irish Catholic fortress looks as lasting and impregnable as Mont St. Michel.

I was glad Roberta had chosen a boy of Tim's type and background—oh dear, my generation was taught to think in terms of type and background and I don't suppose I'll ever completely get over it. I got over it quickly enough with Tim. I soon learned to think of him and count on him as a person. The establishment in which he grew up no longer seems more solid than any other, but I'm not worried. Roberta is safe with Tim.

Tim is solid as a rock, though, thank heaven, he's not stuffy or solemn. He's gay and lighthearted and not even faintly self-important about the fortune his father's will left in his charge.

Timothy Aloysius Farrell built that fortune almost from scratch. A small legacy that his wife received from her godmother gave him his start. He did well in the bull market and got out early in 1929, but he came to public notice and made his first really big killing by selling stocks short when the House of Morgan was trying to prop up the market and old Mr. Rockefeller was announcing that he and his son were buying common stocks.

Farrell continued to sell short at shrewdly chosen moments throughout the Depression. This did not cause him to be loved. He was a notorious success at a time when there were too many failures and his raids on the market were blamed for a number of the failures.

"Taffy is a Welshman," his enemies said, "Taffy is a thief."

Bertie did not agree. Years before we ever laid eyes on Tim, Bertie told me that T. A. Farrell was no more a thief than a Welshman, he simply had an uncanny gift for figuring out how, under any combination of circumstances, the market would react.

It was natural for those not equally gifted to attribute his pyramiding fortune to chicanery and the devil's luck, however in Bertie's opinion they were mistaken. Farrell was ruthless but he was not dishonest.

"T. A. is a more spectacular trader than your father was," Bertie said. "He's a more flamboyant man altogether, but he shares what your father liked to call his knack of seeing how things in general are going. As Pops says, some knack!"

Tim has a sound business head, though he's not as brilliant as his father was. He doesn't need to be. His father took risks in order to get where he wanted to, but by the time he died his wealth was widely and wisely invested. Bertie says it's hard to believe that black Irishman didn't have second sight, he planned for the future like a seventh son of a seventh son.

Tim is respected downtown even by men who had no use for his father and he sees to it that the family companies are capably managed.

I'm pleased that Roberta has this additional financial security, she and the children are as safe where money is concerned as anyone can be, but there's another and more important kind of security and Roberta has that too. And she and Tim have fun together. Sometimes they seem to me as young as their children. They—

Darn it, I've missed a couple of buttons somewhere, I'll have to start over. I better look at what I'm doing instead of that photograph.

Without looking at it I can see the running, skipping, laughing line of children from Nellie to two-year-old Patrick, who is holding fast to his mother's hand. Some are fair and some are dark. Tim's father was black Irish, but his mother is light-haired and gray-eyed.

The children's names run through my head as I fasten the last buttons, Nellie, Aloysius, Robert, Sheila, Sean, Moira, Patrick.

The Irish names are pretty but I'm glad there are Robert and Nellie for us. These children could be a family in a book, though I can't think of a family of seven. Four Marches, five little Peppers, six Bastables. Anyway the family and the book aren't ever quite the same and I can't read the Farrell book. The only book I can read, the only book I know by heart is Bertie's and mine.

I take a quick look in the mirror, put on some lipstick and go into the living room to wait for Bertie.

He shouldn't be too long. It's nice to sit here and watch the fire and wait to hear his key in the door.

The key will turn in the lock and the door will open as he calls, "Nell! You there, Nellie?"

"I'm here," I'll answer, as I have answered for so many years from so many rooms, from cabins on shipboard and hotel suites, from our house on Ninety-second Street, from our first apartment and from this final one. "I'm here, Bertie."